"At b[...]"

New York Times an[...]

KAR[...]

"... is simply outstanding" (*Fresh Fiction*)

Praise for *HUNTED*

"A wild hide-and-seek romantic thriller. . . . There is a reason Robards remains at the top of the lists: fantastic storytelling."

—*RT Book Reviews* (4 ½ stars)

"An adrenaline-pumping adventure of unpredicted dangers and profound emotions. . . . The gift Karen Robards has for creating noteworthy suspenseful stories is evident in every enthralling paragraph. . . . An outstanding and particularly captivating story."

—*Single Titles*

"Karen Robards will have you staying up hours past your bed time just to find out what happens next."

—*The Big Thrill*

"A top-notch thriller full of tension and atmosphere. . . . With its complex plot and excellent characters, *Hunted* is a winner, and I highly recommend it as a fast and satisfying read."

—*Romance Reviews Today*

. . . and for her other romantic thrillers!

"Spellbinding . . . sensual . . . explosive."

—*Publishers Weekly*

"Exhilarating. . . . Edgy and engaging."

—*USA Today*

"Nail-biting suspense and blazing sexual tension."

—*Kirkus Reviews*

"You won't read this book, you will devour it!"

—*RT Book Reviews*

KAREN ROBARDS

HUSH

POCKET BOOKS

New York   London   Toronto   Sydney   New Delhi

Pocket Books
An Imprint of Simon & Schuster, Inc.
1230 Avenue of the Americas
New York, NY 10020

This book is a work of fiction. Any references to historical events, real people, or real places are used fictitiously. Other names, characters, places, and events are products of the author's imagination, and any resemblance to actual events or places or persons, living or dead, is entirely coincidental.

First Pocket Books paperback edition August 2015

POCKET and colophon are registered trademarks of Simon & Schuster, Inc.

For information about special discounts for bulk purchases, please contact Simon & Schuster Special Sales at 1-866-506-1949 or business@simonandschuster.com.

The Simon & Schuster Speakers Bureau can bring authors to your live event. For more information or to book an event contact the Simon & Schuster Speakers Bureau at 1-866-248-3049 or visit our website at www.simonspeakers.com.

Cover design by Lisa Litwack
Cover photograph by Ekaterina Solovieva/Getty Images

Manufactured in the United States of America

10 9 8 7 6 5 4 3 2 1

ISBN 978-1-4767-6660-7
ISBN 978-1-4767-6662-1 (ebook)

Hush is dedicated to my editor, Lauren McKenna.
Lauren, what can I say?
Great editorial advice, calm good judgment,
and grace under fire—you rock.
No one deserves this more.

— CHAPTER —
ONE

The Houston mansion was huge. Dark. Deserted.

Except for the corpse hanging in the living room.

Or whatever the hell rich people called the big, fancy room where nobody ever actually lived. Approximately the size of a football field with the white marble floors and the giant crystal chandeliers dangling overhead. This one, just like the rest of the house, was empty, its furnishings and other accoutrements in storage somewhere waiting for the government to auction them off.

"You should've talked when you had the chance, Jeffy-boy," Finn Bradley said to the corpse as he grimly surveyed it. His voice was soft, but the words seemed to echo off the pale marble walls—hell, for all he knew the ceiling was marble. It soared thirty feet above his head, which made it kind of hard to tell.

The electricity had been cut off, so pale moonlight pouring in through the windows was all he had to go by, but he was confident that the death looked like a suicide.

Except that Finn knew it wasn't.

Jeff Cowan, the twenty-nine-year-old son of disgraced financier George Cowan, who had made off with billions of investor dollars in one of the biggest financial frauds in history, had just become one more piece of collateral damage in the war to recover the missing money. Jeff was slight—okay, so maybe nearly everybody seemed slight when compared to Finn's own six-three, 220-pound self—blond, and classically handsome. He'd had the most expensive of educations. The most expensive of everythings. His parents had doted on him. He had a host of rich-scion–type friends. Yet here he was, his bare feet dangling at approximately Finn's eye level, wearing a pair of gym shorts and a T-shirt, his face contorted in death, the smell of ammonia from where he had pissed himself stinking up the air around him. To all outward appearances, he had wrapped an electrical cord around his neck, attached one end to the wrought iron railing of the second-floor gallery looking down on the room, and leaped over, thus breaking his own damned neck.

Finding a motive was easy: the shame of his father's crime, the unaccustomed poverty into which Jeff had been plunged, the relentless investigations as every law enforcement agency under the sun tried to ferret out who else had been involved in the fraud and *what had happened to the money*, had proved to be too much for the pampered darling of one of Houston's wealthiest families. The ME could bring in a suicide verdict and nobody would question it.

Only a select few would know the verdict was bullshit.

Finn wrapped a hand around Cowan's wrist. He'd seen enough death to know what it looked like, so he didn't bother to check for a pulse. What he was checking for was body temperature.

Cowan was still warm. No sign of rigor mortis. No sign of blood pooling in the extremities. The smell of urine was still strong.

He'd been dead under an hour. Maybe *way* under an hour. As in he could have been killed in the last fifteen minutes or so.

Shit.

It was possible that whoever had killed him was still around. Finn tightened his grip on his gun as he scanned the room, paying particular attention to the nearly impenetrable darkness shrouding the overhead gallery. He didn't get the feeling that anyone was up there, but—

"You find Cowan?" inquired the voice in his head. At least, that was how Finn thought of his unwanted partner, David Baxter. The earwig was almost as bad as having Baxter in there with him. Not quite, though. Bax tended to lose his cool when things didn't go according to plan. If he'd been standing there beside Finn at that moment instead of waiting in a parked car across the street from the ornate iron gates that were closed and padlocked by order of the U.S. government, Bax would be shitting bricks.

"Yep," Finn replied, then added, "he's dead."

The shit bricks started to drop, as Finn had known they would. Bax's voice went shrill.

"Are you *serious*?" He didn't wait for Finn's confirmation, because he knew Finn wasn't a joking-around kind of guy. "Goddamn it! You weren't supposed to kill him!"

Before Finn could reply, the distant, barely audible click of a door being unlocked had him pivoting in the direction from which it had come. There was no mistaking the subsequent sounds: somebody was coming in the front door.

His eyes narrowed. His muscles tensed.

"Somebody's here," he growled at Bax, who was supposed to be keeping watch. "Do your fucking job."

"What?" Bax sputtered. "Me? Me do *my* job? You fucking do yours! You said you thought he was in the house. When we got here, and you went in, you said you wanted to talk to him. You didn't say anything about killing—"

That was all Finn heard, because as he retreated into the shadows at the far side of the room he savagely pulled the damned annoying piece of plastic out of his ear and shoved it into his pocket.

———

"JEFF?" RILEY COWAN called. Her voice was tight with anger.

She knew that flipping on the light switch near the door was a waste of time. The electricity had been shut off weeks before for nonpayment, shortly before the government had seized the house, but out of habit she flipped the switch anyway. Big surprise: the darkness stayed dark. Fortunately she knew her way around. Her former in-laws' former mansion once had been her home, too. She and Jeff had lived with them for nearly a year, until Jeff had finished the in-house training program his father had insisted he complete before buying their own lavish condo in downtown Houston. When Jeff had first brought her here, she'd been a twenty-one-year-old newlywed straight from Philadelphia's poverty-stricken North Side, where she'd been working as a cocktail waitress to put herself through college. Jeff's parents' wealth had been as much of a surprise to her as her existence had been to them. That was seven years ago. A lot had changed since then. To begin with, she and Jeff were divorced, and had been for a year and a half.

Riley waited just inside the front door: Jeff didn't answer, didn't appear. Oakwood—all the mansions in Houston's exclusive River Oaks neighborhood had names—was a big place, eight bedrooms, ten baths, fifteen thousand sumptuous square feet, with its own swimming pool and tennis court and guest/staff house. Given that, even though Jeff was expecting her it was possible that he hadn't heard her calling him. It was also possible that he was drunk off his ass and passed out somewhere, or so drugged up he was practically out of his mind. Actually, knowing him, one of those scenarios was more than possible: it was likely.

The question she should be asking herself was,

exactly how had she ended up becoming her ex-husband's keeper?

He'd tried calling her first. When she hadn't answered, he'd texted her: *I got trouble. Meet me at the house ASAP.*

Typical Jeff: the only thing he ever thought about was what *he* needed. The sad part was, she hadn't followed through on her impulse to text back, *Go to hell.*

Instead, here she was. *Stupid much?*

She'd been finishing up at work when the text had come through. As one of two assistant managers of the Palm Room, one of Houston's most exclusive clubs, she was in charge of closing for the night on weekends, which Jeff knew. This was Saturday—well, Sunday now, because it was after 3 a.m.—and he'd known that she would be leaving work just about the time he sent the text. For about three seconds she'd thought about ignoring it, ignoring *him*—working two jobs as she was doing tended to leave her exhausted at the end of the week, and she'd had just about enough of pulling his chestnuts out of the fire—but Jeff had been so unstable lately that she hadn't been able to bring herself to do it. She hadn't blasted him, either. Instead, she'd come.

Just like he'd known she would.

Because, despite everything he'd put her through, despite the drinking and drugs and other women that had torpedoed their marriage, part of her still cared about him. When he wasn't under the influence of something, he was kind and gentle. He'd been sensitive to her feelings at a time when she'd needed somebody to be. He was handsome, athletic, and sometimes even charming. She was no longer in love with him—thank God; loving Jeff had been a nightmare—but during the tumultuous years they'd been together he'd somehow managed to become family to her.

Didn't mean she couldn't get ticked off at him for dragging her out at this ungodly hour to this place that was full of bad memories and was government property now, even if the authorities hadn't yet gotten around to doing anything beyond officially seizing it, which so far hadn't included changing the locks. The front gates were padlocked, for God's sake: she'd had to park in a neighbor's driveway—she recalled that they always spent the summer in Maine, so no one was home to notice or be disturbed—and walk across about an acre of the neighbor's grounds before coming through the garden gate, which the government either didn't know about yet or didn't care about. Trespassing was what she was doing on Jeff's behalf, and last time she'd checked that was a crime.

The knowledge that she was committing a criminal act for him ticked her off even more.

"Jeff?" Anger sharpened her voice.

Still no answer.

Damn it—him—anyway.

Standing in the cavernous hallway calling to him obviously wasn't going to get the job done. Lips firming, high heels clicking on the vast expanse of white marble floor that was missing the pricey Oriental rugs that had softened it just like the house itself was missing its paintings and furnishings and the bowls of fresh flowers (changed every other day) and the uniformed staff that had made it so intimidating to the new bride she had once been, she walked away from the elongated rectangle of moonlight that spilled through the door she'd left open behind her and into the deepening darkness. The house used to smell of furniture polish and flowers: tonight it smelled of mildew and some indefinable stink. Inside, it was hot as an oven because this was Houston in July, and the air-conditioning had gone with the electricity.

Coming from Jeff, *I got trouble* could mean anything, from *I'm too drunk to drive home* to *I'm dead broke and need to borrow a hundred bucks.* Now that he was no longer vice president of Cowan Investments, the defunct family firm, he was essentially unemployed. To be fair, that wasn't entirely his fault. Nobody in Houston, or in Texas, or possibly even the United States or the whole wide world, was going to employ George Cowan's only son, especially when the feds still suspected that he'd aided his father in his schemes and were investigating him relentlessly. (Jeff hadn't had a thing to do with it; he'd been as clueless about the whole mess as she had been herself.) Of course, there was always employment available at places like McDonald's, or Wal-Mart, as Riley's exasperation had recently led her to snap at him, but she'd known even as she'd said it that the idea of Jeff Cowan working a minimum-wage job was laughable.

It just wasn't in his DNA.

Good thing *she* wasn't such a delicate flower, or they'd all starve. She'd said that to him, too, when she'd handed over most of her paycheck a couple of weeks ago to help pay the rent on the house he now shared with his mother and teenage sister.

The problem was, none of the three of them had ever had to work for money in their lives, and they were floundering. Whereas, until she'd married Jeff, she'd always had to work if she wanted to eat and have a roof over her head, so she had the whole get-a-second-job-if-you-have-to thing down.

Jeff didn't even have the whole get-a-first-job thing down.

When she'd become part of their family, she'd never been anything but poor, never lived in anything except run-down apartments. Her only travel had been an occasional summer trip by car to Florida. The rich, glamorous Cowans had been as alien to her as if they'd been from Mars. Margaret, Jeff's mother, was one of Houston's leading socialites. She could have treated her new daughter-in-law like dirt, could have looked down her nose, could have been snobby and cold to her. Instead Margaret had embraced her, treating Riley like a daughter from the moment Jeff had showed up with her. She'd taught her how to dress, how to navigate the upper echelons of society, how to do the philanthropy thing. When they'd had money, they had showered her with everything that money could buy. Now that they didn't, now that they'd suffered this humiliating, terrifying fall from grace, she wasn't about to turn her back on them. They were her family now. She would help them if she could, any way she could. And Jeff knew that about her. It was, he'd told her, one of the reasons he'd fallen in love with her.

"Jeff?" Okay, she was screeching now.

Her voice was still echoing off the walls as she paused at the first arched doorway to her left. It opened into a corridor that led to the green salon, the sunroom, and the music room. An identical arched doorway to her right led to the library and the card room and the conservatory. When she'd first arrived at Oakwood, she'd thought, *Geez, who has rooms like that?* Now it seemed normal to have pretentiously named rooms that were rarely used.

"Jeff?"

Still no answer. Jeff was probably either in the billiards room, which had built-in cushioned benches that could double as a bed, or out back in the pool area, she calculated. Either choice required her to traverse thousands of square feet of unnervingly empty house. She figured that a better idea would be to first go through the gathering room—a fancy name for what was really a big family room—and check out the pool area, which might save her from needing to go all the way down to the lower level, where the billiards room was located.

It would serve him right if I just turned around and left.

But Riley knew she wouldn't, because to do so would undoubtedly mean spending the rest of the night worrying about him.

Jeff, you ass.

Her phone was already clutched tightly in her hand: she pressed a button and held it up, using it as a flashlight. The faint white beam was woefully inadequate, but it was all she had. She continued on toward the gathering room with dogged determination, refusing to let a little thing like a huge, dark, echoingly empty house spook her.

Yeah, right. Who are you kidding?

"Jeff?" she shouted again.

The twin white marble staircases with their black wrought iron railings curved like swans' necks over her head to meet up on the second-floor landing. Faint sounds—a creak, a hiss, a rattle—made her breath catch. She shot a quick glance upward, then aimed the beam of light that way. Nothing but a whole lot of dark. Any one of the sounds might have been made by Jeff, but then again, they could have been made by anything. Houses settle, she reminded herself firmly as she continued on, but that didn't really help the creeping uneasiness that was making the back of her neck prickle.

The mansion felt . . . alive. That was the only way she knew how to describe it. There was a kind of pulsing energy to it that was distinctly unsettling. It was almost like the house had a heartbeat that was throbbing around her. If she'd been imaginative, which thank God she wasn't, she would have sworn that she could hear it breathing.

That she could hear *something* breathing.

Get a grip, Riley.

If there was any breathing going on, who was it going to be but Jeff? If, say, he was passed out somewhere nearby and hadn't heard her calling him.

On the other hand, it could be anyone—or any-*thing*.

Her heart thumped.

Don't be such a wimp, she told herself impatiently. But as she neared the end of the hall, as darkness swallowed her up and her makeshift flashlight found the closed, arched double doors that opened into the gathering room, she had to admit that she was (maybe just a little bit) afraid. And that ticked her off more than anything else so far.

She'd already texted Jeff when she'd arrived. Now she phoned him, using her index finger to savagely punch his call button. When she heard the muffled sound of his phone ringing—she knew the sound of his ringtone as well as she knew her own—she stiffened, listening.

He was close.

The sound cut off after four rings as his phone went to voice mail, but not before she had zeroed in on its location: the gathering room. Which was directly in front of her. Riley frowned. If he was in there, no way he hadn't heard her yelling for him. Either he'd just come inside from the pool, or he had his earphones in, or he was in there passed out. Or he'd left his phone in there and he was elsewhere, a less likely option because he was rarely separated from his phone.

In any case, she knew where to start looking. She took the few steps needed to reach the heavy double doors and pushed them open.

After the darkness at the end of the hall, the

moonlight flooding the huge room made it seem almost bright.

"Jeff?"

Her shoes sounded especially loud on the marble
as she walked through the doorway and looked
around. In here, the faint musty smell had an acidic
overtone that she couldn't quite place. The room was
the approximate size of a gymnasium, all white marble
with a domed ceiling, half a dozen French doors
looking out onto the pool area, a huge carved-marble
fireplace at one end, and a gallery—the backside of the
second-floor landing—running its length. The modest
two-bedroom brick house she'd grown up in would
have fit in this one room twice over, a fact that she
had once found impossibly intimidating. What she'd
learned since could be summed up in four words:
mo' money, mo' problems. Once upon a time, she
wouldn't have believed that, certainly not when she
was back in Philly scrambling for every dollar.

If Jeff was in the gathering room she couldn't
see him, but then again shadows lay everywhere and
the silvery moonlight didn't quite reach the corners,
which made them as dark as the end of the hall. She
really didn't scare easily but right now, under these
particular circumstances, she discovered that she
was . . . uneasy. She didn't like having her stomach
flutter, or her pulse quicken. She didn't like having her
heart pound like it knew something she didn't.

She didn't like being here, period.

"*Jeff?*" Now *that* was loud. Her voice bounced
off the walls, the floor, the ceiling, the resulting echoes

putting her even more on edge than before. No answer, either, which ratcheted up her annoyance to a whole new level.

This is the last time I go running after you, she promised her ex-husband silently, on the verge of doing what she knew was the smart thing: turning around and leaving him to sort out his own damned mess.

Instead, lips tight with impatience, she scanned the shadowy corners. Could he be passed out on the floor in one of them? Narrowing her eyes and focusing on the darkest part of the room, she pressed the redial button on her phone so it would call him back and pinpoint his (or the phone's) location. At the same time, she stared hard at one corner in particular, on the left side of the fireplace well beyond the reach of the moonlight. She got the jittery-making feeling that someone was there, and directed her phone/flashlight beam toward it accordingly.

Her voice was sharp. "Jeff! Are you—?"

She broke off abruptly as, behind her, Jeff's phone rang, so close it startled her. Doing a quick about-face, she saw nothing but moonlight and shifting shadows.

Puzzled, she peered into the gloom, the words *Damn it, Jeff* just about to fall from her lips.

Then his phone rang again, making her look up. One of the shadows resolved itself into a pair of bare masculine feet dangling limply in the air a little higher than her head.

Riley blinked. The feet were still there.

Her throat tightened.

Long, slim feet. Slightly crooked toes.

She knew them.

Oh, God. She *knew* them.

Riley stopped breathing. She stopped everything. Time seemed to stretch out into an eternity between one heartbeat and the next. She stared at the feet while her stunned mind did its best to reject what she was seeing.

The ringtone blared once more. The sense of being caught in a moment out of time shattered. Riley sucked in air. It was Jeff's ringtone. From Jeff's phone. Following the sound, her gaze slid up over lean bare calves. He was wearing black gym shorts, a black tee: exercise clothes. The phone was *there*, probably in the waterproof pouch he clipped inside his shorts for exercise or swimming, on the lifeless body that hung motionless not ten feet away.

Jeff's lifeless body.

Riley's heart lurched. Her stomach dropped straight down to her toes.

There was no mistake: the moonlight streaming in through the French doors touched on Jeff's blond hair. Fine and pale, it was one of the first things she had noticed about him when he had swept her off her feet in Philly all those years ago.

She must have made some kind of strangled sound, because her throat ached like something wild and fierce had just torn its way out of it. She didn't remember inching forward, but suddenly she was close enough to discover that what she smelled was the ammonialike odor of pee: he had wet himself.

Jeff. My God.

Limp and pale, he hung suspended in midair.

Unable to believe what her eyes were telling her, Riley touched his leg. It was solid, all muscle and bone. Of course it was: Jeff was a runner. The fine hairs on it felt silky. His skin was warm. Did that mean . . . ?

She tried to call out to him, but no sound emerged. His wrist was out of reach. Frantically she grabbed his ankle, felt for a pulse.

Nothing. No beat. His leg was heavy and inert.

She let go, and his whole body moved, but not in a good way. He swung a little, back and forth, from where she had tugged on his leg.

Horror surged through her in an icy tide.

Holy Mary, Mother of God . . .

In this moment of extremis, the teachings of her childhood took over: the Catholic prayer for the dead unspooled with frantic urgency through her head.

Hands shaking now, Riley drew back a step and ran the light from her phone over him.

His head was tilted at an odd angle. Something narrow was wrapped around his neck, digging into the skin beneath his jaw.

His face was dark. Purplish. His handsome features were hideously contorted.

His eyes were open. They gleamed dully as the beam hit them.

He didn't blink. His pupils were fixed. Unseeing.

It hit Riley then like a thunderclap: *Jeff* was hanging by the neck from the gallery railing. He was *dead*.

Agony exploded inside her chest.

Oh, God. Oh, God.

A scream ripped into her already aching throat, where the constriction of the muscles there strangled it before it could escape.

Everything seemed to blur. The room spun. Her phone fell from her suddenly nerveless fingers. Realization merged with grief merged with fear, combining into a deadly lance that stabbed her through the heart.

Jeff. Oh, God. Jeff.

Her knees gave out abruptly, and she crumpled to the floor.

THE CLATTER of her phone hitting marble was unexpected. The sharp sound made Finn stiffen. But there was no threat to him, and his mind recognized that even as his body responded instinctively to the unexpected noise by reaching for his gun.

Chill out. Wait.

His hand dropped.

Still concealed by the darkness that she had almost breached with her makeshift flashlight, he watched her sink to her knees, watched her head drop forward to meet them, watched her shudder and shake. He knew who she was, of course. It was his business to know all the players in the game. Even before moonlight had touched the bright flame of her hair, even before he'd gotten a look at the beautiful, fine-boned face and slender, shapely figure that had prompted the only son of a billionaire to marry Little Miss Nobody from

Nowhere (which was what Houston's catty female upper crust called her behind her back), he'd recognized her voice.

After all, he'd been listening in on her phone conversations with Jeffy-boy for the last couple of days.

Riley Wozniak Cowan. With her blue-collar Philly roots and her matching Yankee accent, which by itself was enough to make her voice a stand-out in this world of the slow Texas drawl.

Watching her now as she huddled there on the floor, clearly in the grip of strong emotion, he felt nothing, no pity, no concern, only a mild impatience as he waited for the shock to wear off, for her to start to cry, to scream, to run away.

She did none of those things. After a long moment, she picked up her phone. Then she got to her feet, stuck her phone down inside the small purse that hung from her shoulder, and stepped close to the corpse. She was wearing a snug little white dress with a short skirt and sky-high heels, and Finn couldn't help but notice the long, slim line of her legs as she went way up on her toes and her hemline rode up her thighs almost to the curve of her ass.

Stretching, she reached up, holding on to the corpse, fumbled around with it doing something he couldn't quite make out, and came back down with— he squinted—Jeffy-boy's phone, in some kind of clear plastic pouch that seemed to have been clipped onto the waistband of his shorts. She said something—her murmur was too low to allow Finn to make out the words—presumably to the corpse. Then she touched

Cowan again—a quick, caressing slide of pale fingers against the equally pale skin of his leg—and turned and headed for the door, head high, those sexy high heels click-clacking purposefully over the floor, moving way faster than she had when she'd come in.

The speed with which she left was the only sign of agitation she now showed.

Having taken Cowan's phone, she was walking away, leaving his dead body hanging just the way she'd found it.

Not what he'd been expecting.

A cool customer. He hadn't pegged her as that.

Finn found himself wondering *why* she wasn't screaming the roof down, or phoning for help.

Along with what was on that phone.

Bottom line, she wasn't behaving the way a woman who'd just found her ex-husband dead ought to behave.

Intrigued, he followed her, careful to keep out of sight.

— CHAPTER —
TWO

The funeral was a nightmare. Not that Riley had been expecting anything else.

"Rest eternal grant to him—"

The final words of the funeral service resonated through the still air, rising over the shuffling of feet, the rustling of the paper programs, the buzz of insects and twitter of birds, the distant drone of traffic. They couldn't have made less sense to Riley than if they were being spoken in Swahili.

Jeff killed himself.

The thought looped endlessly through her mind, tearing her up inside. But her automatic reaction to the idea was even worse, because it was terrifying: *No way in hell.*

It was Thursday afternoon, just after 4 p.m. Blazingly hot. The endless, perfectly groomed green acres of exclusive Glenwood Cemetery seemed to shimmer beneath the cloudless blue sky. The leaves of the single tall oak mercifully shading those closest to the grave from the sun hung motionless, dusty and limp from the prolonged drought that the area had been experiencing. The sickeningly sweet perfume of flowers permeated the air, overwhelming enough to make Riley sick to her stomach. The last time she'd smelled flowers in such profusion had been—*don't think about it.*

She thrust the unwelcome memory out of her mind before it even had a chance to fully form. But, like the heat, there was no escaping that perfume. And that would be because flowers were everywhere. Chrysanthemums. Lilies. Roses. Carnations. Gladiolas. Wreaths, vases, baskets, and sprays of them, massed in undulating drifts of brilliant color behind Father Snyder, the white-robed Episcopal priest who was officiating.

So many flowers. As if by sending them, lifelong friends could make up for the way they had abandoned the Cowans in droves in the nine months since George's arrest. George was the only one who had committed any crimes; but the rest of the family had paid the price, as well, becoming pariahs virtually overnight.

We're sorry now? Is that what the flowers were supposed to say? If that was the message, it was, in Riley's opinion, too little, too late.

The fury that was the reverse side of her grief flamed like a blowtorch through her veins.

Today there were hundreds of people gathered around despite the fact that the funeral ostensibly was private. The shuffling, staring arc of them crowded in among the monuments, covering the sea of grass and spilling out onto the service road bordering this section of graves. Columns of them threaded between the parked cars lining the service road before solidifying into a mass again on the next section of grass on the other side of the road.

The suicide of George Cowan's only son was international news. The TV channels had been talking about it for days. The funeral was the latest chapter in the spectacular downfall of one of the state's most prominent families. Amazing how many people wanted to get an up-close-and-personal look at that.

Most of the onlookers were standing in the full sun. They had to be broiling alive. It was a small, petty consolation, but at the moment it was all she had.

Jeff didn't commit suicide. Riley thrust the conviction out of her mind. She couldn't allow herself to think about that, not now, not until her grief-numbed brain was fully functional again. To know even as much as she thought she knew was scaring her to death. And if her suspicions were correct, it was dangerous, too.

Despite the heat she felt cold all over. Her fingers tightened convulsively around the cool, smooth stems of the bouquet of white carnations she held. Their spicy scent wafted up to her nostrils: not good. Her stomach gave a warning heave.

She'd shared her suspicions about Jeff's death with the cops, for all the good that did. Nobody took her seriously. Nobody wanted to know.

They killed him, she wanted to scream at the assembled company. But she had no proof, nothing to back it up. Nothing except Jeff's own suspicions, which up until she'd found him dead she, too, had firmly dismissed.

Oh, God, why hadn't she paid more attention when he'd told her that he thought people close to his father were being murdered? This faceless *they* he'd kept talking on and on about—she had only the vaguest idea who he might have meant.

There were three new, weird photos on his phone. She'd seen that much, before she'd had a panic-inducing epiphany and taken the phone apart. A couple of men, snapped in the dark, the images blurry, their features indistinct and impossible to identify in the quick look she'd taken before the possible ramifications of what she was seeing burst upon her. They were the last pictures on Jeff's phone: were they of his killers, captured as they'd closed in on him?

Even now, her blood ran cold at the thought.

Of course, they could have been of anybody. His drug dealers. Loan sharks he'd owed money to. Goons hired by the enraged husband or boyfriend of some woman he'd messed with to beat him up. With Jeff, she'd learned never to discount any possibility.

Which was why she hadn't said a word about the pictures to anyone.

Once she'd had a chance to go through everything that was on that phone—Jeff kept his life on it—she might share those pictures with the cops. Even though they'd made it abundantly clear that they didn't want to know.

Because Jeff was George Cowan's son, nobody in

officialdom cared that he was dead. They weren't going to investigate. Suicide, case closed, good riddance.

A fresh burst of anger shot through her.

Jeff's father had ripped off friends, neighbors, business associates. Celebrities. Charitable organizations. Multinational companies. God knew who else. There were thousands of victims. Among the scammed were some pretty unsavory types. *That's* what she knew for sure.

If they thought I could identify them, they'd kill me.

A hard knot of fear settled in her chest as she recalled a conversation she and Jeff had had less than a week ago.

"I believe Marilyn Monroe committed suicide. I believe Lee Harvey Oswald acted alone. I believe Princess Diana's death was an accident." Her flippant reply to Jeff when he'd asked her in exasperation if she was hearing what he was telling her haunted her now.

"Marcus Simms did not die in a hunting accident. Patty Hemming did not 'accidentally' fall down her basement stairs. Diane Schneidermann did not jump from her hotel room balcony. Tom Goodin did not hook up a hose from his car's tailpipe to its front window and kill himself with carbon monoxide poisoning," Jeff retorted. The people he named had worked closely with his father, Riley knew. Besides that, what they had in common was that they had all died from either accidents or suicide since George had been arrested.

Her response was impatient. "For God's sake, Jeff, accidents happen. And Diane and Tom—they were under federal investigation. Maybe they were depressed. Maybe they were *guilty*. Maybe they were afraid of going to jail for the rest of their lives like your father. You don't *know* what was going on with them."

"They didn't kill themselves," he insisted stubbornly. "And Marcus and Patty—those weren't accidents."

Now Jeff was dead. A suicide? No. She would never believe it. Never. She knew Jeff. He would never, ever take his own life.

Standing beside Jeff's open grave, refusing to allow herself to look down at his coffin, which had just been lowered to rest at the bottom of the shaft of raw red earth, Riley could feel the eyes of the mourners—and the reporters, and the gawkers, and the federal agents who made up a sizable contingent of the crowd—on her. The thought that *they* might be among them made her heart beat faster.

Jeff's murderer might be watching me right now. The thought made her skin crawl. She cast a hunted look around.

Everyone seemed to be looking her way. But then again, Jeff's family was beside her. The priest was close. Where else were they going to look?

So much for sussing out the killer like that.

Thankful for the sunglasses that shielded her eyes from the multitude of avid gazes, she kept her spine straight and concentrated on ignoring everything except the progress of an intrepid ant that was making its way across the toe of Father Snyder's shiny black shoe.

On her right, Jeff's mother, Margaret, pressed close to her side, her thin frame shaking, her narrow, patrician face streaked with the tears that regularly trickled from beneath her sunglasses. On Margaret's other side, Emma, Jeff's seventeen-year-old sister, stood unmoving, her face a pale, expressionless mask. Devastated, the three of them in their funeral black dresses and pearls and pumps formed a small, isolated island of grief, united against what felt like the whole world.

Funny that those two should be her family now, but that was how things had worked out. Her marriage to Jeff hadn't lasted. Her ties to his mother and sister had grown as strong as if they were her blood kin. They'd bonded in their mutual heartbreak over Jeff's downward spiral of drinking and drug abuse, and Margaret and Emma had understood her reasons and supported her through the divorce, even as they had continued to love Jeff. In return, when their world had come crashing down, Riley had been there for them.

"Mrs. Cowan, would you like to drop your flowers on the casket now?" Father Snyder asked Margaret quietly.

Margaret shuddered. Her fingers closed almost painfully on Riley's arm, the beautifully kept nails digging into her skin. But Margaret kept her outward composure, nodding jerkily once and then stepping forward. Besides the wet tracks of her tears—something Riley knew Margaret would have hidden if she could have—the only outward sign of distress she showed was the trembling of the bunch of white carnations in her hands.

Riley tried not to think of the cameramen in the crowd, or the millions of people across the world who were undoubtedly watching those trembling flowers live on their TV screens at that very moment. Margaret was such a private person. She didn't deserve to have to grieve the death of her only son in such a shatteringly public way.

Damn you, George, for what you've done to Margaret and Emma—and Jeff. Oh, God, and Jeff.

Once again pain was almost a living thing inside her.

Another spurt of rage, this time at her arrogant bully of a father-in-law, almost balanced out the pain. Then Riley looked at Margaret's bowed head and rigid back, and sorrow once again tightened its icy grip on her heart.

Father Snyder said something, and the crowd responded in the expected ritual reply as Margaret dropped the flowers into the open grave. Riley flinched—she hoped not outwardly—as they landed with a soft thud. At Father Snyder's signal Riley stepped forward and followed suit, watching her flowers hit the surface of the box that held Jeff's remains— *Jeff's remains!*—with a deepening sense of unreality that she actually welcomed, because it kept the worst of her grief at bay. Emma, who looked so like Jeff with her delicate features and build and long, pale blond hair that just glancing in her direction made Riley's stomach tighten, was not as stoic.

Dropping her flowers in turn, Emma choked out, " 'Bye, Jeff," then broke into noisy, racking sobs as she stepped back from the edge of the grave.

Emma had adored her big brother.

Riley's heart ripped open and bled.

"Oh, baby." Margaret wrapped her arms around her daughter, who turned into them and lowered her head to sob openly on her shoulder.

Riley heard the whirr of the cameras, felt the sudden heightening in the crowd's interest as they zeroed in on Emma's heartbreak. She stiffened. Her hands closed in impotent fists.

Vultures.

There was nothing she could do. No way to protect Emma. No way to protect Margaret. No way to protect herself.

Lips tightening, chin tilting up in defiance of the multitudes clearly feeding on this fresh infusion of drama, Riley faced the fact that her only option was to continue to stand beside Jeff's mother and sister and endure as Father Snyder intoned the closing words of the service.

"I can't believe he's dead," Emma sobbed. *"Why?"*

"We're going to be okay, Em," Riley promised her sister-in-law quietly, while Margaret held her daughter close and murmured what comforting words she could. Jeff hadn't told his mother or sister about his conviction that George's associates were being bumped off, because he hadn't wanted to worry them, and Riley hadn't told them that she was actually the one who had found Jeff's body: after she'd gotten well away from the house, an anonymous call (from her, on her ID-blocked cell) had alerted the police, who had officially discovered it. Nevertheless, Margaret and Emma shared her certainty that Jeff had been murdered, because they knew him as well as she did—and because the thought that he had killed himself was just too dreadful for them to bear. If they knew what she knew they would never let the matter rest. She was afraid that delving too deeply into Jeff's death might make them targets.

She was afraid that delving too deeply into Jeff's death might make *her* a target. It was kind of like that if-a-tree-falls-in-a-forest-where-no-one-can-hear-it-does-it-make-a-sound thing: if no one *knew* that Jeff had told her all his suspicions, that she had his phone, which contained the connect-the-dots material he had put together on the other questionable deaths and possibly photos of his killers and who knew what information besides, did that mean she was in danger anyway?

There was no way anyone could know that she had been the one to find Jeff's body. There was no way anyone could know that she'd taken Jeff's phone. There was no way anyone could know what was on that phone.

Was there?

Once the funeral was over, once her brain fog had lifted, she meant to go through the material on Jeff's phone with a fine-tooth comb.

But then she looked back at Margaret and Emma huddled together, and thought maybe she wouldn't.

After all, nothing she found would bring Jeff back. She had herself and Margaret and Emma to think about now. Maybe it would be best to simply let a murdered ex-husband lie.

"I miss him so much," Emma sobbed into her mother's shoulder.

Riley's insides twisted. For the three of them, Jeff's death was the ultimate nightmare, the culmination of nearly a year of terrible events, and if one of them openly broke now under the weight of it, the only surprising thing about it would be that it hadn't happened sooner.

Father Snyder said, "Let us pray."

Riley bowed her head at the priest's directive. But the last thing in the world she felt like doing was praying, and her eyes stayed open. As Father Snyder's voice filled the air, she scanned the crowd. Impossible to say who she resented more: the unabashedly curious who, like her, ignored the directive to pray and kept craning their necks, or the reporters and camera crews that mingled with the crowd as if they had every right to be there, or Margaret's contingent of exquisitely coiffed and dressed high-society friends, only a very few of whom had bothered to stay in touch after George's arrest, or the snotty mean-girl group from Emma's expensive private high school who were obviously eating the whole thing up, or the dark-suited law enforcement types who stood out in this sea of dark-suited men because of their square-shouldered posture, their closed expressions and watchful eyes.

She was equal opportunity, Riley decided: she hated them all.

Her eyes collided with the glance of a tall, powerfully built man who was staring straight at her. His face was harsh-featured, too grim at the moment to be described as handsome, with broad, Slavic cheekbones and a hard mouth above a square jaw. His dark hair was cut ruthlessly short, and he had a deep, real-looking tan, as if he spent a lot of time outdoors. She guessed him to be in his late thirties, and she was as sure as it was possible to be that she had never seen him before in her life. He stood far back in the crowd, and she probably wouldn't have noticed him except that he was inches taller than the people around him and was regarding her intently.

Everything about him, from his haircut to his well-cut black suit to the big, muscular body it covered, to the way he stood with his hands clasped lightly in front of him, made her think federal agent.

Like everyone else, the feds were searching for the missing money. Hard to believe that something in the neighborhood of a billion dollars could just up and vanish, but George continued to insist that all the money was gone, spent in maintaining his lifestyle. She, Margaret, Emma, and especially Jeff had been questioned so often and so extensively about what they knew of its whereabouts that they had come to detest federal agents on sight.

That they'd had the nerve to invade Jeff's funeral infuriated her.

Bastards.

She glared at the man, which she realized a split second into it was a waste of time and effort—he wouldn't be able to tell because of her sunglasses.

". . . Amen," Father Snyder said, concluding the prayer, and Riley's attention shifted back to him as, along with the rest of the crowd, she responded with the obligatory "Amen."

Moments later the service ended, and when she glanced back toward the tall fed he was gone.

———————

FINN'S GAZE swept the crowd again. The tinted windows darkened the scene but didn't interfere with the details. Viktor Arshun was there. So were Tony Millan, Omar Khan, Al Guzman. All serious bad guys, enforcers for the Russian mob, stateside organized crime, Islamic-fascist interests, and the Medellín drug cartel, respectively. He knew them by sight, because it was his business to know them by sight. They didn't know him by sight, because it was his business to make sure they didn't. He had no doubt there were others like them in the mix, as well, circling the family and closest friends of George Cowan like sharks around chum.

Like him, they were after the money. From the look of things, Cowan had picked a lethal bunch to screw over.

No wonder he had practically run into the arms of the FBI when his crimes had been found out, pleading guilty even before he could be put on trial. Federal prison, where he was currently segregated from the general population, was the safest place on earth for him under the circumstances.

If he'd ended up anyplace else, he'd already be dead.

"Anything jump out at you?" Bax asked. He was behind the wheel of the inconspicuous gray Acura that was parked along the service road a few cars behind the limo that had brought the family to the cemetery. Far enough away to remain unnoticed among all the parked vehicles lining both sides of the road, but close enough to allow Finn to keep his eye on his target: Riley Cowan.

Who, to his annoyance, had made him. Her over-sized sunglasses had concealed her eyes, but the way her mouth had tightened as she looked at him, the way her jaw had firmed and her back had stiffened, the whole hostile vibe he'd picked up from her as she'd zeroed in on him out of the hundreds of mourners in the cemetery, had left him in no doubt that she'd noticed him and either taken an instant personal dislike to him (unlikely) or pegged him as a representative of something she had a problem with. Exactly what she had pegged him as, he couldn't be sure, although he guessed it was probably some kind of cop. It didn't matter: he wasn't there to be noticed, and it had prompted his retreat to the car. He'd just slid into the passenger seat beside Bax.

"Nah," Finn replied. He was burning up in his black suit, and not sorry to be out of the blazing heat even if it did slightly hamper his monitoring of the situation. Remote surveillance—hidden cameras, listening devices, etc.—had its limitations: person-to-person encounters outdoors were notoriously difficult to keep tabs on that way. Which was why he'd been standing among the crowd watching when he'd been made. He decided to humor Bax by feeding him what the other man would consider information. "They were talking to people before the service started, but none of it was really one-on-one. Looked like regular funeral stuff."

Jesus, the air-conditioning feels good. Texas in August is hot as hell. Who could live full-time in a place like this?

For an instant Finn thought of Wyoming: the weather would be beautiful, cool and sunny, nothing like this raging furnace. He'd give a lot to be back there right now, working the ranch he'd bought and was slowly whipping into shape. Fixing fences, constructing shelters for the herd of Angus cattle he was building up, tending to the livestock—all that had been therapy for him after his last assignment had gone disastrously wrong. He'd almost been killed, a friend had been killed, and he'd retired. For almost three years, he'd been free. Had thought he was free forever. Then the summons had come: they needed him again.

His lip curled: it was one of those offers you couldn't refuse.

He hadn't even thought they knew where he was.

"You really think one of them knows where the money is?" Bax asked.

"Hard to say," Finn responded noncommittally, knowing that Bax was referring to the Cowan women

who he was watching, too. "George had to know his
house of cards was going to collapse someday. No
way he didn't prepare for the eventuality. No way he
doesn't have a stash. No way he didn't tell somebody
where to find his stash. Was it one of them? I don't
know yet."

"My money was on Jeff. But with him dead and
no activity anywhere . . ." Bax shrugged and his voice
trailed off. Once Finn had informed him that he hadn't
killed Jeff, Bax had been able to take a more objective
view of what had gone down. By no activity, he meant
none of the literally thousands of communication
channels the government was monitoring had lit up in
the wake of Jeff's death.

"Doesn't mean he didn't know," Finn said, glancing at the camera. "Just means he didn't tell anybody
we know about before he died. At least, not so we've
discovered."

If Jeff had talked to whoever had killed him, the
sharks wouldn't still be hanging around. Word spread
fast in a community like theirs, and somebody would
be making a grab for the money. Unless the recipient
of Jeff's confidence was smart enough *not* to make a
move.

His gaze fastened thoughtfully on Riley Cowan,
holding hands with her mother-in-law, whose other
arm was around her wilting and tearful teen daughter.
Despite the heat, and the tragic circumstances,
the three of them still managed to look coolly elegant
as they stood for a moment talking to the minister
with the crowd in motion around them. They were no

longer card-carrying members of the one percent—far from it—but despite the spectacular fall in their circumstances they still had that indefinable air about them that marked the rich. He supposed that wasn't so surprising in the mother, Margaret, who was rail thin with the kind of carefully kept, chin-length blond hair that seemed universal to wealthy women of a certain age, or the sister, Emma, a pretty teen with a long, flaxen ponytail, who incidentally was the only one to show the kind of emotion he would have expected from the deceased's loving family. They'd been born rich, lived all their lives in a silver spoon world. The ex-wife—the joker in the deck—whose bright red hair and killer curves made her stand out in the crowd, was the one who surprised him.

Who kept on surprising him.

For the funeral her sleeveless dress was knee-length, figure-skimming, conservative. A far cry from the short, tight number she'd been wearing when he'd watched her discover Jeff's body. With her milk-white skin and fine features, she looked as to-the-manor-born as any of them.

Not bad for the daughter of a diner waitress and a steelworker. The background check he'd done on her had revealed a gritty past. Her dad had abandoned the family when she was eight. Her mother had died when she was seventeen, after struggling to provide for Riley and a younger, disabled sister. After that, Riley had done it all, going to school, working, taking care of the sister right up until the sister died, about six months before she met Jeff.

And the rest, as they say, was history.

Finn hadn't liked Jeff Cowan. He had zero respect for the guy. But he had to admit that the bogus billionaire's baby boy could pick 'em: the woman was out of the ordinary, and not just because she was smokin' hot.

But did she know where the money was? The jury was still out on that. At the very least, her actions made her extremely interesting to him.

To begin with, she'd squawked her head off to the local yokels about her suspicions that Jeff had been murdered, but she hadn't said a word to anybody about walking inside the family mansion in the middle of the night and finding her ex-husband's body. And as far as he could tell, she hadn't told a soul about taking that phone.

Which ten minutes later she'd disabled by removing the battery, so that if anyone tried remotely locating it they would come up empty.

He wouldn't have expected her to even think of doing something like that, much less know how to do it.

Smart woman. The question was, how smart?

She had a degree in finance. And she'd been building her own investment firm before George's arrest brought the walls tumbling down.

It was a combination that had earned her his undivided attention, unless and until a more viable prospect came along.

"You *sure* Cowan didn't commit suicide?" Bax asked, his tone almost diffident. A chubby five eleven, he had chipmunk cheeks, a snub nose, and smallish blue eyes beneath a light brown brush cut. He was an FBI special agent, but not exactly what anyone would picture when they thought FBI agent: he was a number cruncher, a computer nerd, a geek whose specialty was financial crimes.

Finn had been brought in as the "asset recovery specialist," in alphabet agency speak. With no official government role, he had an unofficial mandate to do whatever he had to do to locate the missing money. Bax was, technically, his supervisor. The handler charged with holding the attack dog's leash.

Good luck with that.

"Yeah," Finn replied without elaborating. Once upon a time, as a deep-cover CIA operative, it had been his business to get men to talk. He knew all the techniques. He had no doubt that Jeff's eventual death might well have been part of the program that night. But someone had gotten sloppy, and it had happened sooner than anticipated.

If whoever had killed him had been good at their jobs, Finn might even have arrived in time to save the little turd's life.

For a price, of course. Everything worth having always came with a price. In Jeff's case, that price would have been information.

He had a feeling that by the time he'd shown up, Jeff would have been more than willing to tell everything he knew.

"Maybe we should just go ahead and question her. Now that the funeral's over and everything, I mean,"

Bax said uneasily. He was referring to Riley Cowan, whose bright red hair made her impossible to miss among the eddy and swirl of the crowd.

Finn watched her walking across the grass.

"Margaret! Emma! Riley! Look this way!" a man shouted.

Finn turned his head to find that TV crews were closing in on the women. Local cops were present to provide security. Not one of them made a move to intervene. Heading off assault by media clearly wasn't why they were there. All three made the classic mistake of looking toward the shout as reporters and cameras converged on them. Their only defense against the onslaught was to avert their faces and hurry toward the limo. A couple of men in suits, rent-a-cop types, got between the women and the oncoming horde. A uniformed driver—part of the package provided by the funeral home, Finn had no doubt—jumped out to open the rear door for them.

The tilt of Riley Cowan's head and her long strides as they ate up the grass radiated anger. Those oversized dark glasses hid her eyes, but her jaw was rigid with tension and her mouth was hard with it.

"I want to hold off approaching her directly for a little longer," Finn replied to Bax, watching as the trio reached the limo.

Stonily ignoring the shouting, swarming reporters that her woeful security team was doing a piss-poor job of holding at bay, Riley got in last, sliding into the car behind her mother- and sister-in-law. He got the impression that she was protective of them, which was another interesting thing under the circumstances. Since she'd divorced the Crown Prince, he would have expected her relationship with her in-laws to be less than cordial.

If nothing happened in a day or two, he decided, he would pay her a visit, but for the moment he preferred to wait and see what, if anything, she would do. Now that Jeff's funeral was over, she might make a move.

He would be waiting if she did.

Softly, softly, catchee monkey.

— CHAPTER —
THREE

"Will this awful day never end?" Margaret murmured as Riley stopped beside her.

Under the cover of the rattling of the air conditioner and the murmur of dozens of voices, it was possible to steal a few moments of private conversation even though the house was packed. The older woman was pale and exhausted-looking, with dark circles under her eyes. Riley's concern for her, already high, ratcheted up another notch.

"The answer was a big 'no,' hmm?" Riley's voice was equally low. She could tell that just from looking at Margaret's face. Margaret had been meaning to ask Bill Stengel, their longtime lawyer, if there was any way around the clause in Jeff's small life insurance policy that precluded a payout for suicide, especially in the face of the family's contention that he was murdered. When Riley had seen them talking a few minutes before, she'd been pretty sure of the topic.

"Bill says the company has to go by the official cause of death." Margaret sounded defeated.

"Figures." Riley wasn't surprised. The way things had been going lately, the surprise would have been any scrap of good news.

They were in the small dining room of the modest brick house that Margaret and Emma had shared with Jeff after George had gone to prison. With a living room, dining room, kitchen, three bedrooms, and a single bath all on one level, the rental was a little run-down but had the immense advantage of being cheap, which was what mattered most to them nowadays.

The walls were painted in muddy earth tones, the floors were scuffed hardwood, and the furniture—because the family hadn't been allowed to keep much more of their previous belongings than a few select personal items and their clothes—had been bought at a secondhand store.

Margaret looked as out of place in it as a peacock in a chicken coop, but she was adapting with a dignity that, to Riley, was the embodiment of what she'd grown up referring to as class in North Philly. (One thing Riley had learned since marrying Jeff was that people with class never talked about anyone having class. It was the poor shmucks without it, of which she had to admit she was still one, who used *class* as a descriptive.)

Case in point: without any outward sign of embarrassment, Margaret was hosting the traditional postfuneral reception in a house that most of her acquaintances clearly, if silently, despised.

In theory, only close friends of the family should have been present, but in actuality the guests were a hodgepodge assortment ranging from a few of Riley's coworkers to Jeff and Riley's onetime couple friends to high school students to members of some of Houston's wealthiest clans. A pair of security guards at the door—they worked weekends at the Palm Room just like she did and Riley was paying them out of her own pocket for tonight—were charged with keeping out undesirables, such as media and law enforcement types. Catty, gossipy socialites were harder to defend against, and Riley had little doubt that the Cowans' reduced circumstances would, like Jeff's death and George's arrest, be an endless topic of conversation among the country club set for the foreseeable future.

"Did you eat?" Riley asked.

"Yes," Margaret replied. Riley knew Margaret was lying but she also knew that there was no point in calling her on it. None of them had been able to eat more than a few bites at a time since it had happened. "I don't think Emma has."

Emma had a troubling tendency not to eat when she was under stress. She'd always been slender, but since George's arrest she'd lost weight until now she was almost too thin. Riley hated to think what kind of long-term impact Jeff's death might have on her.

"She'll be okay," Riley said, both because she wanted to comfort Margaret and because she wanted to believe it was true.

"I hope so." Margaret glanced toward the dining

room table, where several guests were at that moment
loading their plates.

Earlier she'd overheard one of Margaret's couture-
clad friends whisper to another, as she'd picked up one
of the coated paper plates and looked down at it with
distaste, "Honestly. This is just embarrassing. Even if
you didn't have a dime, don't you think you could do
better than *this*?"

While it was certainly true that the spread was a far
cry from the lavish opulence customary at Oakwood—
where the table had been polished mahogany that
seated twenty, the plates were fine china, the silverware
was real silver, and at least two uniformed maids would
have been hovering over a repast prepared by Houston's finest caterers—Riley's blood had boiled, but
for the sake of Margaret and Emma, she hadn't said a
word.

Grimly she'd reminded herself, *Class, baby. Class.*

"Did you eat?" Margaret countered, looking at
Riley again.

"Yes," Riley lied in turn.

The savory aromas that hung in the air should
have made her hungry, should have been appetizing,
especially considering how little she'd eaten over
the past few days, but under the circumstances, to
Riley, they were the opposite of appetizing. She'd
had a knot of dread in her stomach since finding
Jeff's body, and just the thought of food, much less
the smell of it, made her feel queasy. Which was why,
having refilled the potato salad, she had been hurrying out of the room with an empty bowl in her hand

when Margaret had entered, catching her just short of the doorway.

"Riley. You need to." Margaret clearly didn't believe Riley any more than Riley had believed her.

Riley sighed. What was the point of pretending?

"We all do," she said, including Emma in that. "We *will*, once . . ."

Her voice trailed off.

We've gotten used to Jeff being gone, was how that sentence was meant to end. But she couldn't say it aloud, and Margaret didn't need to hear it.

But Margaret apparently understood, because she nodded, then glanced away. "It's getting dark out."

The beige, discount-department-store curtains were drawn to keep out curious eyes, but in this room they didn't quite meet in the middle. Through the gap it was possible to see that outside, twilight was falling. Soon it would be full night.

Riley asked, "Do you want me to start hinting that it's time for everybody to go?"

Margaret shook her head. Her blue eyes were red-rimmed and blurry-looking, but the tears had stopped after the funeral and she looked composed. "It's been good to see people again. And they'll probably start to leave soon anyway."

The thought that it would probably be a long time if ever before Margaret saw most of these particular people—these fair-weather friends, in Riley's humble opinion—again popped into Riley's mind, but she didn't say it.

"You'd think," Riley replied, then hesitated. She

hated to leave Margaret to deal with a houseful of guests on her own, but on the other hand she hated the thought of leaving Margaret and Emma alone after everyone had gone even more. "I'm going to run home and grab some clean clothes, and then I'll be back."

She'd been staying with them since Sunday night. With every fiber of her being she wanted to get back to her own apartment, to her routine, her life, but Jeff's death had shattered any possibility of that: the hard truth was that normal had flown out the window, and whatever eventually took its place would necessarily be different from what had been before.

In any case, she couldn't walk away from Margaret and Emma now: they needed her. Without Jeff in it, with the newness and horror of his death still so raw that it was like an open wound, the house was a sad and lonely place. She couldn't just abandon Margaret and Emma to it.

"You don't have to keep sleeping over here with us." Margaret patted Riley's arm affectionately. Her fingers felt as cold as ice. Riley knew Jeff's mother hadn't been sleeping, and was running on pure adrenaline. She knew, because she was in the same situation. "Aren't you supposed go back to work tomorrow?"

Riley nodded. Her new day job was as a loan officer for a car dealership. She'd taken it, and her night job, as well, in the wake of George's arrest. She'd needed a steady paycheck to help support the family, who'd been rendered penniless practically overnight as accounts were frozen and assets seized. There was no possible way she could stand by and not help. Margaret and Emma had become as dear to her as if they were her own mother and sister, and they, and Jeff, were useless as moneymakers. Family took care of family was how she'd always lived. They were hers now, and she was theirs. Before that she'd been in the process of building her own investment advisory business, using her finance degree from Drexel and the connections she'd made as a member of the Cowan family to establish a small but growing client base. Of course, after George's arrest, her connection to the Cowan family had turned from an asset into an instant poison pill. Her clients had quit her en masse, and her income—she'd been working strictly on commission—had dried up to nearly nothing.

So now she took car loan applications for Simpson Motors by day (Patti Simpson was one of the few friends she'd retained after the Cowan name became mud) and oversaw what was basically a high-end bar by night.

At some later date, she would probably have her maiden name restored, the better to distance herself from what George had done. But even then she would have to move far, far away from Houston, because in the wake of the scandal everybody for a couple of hundred miles in all directions pretty much recognized her on sight.

"I don't want to be on my own yet," Riley lied again. "Are you working next week?"

"Tina told me to take as long as I need." Margaret grimaced. She had taken the only job she'd been offered—as a salesclerk in the high-end resale shop where she'd once sold her own cast-off designer clothes. Riley knew there was no way Margaret didn't hate it, didn't feel the sting of waiting on women who had once been her friends, but she had never uttered a word of complaint. And there it was again, Riley thought: *class*. Something that at this point she was pretty sure she herself was never going to acquire. "I'll probably go back on Monday."

Unspoken between them was the fact that they needed the money. It was near the end of the month, and rent—for the house and Riley's apartment—was due shortly. Margaret still struggled with the concept of "broke"—to a woman who'd always had unlimited available funds, who'd been able to write a check or swipe a charge card for anything she wanted, having to watch every penny was as alien as trying to live on the moon—but to her credit she was learning.

"What about Emma?" Riley asked. Emma, a talented artist, was attending the Houston Museum of Fine Arts Painters' Studio, a prestigious (free) summer program that she had worked hard to be accepted into. At one point her college plans had focused on the Rhode Island School of Design, but without a scholarship that probably wasn't going to happen. She and Margaret were hoping that this summer program might open up some scholarship doors.

Margaret sighed. "Monday? We'll see."

"Okay." Riley nodded again. "Listen, I'm going to head out now. I won't be gone long. I'll bring back ice cream. Strawberry." It was Margaret's favorite flavor.

"And Chocolate Peanut Butter Crunch for Emma. Let's see her resist that."

Margaret smiled. It was a thin, tentative thing, with lips that were a little tremulous, but it was a smile, the first one Riley had seen out of her since she had learned of Jeff's death.

We're going to survive this, Riley promised herself silently.

"Remember how she used to love to stop at Baskin-Robbins?" The smile still hovered on Margaret's lips. Riley did remember: when she'd first come to live at Oakwood, Emma had been a sturdy ten-year-old who would beg to stop for ice cream any time they went anywhere.

And Jeff had still been her Prince Charming, and Margaret had been the kindly fairy godmother who'd taken a wary, jeans and T-shirt clad Riley under her wing and introduced her to the world of fine fashions, society functions, and the life of the uber-rich in general, and George had been the arrogant bully, and had remained so right up until the moment of his arrest.

That had been the thing that she'd brought to the table for Jeff—and Margaret and Emma, too. They were all three gentle souls, easily crushed, easily dominated. She was not. One thing she'd learned to do over the course of her life was stand up to bullies. She'd stood up to George for them.

"Margaret!" Lynn Sullivan, a thin, expensively dressed brunette who was one of Margaret's longtime social set, came up to them and, with a nod for Riley, put a toned and tanned arm around Margaret's shoulders. "Darling, we missed you at the Founders' Ball! You know we would love to have you back at Book Club! Why don't you—"

The Founders' Ball was a charity gala that was the highlight of Houston high-society's summer season. Two years before, Margaret had been its chair. This year she hadn't even received an invitation, not that she would have attended if she had been invited. Her world had changed too radically.

As Margaret listened to her friend extend an invitation to return to the monthly book club that she had once loved but whose members had made it wordlessly clear that they were now made uncomfortable by her presence, Riley moved away, slipping into the kitchen. Like the rest of the house, it was small and crowded, with tired yellow walls and outdated appliances.

She smiled at Bill Stengel, who was just inside the door and glanced over his shoulder as she entered. Stocky and balding, around Margaret's age of fifty-seven, he had a florid complexion and unremarkable features, and in his expensive gray suit looked exactly like the successful lawyer that he was. He was chatting with a couple that she didn't immediately recognize. She would have moved past with only a nod, but he caught her arm.

"Riley. How you holding up?" A Texan born and bred, his accent was strong.

Heartsick. Scared. Broke. "Fine."

Bill nodded like he thought she meant it, and gestured at the couple standing with him. "You know Ted and Sharon Enman?"

If she did, she couldn't place them, but she smiled like the answer was *of course*. As she engaged in the exchange of meaningless pleasantries that passed for conversation at death-related functions, her gaze slid past them and found Emma leaning against the counter next to the sink, surrounded by some of the girls from her (tony private) high school. They were slim and pretty and fashionable, and Emma was looking at them like they were attack dogs and she was a small creature at bay.

"Excuse me," she said, moving away from the small group and heading in Emma's direction, grimacing as she got close enough to overhear the conversation.

". . . so awful for you," Monica Grayson concluded in a sweetly sympathetic tone. With her waist-length black hair and big dark eyes, Monica had a slightly exotic appearance that made her look older than her seventeen years. From Emma's confidences, Riley knew that Monica was the head mean girl. She also knew that Monica was way into boys, who were usually way into her back. "I don't know how you can even hold up your *head*."

"Brent said to say hi. He said to tell you he totally would have come, but he had football practice, or something," Tori Meddors told Emma. She had glossy brown hair that curled up on her shoulders, and a carefully cultivated tan. Like Monica and the other girl who was with them, Natalie Frazier, she was part of the popular clique at Emma's high school. She had been frenemies with Emma since kindergarten. Riley saw Emma visibly wince at that reference to Brent, whom she had just started dating before George's arrest and who Riley knew she still really, really liked, even though Brent had stopped calling after George's arrest. When Brent had invited another girl to the junior/senior prom, Emma had stopped eating for days. She had ended up not going, and Margaret had worried herself sick over it.

"Oh, uh, tell him that's okay," Emma managed. She was gripping the plastic pitcher of iced tea she was holding like it was a life preserver and she was in stormy seas.

"Are you really going to be going to public school now?" Natalie asked in the kind of hushed tone someone might use to inquire about the onset of a fatal disease. Emma looked even more hunted. Riley winced inwardly. George had paid Emma's tuition for the previous year before his arrest, but now there was simply no money. Not for tuition or anything except the necessities.

"She only *hopes* she is. Haven't you ladies heard? All the hottest guys go to public school," Riley said as she reached them. "Have you checked out Pearland's football team? Monica, you'd *die*."

"Oh, hi, Riley," the girls chorused, while Emma shot her a grateful look. Meeting that look with a bracing one of her own, Riley added, "Em, your mother was wondering where you were with that tea."

"Oh, gosh, I forgot she wanted it," Emma said, then added to the girls, "I'd better get in there. Thanks for coming."

She slid away from her friends, and with a smile

for the girls Riley moved on toward the back door. One more reason she was sure Jeff hadn't committed suicide: he knew how fragile Emma was right now, had worried about her state of mind right along with Margaret and Riley, and wouldn't purposefully have shattered his little sister's life yet again for anything. Not when it had already been turned upside down by her good-for-nothing bastard of a father.

Damn you, George.

If she had a penny for every time those words had popped into her mind over the last few months, Riley thought, she would never have to work again for the rest of her life.

Seething with impotent anger was useless, though, so she did her best to put it and her worry about Emma and everything else aside except for her immediate objective of obtaining some clean clothes so that she could go to work tomorrow and pay the rent and utilities and buy food and gas, as she stepped out onto the small back stoop.

The sky was purple now, and the cicadas were singing. Someone nearby was grilling: she could smell the cooking meat, hear the laughing voices of children, the murmur of cheerful adult conversation. Somewhere happiness was in the air, and Riley looked in the direction of the cookout almost wistfully. Then reality bit: in her world, she had things to do, and darkness continued to close in. The sun was gone, and the long shadows that lay across the ground were merging until soon they would swallow everything.

Riley stood where she was for a moment longer,

savoring the solitude, taking a deep breath of the
still-sweltering air as her gaze carefully swept her surroundings.

The one truly positive thing about the scruffy
subdivision where Margaret's house was located was
that, except for the street out front, there was no
place for TV trucks to park, or camera crews to camp
out, or reporters to hide. The small patch of scorched
grass that was the backyard was surrounded by a tired
chain-link fence that was all but hidden by a dusty
vine, and it abutted a number of other tiny yards just
like it. The one-story houses were so close together
that if they didn't keep the drapes drawn at night they
could see into each other's windows. Living in such
unassuming surroundings wasn't a stretch for Riley,
who had grown up in even less prosperous circumstances, but for Margaret and Emma—and Jeff—it was
like being plunked down on the moon.

Pushing Jeff's image away for the time being—
thinking about him hurt too much—she stepped off
the stoop and walked quickly in the opposite direction
from the driveway, which was packed with cars, then
let herself out through the creaky metal gate on the far
side of the house. When they had arrived home after
the funeral there'd been quite a crowd out front, but
by this time it had largely dispersed. Two TV trucks
remained, she saw as she cast a cautious glance toward
the street, but only one camera crew was visible.

They were set up on the sidewalk opposite the
house, apparently conducting a running commentary
on God-knew-what while keeping their camera trained

on the front door, probably in hopes that someone gossip-worthy would enter or leave. A marked police car idled near the camera crew, and another drove slowly down the street, moving away from her. Parked cars lined the curb in both directions and a few people—neighbors or gawkers, Riley couldn't be sure which—stood around on the sidewalks talking as they cast occasional glances at the house.

Being the focus of the scandal-mongers sucked.

Congratulating herself on her foresight in parking her car around the corner and exiting through the back door, Riley slunk through the neighbors' front yards, careful to keep well away from the street. She didn't have far to go, but by the time she was halfway there she'd made the unwelcome discovery that she really didn't like being alone outside in the dark anymore. The shadows seemed to be closing in on her, and she kept thinking she could hear *something* sneaking along behind her. There was nothing there, of course—she checked—but by the time she saw her small white Mazda her pulse was racing and she was breathing way faster than she should have been. A shivery sense of unease kept her glancing over her shoulder even as she unlocked the car. She was starting to mentally chastise herself for being a coward, when it hit her:

Somebody murdered Jeff.

Under the circumstances, being scared wasn't only justified: it was smart.

That thought did not help her calm down. In fact, it made her go cold all over, despite the oppressive heat.

Glancing back, Riley could see the lights of the

camera crew across from Margaret's house. Most of the nearby houses had lights on inside them now. What she took from that was, *there are people nearby*. A scream would bring them running. Not that there was any need to scream: no one had followed her, no one was even close. It was dark, but not so dark she couldn't see well enough to be sure of that.

They don't have any reason to come after you. You never even worked at Cowan Investments.

Unless they knew she had Jeff's phone, and wanted it. Or thought Jeff had told her something. Or were killing Cowans for fun or profit. Or—

Stop it.

Yanking the door open, Riley got in, slammed it shut, hit the lock-doors button, started the car, and took off way faster than she normally would have done toward her apartment. And tried not to let the impossible-to-shake feeling that she was being watched completely terrify her.

— CHAPTER —
FOUR

"You suppose she's in for the night?" Bax asked as he carefully maneuvered the Acura into a vacant spot on the street outside Riley's apartment building.

It was a busy street, full of the kind of tall, boxlike structures that had been built all over Houston in the commercial real estate boom toward the end of the last century. Restaurants and offices and small shops occupied the lower floors of the buildings, and apartments and condos took up the upper floors, so there was plenty of activity, perfect for going unnoticed.

"Don't know." Finn's voice was tight with irritation as he watched her stride across the parking lot and come around the front of her building. Still in her funeral clothes, she looked haunted under the pale glow of the security lights. She was moving fast, and she gave a couple of quick, searching looks around that made him frown. He was confident she hadn't made them, but something seemed to have spooked her. Even from a distance, he could almost feel the waves of tension she was giving off. "We need to get this damned thing fixed or replaced *now*."

He tapped the blank screen of the mobile receiving unit that was propped on the console between the seats. About the size of a portable GPS, voice and/or motion activated, it was designed to monitor the roving bug that had been turned on in her cell phone. The bug allowed Finn to listen in on her mobile calls, of course, and also to track her anywhere she took her cell phone and listen to any conversation anywhere that cell phone was, even if the phone was powered off. He liked the technology because it was simple to use and it was almost impossible to detect.

Unfortunately, not long after they had started following her away from her mother-in-law's house the receiver had stopped picking up her phone's signal, which had led to a harried chase along the freeway and through the city streets. Finn was now discovering that the bug also wasn't working to track her present movements, or pick up any sound.

One possibility was that the receiver was dead.

The other was that during the course of the drive she'd disabled her phone the same way she'd disabled Jeff's.

If that was the case, there could be only one reason: she was afraid of being followed.

And instead of being interested, he was now officially downright fascinated.

To his annoyance, for the moment Finn's only recourse was to track her visually. As Bax picked up

the receiver and started fiddling with it, Riley pushed
through her building's revolving door, slim legs flashing, bright hair gleaming beneath the warm interior
lights. For another moment he was able to watch her
through the building's wall of windows as she walked
quickly across the lobby, heading no doubt for the
elevators. Then she was out of sight.

Invisible to him.

Which was not good.

She could do anything. Talk to anybody. Disappear.

Damn it to hell and back anyway.

———————

HER APARTMENT was cool and quiet and dark. Two of
those things Riley welcomed. The third—darkness—
made her shudder. She banished it by flipping the light
switch the minute she stepped inside her door. The
overhead light came on, as did the two fat white ginger
jar lamps on either side of the couch. A quick scan of
the premises allowed her to relax a little. Her apartment was small, with a galley kitchen, living/dining
room combination, one bedroom, and one and a half
baths—and she could see most of it from where she
stood: unless somebody was under the bed or hiding
in the closets or bath, nobody was waiting to jump
her. Better yet, the place *felt* empty. Engaging the dead
bolt and chain that secured the door, Riley heaved a
sigh of relief. Only then did she realize how on edge
she'd been.

The skin-crawling sensation of being observed

that had been with her from practically the moment she'd left Margaret's house was finally gone.

The living room curtains were open, but since she was on the fourteenth floor and the building opposite was only twelve stories tall she never bothered closing them, as she liked being greeted by daylight when she stepped out of her bedroom in the mornings. The two tall windows were the best thing about the apartment: they fronted the street and let in lots of light. At the moment, she could see the city skyline glowing as it rose like uneven teeth to touch the midnight blue sky.

Her furnishings were minimal—a glass-topped dining table and four chairs, a black pleather couch and chair in front of a small flat-screen TV, a pair of glass-topped end tables, and, serving as both coffee table and storage, a carved wooden trunk. In the bedroom, she had a queen bed with a black and white floral spread, nightstands and chest, plus the desk that she used as her home office. The effect was clean and modern and she liked it. The government scavengers who'd seized everything belonging to the Cowans had come to her apartment, too, on the theory that her divorce was recent and anything she'd acquired during her marriage, like furniture, had been purchased with ill-gotten gains. Just as they'd done at Oakwood, they'd cleaned her place out despite the fact that, except for a few pieces, she'd bought everything new after she'd separated from Jeff. All they'd left her were her clothes and personal belongings. For good measure, they'd seized her bank accounts, too. Nobody had cared that the money she possessed had been hers; she'd taken nothing from the Cowans, nothing from Jeff. Their unfair treatment of her still rankled. Along with their ongoing suspicion of her and Margaret and Jeff, it was one of the reasons she despised them.

When she'd left Jeff she'd been fed up, furious. *You can take your money and shove it up your ass,* is what she'd snarled at him when he'd reminded her of everything she would be walking away from if she divorced him. At that point, all she'd wanted was her life back.

Since then, naturally, her life had gone to hell on a slide.

And she was just as involved with the Cowans as ever.

Grimacing, Riley kicked off her shoes, dropped her purse on the dining table, and padded barefoot across the smooth cushion of the gray wall-to-wall carpet, heading for her bedroom, unzipping her slim black sheath as she went. She felt sticky from the heat, and as she stripped down to her underwear she welcomed the feel of the air-conditioning on her bare skin.

I wish I could turn back time.

That was the useless thought that curled through her mind as she dropped her pearls (fake; the government had taken the real ones, along with the rest of her jewelry except, ironically, the wedding ring she no longer wore or wanted) on the nightstand, put her dress away, then walked into the small connecting bathroom to turn on the taps in the tub, opting for a bath over a shower because she didn't want to get her hair wet. With one bathroom shared between the three of them at Margaret's house, waiting to use it was a given, especially since one of their number was a teen who could spend hours locked in there doing God knows what.

As the water ran she returned to the bedroom, pulled her small suitcase out of the bottom of the closet, and quickly packed enough clothes to last for a few more days. After that, she would reevaluate.

Here, it was possible to pretend that the worst hadn't happened. Her apartment didn't reek of Jeff: he'd visited, but he'd never lived in it. Never even spent the night.

If I'd gotten to Oakwood faster . . .

Impatient with herself, Riley pushed away the useless thought and focused on the task at hand. Conservative suits for the car dealership, sexy dresses for the club. Her work wardrobe reminded her of a mullet: business during the day, party at night.

Packing done, she stripped down to her skin and walked into the bathroom, which was tiny and windowless and strictly utilitarian. The bath was ready: she turned off the taps, twisted her hair up, secured the coil by the simple expedient of shoving the business end of a rattail comb through it, and stepped into the tub.

The water was blissfully hot. As she sank down into it, Riley felt her tense muscles begin to relax for the first time since she had walked into Oakwood that terrible night. She'd needed this, she realized: a little bit of time to herself.

As Mrs. Jeff Cowan, she'd become used to the ultimate in lavish living: gorgeous clothes; six-hundred-dollar-a-pair shoes; thousand-thread-count linens; the finest restaurants; the best clubs; private jets; high-end cars. Most of the materialism hadn't made much of an impression on her. But the one thing she'd come to love was luxurious toiletries.

Now as she lathered her skin with silky white bubbles, the sight and smell of the pink, flower-shaped, rose-scented bar that was one of her few remaining extravagances provided her with a familiar glimmer of pleasure. At least, until all the associations that came with the divine-smelling suds slammed her. Before she'd married Jeff, soap had been soap. Nothing special. Got the job done. The cheapest bar was usually the one she went for.

Their marriage hadn't worked. They hadn't been soul mates, or even compatible life partners. But he had changed her life. *He had introduced her to expensive soap.*

Ah, Jeff.

She closed her eyes, remembering. The first thing she'd noticed about him had been his blond hair gleaming under the light as he'd sat down at the very end of the bar where she was mixing drinks. The second thing, about an hour later, was his smile, rueful and charming, when after running a tab for four old fashioneds he'd discovered that he'd forgotten his wallet. Per bar policy, she'd been on the hook for his tab. She hadn't been happy, and she'd been even less happy when he'd pulled out car keys and informed her that he was going to drive to his apartment, retrieve his wallet, and be right back. Judging him unfit to drive, she called him a cab, and paid for that, too. She hadn't ever expected to see him again. But he'd shown up the next night, reimbursed her, and asked her out to dinner. He'd been sweet and kind and sober and straight, and over the following six months they'd fallen in love.

She'd married him because he'd needed taking care of, and, in the aftermath of losing the little sister she'd raised practically from birth, she'd needed someone who needed taking care of. She saw that now. But then—she'd been in love with him.

At least, with Lorna, she'd been there at the end. Not so with Jeff. He'd died alone.

He must have been so scared.

Don't think about it.

Her throat tightened. Tears stung her eyes. She gripped the soap so hard her nails dug into it.

Crying won't change a thing. I am not going to cry.

Riley let her head rest back against the smooth porcelain and squeezed her eyes even more tightly shut as she fought the tears she refused to shed.

A prickle along the back of her neck was accompanied by the eerie sense that she was not alone. Opening her eyes, blinking to force back welling tears, Riley caught the shadow of movement with her peripheral vision, turned her head so fast it hurt her neck, and saw a man step inside her bathroom and stop. Just like that, there he was, gray sneakers planted on the white tile just inside the door.

Every cell in her body froze.

Average height. Muscular build. Dark jeans. Navy polo shirt. *A black ski mask pulled down over his face.*

"Hello, Riley," he said, and as her heart jumped into her throat and her eyes popped wide he leaped for her.

Terror exploded inside her. Jolted into instant action, she screamed, so loud it echoed off the tiles, and hurled the round little cake of soap at him. It hit the middle of his chest and bounced harmlessly off even as she splashed and scrabbled at the slick porcelain and grabbed the built-in soap dish for leverage, somehow managing to catapult to her feet.

"Shut the fuck up." He snatched at her and got the billowing shower curtain instead as she flung it at him and shied violently away.

Go, go, go.

Shrieking like a train whistle, knowing that she had almost no chance of escape, Riley sprang from the tub. Her only hope was to somehow dodge past him, make it through the door, and run—but the bathroom was small and the sink was blocking her on the left and *he was right there*. Her wet feet slid precariously as they smacked down on smooth tile. Her heart jackhammered. Her pulse raced. She had no weapon, no way to escape.

He's between me and the door—

"*I said shut up.*" He caught her as she tried to barrel past him, his hands—*oh, God, he's wearing gloves, white surgical gloves; this is bad*—big and rough on her waist as he picked her up and threw her bodily back against the tiled wall. She hit with so much force that the breath was knocked out of her along with the scream and she banged her head, hard. The force of it snapped her teeth together, rattled her brain.

"Oh." She fell heavily, landing in the slippery tub, cracking her hip and elbow and shoulder painfully on the way down, splashing into the water, causing it to spill out of the bath in a great wave.

Stunned, she didn't even have time to suck in air for another scream before his hands closed on her shoulders and he forced her down beneath the surface of the water. Desperately she held her breath as she went under, her mouth somehow filling with the taste of the hot, soapy water even as she clamped her lips together.

No, no, no, no, no.

She fought like a wild thing, thrashing and kicking as water closed over her head, shooting up her nose, filling her ears, stinging her eyes. Instinctively she snapped them shut, then a moment later forced them to open a slit so that she could see, because being able to see what was happening seemed somehow paramount to survival. He was leaning over the tub, over *her,* his fingers digging into her shoulders, a blurry dark shape distorted by the waves of churning water sloshing around her. With every ounce of her strength she tried to tear herself free of his grip, to at least get her head above water for a second so that she could breathe, but he held her down against the bottom of the tub like he meant to keep her there forever.

Like he meant to drown her.

The horror of it hit her with the suddenness of a thunderclap.

My God, he's going to kill me! A second later, on a fresh wave of horror, she thought: *Like they killed Jeff.*

Like he *killed Jeff?*

Anger and terror combined to send adrenaline rocketing through her. Surging upward with an urgency born of mortal fear, Riley struggled desperately but still couldn't break free of his grip or get her face above the surface. Dying for air, she went for his eyes, just missed as he jerked back, and wound up raking her nails across the front of his mask and down the sides of his neck.

"You fucking—" He lifted her up by her shoulders— oh, God, thank God, her face was out of the water at last; she sucked in air with a greedy, shuddering gasp— and slammed her head hard against the back of the tub.

Riley saw stars.

Just as quick as that, he pushed her back down under the water and held her there with one hand locked around her throat.

She barely managed to press her lips together. Her lungs were empty. The blow to her head had made her exhale.

No, no, please, I can't breathe.

Panic blinded her. No, it was her hair, loose now, swirling in a dark cloud in front of her face. Her body writhed, twisted, as her empty lungs screamed to be filled. The feel of his rubber-gloved hand squeezing her throat was nightmarish. She grabbed his forearm, clawed at it, tried to knock it aside. As if in retaliation, his hand tightened with excruciating force, and then he let go. She shot upward, only to be caught again before she could reach air and breathe. Clamping on to her shoulders, he forced her down even deeper. Trapped.

He kept her shoulders pinned to the bottom of the tub. Her head swam; her ears rang. The smooth sides of the tub provided no purchase for her desperately scrabbling hands.

I need air. Her burning lungs cried out for her to inhale. It was all she could do not to give in to the increasingly urgent need, but if she did . . .

I'm going to die.

As the reality of that slammed into her, her heart pounded like it would burst out of her chest. Her pulse thundered in her ears.

Without warning he hauled her up so that her head was out of the water once more.

Oh, thank God.

Sucking in air for all she was worth, Riley coughed and choked and hacked up water and sucked more air into her starved lungs in a series of frantic wheezes.

"Pay attention, bitch."

He was talking to her. Water streamed from her hair, which hung down in front of her face and partially blocked her air intake and her vision. She tossed her head, slinging the soaked mass of it back, and to her surprise found herself looking at her attacker's face. In the same shocked instant in which she registered that his ski mask was gone she realized that he must have pulled it off when he'd switched to the one-handed grip on her throat. She'd grabbed his mask:

had she dislodged it somehow so that he couldn't see properly?

It didn't matter: the damage was done. He was no longer making any attempt to hide his features. Her eyes widened on a bony, sallow, thirty-something face with a long chin, large nose, full mouth twisted into a snarl. Short brown hair. Raised scar near the nose. Ugly. Scary.

I can see him clearly. I can identify him. He doesn't care if I can identify him.

Panic made her pulse rate skyrocket. It sent cold shivers racing down her spine.

"You scream again, or give me any more trouble, and I'll make you sorry." His voice grated. It had a faintly foreign intonation. It also left her in no doubt whatsoever that he meant what he said. He pushed her against the back of the tub, gave her shoulders a warning squeeze. As they dug into her flesh, his fingers hurt her. She trembled beneath them. "Understand?"

Dizzy with fear, Riley wheezed and coughed and nodded. She sat waist-deep in the sudsy remains of her still-hot bathwater with her legs stretched out in front of her and her hands braced on the bottom of the tub, rigid with dread and the suppressed energy of the fight-or-flight reflex that she had to control because at the moment she could do neither. His hands pinned her shoulders to the smooth tile wall behind her. The faint scent of roses hung in the air, grotesque to her now. Her eyes stung; she blinked rapidly to clear them.

Crouched beside the tub, her attacker loomed

over her, so close she could see that his eyes were brown. And hard. And mean.

The eyes of a killer.

The tiny hairs on the back of her neck stood up.

She was naked, and her nakedness didn't interest him. He wasn't there for that.

He didn't care if she saw his face.

The truth was inescapable.

He's going to kill me. Oh my God, is this how it happened to Jeff?

Her blood congealed into an icy slush that clogged her veins. Her heart thumped hard and fast.

"Where's the phone?" His fingers dug deeper into her shoulders. Cringing, Riley made an involuntary sound of pain. Fear tasted sour in her mouth. She swallowed, and looked at him out of what felt like enormous eyes.

His grip didn't ease. *"Where's the fucking phone?"*

Jeff's phone. He had to be talking about Jeff's phone. He knew she had it! Oh, God, how did he know?

"Answer me."

"I—I—" she stuttered, caught in a terrible quandary. If giving up the phone was the price of her life, she was willing to part with it that very second. Nothing, no link to Jeff's murder or anything else, was worth dying over. But if the phone was what he was after and she told him where it was, what reason would he have to keep her alive? He could kill her, take the phone, and be gone. What she needed was a plan.

He didn't give her time to even attempt to work

the problem out, or finish her answer. Instead he let out his breath in an impatient *hiss* and shoved her beneath the surface again.

Caught by surprise, Riley swallowed water and choked on it. Her lungs convulsed in protest. Needing to cough, needing to breathe, able to do neither, she thrashed violently.

No, no, no. Please . . .

Just when she thought her lungs would explode, he hauled her back up above the surface. Gasping, shuddering, blinking against the water that cascaded down her face, she inhaled, coughed like she was bringing up a lung, looked at him fearfully, and blurted, "I'll tell you. *I'll tell you,* okay?"

"So tell me." His tone was implacable. His eyes bored into hers, ruthless. Pitiless.

Her thoughts raced as she feverishly tried to come up with some way out.

Think. Think.

"It's—the phone's in my office. At the car dealership. Where I work." It was a lie. Her hope was that she could persuade him to let her get out of the tub. At least then she had a chance at making a run for it. Her voice shook. The rest of her was shaking, too, she realized. "I could take you there, right now. It's after closing, but there's a security guard. He knows me. He'll let me in."

He smiled at her, a slow smile that revealed a gold-edged front tooth. It was a predator's smile. Her heart lurched.

Dear God, I need help—

"We traced the phone's signal on the night your Jeff died. Funny thing—when his phone left the mansion, after the time that we know he was already dead, we picked up another signal that was traveling at the exact same moment on an identical path. Yours. Then Jeff's phone went dead. But yours—it continued on to this apartment with no deviation in the route." His tone was almost gentle. It, plus the look in his eyes, petrified her like nothing had ever done in her life. "I think it is here now. I think you are lying to me."

His eyes gleamed, his hands tightened, and she knew he was about to force her beneath the surface of the water again.

"No, wait!" She pressed back against the smooth porcelain behind her and babbled, "You're right. It's here. I'm sorry I lied. It's—there's a locked drawer in my desk. It's in there. I'll give you the combination." Her voice wavered, broke. "Just don't hurt me."

"You will get the phone for me." His fingers dug into her shoulders.

"Yes," she agreed.

He started hauling her up, out of the tub.

Was this man the last person Jeff had ever seen?

There it was again, the anger, spurting hot, only to be immediately swamped by the iciness of overwhelming fear. It was fear that dried her mouth, twisted her stomach, charged the air around her. Clumsy with it, she got one knee beneath her, pressed a hand to the bottom of the tub for balance—and touched something long and narrow and hard that was lying there on the slick porcelain beneath the water: the plastic tail of her comb. Sometime during her ordeal it had fallen from her hair.

Her breath caught. Her heart tripped. The end was pointed, sharp . . .

Even as he pulled her all the way to her feet, her fingers closed around the comb. Scooping it up, she kept it out of sight, pressed close against her thigh, clutching it so tightly that the teeth dug into her palm.

He warned, "If you lie to me—"

Her heart thumped like a piston, so loud she was afraid he might hear it. She could feel the outline of the comb burning like a brand against her skin.

Oh my God, do I dare?

Stepping out of the tub, she stumbled, catching her foot on the edge and pitching forward—

". . . a second time," he continued, steadying her as she lurched heavily against him. Her weight threw him just a little off balance. He had to let go of her shoulders and grabbed her upper arm instead. "I will hurt you. You will wish to die before—"

It's now or never.

Electrified by terror, she clenched her teeth and reared back and slammed the long pointy handle of her hard plastic comb into the side of his neck with all her might.

The feel of it sinking into his flesh made her think of a skewer plunging through meat.

He screamed, staggering forward. She screamed, too, loud and shrill as a siren, and ripped her arm from his hold and shoved him hard and ran like her life depended on it, which it did. From the corner of her eye she saw him go down on one knee even as he yanked the comb from his neck. Blood spurted out in a thin scarlet stream, spraying over the smooth white porcelain of the tub and adding a splotch of horrible color to the puddle on the floor.

"*Suka!* You fucking bitch!" he howled as she tore into her bedroom.

Without pausing to look back, she raced past the end of her bed even as she heard him coming after her, praying the wound she'd caused would slow her attacker down enough so that she could get out.

Alive.

— CHAPTER —
FIVE

R^{un.} The word ricocheted through her brain. Screaming until her lungs hurt, practically jumping out of her skin with terror, Riley flew through her apartment so fast her feet barely touched the carpet. Out of the bedroom, across the living room—it wasn't far, but the distance to the door seemed to stretch out endlessly. She felt like she was trapped in one of those slow-motion nightmares, being chased by a monster while making no progress at all.

Please God please God please.

A panicky glance over her shoulder found her attacker barreling through her bedroom door. His hand was clapped to the side of his neck. Blood flowed red between her fingers.

"*Koorva! Suka!*" he snarled.

That the foreign words he was hurling at her were curses, she had no doubt.

Oh, God, if he catches me . . .

Her heart thundered. Her pulse raced. Her feet felt like they had lead weights attached. He was closing fast: she could hear him, hear the breath rasping in his throat, the rustle of his clothing, the rushing thud of his footsteps. She could feel the hate and anger rolling off him in waves.

"Help! *Fire!*" she screamed, as a trick she'd been taught in a rape prevention class years before burst into her mind. She grabbed one of the lightweight dining chairs as she passed it, slinging it behind her to land with a crash in his path like it might actually slow him down.

It didn't. Out of the corner of her eye she saw him dodge around it even as she reached the door.

Hurry, hurry, hurry.

Dancing from one foot to the other, so frightened that she felt like her body was electrically charged with fear, she fumbled with the lock—the chain was off, thank God the chain was off!—and twisted it open. Then she grabbed for the knob.

"*Help! Fire!*" she screamed as she yanked the door open.

Risking one more terrified glance over her shoulder, she saw that he was no more than a few feet away, his face contorted with fury, both hands—one horribly red and shiny with blood—stretched out to grab her. More blood covered the side of his neck, disappeared into the open V-neck of his shirt. She could see that it still poured from the wound she had made.

"Get back here!" He snatched at her and missed, the rough warmth of his fingertips just brushing her back as she leaped out into the wide, dimly lit hall with its many closed doors, screaming "Help! Fire!" at the top of her lungs.

"I will kill you! *Suka!*"

"What the fuck?" The roar was loud enough to be heard even through her eardrum-shattering screams. It came from in front of her.

Head snapping around, Riley discovered that (thank God, thank God!) there was a man in the hall. A large man in a dark suit. He ran toward her from the direction of the elevators, responding to her screams, she thought, and *he had a gun in his hand.*

"Help!" She sped toward him with the urgency of a heat-seeking missile. Behind her, her attacker erupted through her apartment door with an enraged cry. Another terrified glance over her shoulder told her that he, too, had acquired a gun. He must have had it on him all along.

"Look out! He's got a—" She screamed a warning at the man racing toward her, breaking off before she got the all-important last word out as he lunged at her, hooked an arm around her waist, snatched her off her feet, and whirled around with her.

Bam! Bam!

The gun—her attacker's gun—fired twice, in rapid succession. Face muffled in her rescuer's chest, Riley screamed. The sound of two hands smacking the wall one right after the other not a foot to her left and the resultant shower of plaster chips told her where the bullets had hit. The man holding her—having already put his back between her and the weapon, she realized—threw her to the ground and dropped down on top of her, shielding her with his body. Hitting the floor hurt and having his considerable weight crash down on top of her hurt, too, but abject fear of her attacker was what had her screaming like a crazy woman into the suffocating curve of the wide chest that now arced above her face.

"Get down!" her rescuer yelled, presumably at someone who'd stepped into the path of possible gunfire.

A woman's cry. A man's shout. Running footsteps. A curse. The sounds were muffled by the big body above her.

From his position—one arm was braced beside her, holding the bulk of his weight off her, while the other seemed to be extended back down the hall toward where her attacker should be—she got the impression that he was aiming his gun but for whatever reason he didn't fire.

As her scream died away, the silence was deafening. She could hear nothing except the thumping of her own—or was it her rescuer's?—heart. A silk tie—black? Dark gray?—dangled in front of her. A smooth white shirt front pressed down against her cheek. She could feel the heat of his body beneath it, feel his chest rising and falling as he breathed. His legs in their suit pants were long and muscular and heavy against hers. She could smell—what? A hint of something fresh: fabric softener? Along with the earthier scent of man.

"Shots fired. Be on the lookout for an armed white male heading down the west fire stairs," her rescuer barked. From the sound of it, he was speaking into a phone or maybe a radio, which confirmed her impression that he was some kind of law enforcement. "Caucasian, short brown hair, about six foot, one eighty, dark polo shirt, jeans. Bleeding from the neck. Get the locals, watch the stairs and elevators, pick him up if you can."

"Is he gone?" A woman's voice quavered from some little distance away.

"Yes, ma'am," her rescuer replied, and then added, "It's all right, I'm with the FBI," and moved, shifting to one side, restoring his gun to his shoulder holster before levering himself off her.

As her field of vision opened up she looked quickly, fearfully past the big body that still hovered above her toward where her attacker had been and beyond, down the long hall in the direction in which he must have fled. He was nowhere in sight, and the relief of it prompted her to draw in a shuddering breath. The college-age couple who lived two doors down— she didn't know their names—were straightening away from where they'd been huddled against the wall just outside their apartment's open door. Mrs. Grant, the nosy, elderly woman who lived across the hall, peered through the gap in her chain-secured, slightly open door. Farther down the hall, she could see a few more barely opened doors with the shadows of people standing cautiously inside them.

"It's over. He's gone. You're safe," Mr. FBI told her quietly, having paused in the act of lifting himself off her, checked by her death grip on him.

It was only as she saw her hands that she realized that she *had* a death grip on him: her fists were
wrapped in his shirt front. There was a soothing note
to his deep voice that both served to reassure her
and, paradoxically, made her start to shake. Her teeth
chattered when she tried to open her mouth. She deliberately clenched them to stop the sound. She was
light-headed with reaction, and breathing way too fast.
Her heart raced. Her stomach churned.

"You're safe," he said again, then added, "He's not
coming back."

Riley could almost feel the adrenaline that had
been rushing through her bloodstream begin to ebb.
She took a deep breath, and just about managed to
regulate her breathing. There was nothing she could
do about the tremors that racked her. She had to work
to let go of the crisp cotton of his shirt, forcing her
fingers to open almost one by one.

"Are you hurt?" he asked, as, freed, he crouched
beside her. He was a big guy, broad-shouldered, long-
legged, muscular: it was like having a mountain crouch
beside her. Riley refocused her attention from the
wrinkles she'd put in his shirt to his face, and found
that she was looking at the tall fed she'd seen earlier at
the cemetery.

His eyes were a calm grayish blue, set beneath
thick dark brows.

She gave a small, negative shake of her head, then
took a breath.

"I saw you earlier. At the cemetery." Her voice
was hoarse, creaky. It hurt her throat to talk.

Before he could reply, the couple from down the hall walked up behind her. Glancing over her shoulder, Riley could see them looming just a few feet away. With her peripheral vision she caught a glimpse of more of her neighbors stepping cautiously into the hall. They moved closer, looking at her and the fed and the damaged wall in fascination, talking among themselves.

"Who is that?"

"The Cowan woman from fourteen G."

"Wowzers."

"What happened?"

"Did she get shot?"

"The wall sure did."

"Was it a robbery?"

"Oh my God, were you raped?"

That last horrified question, louder than the rest and addressed to her by her young female neighbor, was what slammed Riley with the up-to-that-point-forgotten fact that she was naked. It hit her then what she must look like, all pale skin and sprawled limbs, lying on her side on the prickly gray carpet facing the fed, who despite the fact that he could absolutely see it all was, to his credit, keeping his eyes on her face. Her back was turned to her neighbors, but still they were getting quite a view.

Of my bare butt.

The sting of embarrassment gave her the strength to move. Defensively she pulled her knees up to her chest. She wasn't even sure it was enough to make her minimally decent, but under the circumstances it was the best she could do.

"All right, everybody back off," Mr. FBI said, as something warm and dry settled over her—his suit coat, she discovered as she clutched at it, pulling it around herself gratefully. "Give her some space."

Riley got the impression of movement behind her as, not surprisingly, her neighbors obeyed and began to retreat into their apartments. She took a deep breath.

Time to get it together.

"You sure you're not hurt?" he asked, low-voiced, as, with a major effort of will, she sat up, careful to keep his coat wrapped around her. Fortunately, it was large enough to cover about three people her size, and longer on her than some skirts she possessed. Pulling her legs up beneath it, she left nothing of herself on view except her bare feet, and felt marginally better.

"Yes." Light-headed from the effort, which had taken more out of her than she would have imagined, Riley dropped her forehead onto her knees and concentrated on taking deep breaths. She was still shaking, and she suddenly realized that at least part of the reason was that she was freezing. Rivulets of now-cold water dripped down her back from her wet hair. Pulling her hair out of the coat, she slid her arms into the sleeves and hugged the garment closer still, willing the shivers to stop.

The man stood up and put his hand down to Riley. "Help you up?"

She had to tilt her head way back to see his face. On the way up, she couldn't help but notice his powerful athlete's build—and the black shoulder holster that bisected the left side of his white shirt. The gun protruding from it made her breath catch.

Welcome to your new life, Riley Cowan.

"Thanks." She put her hand in his and let him pull her to her feet, careful to keep his jacket closed with her other hand as she moved. As she had thought, it reached almost halfway down her thighs.

"How about we go back inside your apartment and talk?"

"I—"

As soon as he let go of her Riley realized that she'd made a mistake: her knees wouldn't support her.

"Oh," she finished on a note of surprise as they wobbled. Grabbing his arm for support, taking a staggering sideways step, she started to sink to the floor.

"All right, I got you." He caught her before she hit, scooping her up in his arms like she weighed nothing. Riley curled an arm around his shoulders as he carried her back into her apartment. He was solid muscle, and at such close quarters he was almost overwhelmingly masculine down to the hint of stubble darkening his square jaw. Having him carry her like that felt surprisingly intimate, but unless she wanted to stay out in the hall—which she didn't—she didn't seem to have a whole lot of choice.

He closed the door behind them, carried her to her couch, and set her down on it.

"Thank you," she said with assumed composure, as, straightening, he frowned down at her. Conscious suddenly of what she must look like wearing nothing but his sport coat with her bare legs on display, not helped by the knowledge that she was naked beneath it and he knew it and had already seen every inch of her without a stitch on besides, she felt suddenly uncomfortable under that penetrating gaze.

She lifted her chin.

"You're an FBI agent?" It still hurt to talk, and her voice was still hoarse, but she didn't want to just give him the upper hand in whatever interaction was coming. Her tone made it not quite a question. "Could I see some ID, please?"

His eyes narrowed slightly. Then he reached into his back pants pocket, extracted a wallet, flipped it open, and held it out to her.

"Finn Bradley," he said as she looked at the photo ID displayed behind the clear plastic film.

She nodded her acceptance of his ID, and he flipped the wallet closed and restored it to his pocket. "I'm Riley Cowan. But I'm guessing you know that."

He inclined his head. She took that as a big fat *yes*.

"I'm also guessing that you weren't just passing by and happened to hear me scream."

"You're right, I wasn't. I was on my way to talk to you." His eyes swept her.

"What do you want to talk about?" If her tone wasn't quite hostile, it was close. She *knew* what he wanted to talk to her about: the money. That was what they all wanted to talk about.

He held up a hand. "Hang on a minute."

He turned, walked into her bedroom, and disappeared from sight. A moment later he reappeared carrying her bedspread and a towel.

"You're shivering," he said in response to the look she gave him, and Riley realized it was true. He dropped the towel on her lap, then draped the bedspread around her shoulders. Even as she picked up the towel he continued: "There's blood all over your bathroom. Suppose we start by you telling me what just happened."

— CHAPTER —
SIX

"Like I said, I was taking a bath." Riley's thoughts raced a mile a minute as she pulled the bedspread more closely around her, appreciating its weight and warmth. She *was* shivering, long tremors that racked her body. Her throat hurt and her head hurt and she had various other aches and pains, as well, but none of those were her biggest concern at the moment. Far more urgent was this: How much should she tell him? How much *could* she tell him, without causing herself all kinds of trouble? "I looked up, and there was a man in my bathroom. He tried to kill me."

"Why?" The blunt question, coupled with the look that accompanied it, was disconcerting.

"You know, I didn't ask him. I was too busy trying to stay alive." She started blotting her hair with the towel as she spoke, relieved to discover that her heart was slowly regaining its normal rhythm. He watched her with unwavering focus. She found his gaze mildly—all right, who was she kidding, forget the mildly; acutely was more like it—unnerving, and used the excuse of toweling off the rest of her hair to duck her head and escape it. There was a bump on the back of her skull, she discovered with a grimace as she touched it, and recalled having her head slammed into the hard rim of the tub. It was tender, so she avoided it.

He said nothing more until, with her hair as towel-dry as it was going to get, she gave up and tossed her hair back. Their gazes met. His calm blue eyes told her exactly nothing.

Crap.

"He tried to kill you," Bradley prompted. He stood so close she could have reached out and touched him. Now that she was getting a good look at it, she saw that his tie was dark gray, a nice complement to his black suit. His pants leg just brushed the trunk/coffee table in front of the couch. His arms were folded over his chest. By the soft, pale light of her ginger jar lamps, he looked big and dark and dangerous—and way too focused on her for her peace of mind. Riley hated to admit that she found him intimidating, but the truth was she kinda-sorta did. There were damp places on his shirt, and she realized that they must have come from her, when she'd thrown herself naked and stream-ing wet into his arms. *Not* the most steadying memory ever. "What did he do, exactly?" Bradley pressed, pull-ing her out of her momentary diversion.

Remembering made her stomach tighten. The fear of dying was still with her, she discovered, even though she had survived. Probably because somewhere deep inside she was convinced that now that they had targeted her, they would never stop until—

She couldn't finish the thought. Instead she looked him in the eye and said, "He forced my head underwater and held it there until I managed to get away."

"And how did you do that?"

That answer was easy. It even made her feel better. "I stabbed him in the neck with a comb. It's a rattail comb, with a long, sharp end."

His eyes flickered, she thought with surprise.

"Ah," he said, as if that cleared up something— probably the blood in the bathroom—for him. "You know him? Dated him, talked to him, seen him around, anything like that?"

"No." She wasn't just cold on the outside. She was cold on the inside, too. Freezing, actually, as though the blood that was circulating through her veins had been refrigerated. She had almost died, she was terribly afraid of the "they" that she knew was still out there, and now she was being interrogated by a man who looked like he got his jollies from strong-arming people. No wonder she had the shivers. "I never saw him before in my life." She took a deep breath and hurried into speech before he could ask her anything else. "He was wearing a ski mask, at first. Then he took it off. That's when I knew he was going to kill me."

At the memory, her heart lurched.

He inclined his head, which she took as meaning that he agreed with her assessment of what the removal of the ski mask meant.

"Was your door locked?"

"Yes, of course. And the chain was on."

"No sign of forced entry. I looked as I came in. Door's intact, lock's intact. Chain's in one piece, although that's easily managed. Who has your spare key?" He looked at her speculatively.

"My mother-in-law." Her voice took on an acerbic edge. "It wasn't her."

An uptick at the corner of his mouth acknowledged the tone of that last.

"Building maintenance has one, too," she added. "I don't know who else."

"All right. We'll just take it as a given that it wouldn't be that hard to get hold of one." His mouth tightened. His eyes swept her. Something about the look in them reminded Riley that he'd seen her naked. "Did he molest you?"

"No." Her mouth felt like it was stuffed with cotton, and there was a faint ringing in her ears that she put down to reaction. "Nothing like that."

"You were in the bathtub and he immediately jumped on you and tried to drown you."

A jerky nod. "I think it was because of my ex-father-in-law. You were at the funeral today. You know about him. About Jeff." After what had just happened to her, Riley knew she needed help. Jeff had been murdered, she had nearly been murdered, and the bottom line was this guy had just saved her life. Federal agents weren't her favorite people, but she was going to try telling one more law enforcement type the truth about Jeff's death. Her voice hardened. Her eyes challenged him. "He didn't kill himself."

"You got a reason for thinking that?"

"Jeff wasn't suicidal. Not *ever*," she said. "He wouldn't have done that to his mother or sister. There was no note. He—there are all kinds of reasons." She felt her insides twist as the reality of how close she had come to meeting Jeff's fate hit her all over again. "Jeff was convinced that someone was killing people who were close to his father. After what happened to Jeff, after what just happened to me, I think so, too."

"With what purpose?"

"I don't know," she replied with a touch of impatience. "To send a message, I guess."

His eyes stayed fixed on her face. "You think this guy was trying to kill you to send a message to George Cowan? What message?"

Riley suddenly felt as if she were stepping on treacherous ground. "'You rat, you stole my money'? I don't *know*, okay? All I know for sure is that *someone just tried to kill me*."

"Okay." He seemed to be turning something over in his mind. "He say anything? While he was attacking you?" His tone was mild. The look in his eyes—was not. They were as watchful as a hawk's.

She had to fight the impulse to swallow, because giving in to it would have been too big a giveaway. That was the question she'd been hoping to avoid. *What do I say?*

The truth. There's nothing as convincing as the truth. Just not all the truth. As little as possible, until you have a chance to think this thing through.

She was, she discovered, sick of feeling her heart pound. But there it went, pounding again.

"He said, *Hello, Riley.*"

His eyes were narrowing on her face when a brisk knock on the door, followed by a man's voice calling, "Finn? You in there?" diverted his attention.

Riley barely managed not to sigh with relief. The vibe she was picking up from him was growing increasingly nerve-racking. It was like he was waiting—for what? Her to slip up?

But he could only be waiting for her to slip up if he was aware that there was something for her to slip up about.

Which he couldn't be. Could he?

Oh, God, what does he know?

She tried hard to keep her expression unreadable as, lips compressing just enough to be noticeable, he said, "Excuse me a minute," and left her to answer the door.

"You're not wearing your earwig again," the man who walked through the door said reproachfully. He kept his voice low, like he was trying not to be overheard. "If you'd been wearing it, I could have told you this as soon as it happened: we got him."

"You got the man who attacked me?" Not even trying to pretend she hadn't heard, Riley perked up, then clutched the bedspread closer as another long, cold shudder shook her. The news should have made her ecstatic—and it did, it absolutely did, at least she no longer had to fear having that particular bad guy return to try to kill her again—but it also brought a

surge of near panic with it. Would he talk? Would he
tell the authorities that she had Jeff's phone, and he'd
been trying to drown its whereabouts out of her? If
so, what was she going to say to that?

He's lying, and *I have no idea what he's talking about* were the responses that came immediately
to mind, but she needed to think the ramifications
through before she committed to anything. To begin
with, if her attacker had managed to track Jeff's phone
efficiently enough to conclude that it had ended up
with her, what were the chances that the FBI hadn't
done the same thing? Riley did her best to keep her
eyes from widening with horror at the prospect as she
added, "Oh, thank God."

Possibly she hadn't put quite enough conviction
into that, she thought as, having closed the door behind the newcomer, Bradley turned to look at her as
she spoke. Whatever, it was too late now.

Once again, there was something in that calm blue
gaze that she found unnerving.

He looks like he knows. She damped down flutters
of panic by telling herself that she was letting nerves
get the best of her.

*He shows up at almost the exact same time as a
killer who was after Jeff's phone: coincidence?*

*It could be. He said he wanted to talk to me. He
was at the cemetery earlier. The FBI's been showing up
and asking questions for months.*

It didn't help when her mind immediately started
making its own, fear-fueled list of things he might
want to talk to her about quite apart from the phone.

The newcomer was saying happily, "A bunch of patrol cars were just pulling up out front when he came running out through the lobby. Cops were on him like dogs on steak. Not so much as a shot fired." He looked to be a few years younger than Bradley. Riley pegged him as maybe early thirties. Medium height, a little chunky, a little rumpled in his dark gray suit. Round cheeks, snub nose, rosy complexion. Short, bristly brown hair. Friendly expression.

"FBI Special Agent David Baxter." Bradley introduced him. Maybe she was imagining the hint of dryness in his voice, but she didn't think so.

"Bax." Baxter crossed the room to offer her his hand. Extending her own hand out of the cocooning bedspread, Riley took it and shook it, slightly bemused. Her first impression was that this guy was an FBI agent by way of the Boy Scouts. The opposite of intimidating, with about as much in common with his fellow agent, who'd followed him over, as a beagle had with a rottweiler. "Pleasure to meet you, Mrs. Cowan. Oh, and sorry for your loss."

With that he inadvertently confirmed that he, too, knew who she was without the need for any introduction. She guessed that he was Bradley's partner, which meant he'd been on the way to talk to her, too.

She said, "Thank you," while just managing not to narrow her eyes at the pair of them.

He gave a slightly awkward nod in response.

"They ID him?" Bradley asked, looking at his partner.

Bax shook his head. "Not yet. He didn't have

anything on him, no wallet, nothing. And he wasn't talking. At least, not last I saw."

Riley felt a glimmer of hope. *So maybe I'm getting all bent out of shape for nothing. Maybe the bastard won't say a word about Jeff's phone.*

Hope sputtered.

Then again, maybe he will.

And died. *Maybe he won't have to, because maybe these guys already know I have it. Maybe they know everything.*

She battled the urge to wet her lips.

Bradley was still focused on Bax. "Where is he now?"

"Houston PD took him, and, by the way, they want Mrs. Cowan to come down and formally identify him. I said I'd collect her, and we'd bring her."

Bradley looked at her, and then at Bax. "She look like she's up to going down to police headquarters tonight to you?"

Bax looked at her, too. Riley had no idea what she looked like, but he frowned. "I can call them, get them to set it up for tomorrow instead. They've got plenty to hold him on overnight."

They were talking to each other, like she wasn't right there.

Riley said, "I have to work tomorrow." And it occurred to her that going to police headquarters to identify her attacker gave her a really good excuse to get out of the apartment and away from Bradley. Before he got a chance to get going with whatever he'd come to talk to her about. "I'd rather get it out of the way tonight. If you'll both excuse me, I'll just go and get dressed." She looked at Bradley. "Thank you for what you did. I think you probably saved my life."

Clutching the bedspread closer, she stood up as she spoke. She intended it to be a dismissive gesture. Unfortunately, the room immediately tilted sideways. It was all she could do not to stagger. If she hadn't felt this overwhelming need to get rid of them, she would have sat back down again, hard.

Bradley stepped close, caught her arm. She couldn't help it: she swayed as the room whirled, then as he stepped closer still she leaned into him, grabbing his waist, melting against him, allowing him as the nearest solid object to take her weight.

"You're welcome," he said dryly as her forehead came to rest on his chest and she closed her eyes to stop the spinning. His arm came around her to steady her. She registered the sheer size of him, along with the taut muscularity of his waist and the solidness of his chest and the hardness of his arm and could only be thankful he was there. Then as she continued to lean against him because the room was still whirling and there was just nothing else she could do, he picked her up again as if it were the most natural thing in the world and started walking with her.

"Call an ambulance," he said over his shoulder as he carried her into her bedroom. "We need to get her checked out."

"I'm fine," Riley protested, although it was beginning to occur to her that maybe she wasn't.

"There's already an ambulance here." From the

sound of his voice, Bax was right behind them. "The crew's down the hall, checking out this old guy who started having chest pains when he heard gunshots. Cops are here, too, taking statements. Building's crawling with them. They'll probably be knocking on the door wanting to take Mrs. Cowan's statement soon."

"Go get a paramedic. Wait, pull these covers back first."

"What do you think's wrong with her?" Bax sounded anxious as he did as he was told.

"Don't know." Bradley laid her down on the bed. Riley was surprisingly glad of the solid surface beneath her. Her surroundings, including the large man looming over her, were still moving, and keeping perfectly still seemed like her best bet. "Maybe shock. Maybe something else. We'll see." He looked over his shoulder. "What are you waiting for? Go."

Bax went.

Leaving her still wrapped up in his jacket and the bedspread, Bradley pulled the top sheet and satiny blanket over her, tucking them around her as efficiently as any nurse. He was leaning close, and she was able to focus on his face—his mouth was grim, his jaw tight—and that made her realize that the room's shimmying had stopped.

"I got a little dizzy, that's all," Riley said as he straightened away from her. As the pillow embraced the back of her skull, the tender spot from her fall made itself felt once again. She winced. Moving cautiously, she turned onto her side, pillowing her cheek on her hand as she waited to see if the vertigo would recur. It didn't. For a moment she thought about try-ing to get up, but under the circumstances that didn't seem like the smartest idea.

"Twice now," he observed.

"I'm fine as long as I don't stand up. It's probably because he banged my head into the back of the tub."

"That would do it."

Standing over her, Bradley looked . . . formidable. He was frowning down at her, and once again Riley found herself wondering exactly what he knew. Her gut twisted.

He said, "You seem to be remarkably hard to kill."

"What do you mean?"

"Drowning somebody should take about three minutes tops. Hold 'em underwater until they pass out, keep 'em there until you're sure they're dead. For a man of his size dealing with a woman of yours, especially since you were already in a bathtub full of water, it should have been a piece of cake. But he had to bang your head into the back of the tub, and you managed to get his ski mask off and then stab him. With a comb. And you got away." His eyes met hers. "Most forced drowning victims panic and spaz out for less than a minute before they go limp. Sounds like you were able to keep it together a lot longer than that. Long enough to put up an ultimately successful fight. Pretty impressive."

Riley tried to keep her face from revealing the damning truth that the reason she had survived long enough to put up a successful fight was that her attacker had been trying to extract something from her before killing her.

She chose to take the battle to the enemy. "*You* seem to know a lot about forced drownings."

Again that slight uptick at the corner of his mouth that appeared to be what for him passed as a smile. "I know a lot about a lot of things."

Holy hell, she had to stop reading unspoken meaning into everything he said. She was afraid he would be able to see the guilt that surged through her in her eyes.

Forget about taking the battle to the enemy. She just wanted the conversation to end.

"I was fighting for my life," she said with dignity.

"Yeah."

There was absolutely no inflection to that, which of course made her start to read all kinds of nerve-racking things into it. Fortunately, he was no longer looking at her. Instead, he was glancing around the room. Riley felt a tingle of alarm as she tried to work out what he could see. Not Jeff's phone, which was tucked away inside a shoe in her closet, *not* concealed in a locked drawer in her desk as she had told her attacker.

She'd put it there right after discovering Jeff's body, before she'd gotten the call that officially informed her of the terrible tragedy and sent her speeding to Margaret's house.

"You going somewhere?" Bradley's eyes were on her small suitcase, which rested on the carpet near the bed.

"I came home to pack some clothes so I could

spend a few more days with my mother and sister-in-law." Reminded of what she'd left Margaret's house to do, Riley did a lightning calculation: she hadn't yet been gone long enough for Margaret to start to worry, but that time was rapidly approaching. She needed to give Margaret a call . . . It was then that a horrifying thought occurred to her. "Oh, no, I'm going to have to tell Margaret what just happened. She's already been through so much. She's going to go insane."

"Margaret's your *ex*-mother-in-law, right? I'm surprised you've stayed on such good terms." There was absolutely no discernible emotion in his voice. His eyes as she met them were that same calm, unreadable blue.

He wasn't doing anything at all that could be even vaguely construed as threatening, yet he was giving her the heebie-jeebies.

Riley abruptly realized that she was being interrogated by an expert.

This man was even more dangerous than she'd thought.

"She's always been very kind to me." This time Riley didn't resist the urge to wet her lips. She had every (legitimate) reason in the world to be anxious about Margaret. "Jeff's death has just about destroyed her. I hate to have to tell her about this."

Before he could reply, the sound of someone entering her apartment distracted them both. The indistinct murmur of approaching voices presaged Bax's arrival in the room by just a few seconds. Behind him came a pair of blue-uniformed paramedics.

"Right there." Bax motioned in her direction.

As the paramedics bustled to her bedside, Bax, who'd stopped beside his fellow agent, said to Bradley, "I got news. You aren't going to like it."

Overhearing, Riley shamelessly tried listening in on their conversation even as one of the paramedics plopped a medical bag down on the bed beside her and said cheerfully, "I hear you've been feeling dizzy."

"Yes," Riley responded, and at the same time heard Bradley reply in a resigned tone, "So what else is new?"

Then, as one of the paramedics produced a penlight, which he no doubt meant to shine in her eyes, Bradley glanced at her. For the briefest of seconds their eyes met.

Then he looked back at his partner.

"Let's give them some space," he said to Bax.

Riley could do nothing but surrender to the paramedics as the FBI agents left the room.

"They let him go." Bax was bursting with the enormity of it. They'd moved far enough away from the bedroom door that they were in no danger of being overheard, but he kept his voice down anyway. "Diplomatic immunity."

It was a surprise that Finn absorbed in frowning silence. After a moment he asked, "What country?"

"Ukraine."

"If he's entitled to diplomatic immunity, then George screwed over a government agency or somebody connected with the government there on a pretty high level." He'd already run the man's face through his own internal database of bad actors, and drawn a blank. Which meant the guy was either new, or deep cover enough to have not shown up on his radar before now. If the latter was the case, then whoever had sent him was sufficiently concerned about the situation to be deploying the big guns. In other words, some foreign fat cat's ass was in a sling. And that foreign fat cat had enough pull—or knew enough people with enough pull—to get his boy instantly released from police custody.

"Good thing you happened to see a man walk past her window." Bax thrust his hands into his pants pockets, rattling the change there.

Happened to see nothing. Finn had been intently watching the aforementioned windows with binoculars from a vantage point on the roof of the building opposite, which was two stories lower than Riley's apartment. He hadn't been able to see a great deal, even with the curtains open and the lights on. But he had seen the shadowy figure of a man moving through her living room, and as a result had immediately hot-footed it over to her building and grabbed an elevator, meaning to go low-tech and listen at her door.

The moment he'd stepped out of the elevator, her scream had brought him running.

"Yeah," Finn replied. "The receiver functional yet?"

While Finn had been up on the rooftop and then racing through apartment buildings, Bax had been on the phone to tech support trying to verify the status of the receiving unit.

"Nothing wrong with it," Bax said. "Cynthia said it's working fine."

"Okay." Finn wasn't surprised that Bax knew the tech support person's first name. Bax had that same geeky cyber-wonk persona that they did, as well as a lot of relationships with a lot of people he'd never actually met. Finn was equally not surprised to discover that there was nothing wrong with the receiver. It had been patently obvious from almost his first conversational exchange with Riley that she was hiding something. He wasn't quite sure what it was, but one thing he *was* now sure of: she'd disabled her own and Jeffy-boy's cell phones.

And she wasn't talking about it.

"So what we've got here is a Ukrainian with diplomatic immunity who was trying to kill Mrs. Cowan." Bax looked thoughtful while trying his hand at case analysis, which Finn had already discovered wasn't his strong suit. "The question is, why? You think he was hoping to use her to send another message to George?"

"Don't know," Finn replied. He had no real quarrel with Bax, other than the fact that the powers-that-be had set him up to be his minder, but there was no need to go filling his head with too many possibilities. Finn wasn't sure how much Bax was passing on to his superiors, but he was passing on something, and Finn wanted to remain in a position to control just what that something could be.

Knowledge is power. It was also leverage. At some point Finn meant to use it to trade for what he wanted, which was his life back. Permanently, this time.

"By the way, what happened to your coat?" Bax rattled the change in his pocket again. Finn narrowed his eyes a little. The sound was annoying, but right then that wasn't necessarily a bad thing, because it provided a distraction. He didn't like being reminded of why he was missing his coat. That took him to the way Riley had looked when he'd heard her scream and taken off running and she'd come flying down the hall toward him.

Naked.

In those few seconds he'd registered everything there was to register about her body: full round breasts with strawberry nipples, firm but not too firm to bounce; slender waist curving out into unmistakably feminine hips; flat stomach; long, shapely legs. The small patch of hair between them that left no doubt that she was a natural redhead. The smooth sheen of her creamy skin.

He'd unwillingly discovered that her skin was as satiny soft as it looked—and a great many other things about her besides—the instant he'd grabbed her and whirled her around to put his back between her and the gun.

None of those impressions were anything he cared to remember, or be reminded of.

Bottom line? A beautiful woman was a dangerous distraction. A beautiful naked woman who might or might not know where to find what he was looking for? Suffice it to say, he wasn't going there. Not with his mind, or anything else.

He was on board to do a job, and then get the hell out.

Finn shrugged. "She was cold."

Thankfully, he was saved from any further explanation as, at that moment, the paramedics exited the bedroom.

"Could you close the door please?" Riley called

after them. Her voice was still huskier than Finn was used to hearing it, and he wasn't sure if it was from screaming or from something that had been done to her during the attack. He caught a glimpse of her, all curled up in the middle of her bed with the blanket he'd spread over her tucked closely around her, her hair vivid as a splash of scarlet paint amid a sea of white, as the trailing paramedic complied.

"What's the damage?" Finn asked the paramedics when the door was closed and they started walking away from it. They paused, looking at him as he moved toward them. There was a moment there when he could tell they were debating about whether they should reveal any of her medical information to him, but his assumption of authority, bolstered no doubt by the shoulder holster and weapon that shouted law enforcement, carried the day.

"The main thing is, she's got a concussion," the lead paramedic said. "Apparently she took a hard blow to the back of the head: she's got a bump the size of an egg. In addition, she has considerable bruising all over. She'll be sore, but aside from the concussion there's nothing of concern."

"The concussion's the cause of the dizziness?" Finn asked.

The paramedic nodded. "I'd keep her in bed tonight, keep her quiet tomorrow, and she should be fine. If, in the morning, she's still getting dizzy when she stands up, or if any additional symptoms present themselves, you should take her in to see her doctor for a check-up. Or call 911."

Finn didn't reply. Stepping into the breach, Bax said, "We'll do that," and then, as the paramedics left, followed them to the door. After closing it behind them, he turned to look at Finn, who hadn't moved from his spot in the middle of the living room.

"What now?" Bax asked, rattling the coins in his pocket again. Finn's lips tightened fractionally. Bax continued: "Do we stay with her? We have to, don't we? If the guy who just tried to kill her is on the loose, we can't just leave her here on her own."

Asset recovery was another field that wasn't exactly Bax's strong suit. He had no real idea how to go about it. Which suited Finn just fine.

"We're not babysitters," he replied, and considered his options. As the attack on her had shown, Riley was a prime target for more interested parties than just himself and Bax. If she hadn't been before, she certainly was now aware that she was on the radar of those who were seeking the missing money. If she had it, or knew where it was, she should absolutely be thinking about ways to protect herself and the funds. She would almost certainly notify her confederates, if she had any, of what had occurred. His presence, and Bax's, in her immediate vicinity could only gum up the works. Nobody was going to come after her while they were with her—even if no one outside their own small group knew his true identity, the presence of two supposed FBI agents was a considerable deterrent to the kind of attack that was meant to extract intelligence from a target—and, more important, Riley herself couldn't make any moves while they were with her.

Therefore, they were going to go. And stay out of sight. And keep watch.

He said as much to Bax.

Bax said unhappily, "But the perp might —"

He never finished.

The bedroom door opened. They both looked around in surprise to find Riley walking through it. She was fully dressed in a black T-shirt with a pair of white jeans and — surprise, because he'd pegged her as a high-heels-on-every-occasion kind of woman — flat sandals. Her hair, which had puffed out in a cloud of vivid waves around her face as it had dried, had been tamed again and was twisted into a loose updo that made her look younger and more vulnerable than Finn would have liked. She had one hand curled around the handle of her small silver suitcase, which she was pulling along behind her. His coat was folded over her arm.

Having swept her, Finn's gaze returned to her face.

"Going somewhere?" he asked. It was a question, nothing more. Whether or not she went haring around with a concussion was of no concern to him. He was there to find the money, and that was it.

"To Margaret's." She held out his coat to him. "Thanks for the loan." Their eyes met as he took it. As he'd noted when he'd first gotten a good look at them, hers were a green-flecked hazel, wide and innocent-looking. If she felt self-conscious about the fact that he'd seen her naked for a considerable period of time, she wasn't showing it.

"Anytime."

He shrugged into his coat—it was a little damp and smelled vaguely of roses, but the object was to keep his shoulder holster out of sight, and any stray thoughts about the body it had so recently covered he immediately pushed out of his mind—and she resumed walking, moving past him toward the table with the kind of carefully calibrated, deliberate gait that told him she was having to work to keep it steady. Her jaw was set with the effort of it. Her mouth was downright grim.

"You're supposed to stay in bed," Bax said. His eyes were glued to her, too. "Because of the concussion."

"I can't." Picking up her purse, she slung it over one shoulder, glanced at them both, and added, "Margaret's expecting me back. I thought about calling her and telling her I'm going to spend the night here but then she'll want to know why, and I can't tell her about what's happened over the phone. And I have to tell her." She wet her lips, and not for the first time, Finn noticed. And deliberately glanced away.

As far as her calling her ex-mother-in-law was concerned, it probably didn't help that she'd disabled her cell phone: Finn welcomed the thought for the distraction it provided.

What he said was, "You're right. If the idea behind the attack on you was to kill you as a way of sending a message to George, then his wife and daughter are also at risk, and they should know it. In fact, I'm surprised the guy didn't go for one of them instead of you." He smiled at her. "To send a stronger message."

The slight widening of her eyes was all he needed to be convinced that she knew exactly what the motive behind the attack on her was, and it wasn't to send a message to George.

"They let him go," Bax told Riley. He looked, and sounded, worried. "The guy who attacked you. Diplomatic immunity. You really should stay here tonight. One of us can—"

"What?" Her sharp exclamation cut Bax off in midsentence. She looked at Finn, and he gave a nod of confirmation. "They couldn't have! *He tried to kill me.*" Something in Finn's expression must have convinced her that it was true, because she added on a note of horror, "What if he tries again?"

Interesting to note how concerned she generally seemed to be about her mother and sister-in-law's well-being, while in this particular instance, when the threat of a murderous attack on one of them should have seemed especially immediate and real, her own safety was her paramount concern. Which Finn translated as an indication that the attack on her had to do with something she, personally, was connected to. Something that the attacker didn't associate with the others.

Like, say, Jeffy-boy's phone.

"He's not likely to," Finn said. "If all he wanted to do was send a message, just the fact that he attacked you was enough to do that."

Bax frowned at him. "Don't we deport people with diplomatic immunity who commit a crime?"

"Usually," Finn replied. "But this guy hasn't been convicted. He hasn't even been tried."

The whole time they were talking, Finn had been watching Riley turn a whiter shade of pale. It was clear that the news that her attacker had been freed was scaring her to death, and he couldn't blame her: she was damned lucky to be alive. Under other circumstances he would have set her mind at rest. The truth was, he had every confidence that the perpetrator would be rushed out of the country within the next few hours, before any other interested party—like, say, himself—could catch up with him and make inquiries into who he worked for and what he was after.

But it didn't suit him for Riley to know that. What he was hoping was the news would scare her into making a move.

"I've got to go." For support, Riley had been leaning a hand on the back of the dining room chair that had been restored to the set around the table, presumably by Bax. Now she let go to head for the door.

"I'll drive you," Finn said. It would give him time to talk to her, to get more of a feel for what might be getting ready to go down. It would be a far easier way to keep track of her this way than relying on Bax's driving skills and the probably still useless receiver. And it would keep her from falling into the hands of someone with his same agenda and an almost certainly more violent way of finding out what he wanted to know, so it was a win-win for both of them.

As she opened the door and stepped back for them to precede her through it, he thought she was going to refuse. Her brows—delicate wings that were the same sooty black as the thick sweep of her

lashes—twitched together. The look she shot him was
guarded, wary. Walking into the hall with Bax on his
heels, he could almost see the wheels turning behind
those carefully veiled eyes. The whiff of sweet flowery
scent he got as he passed her slammed him with a vivid
image of the first time he'd noticed it, when she'd been
lying naked beneath him in this very hall. Annoyed
with himself, he shook it off.

Then he was in operative mode, conducting a
quick scan of the hallway, automatically assessing
potential threats. To his left, a police technician in the
process of extracting the bullets that had hit the wall
dug a thin silver instrument into plaster. To his right,
a pair of uniforms talked to a bathrobe-clad woman
who stood in her open doorway and cast a curious
look their way.

"Thank you," Riley answered, surprising him. As
she turned her back to lock her door, her voice was all
cool composure. "I'd appreciate that."

"Mrs. Cowan?" one of the uniforms called while
Finn was still processing the implications of Riley's
easy capitulation. The woman the cops had been talking to had disappeared back into her apartment. The
cops had turned and spotted Riley. "Do you have a
minute?"

"No, she doesn't," Finn answered for her, taking her arm and urging her toward the elevators. She
didn't resist. In fact, he got the feeling she was glad of
the support. Her flesh beneath his fingers was firm;
her skin felt silky and warm. The outfit she was wearing covered most of her, but it left her slender neck

bare. From his vantage point beside her, it was impossible to miss the bruises that were darkening on the porcelain skin below her left ear. It wasn't hard to tell that they were fingerprints from a man's hand that had been brutally wrapped around her throat.

Looking at them, his gut tightened.

She would have been easy to hurt. Finn found that he didn't like the idea of it one bit.

"We'd like to get a statement." The cops were following them down the hall. Finn glanced significantly at Bax, who got the message and pulled out his creds.

"FBI," Bax said, waving his wallet at them, and the uniforms stopped.

A moment later the three of them stepped into the elevator. Finn pressed the button for the lobby.

— CHAPTER —
EIGHT

Bradley said, "I was expecting you to give me an argument about driving you home."

It was phrased as a statement, not a question, but Riley answered it anyway.

"No."

If he could be economical with words, why, so could she. She was in the passenger seat of her Mazda, her seat belt fastened securely around her. Without it, she wasn't sure she wouldn't have slithered down into the foot well. She was exhausted, dizzy, headachey, and sore in so many places that her body felt like one giant tender spot. The pills the paramedics had given her had helped some; she'd felt them taking effect. Without them—well, she didn't want to think about how she might be feeling.

Actually, she didn't want to think about anything. But she had no choice.

She'd been getting that cat-at-a-mousehole feeling from him again ever since she'd gotten into the car with him. It was making her nervous as all get-out. Maybe it was her imagination. Maybe not. With her brain not quite as clear as normal, it was hard to be sure.

Bradley was behind the wheel, driving as competently as he seemed to do everything else, looking far too big for her small car. He'd had to adjust the seat all the way back to fit. They were on the freeway, and the swoosh of the tires and the faint rattle of traffic in the lanes around them formed a constant background noise. Despite how dark the night had become, the roadway lighting made it easy for her to see him. His features were as rugged in profile as they were viewed head-on.

He was handsome, she decided, in the kind of aggressively masculine way that had never really appealed to her: she tended to go more for the fine-featured, leanly elegant type. His hands looked large and powerful wrapped around the wheel. His feet in their black shoes dwarfed the Mazda's pedals.

Turned a little sideways to avoid the bump at the back of her skull, her head rested against the rolled top of her seat. Her lids felt heavy—so did her arms, and legs, and head—and the fear that chilled her wasn't nearly as sharp-edged as she knew it should be under the circumstances.

The bastard who attacked me—what if he comes back?

A tiny echo of residual panic caused her stomach to flutter.

"No?" Bradley flicked a look at her. "Why not?"

"You're not trying to kill me," she answered with beautiful simplicity. That, for her, had become the bottom line. The horror of having been attacked was multiplied by the knowledge that her attacker was free, and heightened still more by her conviction that there were more out there like him. Jeff's fate loomed large in her mind. Tonight she could easily have been murdered, too. The only thing that was keeping her from descending into utter, gibbering terror at the thought was, she suspected, the calming effect of the drugs in her system.

She wasn't sure if that was a good thing or a bad.

"No," Bradley agreed, and gave her another of those sideways glances that set her teeth on edge.

When they'd exited her building, Bax had left them. He was behind them now, presumably, in whatever car the agents had arrived in. Bradley had escorted her to the parking lot where she'd left the Mazda, then had had her wait while he'd checked her car for *bombs*. Yes, her life had deteriorated to the point where she had to worry about being blown to smithereens: how had *that* happened? Perched uncomfortably on the bumper of a nearby pickup because her knees were still unreliable, Riley had been acutely conscious of the darkness beyond the lights of the parking lot. *Anyone* could be out there: the knowledge was unnerving.

What am I going to do?

Watching Bradley check beneath her car, then under the hood and finally under the dashboard and seat, had sent her pulse into overdrive and had her stomach wrapping itself into knots. She'd only managed to keep calm by reminding herself that her attacker still didn't have what he'd been after: Jeff's phone.

It wasn't likely that he would kill her before he got his hands on it.

On the other hand, how likely was it that he would come back for a second try?

If he doesn't, someone else will. The thought sent goose bumps racing over her skin. To assume that he was the only one who wanted Jeff's phone—who'd tracked Jeff's phone and linked it to her own—would be stupid. Possibly suicidally stupid.

At the very least, she had to accept that the FBI— the man beside her—most likely had done the same thing.

Luckily, the possibility had first occurred to her while she was still in her apartment, still able to take certain steps to cover her ass. Call what she'd done her contingency plan. The only question now was whether or not to go with it. The alternative was to do nothing, and wait.

The uncertainty of it made her want to jump out of her skin.

It didn't help that he was making her nervous simply by sitting there.

His mouth was unsmiling, and his thick, dark brows formed two straight lines over his eyes. Seen by the uncertain freeway lights, his face was all hard planes and angles. The rugged strength of his jaw belied the calmness of his eyes. He was looking straight ahead, out through the windshield at the busy road, and she saw that his eyelashes were short and bristly and his nose was straight except for a slight bump on the bridge. Crammed into her car, he looked to be about the size of an NFL linebacker. An NFL linebacker who was all muscle and attitude.

Not a man anyone in her right mind would choose to mess with. Or lie to.

Unfortunately, under the circumstances she didn't have a whole lot of choice.

Oh, the tangled web we weave . . .

"So you think George still has the missing money?" Bradley asked. The question, seemingly out of the blue, was startling enough to cause a hitch in her breathing.

Her reply was cautious. "What makes you think I think that?"

"If you think Jeff—and the others; yes, I know about them, four close associates of George's have died violently in the months since he was arrested—was killed to send a message to George to hand over the money, then you must think the money is still available for him to hand over."

His face, and voice, revealed absolutely nothing. Riley felt herself starting to frown and immediately stopped: *it's perfectly logical of him to assume that.*

Isn't it?

Careful, she warned herself, mindful that her brain synapses might not be firing at one hundred percent just at present.

"It's not so much that I believe it," she said. "It's

that I think a lot of the people who George defrauded believe it."

He nodded agreeably. "They find it impossible to accept that that much money is simply gone." Riley didn't say anything, and he continued: "I have a working theory—and that's what I was heading to your apartment to talk to you about—that Jeff wasn't killed to send a message to George. I think he was killed by someone who was trying to torture information about the whereabouts of the missing money out of him." Another unreadable glance slid her way. "What do you think?"

An eighteen-wheeler roared past her window just then, shaking the small car, providing her with a providential reason to glance away, as well as an excuse for any change in expression she might be exhibiting as she dealt with what had just morphed from a worry into an electrifying certainty: *He knows*.

For a moment she couldn't breathe.

Stay calm. Impossible under the circumstances. *Okay, stay focused.*

What *could* he know? At a minimum, everything her attacker knew: that she had Jeff's phone. That she'd taken it from Oakwood.

Maybe a whole lot more.

Then again, maybe not.

In either case, her best move now was to go ahead with the plan. Done right, it should allay Bradley's suspicions while at the same time getting rid of that damned murderer-attracting phone.

Be cool. Then, *Go for it*.

"I think you might be right." Sitting up, ignoring the quick spin the interior of the car did around her at the sudden change in her elevation, Riley did her best to project a wide-eyed recognition of a just-revealed truth along with amazement at his keen intelligence. As that unreadable gaze slid over her face, she continued: "He wanted to know where Jeff's phone was. Right at first, right after he attacked me. He held me underwater until I was just about to die, then pulled me up and asked me where it was. When I told him, he dragged me into the bedroom and made me give it to him. Then he dragged me back into the bathroom and threw me in the tub and started trying to drown me for real. He would have done it, too, if I hadn't managed to get my hands on that comb."

For the briefest of moments, Bradley's face wasn't quite so unreadable. His lashes flickered; his lips compressed.

I was right, Riley exulted. *He knew. He knew I had the phone.*

"He was after Jeff's phone," Bradley said. His face was once again impassive. No inflection at all in his voice. *Hah!* She didn't trust that lack of expression for a minute. He was *interrogating* her. Subtly, thinking she wouldn't catch on. "You had it, and gave it to him."

"That's right." Riley's heart thudded uncomfortably. Lying didn't come all that easily to her, but in this case it was an absolute necessity. The question was, was the fact that she'd taken possession of Jeff's phone *all* he knew?

There was no way to be sure. *Stick as close to the truth as possible. Reveal no more than you have to.*

He asked, "Where's the phone now?"

"In the tub." *True.* Up next: *not*: "He dropped it when I stabbed him."

That penetrated his impenetrable calm for a second time. He shot a narrow-eyed look at her. "He dropped it in the water?"

Riley nodded.

"Did he get it out? Is it still there?" His voice was sharp.

"I don't know," Riley said, although she did. As soon as the paramedics had left, she'd deep-sixed Jeff's phone, sliding it silently into the water remaining in the tub — after first removing the SIM card with all the phone's stored information so that she could check out what was on it, which she meant to do the first chance she got. Any information that wasn't on the SIM card she was counting on the immersion in water to kill. She wasn't sure what that surviving information would be, exactly, but she didn't want to take any chances, especially considering how confident she was that the FBI had formidable data recovery capabilities. And when it was discovered that the phone's SIM card was missing — well, who was to say that her attacker hadn't taken it?

This way, she got to have the phone, and destroy it, too.

All she had to do now was publicly announce that she'd given Jeff's phone to the FBI, and she should be in the clear in the eyes of both Bradley and the scumbag who'd attacked her, as well as anyone else who might have an interest in acquiring that phone.

A slam dunk, if she did say so herself.

"Why didn't you tell me this sooner?" As he spoke, Bradley dug into his pants pocket and pulled out his own phone.

"Right afterwards, I was a little busy running for my life," she reminded him as he punched a button on his phone with a savage jab of his thumb. "Then—well, you know what happened."

A moment later, presumably after somebody answered, he said into the phone, "I need you to go back to Mrs. Cowan's apartment and look for a cell phone. It should be in the tub, in the water. Get it." There was the briefest of pauses. He was, Riley presumed, talking to Bax. "Yeah, right now. And when you have it, call me. And get it dried out."

He listened for a couple of seconds longer, said, "Yeah," again, and disconnected. Shoving the phone back into his pocket, he moved into the far right lane and took the Farm and Market Road exit before shooting another glance at her.

"What was on that phone that would make someone try to kill you to get it?" His tone was more abrupt than any he'd used toward her thus far. Having subsided against the seat again while he was on the phone—she really wasn't feeling well—Riley met his gaze without so much as a blink.

"I have no idea. But if I were to guess—Jeff was looking into the deaths of those four people you mentioned earlier, the ones who were connected to his father." They were off the expressway now, and traffic was light. Margaret's house was maybe ten minutes away. Riley didn't know whether to be glad about that, or sorry. She wanted in the worst way to get out of this car and away from the man driving it, but she hated that she was going to have to add to Margaret's burden by telling her what had happened. "He was convinced they were murdered. He kept the details of his investigation on his phone." She gave a little shrug. "I don't know that that was what the scumbag was after, but it seems likely, doesn't it?"

Bradley's reply was a grunt. "So how'd you wind up with Jeff's phone in the first place?"

Riley was anticipating the question. She had her answer all ready. It was even the truth, as far as it went. But for some reason the words stuck in her throat.

All of a sudden, she could almost see those narrow masculine feet dangling in front of her eyes again. The unnatural stillness of Jeff's body when she touched it, the horrible contortion of his face . . .

Her stomach clenched. She shoved the memories away. Or at least, she tried: they wouldn't go.

"I'm the one who found Jeff's body," she admitted in a constricted voice. As Bradley's brows twitched together and he slid a glinting look at her, she rushed out the rest of what she had to say. That's how she had planned it, to blurt it all out real fast like she was in a hurry to get the confession over with, which she was, although as it turned out the plan had nothing to do with how fast she spoke. She just really, really wanted to get it over with so those terrible images of Jeff would leave her alone. "Jeff asked me to meet him at Oakwood. When I got there he was dead." There was a sudden catch in her voice, and it had nothing to do with any kind of subterfuge. "I took his phone. Then I left, and called 911. Anonymously. I know I shouldn't have gone into the house, that I probably committed some hideous crime because it's been seized by the government, but—"

Her voice broke. For real. She stopped talking because she couldn't continue. The memory of how she had found Jeff was suddenly too fresh, too vivid.

He must have been so scared before he died.

She didn't realize she'd said it aloud until Bradley answered, "It would have been quick. Twenty seconds, and he would have been unconscious."

Oh, wow. Good to know I'm in a car with a man who knows that kind of thing. But this time she didn't say it, or anything at all, aloud, because her throat was too tight to allow any words to get out. The silence stretched as Riley concentrated on putting the terrible memories back where they belonged, in her mind's locked box of things she didn't want to think about.

"You loved him." Bradley slowed the car, then turned into the small subdivision where Margaret's house was located. With the garish lights of the strip malls and fast-food restaurants that had lined the main road behind them, it felt as if they were being swallowed up by darkness.

She felt as if *she* was being swallowed up by darkness.

"Yes."

"You were divorced."

"It was—I wasn't *in love* with him. We stayed friends. Family." Her throat ached. It felt as if her insides were being twisted into a giant pretzel. "I—knowing he died like that is really hard."

"Did he know anything about where George might have hidden the money? Could information like that be on his phone?"

What? He was asking that—why? Riley's mouth dried up. Her stomach turned inside out.

When she didn't answer, he looked at her. "Mrs. Cowan?"

Breathe. Just breathe. Only she couldn't. There wasn't any air. She fumbled at the door to find the button that rolled down her window, pressed it. The window didn't budge. Of course: she'd forgotten the front passenger side window was stuck.

It's my fault that Jeff's dead. That was the thought she'd been avoiding since she'd found him. It slammed into her then with all the force of a speeding train.

"Could you pull over please?" she asked, perfectly polite. "The window's stuck, and I need some air."

He threw her a quick look.

"Hang on," he said. She didn't know what she looked like but it must have been pretty bad, because he immediately pulled over to the side of the road.

As soon as the car stopped, Riley opened the door and got out. The headlights speared a metal mailbox at the end of a driveway about twenty-five feet away, and then as the lights were cut the mailbox disappeared into deep shadow. The whirring of the cicadas was loud, but not any louder than the buzzing in her ears. They were on a narrow residential street lined with small houses with neat yards. Except for a few glowing windows and the uncertain light cast by the fingernail moon, it was now completely dark. No one in sight. She took a few shaky steps away from the car, into parched grass that crackled faintly beneath her feet, toward the protective shadow of a large yew tree that anchored a scruffy hedge that presumably separated one yard from the next. Keeping her back turned to the car, she closed her eyes.

The corollary thought that she'd been doing her utmost to keep at bay hit her then with full force: *I could have warned him. I should have warned him. Then he might still be alive.*

Shivering, she crossed her arms over her chest to ward off the sudden chill.

The twenty seconds of consciousness Bradley said Jeff would have had was plenty of time to be scared. To say nothing of whatever he'd endured before the electrical cord had been wrapped around his neck.

The thought of Jeff experiencing the kind of terror that she had felt when her attacker had tried to drown her made her fists clench. The difference was, after that he'd actually died.

Oh, God, why?

The world wobbled around her. Sorrow joined with fear and guilt to bring a lump to her throat. Her chest was so tight it ached. Even though she was out in the open, she couldn't seem to draw in enough of the warm, pine-scented air to fill her lungs. Light-headed suddenly, she dropped into a crouch, balancing herself with one hand in the prickly grass.

You've got to get it together. You've got to keep it together.

"Mrs. Cowan."

Bradley. He'd turned off the car—she only realized that she'd been able to hear the engine rumbling beneath the noise of the cicadas now that she could not—and was beside her, close enough so that it sounded like he was practically on top of her. In fact, he sounded way closer to her ear than any six-foot, three-inch man should sound to the ear of a woman who was practically huddled in a ball on the ground. Fighting for composure, trying to take another deep breath—her lungs just would not fill—she opened her eyes.

He was crouched in front of her, a large blurry shape in the dark.

Blurry because she was crying.

Damn it.

Even as she blinked furiously, doing her best to rid herself of the tears, his hand curled around her upper arm just above her elbow. It felt warm against her chilled skin. The way he was looking at her—was surprisingly sympathetic.

Riley realized that she was actually starving for a little sympathy right then, a self-pitying thought that made the tears flow faster.

It's too dark: you can't even see his expression. You're imagining it. Damn it! Damn it!

"Do you feel sick?" Bradley asked. Forget sympathy. His voice was totally impersonal.

Gritting her teeth, she shook her head.

"You probably want to get back in the car. Your mother-in-law's house is just a couple of minutes away." He spoke with calm, cool detachment. "Or I can take you to the hospital."

Riley shook her head again. Forcing speech out of her constricted throat was hard. She did it anyway. "I'm fine."

Her voice sounded like it had been dragged through sandpaper.

"Sure?" he asked, and she nodded.

Still holding on to her arm, he stood up, drawing her up with him. It took every bit of willpower Riley possessed to get to her feet, but she managed. Once again she tried sucking in air with limited success. Her knees felt shaky, but she locked them. The ground threatened to tilt, but she knew that if she refused to give in to it the dizziness would soon settle down. Bradley was so close that she automatically used him for support, grabbing on to a handy lapel.

He gripped her wrist, to steady her, she thought.

"You're not going to faint on me, are you?"

Whoa, there was actually an inflection in his voice. Like he was a little worried she might.

"No." Her response came out husky, scratchy. Her chin was tilted up so that she could look at him, but she still couldn't read his expression: the pale slip of a moon was behind him, which meant that all she could see of his face was the faint gleam of his eyes.

He was looking down at her. Belatedly, she realized that if the moonlight was behind him, it was falling full on her face.

His eyes narrowed. His breath eased out through his teeth with a sound like a hiss.

Riley realized he was seeing the tears that were sliding down her cheeks.

— CHAPTER —
NINE

"What? It's been a bad day," Riley managed to get out despite the tightness in her throat. As she spoke, she swiped belligerently at the wet tracks on her face with her free hand. Nothing she could do about the streaming tears other than keep wiping them away. She only wished she could have kept him—or anyone—from seeing them. "You try—"

She was going to say something along the lines of "going to your ex-husband's funeral and then almost getting murdered in the same day," but her voice caught on a sob at the thought of Jeff's *funeral* and she couldn't, could not for the life of her, get any more words out.

"Hey," Bradley said, and there was that damned *am-I-imagining-it* sympathy again, in his voice. Then her knees quivered and she kind of tilted toward him and he caught her and kept her upright. She thought he sighed. His arms came around her and tightened until she lay fully against him. "It's okay."

He felt as solid as a concrete pillar, and something about that, about having someone she could lean on after a lifetime of being the pillar that supported everyone else, got to her. All the pent-up emotion inside her came bursting out. She buried her face in his wide chest, slid her arms beneath his jacket to wrap them around his waist, burrowed into his warmth like a lost child, and cried like she hadn't had a chance to do since Jeff had died.

She didn't do it prettily, either. She sobbed and gasped and sniffled. By the time she was done, his shirt front was damp and he was smoothing loose tendrils of hair out of her face with one hand.

If she could have kept her eyes closed and her face pressed against his chest forever, she would have done it. The fear and grief and guilt had eased; the physical act of crying seemed to have washed away the hard knot that had formed in her chest. But with her tears spent, she was suddenly aware of the man—the absolute *stranger*—in whose arms she rested. The sheer size of him should have been intimidating. So, too, should the shoulder holster that she could just glimpse against his white shirt because her arms were inside his jacket lifting it a little away from his body. To say nothing of the knowledge that he was an FBI agent whose primary purpose for being in her company was to ferret out all her (guilty) secrets. Instead, she felt protected. Safe. And for that brief time while she had been weak, feeling protected and safe was precisely what she'd needed. But that time was at an end: she was ready to be strong again.

She had to be strong again.

Even so, she stayed where she was for a moment longer, regrouping, gathering herself, savoring the unaccustomed luxury of relying on someone else for support. She could feel the heat of his body through the shirt she'd cried all over, feel the rise and fall of his chest, hear the steady beat of his heart beneath her ear, smell the subtle scent of his skin. His legs were long and hard with muscle against hers. The arms around her felt hard with muscle, too, and his chest was as unyielding as a wall.

She didn't know precisely what his job entailed, but he clearly wasn't a desk jockey: he had the body of an athlete. Or a soldier.

The kind of hard, honed body that belonged to a man of action.

Tempting as the prospect was, she couldn't stay in his arms all night.

The real world was still there, still sucked eggs, still had to be dealt with.

Much as she hated to face it, she'd made a complete and utter fool of herself by breaking down like she had.

The only thing to do was own it, and move on.

Taking a deep breath, relieved to discover that she was finally able to do so, she unlocked her arms from around his waist and straightened her spine. God, he was big. In her flat shoes, the top of her head didn't reach his chin. His shoulders were broad enough to block her view of everything behind him.

At this change in the status quo, his hand that was smoothing her hair stilled, dropped away. The arm around her loosened fractionally. As her hands finished sliding around his muscled rib cage to flatten on his chest and push a little so that she wasn't just plastered against him any longer, Riley faced the inevitable and looked up and met his eyes.

His face was still in shadow. She couldn't see his expression, let alone read it.

It was disconcerting to discover that her heart was beating faster than it should have been.

"Better?" he asked.

"Yes." She could have stepped away from him at that point, but she didn't. A sniffle caught her by surprise. She was more surprised when he produced a wad of tissues from a pocket and handed it to her.

"You carry tissues?" she asked on a note of incredulity in between a hiccup and another sniffle. She made good use of them, drying her eyes, wiping her nose, resting comfortably against him all the while.

"They're napkins. Clean ones, don't worry. Courtesy of today's lunch at Burger King."

"Thanks." Finishing with the napkins, she stuffed them in the pocket of her jeans, to be disposed of later. She still felt a little shaky—but that wasn't the reason she didn't go ahead and move out of the circle of his arms. The sad truth was, having a man to lean on felt good. She flicked another look up at him. "I have to confess, I'm embarrassed."

"No need to be."

"I don't usually cry all over people."

"I don't usually get cried all over, so I guess that makes us even." Was that a hint of humor in his voice?

"That answer did not make me feel better," she informed him.

"Sorry."

"I don't usually cry at all."

"Like you said, you've had a bad day."

At the reminder, Riley's stomach started to tighten. "I think me being so weepy has something to do with the concussion. Or maybe the meds."

"Probably."

"Are you laughing at me?" she asked suspiciously. Because the light had shifted enough to allow her to see his face. It was still heavily shadowed, but not so much that she couldn't see that slight uptick at the corner of his mouth that she'd decided earlier passed for his smile.

"God forbid."

She narrowed her eyes at him. "You are. I can tell."

The uptick was gone. "Nope."

She was feeling better, stronger. Standing so close to him, being in his arms like this, was starting to feel unexpectedly intimate. Nestled right up against him as she was, she was suddenly, acutely aware of him as a man, in a way that she absolutely didn't want to be. His size, all those muscles, the very smell of him, was overwhelmingly masculine, and it touched something deeply feminine in herself. To her horror, she found herself speculating about what he would be like in bed, and instantly banished the thought.

Straightening in his hold, she pushed off against his chest.

His arms dropped away, her knees held steady, she

took a step back followed by another, and there she was, standing on her own with a couple feet of space separating them.

She wasn't prepared to acknowledge even to herself what she'd felt between them at just about the time she'd started wondering about him and sex: he'd had an erection the size of a log.

Just thinking about it disconcerted her. It also made her pulse quicken, and her blood heat.

He had to know she'd felt it.

"Ready to go?" he asked, as impassive as always.

So he was going to ignore it. *Good*. Riley found that she wasn't able to meet his eyes. Thanking God for the darkness that made it difficult for him to read her face, she nodded, said, "Yes," and started walking toward the car. She half expected, half wanted to feel his hand on her arm again, but she didn't. Instead he walked silently beside her, opened her door for her, waited until she was seated, and closed it again.

All without a word.

Watching him walk around the front of the car, she felt flustered in a way that was completely foreign to her nature. She noticed that he moved with an easy athleticism. There was a kind of coiled energy about him that reminded her once again that this guy didn't make his living sitting behind a desk. In fact, he made it investigating people like her, a thought that made her nervous all over again and made her sudden attraction to him doubly stupid.

The last thing she needed in her life was that kind of complication. Since her divorce from Jeff, she'd had a lot of men ask her out. Some invitations she'd accepted, some she hadn't, but in the beginning she'd been too freshly out of her marriage to even start to get serious with anyone, and then, after George's downfall, there'd been too much chaos in her life. There was still too much chaos in her life. And given the nature of that chaos, Bradley was absolutely, positively, no-doubt-about-it the wrong guy.

So when he opened the door and slid in beside her, taking up way more than his fair share of space in the small car, she avoided looking at him in the few moments that the interior light was on by pulling down the visor above her seat and checking herself out in the mirror.

What she saw appalled her.

"Oh, gosh, they're going to be able to tell I was crying," she exclaimed dismally, referring to Margaret and Emma, who were probably starting to get worried about her by this time and could be counted on to converge on her as soon as she came in.

"Is that so bad?" Bradley closed the door and started the car.

"You have no idea." The family dynamic worked like this: she didn't cry; instead, she stayed strong for them when they cried. They would be upset—no, *frightened*—by this evidence of weakness in her. She looked at her red-rimmed, swollen eyes and pink nose with dismay. The coil she'd pinned her hair into was all lopsided, and at least half of it had fallen down to straggle around her face. *Not* the cool, calm, and in-control image she wanted to project. As the Mazda pulled away from the curb, she grabbed her purse and busied herself making necessary repairs.

Which also provided her with the perfect excuse not to look at him. Because much as she was trying, she still couldn't get that ginormous erection out of her mind.

"You never answered my question: do you think Jeff knew where George hid his money?" Bradley was back in interrogator mode again, and because it kept her from having to deal with him in a more personal way, she almost—*almost*—welcomed it.

It helped that the question was easy enough to answer.

"I'm almost sure he didn't. George didn't confide in Jeff." Glad of this chance to at least outwardly reclaim her composure, Riley kept her answer matter-of-fact. She tucked the last pin back into her hair, slicked on a bit of lip gloss, called it a day, and flipped the visor closed.

And glanced Bradley's way in time to catch his gaze moving from her mouth to the dark street beyond the windshield. She had the impression that he'd been watching her use her pinky to smooth the gloss over her lower lip.

Looking at his hard profile, she felt a sudden acceleration in her heartbeat. He was aware of her watching him, she knew: she could tell by the slight tightening of his jaw, by the barely perceptible elevation of tension in his body. As she registered those things, the interior of the small car started to feel way too warm. Riley would have suspected a malfunctioning air conditioner, but she could hear the rush of it blowing out through the vents, feel its cold breath on her skin.

Not that it helped.

"I'm kind of surprised at that, seeing as how Jeff was his only son." There was absolutely nothing in his voice to tell her that he was aware of her in the same (unwelcome) way she was now aware of him.

Still, she knew. The evidence was unmistakable.

Fortunately it seemed like he was no more interested in traveling down that path than she was.

"Jeff wasn't always . . . reliable." Drugs and alcohol would do that to a person, as Riley had learned. When he wasn't under the influence, Jeff was sweet and fun and loving, but when he was—well, he had become a different person. Riley said none of that. Instead, years' worth of memories of her ex-husband crowded into her head. A lot were good, many more were bad, but the fact remained: eternity could pass, and she still would never, ever get over the horrible manner in which he had died.

My fault. Her stomach tied itself into a painful knot.

"Who would George have confided in? His wife? An associate?"

Bradley's questions were no longer in the least bit subtle.

In this cat-and-mouse game he hopefully had no idea they were playing, that meant advantage: Riley.

"Not Margaret," Riley said. "If he confided in an associate, I wouldn't know."

"He have a girlfriend? A mistress?"

"I don't think so. But I wouldn't know that, either."

He didn't reply, and Riley got the impression that he was deep in thought. She looked away from him, out the window. The houses were of the same type as they had been on the previous street, as they were on Margaret's street, as they were throughout the subdivision: small ranches and split-levels. They were almost to Margaret's house now.

Riley was both glad and sorry.

"So when did you disable Jeff's phone?"

The tone of his question was so casual, such a throwaway, that it took Riley a second to internalize the question itself, to accept that, maybe, Bradley might still be harboring a suspicion or two where she was concerned after all. The question also confirmed that she'd been right all the way down the line: he, or his agency, had tracked Jeff's phone just like her attacker had. *That* was the real reason he'd been on his way to her apartment, she had no doubt.

She definitely was not the only one with an agenda here.

She replied easily. After all, there was nothing tricky about telling the truth.

"Right after I called 911. That's when it really hit me that Jeff had been murdered. Then I just got completely paranoid about being followed, and I took the battery out of his phone."

"I'm surprised it occurred to you to do that."

"Are you kidding? Do you ever watch TV?"

He gave a little grunt. "Not much."

Riley got the impression that she had allayed

his suspicions once again, and gave herself a mental thumbs-up.

Then they turned the corner that took them onto Margaret's street. Riley took one look at the quartet of news trucks gathered outside the house, at the gaggle of reporters, at the klieg lights and crowd of gawking neighbors, and felt her stomach drop. Her eyes widened in alarm.

"Something's happened," she said.

"Shit," Bradley said at the same time, and turned down the nearest side street. It was, as it happened, the street Riley had parked on earlier in an effort to avoid the cameras. As Riley stared at the fresh swarm of media, he added, "Relax. They're probably here because the word's out that you were attacked in your apartment tonight."

"Oh." In a way, that was a relief. She frowned, and started to say, *Margaret would have called me*, then bit back the words because in the nick of time she remembered that she'd popped the battery out of her phone, too.

That thought was quickly followed by another: *Margaret will be going nuts*.

"I have to go in." Riley looked worriedly at the gathering on the street.

"Yeah." Bradley was already parking, pulling over to the curb not far from the spot Riley had vacated earlier. He cut the engine and the lights. A house blocked their view of most of the activity in front of Margaret's house, but the glow of the lights was impossible to miss.

"Probably your best bet is to go in through the back door," Bradley said. He looked at her. "You up to cutting through some yards?"

Up to retracing the route by which she'd left Margaret's house?

But of course, he didn't know that—she didn't think.

"Yes."

He got out, retrieved her suitcase from the trunk, and joined her where she stood waiting beside the car. He handed her keys to her.

"Come on, I'll walk you," he said.

The knot of dread that had settled in her chest as she got out of the car was due to far more than the prospect of sneaking across a number of dark yards alone, but still his offer was welcome.

She nodded, and they started walking, staying in front yards to avoid fences, keeping close to the houses to make use of the denser darkness of the buildings' shadows. Instead of pulling her wheeled suitcase as she would have done, Bradley carried it by its handle as if it weighed nothing at all. His other hand curled around her upper arm. She was glad it was there, and not only because, with her knees still not being completely reliable, she needed the support.

The thing was, the feel of his warm, strong hand gripping her arm had become familiar by this time. Like his presence beside her in the dark, she found it comforting. She discovered that she hated the thought that he would shortly be going away.

The closer they got to Margaret's house, the more

unnerved she became by the situation she knew she was walking into.

"We're not safe here, are we?" Riley kept her voice low. The grass was so dry their footsteps crunched. They skirted patches of light thrown into the yards by the curtained windows, and at the same time Riley kept a careful eye on the media circus down the street. If they were spotted . . . "Margaret and Emma and me, I mean."

"Maybe you should think about getting out of town for a while," Bradley replied, tacitly confirming what she suspected: that she was right to be afraid.

Riley gave a huff of bitter amusement. "And go where, exactly?" She'd already considered, and discarded, the idea of gathering up Margaret and Emma and fleeing somewhere far, far away. The conclusion she'd reached was, there was nowhere that was far enough. "George ripped off a lot of people. I'm not sure there's anywhere that would be safe."

His slight grimace acknowledged the probable truth of that.

"I'll see what I can do to get you and your mother- and sister-in-law police protection."

"Since Jeff's death, the police already drive down our street every few hours. I think it's as much to make sure the press isn't disturbing the neighbors as anything."

"Should be able to get a patrol car parked in your driveway for the next few weeks, at least at night."

"That's something." Although Riley was terribly afraid that it wouldn't be enough. "Thank you."

He nodded, seemed to hesitate. "Listen, the bastard who attacked you—he's probably long gone. I don't think you have to worry about him coming back."

"Really?" When he gave a brief, affirming nod, she felt a flutter of relief and added, "That's good to know." But there was no way to be sure that her attacker and Jeff's murderer were one and the same, a thought that made her heart lurch at its implications for her, Margaret, and Emma.

"There are a lot more people who could potentially be coming after us than just that one guy tonight, aren't there?" Riley asked in a hollow voice, after outlining her conclusions for Bradley. They were in Margaret's backyard now, having just stepped through the gate. Bradley's hand had dropped away from her arm: the skin it had warmed was already starting to feel cold.

She was already starting to feel cold. Riley attributed that to the fact that without him, she was afraid.

"Maybe." He stopped walking and held out his hand. "Give me your phone. *And* the battery."

That dry add-on told her that he knew she'd disassembled her phone, too. Big surprise. Riley stopped walking, as well, fished both pieces out of her purse, and handed them over without a word.

He snapped the battery back into place far more easily than she'd taken it off.

Then he said, "Type in your code," and handed her phone back to her. She did as he asked, then without question gave her phone back to him when he held out his hand again.

She watched him punch a button, type something in.

"I just gave you an emergency contact number," he said, showing her what he'd done. "All you have to do is hit this. Think of it as your own personal 911. If I'm around, it'll get me. If I'm not, it'll call out the cavalry. You'll have help just as fast as it can get to you."

"Thank you." She accepted the phone with a quick smile and a surge of real gratitude as he handed it back to her. At this point, the prospect of even speed-dialed protection was better than no protection at all.

"Keep it on you," he cautioned when she moved to put her phone in her purse, and she nodded and slipped it into her pocket instead.

"I will."

Although the section of the yard they were standing in was dark, all the lights in Margaret's house seemed to be on, which was unusual. The effect was to send stripes of illumination cutting across the grass. She doubted that the house was still full of guests. More likely Margaret and Emma, having been alerted to what had happened by the growing media presence out front, were pacing the floors, out of their minds with worry about her.

"I have to go in." She said it with a surprising degree of reluctance as she glanced toward the back door. Then she had a thought and exclaimed, "I forgot the ice cream!"

"Ice cream?"

"Strawberry for Margaret, peanut butter crunch for Emma," she explained, and hung her head. "I promised I'd bring some back."

"Ah."

Something about his tone caused her to give him a searching look. They were standing so close their arms brushed, but once again she couldn't read a thing in his face. And that wasn't because of the shadows that enveloped them, either.

She said, "Thank you. For everything."

"Not a problem," he said.

With no more warning than that, his hand came up to cradle her jaw, and he bent his head and kissed her.

— CHAPTER —
TEN

Riley was so surprised that at first she couldn't move.

His kiss was as uncompromisingly masculine as everything else about him. Firm-lipped, hungry. And hot. So, so hot.

Her heart thudded. Deep inside, her body clenched.

His mouth moved persuasively on hers, and just like that the night went out of focus around her. His tongue slid past the lips she instinctively parted for him, taking expert possession of her mouth. She gave a little shudder, closed her eyes, and found herself kissing him back.

His hand felt warm and strong against the side of her face, and with the tiny part of her mind that remained functional she was aware that he was keeping control of the kiss by positioning her mouth exactly where he wanted it, positioning her exactly where he wanted her. Not that she objected. Hooking an arm around his neck, she let him tilt her back until her head found a pillow on his broad shoulder. He explored her mouth, the hard urgency of his kiss a revelation. It made her dizzy, made her cling to him. His arm tightened around her, pulling her lower body fully against him.

She went up in flames.

That enormous erection was back, making it obvious what he wanted from her.

The truly mind-blowing thing about it was, with that thriller of a kiss setting her on fire like it was, she wanted it, too.

The heart-stopping intensity of the way he was kissing her rocked her to her toes. It made her pulse pound. It made her bones melt. If he'd lowered her to the grass right there and then and come down on top of her, she would have started tearing off her clothes. She wanted to get naked with him. No, get real: she wanted to have sex with him.

It had been a long, long time since a man had been able to turn her on so fast. In fact, she wasn't sure a man had ever been able to turn her on so fast.

What she was experiencing was nothing short of a blast of sheer, burning sexual desire.

For the first time in her life, she understood how people wound up falling into bed with complete strangers. Given a bed and privacy, she would have absolutely been there.

He was the one who broke it up. He lifted his mouth from hers and straightened, setting her firmly on her feet and putting a small bit of distance between them while his hands on her waist helped her keep her balance.

For the briefest of moments her arms stayed wrapped around his neck. She stared up at him in bemusement, drinking in the dark, hot gleam in his eyes, the tension around his hard mouth, while she recalibrated. Then she removed her arms from around his neck and deliberately stepped back, out of his reach.

And to hell with her wobbly knees.

"Agent Bradley," she began, her voice embarrassingly huskier than it should have been, then thought, *God, that sounds idiotic after he just kissed me into next week*, and amended it to a firm, "Finn."

His eyes narrowed slightly at her. To her annoyance, that was all the response she got.

Didn't seem to make a difference: she was still wildly aroused, still wanted more. She was breathing way faster than she should have been. Her heart pounded and her pulse raced. He was feeling the intensity of the attraction between them, too. She could tell, although he didn't say anything, didn't make any kind of move. Electricity arced between them. There was a sizzle in the air, an almost tangible heat.

What she wanted to do, more than she had wanted to do anything in a while, was move back into his arms and pick up right where they had left off.

But then the memory of how the rest of her day had gone came crashing into her consciousness, and all those hot, tingly feelings got doused by a wave of cold reality.

"What was that?" She was proud of the undernote of acerbity in her voice.

"A kiss," he said, and jerked his head toward the

back door. "Go on in. I'll watch until you're safely inside."

Her brows snapped together.

"What—?" she began. —*do you mean, a kiss?* was the rest of what she was going to say, and pretty hotly, too, because that was no answer at all and sounded infuriatingly dismissive to boot, but she never got the chance to finish.

The back door opened.

"Whoever's out there, this is private property. You need to leave right now. I've called the police."

"Margaret, it's me," Riley called.

"Riley? Oh, thank goodness!" Margaret stepped out onto the stoop, her slim form backlit by the light spilling from the kitchen. She was still dressed in her funeral clothes, which made Riley wonder if maybe some of the guests had lingered. She was looking in Riley's direction, but because of the pool of light she was standing in and the darkness that blanketed the yard, she was unlikely to be able to see much—like the fact that Riley wasn't alone. "Come inside."

With a salute that might have been somewhat mocking—it was too dark to be sure—Finn gifted her with an infuriating glimmer of a smile and melted away into the shadows.

Riley frowned after him, surprised at how much she hated to see him go. Over and above that blistering kiss, he'd made her feel safe. Without him, she felt . . . vulnerable. Exposed.

In danger.

Like the dark was closing in again.

But with him gone, there was nothing else to do: she turned and walked into the house.

The second she stepped through the back door, Margaret closed and locked it behind her.

Then Margaret's gaze dropped to her neck, and she started exclaiming over the bruises that even Riley's high-necked shirt couldn't cover. Emma, who'd been sitting at the kitchen table, jumped up and ran over to hug her.

Hugging Emma back, Riley registered how thin she felt. At the same time, she was doing her best to thrust all thoughts of that blazing kiss and everything associated with it out of her mind. It shouldn't have happened, and her response to it had been an aberration, a sign of the extreme stress she was under. Or maybe it had stemmed from the concussion. Or the meds. Whatever the underlying catalyst, she refused to think about it again.

"We were so scared for you," Emma said as she stepped back. Like Margaret, she was still wearing the black dress she'd worn to the funeral, but her shoes were off and her hair hung straight and sleek down her back instead of being caught up in a ponytail as it had been earlier.

Margaret chimed in with, "A reporter came up and rang the doorbell and when Bill answered the door to order him off the porch, he told Bill someone had tried to kill you! Is that true?"

Bill had walked into the kitchen a moment earlier and now stood frowning at the three of them as they stood in a tight little group near the refrigerator. Riley wasn't particularly surprised to see that he had stayed with Margaret and Emma until they'd found out whether Riley was safe.

Riley breathed an inward sigh of relief: if Margaret had seen the man she was with, she would have immediately said something—and she didn't, so Riley knew Finn hadn't been spotted. "I'm all right," she assured them, and glanced toward the living room. "Is anyone else here?"

"Brent left about fifteen minutes ago." Emma's lips didn't quiver, but the bruised look in her eyes told Riley that Brent's visit hadn't exactly left her with the warm fuzzies. "Right before the reporter came to the door. He was with Julie and Sarah Mason and Andrew Brown." Julie being one of Emma's (former) close friends. Sarah Mason and Andrew Brown were schoolmates. "They stopped in on their way to get a pizza. To say, you know, sorry about Jeff. They were the last, I think. I mean, accept for Mr. Stengel."

Reading between the lines, Riley deduced that Brent and Julie had shown up as a couple. Aching for Emma, she gave the teen a sympathetic pat.

"Sucks." Riley's summation was succinct, and Emma grimaced in acknowledgment.

"I'm just glad you're okay," Emma replied. "I couldn't take it if—"

"So tell us everything," Margaret interrupted before Emma could finish with something on the order of, *you died like Jeff.* Riley thought it was probably because she didn't want Emma's thoughts going any farther down that path than could be helped. "The reporter said you were surprised by a man who was waiting in your apartment."

Margaret's normally low-pitched voice was shriller than usual. Her arms were crossed over her chest, and her face looked pale and pinched. Riley would have given pretty much anything not to have to add to her, or Emma's, distress, but this was something she simply couldn't keep to herself: the attack constituted a dire development that had to be shared.

"There's something I have to do first," Riley said, because she knew she needed to get it over with while she was still feeling strong enough, and while the op portunity was there. "Hang on a minute, and I'll tell you the whole story."

With them peppering her with questions even as they followed her, she headed for the front door. After warning Margaret and Emma to stay inside and dismissing with a wave of her hand Bill's sharp query as to what in the world she was doing, she stepped out onto the front porch and closed the door behind her.

The response she was anticipating took maybe five seconds.

"It's Riley!" one of the reporters shrieked.

"Look, it's Riley!" another yelled half a beat later.

With that, they rushed her, pounding through the front yard, focusing their blinding lights and cameras on her, thrusting their microphones toward her, hurling so many questions at her that it was almost impossible to separate them into anything coherent. Before, she'd avoided them like the bloodsuckers they were, ducking from their cameras, ignoring their questions.

Now they constituted the ideal way for her to send a message.

The questions came thick and fast.

"Were you the target of the shots that were fired in your building earlier?"

"Did somebody just try to kill you?"

"Were you attacked by a man in your apartment tonight?"

Riley could barely make out the faces behind the barrage of lights.

"Yes, I was attacked tonight in my apartment—possibly by the same man who murdered my ex-husband," she said directly into the lens of the closest camera, her hand curling around one of the wrought iron roof supports. Using the media to tell the public the truth about what had happened to Jeff felt good. She desperately wanted whoever had killed him to be caught, and since she'd already been targeted, she no longer had to fear making herself one. "The man who attacked me demanded that I give him Jeff's cell phone, which was in my possession. I was able to get away, alive and reasonably well as you can see, and have since turned Jeff's cell phone over to the FBI. It's with them now." She raised her free hand to shield her eyes from the glare, and added, "That's all I have to say. The cell phone's with the FBI. Good night."

There was a collective wail of protest.

"Riley, no! Come back!"

"Why was he after Jeff's phone?"

"Was he trying to kill you?"

"Is it true he's in police custody?"

Steadfastly ignoring the increasingly frantic tenor of the shouted questions, she waved, stepped back inside the house, and shut and locked the door.

Whew.

For the briefest of moments, she allowed herself to lean against the door. Her head spun. Her knees felt weak. She felt like every last bit of strength she had remaining to her had just been spent. But she'd done what she needed to do. Now anyone else out there who thought there might be some kind of answer on Jeff's phone would know that, whether that was true or not, she no longer had it. She'd just made herself and Margaret and Emma at least a little bit safer.

"You talked to the media," Bill said in a dumbstruck tone as Riley pushed off from the door, took the few steps needed to reach the dark brown, floral couch and sank bonelessly down on it.

Since their lives had come crashing down around them, one of the things Bill had told all of them so often that they were sick of hearing it was, "Don't talk to the media."

"I had to." Feeling inordinately tired, Riley fought to clear her head. There was a fine line to walk here, between what to tell and what not to tell, and at the moment her thinking wasn't the sharpest it had ever been. She needed to be careful. "I wanted to get the word out that I don't have Jeff's cell phone. That's what the man who was in my apartment was after. The sooner everybody knows it's in the hands of the FBI, the better off we'll all be."

"Why would someone attack you for Jeff's

phone?" Bill asked. He stood in the middle of the living room frowning at her. "What in the world could be on it?"

Riley shook her head wearily. "I don't know. I guess the FBI will find out. I think—"

She was interrupted by the ringing of the doorbell.

Bill turned and snatched open the door before anyone else could make a move, snapped at whoever was on the other side of it, "I'm Mrs. Cowan's lawyer. You're on private property. If you don't leave immediately I'll have you arrested for trespassing," and banged the door shut again.

As he locked it, he sent a reproachful look at Riley, which she ignored. Whatever Bill thought about what she'd just done, she knew that getting the news that she no longer had Jeff's phone out there in the public arena was the smartest thing she could do.

"Tell us what happened," Margaret ordered. She perched on the edge of the tan corduroy recliner beside the couch, her hands clasped tightly in her lap.

Emma, meanwhile, had flung herself down on the cushions next to Riley and was looking at her wide-eyed. She said, "Those bruises on your neck—did he, like, try to choke you or something?"

Riley gingerly touched the tender area. The last thing in the world she wanted to do was give Emma more disturbing images to carry around in her head. But there was no denying the already-purpling bruises.

"He grabbed me by the neck," Riley replied, ignoring the shiver that ran down her spine at the memory. Then, downplaying everything she could for

Emma's sake, she gave them a judiciously edited version of the attack, fudging such details as the fact that she had run for her life while naked—in her revised version she'd managed to snatch up a towel—and almost everything about the time she'd spent with Finn, with the exception of the fact that she'd broken down in tears, or the kiss that she now shied away from even thinking about.

"Dear God," Margaret said when she was finished. "I shudder to think what might have happened if you hadn't gotten away, or those FBI agents hadn't been there."

"He would have shot her." Emma's tone was stark. She huddled in a corner of the couch with her knees drawn up tightly beside her. The ends of her long blond hair swung over her shoulder, almost brushing her pink-manicured toenails. "You have to face it, Mom. We're all at risk."

"No," Margaret protested as her eyes met Riley's. At the expression on Emma's and Margaret's faces, Riley felt her insides contract. Both, in their different ways, looked afraid.

The worst thing about it was, they were right to be afraid. *She* was right to be afraid.

"I can try to get some private security—" Bill began, only to be interrupted by another peal of the doorbell.

Muttering something under his breath, Bill strode to the door and yanked it open.

The bristling belligerence of his stance changed almost instantly.

"What can I do for you, officers?"

Officers?

Alarmed, the women looked at each other and then toward the door, but the way they were situated precluded them from seeing whoever was on the porch. Tensing in instinctive anticipation of more bad news, too exhausted to get up and check out what was going on for herself, Riley could hear a man's voice, although not distinctly enough to make out the words. Bill listened, nodded, then stepped back. As he closed the door, Riley saw that he held a white plastic grocery-type bag in his hand.

"What—?" Margaret began, her hands pressed to her heart, speaking for all of them.

"There'll be a patrol car with two officers in it parked out in your driveway every night starting now until they tell us otherwise," Bill said, sounding as relieved as he did surprised. "That will certainly make us all feel better, won't it?" His gaze took in Emma as well as Margaret, then shifted to Riley. "The officer also said he was told to give you this."

He handed her the bag. Mystified, Riley looked inside.

The two pints of ice cream were clearly labeled: one was strawberry; the other was chocolate peanut butter crunch.

— CHAPTER —
ELEVEN

"The problem's been taken care of." That was how the conversation started. No greeting, no self-identification from the speaker. But Finn knew who it was, and what he was talking about. Because Riley's attacker had seen Finn and could potentially—with sufficient digging and the right facial recognition software—identify him, he'd been eliminated before he could escape the country.

"It's looking like the surviving family members are in the clear." Finn spoke into the pay phone that in this world of ubiquitous electronic eavesdropping was, ironically, the most secure means of communication with his superior. His words were as to-the-point as the other man's. "I'm going to move on."

What he was moving on to were the chairmen of the investment firms that had been most heavily involved with George Cowan's company, referring clients to him, funneling a substantial amount of dollars from their own investment funds for him to manage along with those of his own clients. Two of those men, both longtime close associates and personal friends of George Cowan, were currently at the top of Finn's getting-to-know-you list. With all the high-tech searching that was going on in every possible money repository throughout the world still drawing a blank, human intelligence was looking like their best shot at finding the missing money.

Human intelligence, in this case, meaning Finn.

Always assuming, of course, that the money was there to be found. And people way above his pay grade were convinced it was.

"We're getting down to the wire on this thing," Eagle warned.

Eagle was not, of course, his real name. Having worked for him for twelve years, since being recruited right out of college until he'd "retired" not quite three years before, and having almost died protecting him in the giant screwup that had led to his leaving the life supposedly forever, Finn was well aware of Eagle's true identity: CIA Assistant Director William Loring. But security dictated that operatives be referred to at all times by their code names, and like the rest of them, Finn subscribed to that. Finn referred to Loring as Eagle just as Loring referred to him as Kestrel. The cell of operatives, of which Finn was one of a number of loosely connected parts, also used code names Falcon, Hawk, Harrier, Osprey, Shrike, and the big dog, the director himself, was code-named Condor. The code name for the suite of offices in D.C. that was their unit's headquarters? The nest.

Never let it be said that the CIA was not cute.

Highly elite, highly compartmentalized, his unit was the Agency's troubleshooters: they went wherever the Agency needed them to go, and did whatever the Agency needed them to do, no questions asked. Only the highest echelon of Agency leadership even knew that they existed, which added to the ease with which they could be cut loose if an operation went south. Finn had no illusions as to why he had been tapped for this particular job: aside from his long association with Eagle, during which he had earned as much of the man's trust as anyone ever did, he no longer had any affiliation with the government, and if the shit hit the fan he'd be easy to disavow.

Or worse.

Unlike the Marines, the Agency left men behind as was deemed necessary. Every operative knew that going in.

Finn was outside at the moment, leaning a shoulder against the brick wall of a nondescript building on the edge of downtown Houston after having been picked up by Bax at the Cowans' house. The building had once housed medical offices and a pharmacy. Now its lowest level was a payday loan operation, currently closed for the night. But it had one of the few surviving pay phones in the area still affixed to the wall, and that plus its location made it ideal for Finn's purpose of checking in with Eagle and updating him on his progress so far. The time was just past 11 p.m., dark except for the dim glow of security lights in a parking garage a couple of buildings down the block. The only other people he could see were a homeless man pushing a rattling grocery cart in the opposite direction and a guy in a sport jacket heading toward his pickup, which was parked curbside across the street. Finn kept an eye on both of them—he didn't expect any problems, but experience had taught him to be wary and that wariness was more natural to him than breathing now.

"I'm aware of the time constraints," Finn answered. "If it's anywhere to be found, I'll find it."

It referring to the money, of course.

"Make sure you get to it before our friends do," Eagle said, and disconnected.

Listening to the sudden buzz of dead air in his ear, Finn frowned. The *friends* Eagle had referred to were other countries plus all the non-government-sanctioned players in the game, all of which were hunting the missing money with as much zeal as his own government. Technically, the money belonged in the custody of the United States, to deal with as it saw fit; realistically, it was finders keepers. Whoever got there first got the money, and if it was anyone besides the United States they were going to make that money disappear.

It was sort of like *The Amazing Race,* only with billions of dollars as a prize and every single contestant prepared to kill or die or do whatever it took to win. Finn included.

That was how he served his country. Bring on the brass band.

The thing was, over the last few years he'd gotten

a taste of how good a normal life could be. Waking up in the same place every day, working hard at something with a future, talking to people when their paths crossed in town or in a store, having neighbors. He'd even made a few tentative steps toward starting a relationship with a woman that was more than a night or two of no-strings-attached sex. He'd taken the female vet who'd come out to treat one of his steers to dinner, he'd gone to the movies with a pretty hostess from the local IHOP, he'd been to a party with an elementary school teacher who'd bumped his car in traffic.

Sure, none of those dates had developed into anything more, but the point was he was trying. Trying, after a dozen years spent serving his country in secret, to assimilate back into the world he'd left behind at twenty-two.

Nothing big, nothing earthshaking. But even those small steps added up to something so different from the life he'd been used to as a clandestine operative that it was like stepping into the noonday sun after a decade and a half spent skulking in the dark.

Hanging up the phone, Finn scanned the area reflexively. The homeless man was almost out of sight. The other guy was in his truck pulling away from the curb. Other than that, the block was dead.

He turned and started walking.

The building he was heading for looked as dark and deserted as every other office building in the area.

It wasn't.

Inside the shabby brick building, the FBI kept offices that no one officially knew about. The offices were used by agents who were on special assignments that for one reason or another were off the record—in this case, it was the FBI wanting to keep an eye on the CIA in this under-the-radar government search for Cowan's missing billions.

The people in the building didn't know each other, didn't interact, just got their jobs done and stayed out of each other's way. Since Finn was not an FBI agent—the FBI and the CIA were about as friendly as a snake and a mongoose—and he preferred to remain as anonymous as possible, he had elected to remain outside while Bax went in to do his thing. As he'd told Bax, it gave him a chance to stretch his legs. What he hadn't mentioned was that it also gave him a chance to check in with Eagle without worrying about what Bax or anyone else might overhear.

Meanwhile, his absence gave Bax a chance to file his report—the second one in the not-quite-two weeks he and Finn had been together—without worrying about what Finn might overhear.

A win-win for both of them.

The reason the building appeared empty at this hour when it was really fully staffed and operational was that the interior space had been configured so that there were offices within offices, and the real offices had no windows. The windows looking out onto the street opened into shell offices of a supposed oil drilling company, the lights of which went on and off at appropriate open-of-business and close-of-business hours.

At the moment, Bax was inside one of those secret

offices, filing his report on major developments in his
assignment that had to be dropped into his supervisor's
email inbox as soon as possible after they occurred.
Finn wasn't supposed to know the contents of the
reports, but he did—despite the encrypted computer
setup Bax was using. Why? Because he'd put the same
kind of bug in Bax's phone that he'd placed in Riley's.
It tracked Bax, captured his conversations, and in a
happy little bonus, since Bax relied on a dictation
program loaded into the computer to place his reports, captured those, as well. (Finn was confident the
Agency was also monitoring them, but he liked getting
information that affected him firsthand.) It amused
Finn to think that the tech-savvy numbers nerd he'd
been saddled with hadn't thought to check his own
phone for a bug, but Bax hadn't, and Finn had gotten
some enjoyment out of hearing himself described as
"not much of a talker," "stone cold," and, his favorite,
"dude's fucking scary, man!"

Nonc of which gave Finn a problem with Bax.
The reports themselves had been factual. That was
what he was interested in, and as far as he could tell
Bax was playing it straight and wasn't engaging in any
kind of double-dealing. Not that Finn trusted him,
or the FBI, but then again he no longer really trusted
anyone—including members of his own crew.

Words to not die by: everybody lies.

Finn wondered if Bax had any real idea what the
Bureau had gotten him into. He doubted it, but that
was not his problem.

He was there to do his job and get the hell out.

Putting in the earwig that he'd taken out when he'd placed the call to Eagle, Finn was in time to catch the end of Bax's report.

"—then drove to Margaret Cowan's house, where I picked up Bradley. Together we proceeded to drive to this location. We made one stop on the way, to an ice cream store, where Bradley purchased two pints of ice cream. The ice cream was sent to Margaret Cowan's house via a patrol officer whose unit was being dispatched to provide security for Margaret, Emma, and Riley Cowan at night from this date until an indefinite end date as a result of the previously described attempt on Riley Cowan's life. The purpose of the ice cream is unknown. Bradley's future line of investigation is unknown."

Bax kept on talking, but Finn listened without really registering what was being said. He found himself instead mentally following the ice cream to its destination. Riley would have known it was from him, just like she would have known the squad car stationed in her driveway was from him.

What she wouldn't know was that the ice cream was his way of saying he was sorry about the kiss, which he absolutely should not have engaged in. She also wouldn't know that the kiss had been his way of saying good-bye. Her fessing up to finding Jeff's body and taking his phone, coupled with her explanation for why she'd disabled it and the fact that she had voluntarily handed it over, had moved her down enough notches on his hit parade that he was turning his focus elsewhere. He was only interested in pursuing people who could take him where he wanted to go. Unless something new came up, he wouldn't see her again.

The realization that that didn't sit well with him told him it was an intelligent decision.

Letting his attraction to a subject he was investigating get out of hand like he had done tonight was something that had never happened to him before. It was unprofessional, and he regretted it.

The problem was, the way she had looked running toward him naked seemed burned into his brain. He was human, after all, and she was beautiful. No amount of training could counteract that.

No amount of training could counteract the memory of how her full, firm breasts with their hard little nipples had felt pressed up against his chest, or the slender, supple, unmistakably feminine shape of her as she clung to him. No amount of training could counteract the effect of the silken warmth of her skin beneath his hands, or how sexy she'd felt in his arms, or the sight of her bare, truly world-class ass. No amount of training could—

Keep him from getting a boner the size of a Louis-ville Slugger every time he remembered, he concluded wryly.

Obvious solution: don't remember. But he was having a hell of a time getting her—the look of her, the feel of her, the smell of her, and most of all the passionate way she had kissed him back—out of his head.

She'd known he wanted her. From just before she'd finished, in her words, crying all over him, the evidence had been right there in front of her. She hadn't missed it. He'd seen the moment the knowledge had dawned on her in her eyes.

Her only reaction had been to step out of his arms.

A cool customer.

Same conclusion he'd reached about her before.

Until he kissed her. Then she'd caught fire in the blink of an eye.

And he'd been consumed with the urge to take her to bed.

He was still consumed with the urge to take her to bed.

That was what was bothering him the most.

That, plus the fact that taking her to bed just wasn't going to happen.

Almost as bothersome was the knowledge that he hadn't liked seeing her cry.

Years in the field had hardened him so that he rarely felt emotion. But he'd felt—what? A twinge of an unfamiliar kind of unease when the moonlight had hit Riley Cowan's face and he'd seen that it was streaked with tears.

He hoped it wasn't a sign that he was getting soft.

Softness could be exploited. Softness could get you killed.

Whether he liked it or not, she'd slid way down the hit parade. He wouldn't see her again.

It was for the best.

Finn was just reaching the car when Bax walked out the building's side door into the parking lot.

Perfect timing.

Bax was driving, so Finn got in beside him and said, "You get your report filed?"

"I did," Bax replied. He was pulling out into the street, heading toward the nondescript hotel where Finn and he, in his role as Finn's babysitter, had side-by-side rooms, when Bax added, "I also got a message from the lab about Jeff's phone while I was in there. They're not going to be able to get anything off it."

"Water fry it that bad?" Finn was mildly surprised. He'd figured the FBI techies could get data off anything.

"Turned out it didn't matter. The SIM card was missing. The Ukrainian must've taken it."

Finn didn't stiffen. He never gave that much away. But his gut tightened.

"Yeah," he said, and that was all. Bax's interpretation was certainly possible. But call him suspicious: he had a whole nother possibility in mind.

— CHAPTER —
TWELVE

After Bill left, they ate ice cream, the three of them. Or, rather, Riley and Margaret ate ice cream, spooning it up (with Margaret making the occasional exaggerated little sound of pleasure as if she were trying to encourage a baby to eat), while Emma, after taking a couple of tiny bites to please them, stirred her spoon around the melting contents of her bowl as if they wouldn't notice what she was doing.

It was a desperate attempt at normalcy, undertaken solely for Emma's benefit.

And, except for the fact that Emma wasn't eating and Jeff wasn't there and they were sitting at a secondhand table in a small, crowded kitchen in a dreary ranch house rather than a custom-made banquette in the bow-windowed breakfast room of a mansion where they'd once habitually adjourned to eat ice cream, it was almost like old times.

Also, back then there hadn't been a squad car parked in their driveway that might possibly be all that stood between them and being murdered in their beds. And Riley hadn't had a perpetual knot in her stomach. And Margaret hadn't had that haunted look in her eyes.

And none of them had been afraid. She knew they were both thinking the same thing: *What have we done?*

"So who sent the ice cream?" Emma asked, stirring.

Glad to have something so innocuous to talk about, Riley swallowed her mouthful of chocolate peanut butter crunch. The flavor wasn't her favorite, but she hoped that seeing her enjoying it would encourage Emma. Anyway, the cold smoothness of it felt good going down her bruised throat. "I told the FBI agent who drove me home that I'd meant to pick some up. I'm sure it was him."

"That was thoughtful of him," Margaret said in a falsely bright tone.

"We're never going to get away from this, are we?" Emma asked in a subdued tone. "People think we were part of what Dad did."

"No one thinks that," Margaret protested.

Emma looked impatient. "Oh, yes, they do. Even the kids at my art program keep asking me things like, *so where's the cash?* They all think we know. Everybody thinks we know." She looked at Riley. "That's the reason that asshat hurt you. That's why somebody killed Jeff. That's why there's a cop car parked outside right now. We're all in danger because Dad scammed all that money and everybody thinks we know where it is."

"The cop car's a precaution," Riley said. "The ass-hat who attacked me was after Jeff's phone. You heard me go outside and tell everybody in the whole world who's interested that I gave it to the FBI. I don't think anybody's going to come after me again, because I no longer have anything they want. I don't think anybody was ever going to come after you, or your mom."

Emma said, "But you don't *know*."

Margaret was looking distressed. "Honey, it won't always be like this. Time heals. People will forget."

Emma looked from her mother to Riley and back. "That is such bullshit," she burst out. "This whole thing is such *bullshit*. Everything is *ruined*. For the rest of my life, people are still going to be calling me '*that crook George Cowan's kid*.' And Jeff will always, always be dead. And we didn't even do anything *wrong*."

With that she shoved her chair back, jumped up, and ran from the room. A moment later, the slam of her bedroom door echoed through the house.

Margaret's shoulders slumped. There were circles beneath her eyes that hadn't been there before, and the lines running from her nose to her mouth suddenly seemed more pronounced. She appeared utterly defeated.

Riley hurt for her. For Emma, too. For all of them.

"You're right, you know," Riley said quietly. "People will forget, and time does heal. Emma's just too young to realize it."

"I wouldn't say this to anybody but you but—oh, I *hate* George for what he's done to us." Anger blazed suddenly from Margaret's eyes. Riley's own eyes widened. In all the time she'd known her, she could count on one hand the number of times she'd seen Margaret angry. Margaret's voice shook as she continued: "He's the reason Jeff's dead. And the reason you were almost killed tonight. And Emma—dear lord, what if someone comes after *her*?"

Her pale, slender hands lay palm down on the table on either side of the bowl that held the melting mound of pink ice cream. As she finished they clenched into fists.

"There's a cop car in the driveway," Riley reminded her. "With two armed cops in it. And *no one* could think Emma knows anything."

Margaret wet her lips. "They could hurt George through Emma. Far more than they could through Jeff. He—she was his little girl. We've got to do something."

Fear twisted inside Riley like a knife. Meeting Margaret's eyes, she could see the same fear reflected back at her.

Panic did no one any good. Covering one of Margaret's clenched fists with her hand, Riley said steadily, "There's no way anyone could think that any of the three of us know anything. What happened to me tonight was strictly about what was on Jeff's phone."

The fear in Margaret's eyes didn't abate. "What *was* on it?"

"I don't know," Riley replied wearily, and made a gesture indicating that she didn't want to talk about it right then. She'd been right in her suspicions so far. It wasn't that much of a stretch to conclude that

someone—like, say, Agent Finn Bradley of the FBI—
might be listening in on everything they said, even
inside the house.

"This is a nightmare," Margaret whispered, and
closed her eyes. Riley could see that she was fighting
for composure. Riley knew that Margaret was being
shaken by the same terrible thought that had hit Riley
earlier—had their actions somehow brought Jeff's
killer down upon him?

A hard, cold knot formed in her chest.

The next question—would it bring a killer down
upon *them*?—sent a shiver down her spine.

After a moment Margaret's eyes opened and her
hands unclenched. Riley patted those pale fingers then
pulled her own hand away. Glancing toward the hall
that led to the bedrooms, Margaret said in a more normal tone, "Emma's like me. We tend to stick our heads
in the sand in times of trouble. We've both been thinking that one day things would get back to normal. Now
that Jeff—" Her voice quivered, and she didn't finish
the thought. "I guess Emma and I are both just now
facing up to the fact that nothing can ever be normal
again."

"Things won't be the same," Riley said around the
sudden constriction in her throat. "But you'll adjust.
So will Emma. We all just need to hang on."

Margaret pushed back from the table and stood
up. "I'm going to go talk to her. Even though she
probably doesn't feel like talking to me right now."

Riley nodded. As Margaret left the room, Riley
saw that for once her usually perfect posture had

forsaken her. Her head was bowed, her shoulders hunched. She walked like she was carrying the weight of the world on her back.

With Margaret gone, Riley did the only thing that was left for her to do: she cleared away the ice cream bowls, rinsing them and putting them in the dishwasher. Then she headed down the hall to get ready for bed. Through Emma's closed door she could hear the murmur of Margaret's voice, along with other muffled sounds that she thought had to be Emma, sobbing. Riley's stomach turned inside out all over again.

No matter what any of them did now, the hard truth was there was no going back.

An hour later, Riley tossed aside the light blanket she'd been curled beneath on the living room couch and stood up. As exhausted as she was, sleep refused to come. The house was quiet and dark, except for the light she'd left on in the kitchen because darkness now made her uneasy.

Lifting one edge of the closed front curtains, she peered out to reassure herself that the cop car was still in the driveway. It was: she could see the shape of it, pale against the night. She felt a rush of gratitude toward Finn for sending it, but as quickly as it came she shied away from it: he was the last thing she wanted to think about right now. She looked past the cop car to see that the TV trucks were gone. As far as she could tell, no one was out and about. The street was still. A lighted window here, a porch light there, provided only small points of illumination in the blackness.

Letting the curtain drop, she turned and padded into the narrow hall. Her destination was the bathroom, which was the first door on the right. Margaret and Emma each had bedrooms at the end of the hall. The other bedroom, the one Jeff had used, was almost directly across from the bathroom. Like the others, its door was closed. She couldn't bring herself to sleep there, in the bed he had used, so she'd been sleeping on the couch. Since she was the first one up every morning, she wasn't sure the others even knew.

She had almost reached her destination when the sound of a door opening made her glance swiftly toward the end of the hall.

Margaret stood in her bedroom doorway, shadowy and indistinct except for the faint gleam of her white satin robe as it reflected the dim glow of the kitchen light. The kitchen was behind Riley, and her pale blue nightgown was soft cotton and wouldn't reflect the light; still, she had no doubt Margaret could see her, too.

Margaret came toward her. Riley stopped, waiting.

"I can't get it out of my mind," Margaret whispered as she reached her. "Was Jeff killed because—?"

"Shh." Catching the other woman's arm, Riley pulled her into the bathroom, which was tiny and ordinary: white tub, sink, toilet, fifties-era avocado green tiles on the floor and walls. She flipped on the light, closed the door. Putting a finger to her lips, she then turned on the tap in the sink as high as it would go. Cold water so it wouldn't steam up the room, making it even warmer than it was because the central air-conditioning unit was in the last stages of its life cycle. Like she'd told Finn earlier, she watched TV, and sometimes even learned from it: in one of the police procedural shows she favored, the sound of running water had been used to provide the kind of white noise that could foil eavesdropping devices. Not that she was convinced that the shows were accurate, and not that she was convinced that they were being eavesdropped on, but under the circumstances she thought it would be smart to do what she could, just in case.

Margaret looked at her with surprise.

"So we won't be overheard," Riley explained, low-voiced.

"Emma's asleep." Margaret's arms were folded over her chest, and by the bathroom's stark light, without makeup, she looked old. The fine lines in her face were readily apparent. Her lips were pale and dry. Her eyes were red-rimmed. Tension made the tendons in her neck stand out above the lace-trimmed edge of her floral nightgown, which was just visible above the lapels of her tightly tied robe. The running-water precaution wasn't about Emma, but Riley had no time to explain as Margaret rushed on, quietly but with an edge of near hysteria in her voice. "Could Jeff have known? Could anybody know, and think it was him? Oh, dear God, was he killed because of what we did?"

— CHAPTER —

THIRTEEN

That was the question that had been hammering at Riley since she'd found Jeff's body. It had chewed holes in her heart, clawed its way through her mind.

It was the primary reason she had originally taken his phone, and, earlier tonight, the SIM card: in case somehow, in some way, there was something incriminating on it, some kind of clue, some kind of link that might lead to what she and Margaret had done. In case there was something on it that might provide an investigator—or someone even worse—with the kind of *aha* moment that she had experienced.

The idea had terrified her even as she had crouched in shock below Jeff's dead body, and it terrified her still. But having had time to consider, she thought the chance of that being the case was somewhere between slim and none.

At least, that's what she thought when it wasn't the

middle of the night and all kinds of horrific scenarios were invading her dreams.

Once she'd had a chance to plug the SIM card into an e-reader and make a thorough search of the contents, she'd know for sure. But she had to wait until she could figure out a way to make certain that accessing the information on that SIM card wouldn't send a flaming look-at-me arrow shooting out through cyberspace.

But for now, for the sake of Margaret's peace of mind, she was going to go with pure logic.

"If Jeff had even suspected, he would have said something." Riley had already mentally reviewed the manner in which Jeff had summoned her to Oakwood on that last night, in case he'd stumbled onto something just before he'd died. If so, it had to have been after he'd texted her, because he'd given her no clue in his message. But she didn't think that's what had happened: unless he'd been incapacitated, he would have phone-blasted her with excitement at the discovery as soon as he'd made it. Unless, of course, he hadn't had time. "I'm almost positive he didn't know. That's not why he was killed."

Margaret sat down abruptly on the closed lid of the toilet and looked up at her with torment in her eyes. "Then why?"

Riley had no answer to that, so she just shook her head.

"Jeff's the one who found George's calendar on that cloud thing in the first place," Margaret persisted. "Wouldn't there be some trace of him looking at it?"

"iCloud," Riley corrected automatically, adding, "I don't think so," as she thought back to a Friday night, *that* Friday night, a little more than a month ago. She'd been giving Jeff a ride home from the Palm Room after he'd stopped in to share the latest results from his investigation into the supposed murders of George's associates, and, not incidentally, cadge some free drinks (from one of the waitresses who had a soft spot for him, not from her). Accessing the Internet from his phone while she drove, using old usernames and passwords he knew his father had once used, he'd unexpectedly hit pay dirt: a cache of George's emails, photos, notes, etc., that everyone had believed no longer existed. They were in an account that apparently automatically backed up to the cloud, which would have floored George if he had realized it, because in the days before his arrest, suspecting it was imminent, he had deleted all his files and then destroyed the devices they were kept on in an attempt to prevent them from falling into the hands of investigators.

Jeff had whooped gleefully upon discovering that at least some of that material was still around. At his insistence, she'd pulled into a McDonald's parking lot while he went through it, looking for clues that might corroborate his theories about the deaths of his father's associates being murders, or, alternatively, lead to the missing money. He'd been careful not to download anything since the feds were still suspicious that he'd been involved in his father's crimes. He didn't want to leave any cyber trail that would lead back to him in case an investigator should subsequently come across the files and accuse him of some kind of prior knowledge. But he'd shared bits and pieces with her, probably in a bid to defuse her impatience to get going again.

None of it had seemed to have anything to do with what he was looking into, as Riley had pithily told him. None of it had seemed to have anything to do with anything worth talking about, in fact. It had all been seemingly minor, personal stuff.

One of the items had been George's calendar for the month in which he'd been arrested. All the appointments he'd jotted down were business-related, and if they held some significance other than a frantic winding up of his affairs, Riley was too tired to spot it, or care.

"You know, it's after three a.m., and I've been working for something like eighteen hours now. You want to explain to me why I'm sitting in a parking lot looking at this stuff with you?" she'd growled. "Remind me, next time you come to my club and drink too much, to call you a cab."

"You're the one who insisted on driving me home. And I can't afford a cab." Jeff was still paging through the calendar, utterly absorbed. "I don't want to do this at my mother's house. Now they can track everything everybody does online. You know these phones have a GPS, right? You never know if maybe the location of whatever device is looking at this stuff is getting embedded somewhere. I want to make it as hard as possible for them to actually trace it back to me."

"Oh my God, there you go with the 'them' again. You are totally paranoid." Riley had rolled her eyes and restarted the car. "That's it. I've had enough. We're out of here."

"Riley—"

"Forget it." She drove to the exit, pulled out onto the dark street, headed west.

That's when Jeff had said, "Even in the midst of everything that was going on, Dad put a note on his calendar about Emma's birthday." Which, to add to that particular month's fun, had been only four days before the FBI had hauled George out of his office in handcuffs. *Happy sixteenth to my baby girl. Whatever happens, we'll always have Paris.* Riley could still remember the sudden flash of emotion with which Jeff had added, "How did the mean old bastard even have the balls to write that, knowing that he'd done everything he could to basically destroy her life?"

Riley couldn't remember what she'd replied to that. Her thoughts were already skipping ahead to three days after that conversation had taken place, when she'd been standing in the doorway of Margaret's bedroom chatting with her while the other woman finished getting dressed. Riley's gaze had happened to rest on the small painting propped on a decorative gilt easel that occupied a corner of Margaret's dresser. It was one of the of-no-value-to-anyone-outside-the-family personal items the government had had no interest in confiscating.

It was a five-by-seven unframed canvas, an oil in

soft pastels. Emma had painted it, from a photograph, Riley thought. In it, Emma and Margaret stood arm-in-arm in front of the Eiffel Tower.

Riley remembered that trip: it had been over spring break in Emma's freshman year. Emma and Margaret had gone alone.

Whatever happens, we'll always have Paris.

George had written those words presumably about himself and Emma. But Riley was as sure as it was possible to be that Emma had never spent a day in Paris with George in her life.

George never did anything without a purpose.

Since Emma had painted it, that painting had been on Margaret's dresser, first in the vast master suite at Oakwood and, later, in this small house.

While Margaret slipped into her shoes, Riley crossed to the painting and picked it up.

Even now, she could remember the way her heart had started pounding when she'd looked at the brown paper backing stapled to the wooden frame the canvas was stretched over: four of the staples on the left side were missing. Although the paper still lay flat against the frame, the absence of the staples created an opening.

Being careful not to rip the paper, she slid a finger inside. There was something there, in the space between the painting and the paper backing. It felt like the cavity was stuffed with tissues. Soft and silky tissues. As in, Kleenex.

Frowning, withdrawing her finger, Riley shook the painting. Nothing. No sound, no movement.

It seemed likely that the tissues were put there for just that purpose: to keep something that was inside from moving around, or from making a sound if the painting was moved around. Riley was familiar with Emma's paintings. To her knowledge, they weren't routinely stuffed with tissues.

"What are you doing?" Having finished dressing, Margaret came to stand next to her, frowning at her through the mirror that hung over the dresser.

"I think something's in here," Riley said.

A moment later, with Margaret's permission and the help of a nail file, she'd removed enough of the staples to allow her to see that the painting was indeed stuffed with ordinary white Kleenex. More tissues were wrapped tightly around a small, flat, rectangular object that was held in place by the wadding.

That object, she saw when she pulled the tissues off, was a small black notebook. Pulse pounding, Riley flipped through it.

"Is that—?" Margaret broke off, swallowing convulsively, clearly unable to finish. She'd seen the small, precise handwriting, too. It was unmistakably George's.

"Yes. I think it is." Riley peered more closely at the neat lines of numbers and scribbled notes on the pages, then looked at Margaret, dry-mouthed.

She was almost certain that what she held in her hand was a list of bank accounts, along with their locations and the information needed to access them. It was, in other words, a map to the missing money.

A twenty-first-century treasure map.

Her heart pounded like she'd been running for miles.

Margaret recognized it for what it was, too. The knowledge was there in her eyes.

"Dear Lord, what do we do?" Margaret sounded like she was short of breath.

"Hand it over to the FBI, I guess."

Margaret said, "They'll think we were part of it. They'll think we knew."

It took the fear in Margaret's voice to make Riley realize that the little notebook she was holding was the equivalent of a suicide bomb. If she turned it over and things went badly, it could destroy her, Margaret, and Jeff, which would in turn also destroy Emma. The investigators had been so viciously aggressive in trying to spread blame to the family. Would they believe that they hadn't had the notebook and known the whereabouts of the money from the beginning? Would they believe they hadn't been part of the scam all along?

Riley wasn't prepared to bet the rest of her life on it.

"I don't think I could face going to prison," Margaret said in a thin little voice that was like nothing Riley had ever heard from her before. Like Riley and Jeff, Margaret had been threatened with decades behind bars if it could be proved she'd known anything about what George was up to. The prospect obviously scared her to death. If truth be told, it scared Riley to death, too.

As they'd already learned to their cost, innocence

was no protection. It was all about what the investigators suspected, and felt they could prove.

Looking down at the notebook, Riley said slowly, "Nobody knows we found this. We don't have to give it to anyone. We don't have to tell anyone. We can throw the notebook away. Or burn it."

"Maybe the money's not even there anymore. Maybe those accounts are empty." Margaret must have caught a glimpse of the clock sitting on her nightstand, because she seemed to gather herself together as she exclaimed, "Oh my, look at the time! We've got to leave. We can't be late for Emma's exhibition. She's so nervous. She needs us there." They were headed to Tate Gallery, where Emma's paintings, along with those of other talented teens in the area, were being exhibited and judged by some of the most respected artists in the country.

Riley felt like her insides were cramping up. "Okay. We don't have to decide anything about this right now. I'm going to put it back inside here, and we're not going to tell anybody about it until we figure out what to do. Not anybody. *Not Jeff.*"

As she spoke she slipped the notebook back inside the painting, wriggled enough of the staples back into their holes to secure the backing, and returned it to its easel on the dresser.

Margaret nodded agreement.

"Not Jeff," she repeated.

Neither of them had to say anything more. They both knew that with his sporadic drinking sprees and drug use, Jeff was too volatile to be trusted with any secret, much less one as potentially explosive as this.

Throughout the rest of the day, even when Emma won first place at the exhibit and a trip to compete at the international level at the Bermuda National Gallery two weeks later, Riley wasn't able to get the notebook out of her mind for more than a couple of minutes at a time. Neither, as she confessed later, was Margaret.

In fact, over the next few days, their secret knowledge made them both so jumpy that they had trouble concentrating during the day and sleeping at night.

They discussed what to do until they were both sick of the topic.

Riley finally fished the notebook out and, afraid of somehow being discovered with it in her possession, copied down some of the information in a ridiculous code that she alone could decipher. (On paper—by that time she was as paranoid as Jeff, and the idea of copying anything into the notes app on her phone or taking a picture of the pages or doing anything digitally with the information at all spooked her.) Using one of the computers at the library, being oh-so-careful not to disturb anything on the sites she had to navigate through, she checked to make sure that what they'd found were indeed bank account numbers and passwords and locations.

They were. As it turned out, there were a total of 137 accounts, some numbered, some in the names of various trusts and corporations, in such far-flung places as Singapore, Hong Kong, the Isle of Man,

Liechtenstein, Luxembourg, the Channel Islands, the Caymans, and Panama.

The total in the accounts was a tad over a billion dollars. More than twenty times that sum was missing, either spent or in other vehicles that George hadn't recorded in his notebook, but still the accounts held so much money that Riley was staggered as she added up the figures.

When Riley told Margaret what she had found, Margaret turned around, walked into the bathroom, and vomited.

Later, after much discussion, they decided that the best thing to do was nothing. Sooner or later, they felt, investigators were bound to find the accounts on their own, and when they did it wouldn't have anything to do with them. They would act as surprised as everybody else.

That's when Margaret had uttered the fatal, wistful, words: "That's so much money. If we had even the smallest sliver of it . . ." Her voice trailed away. Then she looked at Riley and said, "Could we somehow get hold of a little bit of it, do you think?"

Shades of the apple tree in Eden.

As it turned out, they could. With Riley's background in finance, it was easy, actually, given that they had the account locations and numbers, the log-in codes, the passwords, and everything else they needed, written right there in George's little black book. As a precaution, Riley bought a refurbished computer at a secondhand store, for which she paid cash. Using it to access an account in Luxembourg, chosen because the

amount of money in it was at the middling level for
the accounts, Riley authorized a wire transfer from
that account to an account she opened in Switzer-
land to receive it. From there, she quickly pinged the
money through various bank accounts until she felt
the trail was sufficiently muddied that no one could
follow it even if, at some point, the withdrawal was
discovered along with the existence of the Luxembourg bank account. Finally she let the money settle,
permanently, in a corporate account she created in
Bermuda, chosen for its banking secrecy and because,
as far as she could tell, George hadn't parked anything
in that locale. Then she closed all the accounts she'd
used to get it there, making Margaret's "sliver" completely (she hoped) untraceable.

Since everything had been done online, the whole
thing had taken less than a day.

"Ten million dollars of that was *mine,* nothing
to do with George or anything he did. I inherited it
from my parents before we got married." That's what
Margaret had told her, when they were still discussing
whether or not they should even think about trying
to skim something from the accounts they had discovered.

Ten million dollars was the amount Riley ended
up transferring into the Bermuda account.

It was so small, compared to the amount left behind, that taking it to ensure Margaret and Emma's
future security wouldn't make any difference to anybody. Riley knew that whatever happened, she could
take care of herself. But Margaret and Emma were a

different story. Margaret was nearly sixty years old
and had spent her entire life in the rarified environs of
the superrich. Money had always simply been there
for her. Emma was young, with her future still to be
provided for. They didn't deserve the circumstances
they were in. They'd had nothing to do with George's
crimes.

So Riley had done it. She'd siphoned off a tiny
stream of money. For them.

Since then, she'd been as antsy as the proverbial
cat on a hot tin roof.

She felt like a criminal. *Was* a criminal. She
could tell herself that the money had originally been
Margaret's—no ill-gotten funds involved—all she
wanted to, but the fact remained that transferring that
money as she had done would get her in big trouble if
it was ever found out.

She could go to jail.

"If the man who attacked you didn't want Jeff's
phone because he'd found something on that cloud
thing linking it to George's files, then why did he want
it?" Margaret said, snapping Riley out of her reverie
and back to the present.

Riley was glad to leave the past behind. She focused with fierce concentration on Margaret, who was
almost as pale as the toilet on which she perched.

"I don't know," Riley said again. "I only got a
quick glimpse of a few things that were on it before
I shut it down. There were three pictures of a couple
of men moving around in the dark that looked like
they had been taken right before Jeff died. Maybe

they were of Jeff's killers, maybe not. Maybe Jeff did end up downloading some of George's files, and they were on his phone, and the scumbag somehow knew and wanted it for that reason. But the thing to keep in mind is, the man who attacked me and whoever killed Jeff are not necessarily one and the same person. I was attacked because he wanted Jeff's phone." Riley took a deep breath, and put it out there. "But I don't think Jeff was killed for his phone. It was still on him when he died. I know, because I found his body that night and took the phone off him, just in case there was something on it that could lead back to us, to what we did. What are the chances that his killers would have missed the phone if that's what they were after?"

Margaret stared at her, wide-eyed. "*You* found Jeff's body?"

"He texted me to pick him up at Oakwood." Riley had hoped to spare Margaret the details, but they were past that now. She told Margaret the whole story, concluding with, "The bottom line is that there's no way Jeff knew that we found the money. Nobody could have killed him for that reason, because even if Jeff ended up downloading every one of George's files he still would've had to make the connection from the calendar to Emma's painting, and he never did. I'm sure of it. And nobody outside the family could possibly make that connection."

For a moment Margaret seemed to mull that over. Then her lips quivered, and her eyes shone with a sudden welling of tears.

She said, "If we had turned George's notebook over to the authorities as soon as we found it, Jeff would be alive right now."

Her words hit Riley like a fist to the stomach. That was the truth that had been crawling around the edges of her consciousness and whispering to her in her sleep. That was the truth that had been staring her in the face ever since she'd found Jeff dead, the truth that she hadn't wanted to see, had refused to recognize.

Unable to speak, Riley stared mutely at Margaret, aware that the dawning horror of realization was probably visible in her face. The tears that were now sliding down the older woman's cheeks broke her heart at the same time as they brought tears to her own eyes.

"We didn't know. We couldn't have known." The words forced their way out of Riley's constricted throat even as Margaret covered her face with her hands. Heart breaking, Riley sank to her knees and put her arms around Margaret.

Holding on to each other, they cried.

Finally, when they were spent, when Riley sank back on her heels and they were both wiping their eyes with folded squares of toilet paper, Margaret gave a deep, shaky sigh.

"There's something you don't know." Margaret's voice was thick in the aftermath of her tears. Still on her knees on the hard tile floor, Riley looked a question at her, and saw that Margaret's hands were clasped together so tightly her knuckles were white. Riley's internal alarm-o-meter immediately started screeching at about a thousand decibels. "When I was in Bermuda with Emma, I went to the bank and withdrew some of the money. I know we agreed not to touch it for years, but—I took out thirty thousand dollars: I thought I might use it to pay Emma's tuition. Because it's her senior year, and—well, I don't have to tell *you*. It's in the suitcase in my closet right now."

The Palm Room was one of those places Finn would never have gone to voluntarily. It was dark and smelled of booze and perfume and he had no doubt at all that any cop with the inclination could make a dozen drug busts within his first five minutes inside. The pounding beat of the music assaulted his ears as soon as he cleared the second set of heavy steel doors through which customers had to pass to join the ranks of those privileged/connected/rich/good-looking enough to be admitted to the converted warehouse just off Katy Freeway. It was Friday, or rather Saturday now, almost 1 a.m., and the line to get in stretched around the block. The quartet of burly bouncers guarding the doors had to be persuaded to let him in by a flash of his creds.

Once inside, Finn prowled through the various rooms the 25,000-square-foot, two-level space had been divided into, a predator in search of a very specific prey. He was all but deafened by the blasting music and the underlying combined roar of clinking glasses and laughter and the voices of hundreds of people all talking at once. Out on the huge dance floor that was the centerpiece of the space, boots scooted and short skirts twirled as laser beams of colored light sliced through the darkness to highlight various couples getting down. A live band played on a dimly lit, raised stage. Fake palm trees pulsing with green Christmas lights filled the corners.

The mezzanine overlooking the dance floor was lined with people leaning against the rail watching the action below.

"Can I get you a drink, sir?" a waitress asked, her voice raised to be heard over the din. She looked to be barely of legal drinking age, a pretty, dark-haired girl with a lithe, tanned body all but bared by a tiny pair of black shorts and a long-sleeved white shirt that failed to provide her with any degree of modesty because it was unbuttoned, rolled up as high on her torso as possible, and tied in a knot between her breasts.

Finn shook his head. He could have used a beer— he could have used several beers—but he was working.

"I'm looking for Mrs. Cowan." He had to raise his voice to be heard, too.

"Riley?" She swept a speculative glance over him. Her name tag read Katie, and she was carrying a round tray with a couple of bottles of Lone Star beer on it, which was probably what had made him think of the beverage in the first place. "She's probably over there in the Sports Bar." She pointed across the dance floor. "That's where the big spenders hang out."

Finn nodded, tucked a couple of singles into the squat, heavy highball glass that was already brimming with them on the tray, and, skirting the dance floor, headed in the direction Katie had indicated.

She—meaning the object of his search—hadn't really said anything incriminating, Finn reminded himself in an effort to retain the necessary degree of objectivity.

Ah, but it was what she didn't say.

His gut had been telling him all along that she was involved in this thing up to her eyeballs. What he'd heard tonight had confirmed every twinge of instinct he'd had.

After a long, exhausting, and ultimately fruitless day of running down all the intelligence he could get his hands on concerning the recent activities of the men whom Riley's confessions had pushed to the top of his hit list, he had returned with Bax to their hotel rooms about two hours previously. Leaving an out-of-the-loop Bax securely tucked away in his own room for the night, Finn had headed downstairs again to collect an envelope waiting for him at the front desk. The envelope had contained the CD from the sound amplifier recorder that he had affixed to the roof of the police cruiser that had spent the night in Margaret Cowan's driveway. Voice activated, it had served as a supplement to the bug in Riley's phone, the effectiveness of which was hampered by the fact that it covered only its immediate vicinity. The sound amplifier recorder captured everything that had been said in Margaret's house from the time the cruiser had arrived until it had left that morning after the ladies were all out of the house. The cruiser was there again tonight, with the recorder busy doing its thing.

The CD had contained maybe forty minutes of actual conversation. He had kicked back in the armchair in his room and listened.

The lawyer left; Emma had a breakdown; Riley and Margaret talked, but revealed nothing he didn't already know; Margaret talked to Emma, presumably in the teen's bedroom, again revealing nothing new; then, at 2:07 a.m. according to the voiceover on the recording, Riley and Margaret talked once more, with Margaret saying, "Was Jeff killed because—?" and Riley answering with, "Shh."

That had been followed almost immediately by the sound of a door closing. After that, the recorder had picked up a few barely intelligible words masked by a muted roar. There'd been more talk in the morning when they'd gotten up, typical getting-ready-to-go conversation, but it was Riley's middle-of-the-night exchange with Margaret, coupled with that masking roar and underscored by some information he'd received earlier, that had brought him out to the Palm Room in search of her.

He knew what that muted roar was: running water. He knew what its purpose was: to mask a conversation. It was a guess, but he thought it was a good one: Riley and Margaret had continued the conversation that had been interrupted by Riley's sharp "Shh" in the bathroom. With the water running—the purpose of which could only have been to foil any listening devices.

Given Riley's propensity for messing with electronics, he did not imagine that the running water had been Margaret's idea.

And there would only have been a need for running water if the conversation was something Riley absolutely did not want anyone to overhear.

In his experience, people weren't that wary without a reason.

"Was Jeff killed because—?"

The answer he did not hear tantalized him. It also pissed him off.

His anger was directed more at himself than her.

He'd known from the moment he'd watched her take that phone off Jeffy-boy's body that she had something to hide.

But he'd let the fact that she was a woman—a young, beautiful, sexy woman who seemed to possess the effortless ability to turn him on to his back teeth—influence him.

Which was why, even before he stepped through the garage-sized open door of the Sports Bar—the name hung in neon over the opening—he was feeling grim.

He glanced around. It was a smallish space, maybe twenty two-person tables, most of which were occupied, with half a dozen big plasma TVs fastened to the wall—all tuned silently to various sports games; headsets for anyone who wanted to listen hung on hooks beneath the TVs—and a long mahogany bar with a mirrored wall behind it, a green glass lighting fixture hanging above it, and a dozen bar stools in front of it. Another of the scantily clad waitresses flitted from table to table, serving drinks and what looked like tiny bags of popcorn. The bar stools seemed to be all occupied, mostly by men. Two bartenders, one male and one female, were busy pouring drinks.

His quarry leaned against the far end of the bar with her back to him. Standing as she was under one of the lights, there was no mistaking the bright blaze of her hair. It hung loose around her shoulders in a profusion of waves. Her dress was black, short, sweater-girl tight, and glittery with sequins. The way it clung to her ass should have been against the law. She was wearing sheer black stockings, mile-high heels. The burly older guy in a business suit and a cowboy hat who was spilling over the bar stool beside her was running his hand up and down her bare upper arm as they talked.

Watching that, his grim got a whole lot grimmer.

He walked over, leaned against the bar beside her. Close, so she'd know somebody was there.

She turned a little, glancing his way, and met his eyes. The sooty black of her lashes framed big green-hazel eyes as they widened. Her lips parted in transparent surprise.

Then she smiled, a dazzlingly genuine I'm-so-glad-to-see-you smile that hit him with the approximate incendiary effect of a surface-to-air missile.

If he'd been standing upright, it would have rocked him back on his heels. As it was, his heart kinda jumped. His balls definitely tightened.

And his grimmer grim morphed into something way hotter and more dangerous.

She'd been about to say, *Thank you for the ice cream.*

Then he smiled a not-nice smile and said, "I don't like it when people lie to me, Mrs. Cowan."

His gray-blue eyes were hard as steel. His posture appeared deceptively casual as he rested one elbow on the bar, his big body seemingly at ease, his heavy shoulders wide enough to block most of her view of the goings-on on the dance floor in the main room beyond him. In his FBI-typical dark suit and white shirt—tonight he was minus the tie—he looked exactly like what he was: a federal agent. He also looked tough and in a bad mood and not like anyone you wanted to mess with.

He was so close his arm brushed hers. Looking at his expression, she knew he'd gotten that close on purpose.

And that purpose wasn't to try to make her little heart go pitty-pat.

His words made her stiffen. On her other side, Don Osborne was, thankfully, talking to Chip the bartender as Chip set Don's third scotch on the rocks in front of him. That, plus the pulsing music, was almost certainly enough to keep him from overhearing.

Unlike Finn's smile, her answering one was sweet as sugar. "I don't like it when people try to intimidate me, Agent Bradley."

His eyes narrowed. Her smile sweetened.

"So you want to tell me how that phone really got in the bathwater?"

Her heart skipped a beat. She prayed her sudden spurt of alarm didn't show.

Just because she kept her voice necessarily low didn't mean it was any less hostile. "I don't want to tell you anything at all. In case you haven't noticed, I'm at work. Excuse me."

As she turned away from him, he straightened to his full height and caught her arm.

"You took the SIM card out. Don't deny it."

Her stomach clenched, but she wasn't about to show it if she could help it. Even as she flashed a let-go-or-die look at him, Don swiveled his stool in her direction and frowned.

"There a problem, Riley?" he asked, glancing from the hand on her arm to Finn. What he saw in Finn's face made his weather-beaten features harden.

Riley shook her head.

"I'm an FBI agent," Finn said. His tone had a *you want trouble, I'm it* edge.

It was all she could do to resist the urge to kick him.

"He's investigating what happened last night. He just wants to ask me a few questions," Riley said. "If you don't mind, I'll walk him out and answer them for him on the way."

"That's fine. You do what you need to do." He patted her arm again. "Like I said, I'm awful sorry about Jeff." He looked at Finn. "This here's a real fine lady. Think the world of her. You be sure and treat her like it."

Finn's hand tightened on her arm. Riley couldn't see his face, but getting him out of there while the getting was good seemed like the best option.

"Thanks, Don," she said. "I'll see you before you leave." Smiling at Don, Riley moved away from the bar with Finn a step behind her, still holding on to her arm like she was a prisoner and he was marching her away.

"You know, you didn't strike me as the type to go hunting a sugar daddy," Finn said in her ear.

They'd just stepped outside the Sports Bar into the main room. It was louder, darker, and way more private.

Giving him the poisonous look she'd been holding back on, she jerked her arm from his hold.

"*Keep walking*. Don's my boss. Actually, my boss's boss. He *owns* the Palm Room," she hissed at him. To her relief he fell in step beside her as she headed for the exit. "He's married with five children and ten grandchildren. It's been really good of him to give me a job and keep me on despite all the horrible things that have happened, and I appreciate it. But even he has his limits, and having an FBI agent hanging around because of me just might be it. Since I really don't want to get fired, I'd appreciate it if you'd leave."

"Want to get rid of me? Answer my questions." He stopped walking. As she turned to glare at him, the smile he gave her verged on the diabolical. "Let's start with what's on Jeff's phone."

"I don't know what's on Jeff's phone," she blazed back. Her voice must have been louder than she'd intended, because several patrons at the surrounding tables glanced at her.

Aware that to a number of them she was

undoubtedly a recognizable figure, she clamped her lips together, turned on her heel, and started walking again. Not that she expected to be able to just walk away from him. She was pretty sure that wherever she went, he meant to follow.

But the closer she could get him to the door, the closer he would be to leaving. She was good friends with all the bouncers. If he'd been anybody else, she would have happily had them escort him out. But throwing out a federal agent probably wasn't something she even wanted to attempt.

She had no hope whatsoever that he would go quietly into that good night.

"Oh, Riley, there you are!" Ana Torres, who oversaw the Hip-Hop Room, which like the Sports Bar was another of the Palm Room's clubs-within-a-club, touched her shoulder, making her jump even as she glanced around. Ana looked taken aback. "I'm sorry, I didn't mean to startle you." Ignoring Finn, who'd stopped so close behind her that her back practically brushed his front, Riley waved a hand to say *it's okay.* Casting a curious glance over Riley's shoulder at the man who was no doubt looming like a mountain behind her, Ana continued: "Our card scanner's broken. Do you want me to move to cash only, or . . . ?"

Don had a strict policy requiring that each club room maintain its own sales records. Since he was on the premises, Riley could've asked him, or sent Ana to ask him, but part of her job as assistant manager was to take care of such issues.

"Use the one in the Star Lounge." It was the club

room closest to the Hip-Hop Room. "Be sure and have everyone sign in with their sales number before ringing up a charge."

Ana nodded. "Will do."

While Riley was talking, Finn curled a hand around her arm again. Ana glanced from it to her face to him curiously. But she didn't say anything before hurrying off.

That didn't mean that the whole club wouldn't soon be gossiping about the big, bad FBI agent who was manhandling her.

"Are you *trying* to make people think I'm in trouble?" Riley turned on him to growl once Ana was out of earshot.

"I'm trying to get you to answer my questions."

"I want a lawyer," Riley snapped. Once again people at surrounding tables glanced her way. This time she was sure she saw recognition in some of their faces.

"You really want to go that route? 'Cause if that's the way you want to play it, I could have you placed under arrest and taken downtown and ask my questions there."

"I wouldn't answer. Anyway, arrest me for what?"

"Think I couldn't come up with something?"

Riley saw Don emerge from the Sports Bar and glance around. She really didn't want to have his attention drawn to her and her FBI escort again.

Glowering at Finn, she grabbed his arm and hauled him away from the exit where they'd been heading and out onto the dance floor. As dark as it was, as erratic as the lighting was, and as unexpected as her presence on it would be, it was the one place in the building where she was reasonably sure she could escape notice.

Finn stopped dead, and she turned to face him.

"You want to ask me questions? Fine. Ask away," she said, and put her arms around his neck.

— CHAPTER —
FIFTEEN

Her fingers automatically followed the path of his shirt collar, encountering both the warm skin at the nape of his neck and the short, crisp hair on the back of his head. Reluctantly she recognized how much she liked the feel of both. Along with the sturdy, shelflike quality of his broad shoulders that her arms were draped over. And his height, which had her stretching upward even with her four-inch heels. And . . .

The feel of the gun beneath his jacket? Not so much.

That just underlined why she needed to be wary of him.

"I don't dance." Finn's voice grated. His eyes were heavy-lidded and impossible to read as he looked down at her.

"What's so hard about it? Put your hands on my waist and sway." His hands found her waist even before she finished speaking, settling on either side of it at the narrowest part just above the flare of her hips. She could feel the size and shape of them holding her lightly through the stretchy knit of her dress. High-necked, with tiny cap sleeves and an Oriental vibe, it wouldn't have been her first choice given the heat, but in conjunction with the pantyhose she was wearing it had the primary advantage of hiding most of her bruises. "You can sway, can't you?"

"Maybe." It seemed he could, and even pick up his feet at the same time, although recalcitrance practically oozed from his pores. "I want that SIM card, Riley."

The sudden guilty jump of her heart was not, she reminded herself fiercely, outwardly visible. She kept calm by focusing on his use of her given name. She wasn't positive, but she thought it was the first time he'd ever called her by it.

Was *swoon* even a word people used anymore? Because to her surprise, and annoyance, the gravelly way he said her name made her want to.

"I can't hear you," she mouthed, although she could. But using the heavy-metal music as an excuse gave her a second to recover.

Looking irritated, he dipped his head—she got a whiff of soap, felt his warm breath on her ear—and repeated the demand.

As he straightened, her heart was still behaving oddly, but for an entirely different reason.

"I want a Porsche Carrera, but I doubt I'm ever going to get it," she replied. Her eyes mocked. Never mind the fact that the chemistry between them was raising the temperature in the air. She'd made up her mind that the only thing to do was lie her butt off, and if her stomach twisted tighter than a loaf of challah bread at the prospect of lying to the man, she was prepared to ignore it.

"I'm not playing," he warned. His jaw had hardened, and she found herself noticing with interest the faint shadow of stubble that darkened it and his cheeks. How was it that she'd ever thought she didn't like overwhelmingly masculine men? In a possible example of the worst timing ever, she was discovering that she did.

"Me, either." She gave a playful, one-fingered caress to the warm skin at the back of his neck, and felt every muscle in his body go taut as a bowstring in response.

Every muscle. There was enough space between them that the tips of her breasts only barely brushed the bulge in his jacket that was his gun.

Her abdomen now brushed a bulge of a totally different sort.

Big Boy was back.

Her lips parted as she made the discovery. Her gaze slid up over his face.

His mouth was grim. His eyes had a hard, restless glitter at their backs.

For a moment their eyes held.

Mutual acknowledgment.

The air around them felt like it was slowly turning to steam.

"You ever hear of iCloud?" The edge to his voice

was underlined by the tightening of his grip on her waist. She could feel the blunt tips of his fingers digging into her flesh.

Another terrifying question. As she registered the possible implication of that terrifying question, her heart leaped into her throat and her knees went weak and she was very much afraid that her eyes widened in shock.

Thank God for the darkness. She hoped it was enough to hide any reactive change of expression she might have experienced. They were moving, kind of basic box step stuff, to the sexy, throbbing beat of Second City's "I Wanna Feel." Glancing at the gyrating throng around them in a desperate bid to give herself a moment, observing entwined couples practically making out on the dance floor on all sides without really seeing them, she focused on getting her reactions under control.

How much does he know? was the panicky question that pulsed in her brain. She tried to thrust it away but without notable success.

"I can't hear you," she mouthed again.

His eyes narrowed. "Funny, I can hear you."

She shook her head in mock bewilderment, and he leaned closer to repeat the question in her ear. This time, his cheek brushed hers. The sandpaper feel of his stubble against the softness of her skin made her go all melted-marshmallowy inside.

It was almost enough to cause her to forget the clutch of fear she'd experienced when he'd asked if she'd ever heard of iCloud.

As he straightened, her reply was airy. "What about it?"

He leaned close again. This time she was prepared for the rasp of his cheek against hers, for the feel of his warm breath against her ear, for the smell of soap with a hint of menthol—a shaving cream, no doubt—and man.

"A phone like Jeff's usually automatically uploads to it. I've got people checking that out now. If it did, I don't need the SIM card. I'm giving you the chance to hand it over before I find out what was on that phone some other way."

The wave of relief that washed over her was enormous. It cleared her head, gave her her mojo back.

He might be threatening her with iCloud, but in the context of Jeff's phone he was threatening her with the absolute wrong thing.

He didn't know Jeff. He had no idea of the degree of paranoia Jeff had experienced after discovering George's iCloud-stored information cache. Enough so that Jeff had taken steps to make sure that his phone would do no such thing.

Which, in turn, meant that the big, bad FBI agent was shit out of luck.

"Thanks, but I think I'll pass," she said as he straightened, and smiled at him.

His face darkened. His eyes flared. "I won't make the offer again."

In pretend deafness she asked, "What did you say?"

The hard angle of his jaw was only a little above

the level of her eyes. She watched it clench, watched his mouth thin and harden. The aggravation defense: nothing she ever would have employed with premeditation, but it seemed to work. Next time she found herself on the wrong end of an interrogation, she'd remember it.

Then his arms encircled her, tightened. He pulled her fully against him and swung her around, lifting her clean off her feet in the process. It might have been a defensive move, designed to keep them from being bumped by a wildly boogying couple on their right. But she thought it was an offensive one, payback for her pretense. Whatever his motive, it was an unexpected enough move to cause her to lock her arms around his neck and cling to him, then leave her plastered right up against him like jelly to peanut butter, even after her feet were firmly back on the floor again.

It was something that, in retrospect, she would have been better off avoiding.

Too late.

Who would have guessed that she was such a sucker for a big strong man who could sweep her off her feet?

Apparently she was. Once she had her feet beneath her again, she could have put some space between them. She could have unlocked her arms from around his neck and taken a half-step back.

She didn't. She didn't want to.

She felt as if tongues of flame were licking at her skin.

The feel of him, warm even through his clothes

and all solid muscle, was intoxicating. The unyielding firmness of his chest against her breasts, the brush of his long, powerful legs in their suit pants against her nylon-sheathed, much more delicate ones, but most of all the unmistakable evidence of his arousal that was now wedged between them, made her burn, made her quake.

She never even realized her smile was gone until his eyes slid down to fasten on her mouth.

A wave of heat hit her, as tangible as if it had come rolling off a fire. Her heart pounded. Her pulse raced.

The music and darkness swirled around her, blocking out everything except him. Except them.

She watched him looking at her mouth, and her bones turned to water.

Shrouded in the deep purple gloom of the dance floor, with neon shafts of light shooting like meteors through the darkness high above his head, he looked big and dangerous and sexy as hell.

He felt big and dangerous and sexy as hell.

All of a sudden all she could think about was that blistering kiss they had shared.

What she wanted, so much that it surprised her, was for him to kiss her again.

Their eyes met. His were hooded, restless, gleaming. They made her mouth go dry. They made her insides clench. His face was close to hers. It was all she could do not to turn her head so that her mouth brushed his sandpaper cheek.

Wrapped in his arms, with the evidence of how much he wanted her right there between them and the

electricity they generated throwing off sparks everywhere, she almost forgot why they were on the dance
floor in the first place.

Then his head dipped closer still.

"The way I figure it, you took the SIM card out
and tossed the phone in the tub right after the paramedics left your bedroom," he said in her ear.

By the time he straightened, she'd made a considerable amount of headway toward regaining her focus.
Forget sexy. Now he looked predatory. Okay, sexy *and*
predatory. Who would've thought she could find *that*
combination hot? But despite everything, it seemed,
she did. His arms felt hard and possessive around her.
Her breasts were snuggled right up against his chest.
She could feel the unmistakable shape of his gun against
her shoulder. She could feel the buttons on his shirt, the
outline of his belt buckle. Their hips and thighs were
molded together so that she could feel the hard shape of
everything pressing into her. They were barely moving
now, just swaying in time to the pulsing music, and she
felt like she was in free fall, going down fast.

She wanted him so much that it was scary. Her
body tingled and throbbed and ached.

Forget dancing. This was foreplay set to music.
Delicious. Intense. Pleasurable.

And absolutely *not* going to end in red-hot sex.

No matter how turned on she was, she wasn't
about to forget who he was and what he was after.

Short answers: FBI agent; information she
couldn't, wouldn't, give.

She lifted her chin at him. "Anybody ever tell you

you have a great imagination?" To her dismay, instead of being light as she'd intended, her voice came out sounding throaty, thick.

This time his mouth got so close to her ear that she could actually feel his lips moving. "Are you denying it?"

She shivered, and not from guilt or fear. It was from the butterfly touch of his mouth on her skin. As he straightened, her arms stayed wrapped around his neck. Her head tilted farther back as if to offer up her lips for his kiss.

"Yes."

He looked like he was barely managing to swallow some choice curse words. His arms hardened around her, shifted. One hand slid down to rest in the small of her back. She could feel the size and shape of it through her dress. Another inch or so, and he'd have his hand on her butt. Difficult as it might be to face the truth, she *wanted* his hand on her butt. She found herself pressed even more firmly against the hardness that told her that, despite his terse questions, he was at least as aroused as she was, and she wasn't sure if it was his doing or hers.

He bent his head again, only this time he didn't say anything. Instead his lips brushed her ear, and then they settled against the tender skin just below it.

They were warm and firm and totally mind-blowing. She could feel the rasp of his stubble against her skin.

He kissed her there, lingered, kissed some more. She sucked in air.

His mouth was hot, and damp, and a revelation in the way it made her feel as it crawled tenderly, searchingly, thrillingly, along the underside of her jaw before returning to nuzzle her beneath her ear again.

Her heart thumped. Her loins tightened. Her bones turned to water. The world spun away. If she hadn't managed to clamp her lips together just in time, she would have moaned out loud. She was on fire, burning up, hungry for more. There it was again, the same blazing chemistry that had sprung up between them when he had kissed her before, and if there'd been a bed handy she would have been falling into it with him just as fast as she could. Her arms tightened around his neck and her body arched up against his and she told him in every way but words how much she wanted him. But even as she was melting inside from the heat the two of them were generating, the thinking part of her, the logical, reasonable, rational part of her, whispered a killjoy warning: *You need to put a stop to this.*

The thing was, she didn't want to.

His lips were at her ear again. "Think I can't tell you're lying? All I have to do is feel how fast your pulse is pounding."

Not what she had been expecting.

Her eyes popped open. Her fingers, which had been threading through the thick hair on the back of his head, stilled. The heat, the urgency, the sheer reckless desire that had brought her to the brink of possibly doing something really stupid, was blasted by a wave of cold reality.

He'd been kissing her neck as a kind of lie detector test.

Outrage didn't begin to cover it.

Two could play at this game. His ear was within easy reach of her mouth. Sensuously she ran her tongue along the sturdy outer curve of it, nibbled his soft earlobe, enjoying the harsh intake of his breath, the way he stiffened.

Then, in the spirit of sweet revenge, she whispered throatily into it, "You ever think that maybe you just really turn me on?"

She felt the impact of the words hitting him. For a moment he went still as stone in her arms. His every muscle tensed. He seemed to stop breathing. His reaction was everything she had hoped for, and more.

He lifted his head just enough so that he could look down at her.

A dark flush rode high on his cheekbones. His eyes were narrow and glittering, their blue-gray no longer calm. The look in them told her everything she needed to know: he might have been trying to seduce her secrets out of her, to gauge her truthfulness with kisses, but he was even hungrier for her than she was for him.

A second later, it became obvious from the hardening of his expression that he'd figured out that she'd just slapped some payback on him.

His brows twitched together.

"Enough of this. You need to start telling me the truth." His voice was harsh, with a rough edge to it that, despite everything, still managed to do funny things to her insides.

"*You* need to start trying to find out who killed my ex-husband instead of constantly harassing me," she snapped, and pushed free of his arms. Standing in front of him on the dance floor with couples crowding around them on all sides, she folded her arms over her chest and glared at him. "I have to go back to work. I can't make you, obviously, but I wish you'd leave."

Then she turned on her heel and walked off the dance floor.

———

FINN CURSED himself all the way back to his hotel room. From the moment he'd seen Cowboy Bob's hand sliding up and down Riley's bare arm, his plan had gone to hell right along with his temper. Instead of calmly confronting her with what he knew and demanding that she tell him the truth under threat of arrest, which was the gist of what he'd intended to do when he'd left the hotel to pay her a visit, he'd gotten hung up on his dislike of the old guy touching her and the way she didn't seem to have a problem with it. He'd lost his cool, and then, when he'd been stupid enough to let her pull him out onto the dance floor, lost his head entirely.

Difficult to interrogate a suspect when all you wanted to do was fuck her senseless.

Difficult to rationally evaluate anything she'd said when all you still wanted to do was fuck her senseless.

Every time he remembered the warm glide of her tongue along the outside of his ear, he got hard as a rock.

The easy solution—stop remembering—wasn't as easy as it sounded.

He couldn't seem to get it out of his head.

Any of it.

Her.

So much for saying good-bye. She was officially top of his hit parade again.

She knew something. Something big. No longer any doubt about it in his mind.

He'd been doing this too long not to have developed a nose for guilt.

And tonight she'd been throwing off guilt like skunk scent.

Even while she smelled of roses.

This time he'd recognized the scent. Same one she'd smelled of before, which he'd finally identified, although it had taken him a while to figure out exactly why some kind of flower seemed to be perfuming the air everywhere he went. Finally a lightbulb had gone off: it was his damned jacket, which had smelled like her all last night. This morning he'd dropped that particular suit off at the cleaners. He needed it to be minus any trace of Riley Cowan before he wore it again.

The better to put you out of my mind, my dear.

Thing was, it wasn't looking like he was going to be able to do that anytime soon.

Other thing was, he wasn't the only player in the game.

At least *he* wasn't going to do her any physical harm.

She'd made a nice move by announcing on world-wide TV that she'd given Jeffy-boy's phone to the FBI.

Smart girl.

He wasn't sure it was enough.

His driving fear was that somebody else might start to wonder about what secrets she was keeping.

To that end, he'd made arrangements for a pair of undercover cops to be in the parking lot when she got off work at 2 a.m. Keeping discreetly out of sight, they would watch her walk from the door of the Palm Room to her car, then follow her home where the squad car was already in her driveway keeping tabs on everything that was happening in Margaret's house.

The good news was, somebody placing a bomb in Riley's car probably wasn't going to happen. No point in killing the secret keeper until you knew the secret.

Letting himself into his hotel room—quietly so as not to disturb Bax next door—Finn headed straight for the bathroom, stripping his clothes off as he went.

What he needed was a long cold shower, followed by a few hours' sleep.

———

AFTER SNAPPING at a customer who'd come up to her to complain that his drinks were watered (they weren't), and being terse with a limo driver who tried to insist on parking right outside the front door as he waited for his VIP client, and threatening to call the police on a table of big drinkers who tried to sneak out without paying their tab, Riley was forced to face it: she was something less than her usual even-tempered self. And that would be because she was both worried sick and mad as hell at Finn. Ordinarily she would have fixed all those typical Friday night problems with her typical poise and finesse, but since she'd walked away from him on the dance floor and he'd subsequently (color her surprised) left the club, she'd been edgy and irritable and a whole lot quicker to jump than she normally would have been.

Fortunately, Don had left the club. Also fortunately, it was getting on toward one thirty. The club shut down at two. Closing up would keep her another half an hour after that, and then she would be free to go home.

Until ten o'clock Saturday morning, when she was due at her first job again.

At the thought, she barely swallowed a groan.

She hadn't slept much last night, and she'd put in a full day's work at the car dealership before coming in to the club tonight. She was bruised, thoroughly traumatized, and a little sore. The thought of calling in sick to both jobs had been tempting, but with the economy like it was, jobs were hard to come by. For her, with her baggage and especially with the fact that she'd been all over last night's 11 p.m. news and, for all she knew, the news today, jobs were especially hard to come by. She hadn't wanted to push it with either employer.

Of course, if she'd known Finn was going to stop by the club, she would have called in sick in a heartbeat.

I was glad to see him. That was the really galling part.

I must be insane.

He was an FBI agent, an investigator. He wasn't hanging around her because he was smitten with her big green-hazel eyes.

He was doing his fricking job.

He probably thought of making out with her as a nice perk, like dental insurance.

That thought made her mad all over again.

So get over him already.

He knew way too much about what she'd been doing. He was suspicious of her, nosing around, and she was as sure as it was possible to be of anything that he wasn't going to just go away.

Unless he was psychic, though, she didn't see any way he could find out about George's notebook, or discover what she and Margaret had done.

Didn't keep her from being scared to death anyway. Not of Finn, but of being found out.

To say nothing of whatever murderous characters might be lurking around as they hunted the money.

The knot her stomach had wrapped itself into after last night's conversation with Margaret kept twisting tighter.

Cissy Barry, the head waitress from the Star Lounge, came hurrying up to Riley. Maybe thirty-five, with short blond hair, she was still able to rock the club's body-baring uniform, which only the two female assistant managers and the hostesses were exempted from wearing. "The ice machine in the Star Lounge is on the fritz. I've scooped all the ice out, but it's going to need to be fixed before tomorrow night."

Riley nodded. "I'll leave a note for Stephan"—the handyman who worked days to keep the club functional at night—"to check it out." Maude Clemons, one of the hostesses, was beckoning to her as she finished speaking. With a quick smile for Cissy, Riley headed toward the hostess' station, threading her way among a crowd of rowdy Astros fans (she could tell by their T-shirts) heading for the dance floor.

The hostess station was twenty feet back from the second set of doors that constituted the entry. Paneled in bronzed mirrors, with a carefully tended live palm tree in one corner and a black leather hostess stand as the central feature, it was where the club's four hostesses took turns greeting guests and showing them to tables, among other duties.

Maude, a beautiful twenty-something brunette who worked days as a model, said, "Phone for you," and nodded toward the landline on the credenza behind the podium. Riley waved her thanks as Maude stepped away to greet a pair of just-arriving businessmen.

Walking over to the credenza, she saw the flashing light that indicated a call on line one, picked up the receiver, and pushed the button.

"Riley Cowan," she said into the phone.

"Can you come and get me?" It was Emma. Her voice sounded small and thin and shaky.

— CHAPTER —
SIXTEEN

L ess than twenty minutes later, Riley drove through the dozen or so four-story brick buildings that made up the Heywood Plaza apartment complex, jittery with nerves, taking in the relatively late-model cars all lined up in the parking areas, the green space complete with playground and swimming pool between the buildings, the dim and yellowish, but present, security lighting that kept these wee hours of the morning from being overwhelmingly dark. The complex was not particularly upscale, but it didn't scream danger, either. The area of town was decent, not too far from River Oaks.

The surroundings weren't the reason she was feeling so anxious.

It was the fact that Emma might be out here alone at this time of night that was giving her a spasm. Coupled with the fact that *she* definitely was out here alone. After last night, to borrow a phrase from Disney's *The Little Mermaid,* which Emma had watched so often years ago that the songs were permanently implanted in the family consciousness, Riley wanted to be where the people are. Although she thought (hoped) she'd headed off any more attacks on her by telling the world that she no longer had Jeff's phone, she couldn't be sure that she wouldn't be attacked for some other reason. Or that Emma wouldn't be attacked.

Simply speculating about the possibilities was enough to make her blood run cold.

That old adage about there being safety in numbers had never been more true.

Em, what were you thinking?

The complex was laid out in a square with a single entrance off Willowick Road. Despite the lateness of the hour, a few people were outside—heading to or from their cars, walking leashed dogs, carrying out trash—but there was no sign of Emma. As Riley scanned the shadowy sidewalks and parking lots and front-yard space and vestibules, the ever-present knot in her stomach was joined by a tightness in her chest.

Emma hadn't said much over the phone, just "come and get me" and the address, after which Riley had asked Cissy Barry to close for her and flown out the back door so no one but Cissy would realize she was leaving early. It had been obvious from Emma's voice that she was near tears. Last time Riley had seen Emma was around seven thirty, when, after grabbing dinner and changing clothes to go to work at the club, Riley had headed out. Emma and Margaret had, she thought, been settling down for a night of TV.

Apparently not.

What she'd said to Emma, along with *I'm coming right now*, was *Stay inside until I get there. I'll text you.*

But knowing Emma, and knowing that she was upset over everything that had happened, and considering that even driving like a maniac it had taken Riley almost fifteen minutes to get there, she wouldn't be surprised at all to find Emma walking down a sidewalk or huddled in a vestibule.

The particulars of what Emma was doing at an apartment complex in the middle of the night could wait until Riley had her safe.

Craning her neck to look for addresses on the buildings as she drove, Riley found 2004, then 2006—she was looking for 2010—and then spotted Emma. Even as relief washed over Riley, some things, if not everything, became clear.

Emma was standing in the tiny patch of front-yard grass in front of 2010 talking to Brent. Brent was a cute kid, tall, black-haired, boyishly lean, but with some muscles from his position on the football team. Emma, her long blond hair tucked behind her ears and shining like moonbeams in the glow of a nearby security light, wearing a pretty blue romper that left most of her long legs bare, was nodding and smiling at something he was saying to her.

Riley hoped that she was the only one who appreciated what a good performance Emma was putting on. Brent had an arm around petite brunette Julie, who was nestled right up against him like she belonged there. Surrounding them, drinking it all in like vultures, was the mean girl triumvirate of Monica, Natalie, and Tori, along with a couple of Brent's friends whose names Riley didn't know.

Except for Emma, they were all wearing swimsuits: teeny bikini tops with towels for sarongs for the girls, surfer shorts for the boys. Brent's towel was slung around his neck. Riley assumed they were heading toward the complex's pool. Given that Emma wasn't wearing a swimsuit and had called her to get picked up, Riley also assumed that she wasn't planning to participate in the 2 a.m. swim.

And she knew Emma must be dying inside.

She didn't know whether to honk, park, or circle. The last thing she wanted to do was embarrass Emma.

Compromising, she drove around the corner, pulled into a parking spot out of sight, and texted Emma where she was.

A moment later, Emma came running around the corner. Hesitating, she looked around, saw the car, ran toward it, and threw herself inside.

"*Go.*" Emma dropped her bag in the footwell, grabbed her seat belt, and pulled it on even as Riley obediently started the car and backed out of the space. "I don't want anybody to see you."

"Why?" Putting the car in drive, Riley headed out of the complex.

"I told them a hot football player from Pearland was picking me up."

Considering that Emma did not as yet know any football players from Pearland, much less any hot ones, Riley recognized the lie for what it was—an attempt to save face with Brent and the others—and made a sympathetic face at Emma in acknowledgment. As Riley pulled out onto Willowick, Emma lifted her hair away from her face and with quick, jerky movements twisted it into a knot at her nape. Then she blew out a sound that was part groan, part sigh.

Braking for a red light, Riley caught the scent of booze. "Have you been drinking?"

"Don't start. I had like half a beer. It was a *party*." She leaned her head back against the top of the seat and stared at the ceiling. "I hate my life *so much*."

"How did you even get there?" Riley pulled out through the intersection, heading for the freeway. Traffic was almost nonexistent—she could see the lights of maybe three other vehicles, none of them close. They were out of the residential area now, and commercial establishments, most of them closed, lined the road on both sides. It was too dark inside the car to allow her to see Emma's expression, but she could hear the unhappiness in her voice.

"Jen Combs and Sara Loomis picked me up. It's Neely Shafer's birthday. Her sister has an apartment there, so she was able to use the party room, and everybody was invited to spend the night."

"Did you say anything about this earlier?" Because if so, Riley had missed it.

"I didn't know about it until Jen called and asked if I was going. I mean, I knew it was Neely's birthday, but I didn't know about the party." Turning her head, she looked at Riley. There was a despairing note to her voice. "I wasn't even invited. I just—when Jen called I just—I'm so sick of staying home and not being a part of things anymore and . . ."

Her voice trailed off.

"And you thought it would give you a chance to see Brent," Riley finished for her. Reaching the expressway entrance, Riley discovered to her annoyance that it was blocked off: damned road construction. She drove on, into the uber-darkness beneath the overpass, heading for the next on-ramp, which was about three miles away.

"Yeah," Emma admitted.

"Didn't work out so well, huh?" There was sympathy in Riley's voice, and in the glance she shot Emma, who shook her head dispiritedly.

"It was awful. Everybody's just *different* with me now, like I have a fatal disease or something. They're either way too nice, or they kind of stay away and *look* at me. Neely even came up to me and said this thing like, 'I'm so sorry I forgot to invite you, there's plenty of room, please stay the night,' which was so *humiliating*." Emma took a deep, shuddering breath. "And the only thing Brent said to me all night was *hi* like he barely even knew me, until right there at the end when I was outside waiting for you and they all came out. When he saw me standing there he said, 'Hey, we're going swimming, should be a blast, you ought to stay,' like he *pitied* me. And he had his hands all over Julie just like he'd had them all over her all night and when I ran into her in the bathroom right before I called you she told me they're going out." That last bit that came out in a rush told Riley how painful even talking about it was. As she finished, Emma folded her arms over her chest like she was cold. Riley knew that wasn't it, but still she automatically reached out to turn down the air-conditioning. "Jen and Sara couldn't give me a ride home because they were spending the night and I didn't want to go around asking everybody if they were ready to leave and I—I just couldn't stay."

Riley hurt for her. "I'm sorry, Em."

"I know." Emma slumped in her seat. "Thanks for coming to get me, by the way."

"Any time." Riley glanced at her and asked, "Did you tell your mother you were going out?"

A negative shake of her head. "She was in bed."

"Emma—" Riley started to remonstrate, but Emma looked so woebegone that she changed what she had been going to say to "There really will be hunky football players at Pearland, you know. I'll bet you a mani-pedi at Timothy's that you'll be all like, 'Brent who?' two weeks after you start."

Emma made a skeptical face. "Yeah, but they'll all know about Dad, too. *Everybody* knows. It's like I'm branded or something."

"Anybody that makes a difference to is somebody you don't want in your life anyway." Riley braked for another red light. They were close to the express-way on-ramp in an area lined with warehouses that appeared deserted at that hour. The long, corrugated metal buildings were enclosed by a succession of tall, chain-link fences. A few security lights glowed close to the warehouses and thus far away from the road, but other than that and the headlights of a van that had passed them a few minutes ago and was already stopped at the light, and their own headlights, which basically illuminated the back of the van, this part of the four-lane road was dark as a cave.

Emma said, "Yeah, right."

"It's—" Riley began, but never finished. A blur of movement outside Emma's window made her look sharply toward it. Riley's breath caught: there was a kind of dense shadow right beside the car—

Crash.

Emma's window caved in, shattering faster than Riley could process what was happening. Heart lurching, scream tearing out of her throat, Riley jumped what felt like it should have been a foot in the air only to be restrained by her seat belt. Emma screamed, too, surging toward Riley, doing her best to get out of the way of the exploding window but held in place by her seat belt as pebbles of glass rained in on her. Riley's gaze riveted on a black-clad arm as it shot through the now-missing window to grab at Emma's door handle.

Of course, the doors were locked. Thank God the doors were locked. They would be impossible to open from the outside.

"Oh, God! Oh, God!" Panicking, Emma leaned away from the door as she fought to free herself from her seat belt. "Riley, *help*!"

"Em!" Pulse thundering, Riley released her own seat belt and lunged across Emma to beat at the arm—it was a man's arm, black windbreaker, black glove— while Emma, still scrabbling at her seat belt, let loose another sirenlike blast almost in Riley's ear.

A carjacking? A random crime? Or someone else after the missing money? The terrifying possibilities sent an icy chill shooting down Riley's spine.

"Help!" Riley screamed, shoving the gloved hand away from the door handle. In the process, her foot slipped off the brake. She only realized what had happened as the car rolled forward to hit the back of the van with a jarring thud that catapulted her sideways, sending her shoulder smacking into the dashboard and stopping the car dead.

The Mazda's headlights reflecting off the van's white double doors drew her attention and caused the interior of the car to be lighter than it had been a moment before.

The van—now the driver will get out, see what's happening, help us.

That was the desperate hope revolving through her head as the gloved hand once again grabbed for the door handle. Throwing herself back into the battle, Riley could feel Emma's body twisting with panic against her as Emma fought to get out of her seat belt and away from the door. Blows weren't working; Riley viciously pinched the man's forearm. He yelped, and the arm whipped out of sight.

Adrenaline pouring through her veins, Riley shouted at the shadowy figure looming outside the window: "Get out of here! We don't have anything you want! Go on, go away!"

The arm shot back inside the window in a lightning punch that struck Riley in the forehead just above her right eye.

"Riley!" Emma tried and failed to catch her as Riley was knocked back into her own seat. Emma's head swiveled toward the window. *"Leave us alone!"*

Forehead tingling, momentarily a little disoriented by the punch, Riley was aware of Emma screaming like a banshee and flailing away at the dark figure of the man outside the window, who was once again reaching for the inside door handle.

"Help! Somebody help us!" Emma shrieked, struggling with her seat belt latch. *"Help!"*

Glancing wildly at the closed back of the van, Riley thought, *Where's the driver?*

To Emma she cried, "Don't let him unlock the door!" and smashed her palm down on the horn—the resultant blast split the night—in an attempt to attract attention. Then she grabbed for the gearshift.

Can't go forward, must reverse.

Nothing happened when Riley jerked the gearshift. The metal shaft didn't budge. *What . . . ?* Her pulse pounded. Her stomach dropped. She experienced a split second of blind panic in which she yanked at the gearshift with all her strength while Emma's screams exploded through the car. Riley was so flustered and frightened that it was almost impossible to think, but then she remembered that she had to depress the brake first. She did that and yanked the gearshift back just as Emma, shrieking, succeeded in unbuckling her seat belt at last.

Crash.

Riley screeched and jumped like she'd been shot as her own window shattered. Her heart catapulted into her throat. Even as she was showered with marble-like chunks of glass, part of a man's torso plunged through the broken window. A long arm shot past her to turn off the ignition and snatch her keys. Her instant impression was of a black-gloved hand and a shiny black sleeve.

"No, no, no!" she cried, grabbing futilely for the keys, which were protected in a closed, gloved fist. "Em, quick, jump in the back!"

It was too late. Even as Emma scrambled over the console toward the space between the front seats, a tiny beeping sound—the unlock button on the key ring being depressed; Riley recognized it with a thrill of pure horror—sent Riley's pulse rate skyrocketing.

That was the only warning she got before her door and Emma's were jerked open almost simultaneously.

Riley's heart seemed to stop.

As the interior light blinked on, Emma screamed with fresh intensity and tried to hurl herself into the rear. Too late: struggling wildly, she was grabbed and hauled backward toward the open door.

"Riley! Riley!"

"Emma!"

Mouth sour with fear, Riley grabbed at her, caught at her slim, cool arms, her frantically grasping hands, tried to hold her, to pull her back, then screamed with surprise and pain as a hand fisted in her own hair, snapping her head back, and another one closed ferociously around her arm. Panic surging through her, she fought desperately to hang on to Emma, who was jerked free of her to vanish, shrieking, through the door.

"Riley!"

Screaming, Riley, too, was dragged from the car. *"Emma!"*

Outside, the headlights cast weird shadows across the blacktop. The smell of exhaust was strong. In concert with Emma's, Riley's screams pierced the night, almost drowning out the sounds of their struggles and their abductors' threats and curses. Her hair felt like it was being ripped out by the roots as she was kept from falling to her knees by the fist tangled in it. A muscular arm grabbed her, managed to pin her arms to her body. Despite the heat, cold sweat poured over Riley in a wave as she got a lightning glimpse of the black ski mask her captor was wearing and was hit by an instant, horrifying flashback to the attack in her apartment.

No carjacking, no random crime—this is about the money. Deep down, she'd known it all along. Her heart pounded so hard it slammed against her breastbone. Her pulse sounded loud as thunder in her ears.

"Get off me!" she cried, throwing her head back in an attempt to head-butt her captor, trying everything she knew to break away. *"Emma!"*

Yanking her hair so hard she saw stars, her captor snarled, "Quit fighting or I'll break your damned neck."

Forget that. Riley fought like a tigress as she was half carried, half shoved a few steps, then bodyslammed facedown against the Mazda's trunk with such force that the breath was knocked out of her.

"Riley! *Help! Help!*" Emma's panicked cries turned into a shrill, terrified scream that was abruptly cut off.

"Emma!" Despite everything, Riley rallied enough to respond, to lift her head in time to watch Emma, a gloved hand over her mouth, a black-clad arm around her waist, being borne, struggling for all she was worth, around the back corner of the van and out of sight.

"*Emma!*" Galvanized, Riley summoned every last bit of strength she had.

Aiming the heel of her shoe in a vicious kick back at the right knee of the man holding her and just missing as he dodged at the last second, Riley screamed like a steam whistle, fought to get free—and had her head slammed into the trunk so hard her jaws snapped together and the world went out of focus around her.

"You listen." Her captor bent over her, holding her in place with his hand in her hair and his body weight pressed against her back, his tone brutal. Too woozy to struggle, Riley lay panting and shuddering against the warm trunk of her car. "We know George has the billions he stole hidden somewhere. You have three days to find out where it is. You find it, and you tell us. Exactly where the money is, and how to get access to it. If you don't, George will be burying his daughter beside his son. Understand?"

Riley's blood turned to ice in her veins. She sucked in a wheezing breath. For Emma, she would turn over the information, the notebook, everything. Anything. Now.

"I have—" she began, meaning to add "the information you need."

"Shut up." He cut her off by the simple expedient of slamming her head into the trunk again. Riley cried out, went limp, breathed.

"I said *listen*. Three days. No cops, no FBI, no authorities. You go to George, tell him what I said. We'll contact you on your cell phone on Monday night. If you give us what we want, the girl will be released. If you don't . . ."

Without warning, he shoved her violently away from him. Crying out in surprise, Riley went flying, sliding along the side of the car, stumbling, falling to her knees on the rough pavement.

Looking up, she saw her captor running toward the van.

"*Wait!*" she cried, but it was too late: he reached the van, hopped in.

She was still struggling to her feet as, with a squeal of tires, the van sped away.

— CHAPTER —
SEVENTEEN

Panic. Desperation. Fury. Shock. As the van disappeared into the night, Riley would have collapsed from the gamut of emotions that engulfed her, but she simply didn't have the time.

Screaming was out, too. Worthless, worthless screaming.

Emma's life was in danger. She had to pull herself together fast, to think, to deal.

Heart pounding, breathing like she had been running for miles, insides curdling with terror, Riley leaned against the now-dark Mazda and sent a fervent prayer winging skyward: *Please, God, keep Emma safe*.

Beating back the hysteria that threatened, Riley grabbed onto the tatters of her composure and took swift stock of the situation. It was the middle of the night, no other human being in sight. Emma was gone, kidnapped. She was stuck on a deserted road in a closed-down industrial area with a car that, minus its keys, was useless. Running back the way they had

come, she might reach help in, say, fifteen minutes.
Running forward, she was probably looking at the
same time frame. Another car would almost certainly
come along, but there was no saying when, or if, it
would stop for her.

None of that would happen fast enough to save
Emma.

She needed help. She needed it now.

No cops, no FBI, no authorities. She could hear the
warning still.

That left her and Margaret to deal with the situation. That put Emma's life squarely in their hands.

Riley felt dizzy. Her heart felt like it would beat
its way out of her chest. Cold sweat poured over her
in a wave.

She had what the kidnappers wanted: she knew
where the money was, how to access the bank accounts,
the whole nine yards. She would have told them so if
they'd given her the chance.

*We'll contact you on your cell phone on Monday
night.*

When the kidnappers did that, she could give
them the information. She would gladly give them the
information.

Anything, if they would let Emma go.

But what if they didn't let Emma go? What if
she handed over the information and—nothing? The
thought froze her to her bone marrow. What would
she—she and Margaret—do then?

Go to the authorities at that point? It might very
well be too late.

Emma could be killed. Oh, God, no matter what she did, Emma could be killed.

That was when Riley started to shake. Her knees were suddenly so unsteady that she had to sit down hard in the driver's seat. Chunks of safety glass from the broken window littered the seat, but she never even felt them.

Her only option seemed to be to hand over the information and trust that the kidnappers would keep their word.

Trust? Kidnappers? The very people who had just dragged her and Emma out of their car in the middle of the night? Get real, Riley.

Emma's life is at stake.

Riley felt like an icy hand had just closed around her heart. Deliberately she slowed her breathing, determined not to hyperventilate.

She dared not try to handle this on her own. Margaret would be no help at all. Margaret would have a breakdown. This was beyond anything either of them, or both of them, were qualified to take on.

I need help. We need help.

Casting a hunted look around, she felt her skin crawl as she tried to confirm that she was indeed absolutely, totally alone. Darkness stretched silently around her. The warehouses crouched on one side of the road, unspooling in a seemingly endless line beneath pale, wavery security lights. On the other side, a drainage ditch, an empty, trash-strewn field, what looked like an abandoned storage facility, the distant flash of headlights on the expressway.

Her surroundings gave fresh, sinister meaning to *not a soul in sight*.

She didn't know if it was her imagination but—it was almost like she sensed a presence.

What if they're watching me? Remotely? Listening to me? Like, say, through a bug? Monitoring a police scanner? Suppose they have a contact in the FBI?

Panic flooded her. It required an almost-physical effort to beat it back. She didn't know if any of those things were reasonable, possible. She *did* know that she didn't want to do anything that might jeopardize Emma's life.

Stay calm. Think it through.

What she came back to, after swiftly taking into consideration every possible danger that she could foresee, was *I need help*.

There was only one person she could think of to call.

Her own personal 911 hotline.

———————

THE SHARP blare of a trumpet—a ringtone he'd deliberately chosen for one particular caller—woke Finn up out of a sound sleep. His eyes opened on pitch blackness. His senses told him that he was in an unfamiliar bed, an unfamiliar place. Still, he knew immediately where he was and what that blasting trumpet portended. Waking fast and in full possession of his senses was a necessary ability he'd acquired over the years. Didn't prevent him from experiencing a thrill of alarm as he scooped his phone off the bedside table and answered. If Riley was calling him after that little disaster of an encounter earlier, something majorly bad must've gone down.

"Yeah," he said.

"I need you." Riley's voice was unsteady. His gut tightened in response. "Can you come?"

"What's happened? Where are you?"

Without answering the first question, she said a street name and location that meant nothing to him, and added, "Hurry."

"You in danger?"

"No, not me." Her voice still had that wavering quality that affected him like a jab to the stomach. It had him throwing his legs over the side of the bed and reaching for his pants like the hotel was on fire. "I'll fill you in when you get here."

"Quick as I can," he promised, but hadn't even finished speaking before she hung up.

He glanced at glowing green numbers on the digital clock—2:20 a.m. He'd been asleep for all of half an hour.

Five minutes later he was dressed, in the Acura and speeding toward where the blinking light on the mobile receiving unit told him she was. On the way, he hit the button that allowed him to listen to everything that had been recorded by the bug in Riley's cell phone since he'd left her in the Palm Room.

By the time he spotted the Mazda's emergency blinkers flashing through the darkness on the deserted stretch of road that ran parallel to the expressway, he knew what had transpired, why Riley sounded so distraught. Grimly he'd placed the phone call needed to get an all-out search-and-rescue effort for Emma Cowan going, then another one to find out what the hell had happened to the team that was supposed to keep Riley under visual surveillance as she left work.

They were, as it turned out, still in the parking lot outside the Palm Room. Been there since 1:55 a.m., according to Detective Tim Smith, who answered the call from the car in which he and his partner were watching the club's entrance.

"She hasn't come out yet," Smith reported.

Finn clamped down on all kinds of unpleasant replies, said, "She's covered, you can stand down," and disconnected.

Pulling onto the shoulder behind Riley's car, which was stopped in the slow lane, he shut off the mobile receiving unit and shoved it under his seat, pocketed his phone, slammed the car into park, and got out.

She was sitting in the driver's seat. The Mazda's interior light flashed briefly as she got out to meet him.

Striding around the back of her car, he took in the slim, sexy shape of her silhouetted against the darkness as she walked toward him, swaying slightly on those killer high heels. As he got closer he saw that her stockings were ripped all to hell, her dress was covered with pale dust, and her hair was a disheveled mess. Another couple of strides, and he could tell that her face was white as a corpse's, her eyes were huge and dark, and her mouth was shaking.

"Emma's been kidnapped," was how she greeted him.

"Are you hurt?" he asked sharply.

"No." There was impatience in the way she shook her head, even though all evidence pointed to the contrary. Her voice was hoarse, but surprisingly steady given the circumstances. "Two men in a van—they took her. For the money." She took a breath, and he heard the hitch in it, which told him everything he needed to know about the state of her emotions despite the brave front she was putting on. "There was no license plate. A plain white van. That's all I can tell you."

"We'll get her back," he said, and slid a hand around her elbow to steady her as she wobbled and then stopped walking, maybe two feet in front of him.

"Will we?" Her eyes met his, begged. She was looking at him like he was her one hope of salvation, and something about having her look at him like that, about *her*, period, did something unexpected, something he didn't like at all, to his insides.

"Yeah." His reply was terse.

"Okay." She closed her eyes like she took that single, bitten-off syllable as a promise, like he'd lifted a weight off of her, like she was placing her complete faith in him. She looked vulnerable, and beautiful, and as his eyes slid over her face his insides did that weird twisting thing again, which alarmed him almost as much as it pissed him off.

"God damn it," he muttered, meaning it, and pulled her into his arms.

She went to him as though in his arms was exactly where she wanted to be.

———————

HE WAS a hard-eyed, suspicious-minded federal agent who was only in her life because he was investigating her. He'd made it abundantly clear that he thought she was guilty of something, and the thing about it was, he wasn't wrong. If he found out the truth, she had no idea what he would do, but her expectations included handcuffs and jail. Maybe a long time in jail.

Turned out that none of that mattered.

In this moment of terrible fear and grief and danger, he was her port in the storm. It had been a long time since she'd allowed herself to depend on anyone, but she was depending on him now.

She felt like she *could* depend on him. For her, that was huge.

Calling him had been the right choice. Riley was sure of it the instant she saw him step out of his car. Shrouded in thick gray shadows, he looked big and tough and capable, and if she'd been up to running she would have run to him on sight.

Please God please God please keep Emma safe.

He nodded as if it was no more than he had expected when, from the shelter of his arms, she urgently repeated the kidnappers' warning not to call the FBI or any other authorities and worried aloud that there might be some way they could *know*.

He said, "The number you called to reach me is untraceable. No one is going to know you got the FBI or any other authorities involved. You did the absolute smartest thing you could have done by calling me."

Then he wrapped his jacket around her—until then, she hadn't even realized she was shivering—put her in his car, told her to sit tight, and left her briefly to push the Mazda out of the road. She assumed that's when he made some calls, because when he got back in the car he told her that a crack team of agents was already looking for Emma and that everything possible was being done to find her. That didn't make her relax—nothing could—but she believed him, and a tiny portion of the driving fear that had her in its grip eased.

As they pulled away, she glanced back and said, "My car—" because it had occurred to her that she couldn't simply abandon it.

"A tow truck's on the way," Finn replied. "A forensics team will check it for fingerprints—"

"There won't be any," she interrupted, too ramped up on adrenaline still to let him finish. "The kidnappers were wearing gloves."

"They'll also check for any other evidence. The windows will be repaired, and it'll be returned to you. Shouldn't take more than a day or two."

Any kind of quip about fast or five-star government service was beyond her. Relieved to have the problem of her car solved, Riley simply nodded.

"Emma must be scared out of her mind," she burst out a moment later. That was the terrible thought she couldn't escape. It turned her insides to jelly, reduced her brain to mush. Then, because, though she'd been trying not to think about it she couldn't help herself, she added in a voice that even to her own ears sounded strained, "Do you think they'll hurt her?"

He glanced at her, shook his head. Another car passed them, traveling in the opposite direction. As its headlights slashed through the Acura she saw that his eyes were hard and his features were set in grim lines. His was the face of a man born to deal with bad guys and mayhem and crises, and she recognized that thankfully.

He said, "They don't have any reason to hurt her. They're after money, and they think she's their ticket to getting it."

Riley knew that his answer couldn't be anything other than speculation, that there was no way he could know for sure, and he certainly wouldn't say anything else anyway because he wouldn't want to further upset her, but still she felt the slightest lessening of the terrible fear that had her nerves stretched tight as piano wire.

"So you think they'll let her go, once they get it?"

The compression of his lips was all the reply she needed. Alarm spiked through her, setting her nerves jumping all over again.

"You don't, do you?" Even she couldn't miss the edge of panic in her voice.

"If you're asking me if I think Emma's going to wind up dead, the answer is no, I don't." He glanced at her. His face was unreadable. "We'll get her back. Trust me."

— CHAPTER —
EIGHTEEN

The thing about it was, Riley did. Sort of. To put her feelings in a nutshell, she trusted him about this.

"I am," she told him, meaning trusting him. "I do."

The look Finn gave her was impossible to read in the dark, but she didn't miss the tightening of his hands around the steering wheel.

Whether it was designed to distract her or not, Riley didn't know, given that she'd already told him most of the pertinent facts, but what he said next was, "Tell me everything that happened, from the beginning."

Riley took a deep breath.

Then, looking unseeingly out through the windshield at the closed-for-the-night strip malls and office complexes and small businesses that surrounded them, she started with Emma's phone call and told him the whole story, in a flat voice that she doggedly stuck to in an effort to keep herself from getting emotional. She was still talking when he braked and rolled down his window. Blinking at the sudden rush of warm night air, she only realized that they were at a McDonald's drive-thru as he looked at her and said, "I could use some coffee, and I'm thinking you could, too."

A second later, a tinny little disembodied voice said, "Welcome to McDonald's. May I take your order?"

Riley accepted coffee, declined food, and then sipped the strong hot brew gratefully despite the two extra sugars he dumped in hers. The Styrofoam cup felt warm against her cold fingers, and she cradled it. The bracing smell of the coffee was comforting in its familiarity.

"Better?" Finn pulled back out onto the road. It was a six-lane artery that led downtown, busy during the day but nearly deserted now. Riley frowned a little as, for the first time since he'd picked her up, she became aware of her surroundings: they'd passed the expressway entrance that she'd been heading for when Emma was taken sometime back.

Sipping her coffee, she looked at him.

"Yes. Where are we going?" She'd assumed he was taking her back to Margaret's house, but if so he was heading in the wrong direction. At the thought of what she would have to do when she got there—tell Margaret about Emma—Riley felt sick. Such horrifying news—she didn't know how Margaret was going to bear it. At the very least, Margaret would be hysterical. The worst part about it was, she would have every reason to be. *Riley* felt hysterical. Only for Emma's sake was she managing to keep a lid on it.

"To my hotel room."

"Why?" It was a simple question, nothing more. The fact that she wasn't stiffening up, or protesting, or even thinking about protesting, told her everything she needed to know about their relationship at that moment: in a nutshell, she trusted him enough that she was prepared to do what he said.

"Nothing to do with sex, so you can put that out of your mind." His voice was dry. "We both need to grab a few hours' sleep. My hotel room is the best place to do that."

It said a lot about the state she was in that Riley barely registered his reference to sex. Under the circumstances, and to his credit, she hadn't thought he was coming on to her. The wasting of time was the part that was bothering her. With a quick, agitated shake of her head, Riley said, "Sleep? Are you serious? With Emma—"

He cut her off. "The people we've got looking for Emma are top-notch at their jobs. We can't add anything to what they're doing right now. The best thing you can do for Emma is keep yourself functional. You not sleeping, or eating, or doing anything else that keeps you going, doesn't help her."

Much as Riley hated to accept it, that made sense. For her to go running around like a chicken with its head cut off could do Emma no earthly good.

He continued, "I need sleep, too, and I can't sleep if I'm worrying about you. The only way I can know for sure you're safe is if you're with me, so we're both going back to my hotel room and going to sleep."

He shot a glance at her. "Your ex-husband dead, you attacked, Emma kidnapped—that's a lot of violence aimed at your family in a short period of time. It's making me think that maybe something happened to stir the pot. There are a lot of players in this game. The people who grabbed Emma are probably not the same ones who went after you, and it's possible that neither of them were behind what happened to Jeff. Somebody could come after you again. I don't have time to worry about you, and do my job, too, so you're with me for the duration."

Again, Riley didn't protest. His assessment of the situation was chilling, but it made sense, and the thought of how she would feel if she wasn't with him—in a word, terrified—was enough to make her willing to stick to him like Velcro.

"Okay."

Then another fear arose that made her stomach cramp. "What about Margaret?"

"She's covered. She's been put under surveillance. Nobody can get to her. Like I said, if I'm worried about people's safety, I can't do my job."

Riley breathed a little more easily. "What is your job, exactly?"

"Finding the money. Finding out if Jeff and/or any of those other four individuals whose deaths he was interested in were murdered, and who did it. And now, making sure Emma gets home safe and sound." He glanced at her, and something flickered in his eyes that she was too agitated to even try to identify. "So the kidnappers told you to go see George. Tomorrow, that's what we'll do. Assuming George knows where the money is, do you think he'll tell you?"

"I don't know."

"Would he be more likely to tell his wife?"

Okay, Riley told herself, *focus.* This was where things started to get tricky. This was where she had to keep her cool, be strong, play it smart.

"He and Margaret are estranged. She'd been planning to divorce him even before his arrest, and he knows that. But he loves Emma. If I go to him and tell him what's happened, I think he might tell me where the money is. Assuming he has it, of course, and knows."

"Assuming that." There was no mistaking the faint note of dryness in Finn's voice.

The thing was, she had no idea how George would react if she showed up demanding he tell her where the money was hidden on pain of Emma's life, but the other thing was, it didn't matter. *She* knew where the money was hidden, and exactly how to access it, and now she thanked God for that. She was prepared to do anything it took to save Emma, even if it meant exposing herself and Margaret completely, and she knew Margaret would agree wholeheartedly.

But she thought there might be a better way.

During the brief period between the time she'd called Finn and when he had actually shown up, she'd come up with a plan that she hoped might save them all. Her first thought had been that she would simply give George's black book to Finn, pray it was enough to ensure Emma's safety, and at the same time hope that investigators would believe she and Margaret had only just discovered it themselves, and would likewise fail to notice the ten-million-dollar sliver she'd taken from it. But if investigators didn't believe it, if they were suspicious (which they were) and eager to send more people to jail (which they seemed to be), and looked into the matter in any depth, they would undoubtedly learn that Margaret and Emma had recently returned from Bermuda, and probe around in the banks there to see what they could find. Riley would have still entertained a fair degree of hope that they would miss the numbered trust account she had created, except for the fact that any investigators worth their salt would look especially hard at new accounts. While she thought the account she'd set up could withstand their scrutiny even then (there was nothing to tie it to the Cowans, after all), they would almost certainly review withdrawals and possibly bank security footage for the dates Margaret had been in Bermuda, which was a tiny island with a limited number of banks. When they did that, they would find the thirty-thousand-dollar withdrawal, and see Margaret making it.

To imagine any other outcome would be foolish.

When that happened, she and Margaret would both look guilty as hell, and the wrath of the law would almost certainly descend on them with a vengeance. Both of them might very well go to jail, and Emma's life would be shattered once more. Though, again, it was a small price to pay for Emma's survival.

Riley had anxiously rubbed at the sore spot on her forehead, commanding herself to think this through.

And then the solution had hit her.

If she went to visit George, had him tell her where he'd hidden information about the secret bank accounts (whether he really did tell her any such thing or not didn't matter, because she would pretend he did), and then pretend to discover the little black book all over again, she could keep the attention off her and Margaret and on the sudden discovery of so much money. Everything would go down under full view of Finn, so there would be no suspicion whatsoever of any prior knowledge on her or Margaret's part, and the ten million dollars she'd skimmed would almost certainly go unnoticed under those seemingly straightforward circumstances.

The best part was, once the money had been officially discovered, no one would be looking for it anymore, which meant that the bad guys would all go away along with the government and its agents. Nobody would be at risk of being murdered any longer, Margaret and Emma would have the ten million, which was enough to make them secure, and the three of them could hopefully live in peace for the rest of their lives.

Going over the plan for possible flaws, Riley had come up with a few: her fingerprints, and Margaret's, would undoubtedly be all over George's black book; in her first burst of horror in hearing about Emma, Margaret might well blurt out something that revealed their guilty secret; and the information on the illicit bank accounts would have to be discovered in a place that George would have had access to *and* that did not bear signs of her and Margaret's recent tampering, which left Emma's Paris painting out.

All manageable problems, Riley concluded, even as she worked out ways to manage them.

All of a sudden, as the plan scrolled through her brain one more time, a huge problem flashed before her, obvious as a neon sign. How had she missed it the first time around?

"Wait a minute." She frowned at Finn in sudden stark suspicion as fear once again flooded her heart. "You're an FBI agent. You work for the government. Even if George does tell me where the money is, even if it is found, you're not just going to give it to the kidnappers to ransom Emma, are you? What happens to it after that will be up to the government!"

"Whatever happens, saving Emma is my top priority." Finn looked at her steadily. "I give you my word on that."

"If I help you find the money, you promise you'll use it to get Emma back." Riley gave him a hard look as she sought clarity.

"I promise I will if necessary. What I'm hoping is, she'll be recovered fast enough that the money won't need to play into it. But if giving the kidnappers the money is what it takes to save Emma's life, then that's what will happen."

There was enough light now that she could see his expression. Security lights, Riley saw, and realized that they had pulled into a parking lot. His face was hard and set. He looked tired and, with his hair ruffled and his jaw darkened by stubble and his white shirt open at the neck and slightly wrinkled, disheveled. Then he turned his head and looked at her, and in the calm, steady gaze of those blue-gray eyes Riley saw enough to make her believe him.

"Okay," she said. Then as he cut the engine and she saw the time flash on the dashboard clock as it died—it was 3:17—she added, "Margaret gets up at eight on Saturdays. I need to be home by then. I have to tell her what happened."

The thought made her nauseous, but that was the very longest she felt she could wait. The only reason she hadn't already insisted that she needed to rush instantly to Margaret's side was that telling her wouldn't change a thing. And jolting the poor woman out of what little sleep she was managing to get these days to relay the horrible news wouldn't exactly be a help, either.

"Fair enough."

Finn got out, and Riley followed. A glance told her that it was a chain hotel, eight stories, inexpensive. The parking lot was dimly lit, deserted, no attendant. The darkness beyond the parking lot was enough to make her shiver. Overhead, the moon barely lit the sky. Even the stars looked muted and cold.

Her legs felt rubbery, but Riley managed to walk across the parking lot and through the lobby unaided. They didn't talk, but she was aware of him looking at her as they rode up the elevator. His room was on the sixth floor; the hall was quiet, deserted.

When he opened the door to his room, she walked inside, glanced around. A typical hotel room: ugly green carpet, nondescript wallpaper, a chest with a flat-screen TV on top of it, a chair. Under any other circumstances, the single king-sized bed would have made her eyes narrow. But she merely glanced at it in passing, then looked at him as he closed the door and turned to face her.

The room suddenly seemed much smaller with him in it.

"Bathroom's all yours," he said.

— CHAPTER —

NINETEEN

Riley nodded, and started walking toward the bathroom that was just off the room's door, bringing her closer to Finn.

He stood in the small, corridor-like part of the room just inside the door, his hand still on the light switch, facing her. The bathroom was to his left.

His eyes narrowed as he watched her coming toward him.

"Hang on, I'll get you something to sleep in." He opened the closet door next to the bathroom, and crouched. As she reached him she saw two more dark suits and a couple of white shirts on hangers, and that he was rummaging in a small black suitcase on the floor of the closet.

Of course, it wasn't the kind of hotel that would offer guests the use of complimentary bathrobes. But her dress was covered with grime from the car and the road. Her stockings were ripped and dirty. Unless she wanted to sleep in her undies—a silky pink bra and matching panties, expensive like almost all her clothes because they'd been bought before the world had gone to hell and she hadn't had the money to buy anything since—she needed something of his.

A moment later he pulled a white garment from the suitcase. As he stood up with it clutched in one hand and turned to face her, they were so close that their bodies brushed. The contact was inadvertent, she knew, but the electricity that sparked between them was instant and real and there was no way either of them missed it. In sheer self-defense, she took a step back to put some space between them and saw in the hardening of his mouth that he knew what she'd done and why. Like on the dance floor of the Palm Room, Riley was supremely conscious of his size, and of the solid strength of his body, and not just because all those manly muscles turned her on. He looked like he could take on an army single-handedly, and under the circumstances she found that supremely comforting. The shoulder holster he was wearing helped, too: a big, strong, *armed* federal agent was probably about as good as it got, protection-wise.

If he'd been in the car with them when Emma was grabbed . . .

A wave of coldness hit her, and she shivered. The hard knot that had been lodged in her chest ever since Emma had vanished in that van expanded so that she suddenly couldn't breathe.

His eyes narrowed as they slid over her face.

With no warning at all, he bent his head and kissed her, moving his lips against hers, sliding his tongue along the line where her lips met, in a soft, deliberate tasting that never penetrated but still acted on her like a defibrillator, jolting her back into the moment, slamming fireballs of awareness through her system, making her gasp and breathe even as he broke the contact and lifted his head.

The increased rate of his respiration was scarcely noticeable. The hard glitter in his eyes was impossible to miss.

Suddenly dizzy, Riley steadied herself by clutching at his arm. The feel of his taut bicep beneath her hand seemed to burn itself into her palm.

Heat blazed between them as tangibly as if the air had ignited.

"Quit thinking about what happened," he said, as she stared at him. "You'll make yourself crazy, and it won't do any good."

That was when she understood that he'd kissed her to get her mind off Emma. The knowledge didn't do anything to calm the hungry quickening he'd awakened, but it did give her the presence of mind to let her hand drop away from his arm, to break eye contact with him, to center herself and remember why she was there. For protection. And to save Emma.

Sleeping with him wasn't it.

"Here." He thrust the wadded-up garment in his hand at her, and as she took it she saw it was a plain white T-shirt, size extra-large. "Best I can do. I don't sleep in pajamas, and everything else I've got will be way too big for you."

Talking, Riley discovered, was beyond her. She

nodded, went into the bathroom, and closed and locked the door. Then she gave in to nerves, exhaustion, and stark, icy terror. Bracing both hands on the vanity, she leaned heavily against it while long shudders of reaction shook her. Staring into the mirrored wall above the twin sinks without even so much as seeing her reflection, she sucked in a series of ragged, unsatisfying breaths. Her shoulders sagged, her legs wobbled, and her stomach threatened to turn inside out.

The thought of Emma, terrified and in danger, that took possession of her mind would have been enough to take her to her knees if she hadn't deliberately forced it from her head.

Stop it. Get a grip.

As Finn had said, thinking about it wouldn't do any good.

Thinking about his kiss was equally unproductive, so she shoved that out of her head, too.

Instead she gritted her teeth, straightened away from the vanity, kicked off her shoes, and turned on the shower.

Putting one foot in front of the other and getting on with it: that's what she'd done all her life.

She could do it now, too.

Having taken a quick shower, brushed her teeth with his toothpaste and her finger, swallowed a couple of Tylenol from her purse to combat the throbbing headache and various other aches and pains that afflicted her, and checked her face for damage from that punch—she was relieved to find nothing more than a red mark up near her hairline—she emerged from the bathroom to discover that he'd made himself a bed on the floor: a beige blanket and a pair of pillows were spread out on the carpet at the foot of the bed.

He stood beside the chest that held the TV, his back to her. As she tucked her clothes inside the closet and dropped her shoes on the floor, a glance told her that his shoulder holster was gone now, although he was still fully dressed in the same rumpled dress shirt and trousers. She took in how nearly black his hair actually was, the color of the darkest coffee, along with how broad his shoulders looked above the trimness of his waist and the athletic tightness of his butt. Her gaze was sliding down his long, muscular legs when he turned around and held something out to her.

"Take it," he said abruptly.

She stared at the object in his hands. It was easier than looking at him.

What he was holding out to her was a clear plastic glass, one of the two that had been wrapped in paper beside the ice bucket, she confirmed with a glance at that hotel room staple, which sat on a tray beside the TV. The glass appeared to be about half full of orange juice.

"What is it?" Her voice sounded croaky, a result no doubt of all the screaming she had done earlier. But she refused to think about that. Instead, she stepped forward and took the glass from him, eyeing its contents with a skeptical frown.

"A screwdriver. The minibar had orange juice and vodka." His gaze swept her. She'd kept her hair dry, and brushed it out after her shower with the small brush she kept, along with a few cosmetics and other essentials, in her purse. The soft fall of it hid the bruises on her neck, as well as the fresh mark near her hairline. Her face was washed clean of any makeup except for a slick of rosy balm on her lips. She was wearing his T-shirt, which was far too large. It hung on her like a sack and hit her at approximately mid-thigh. For modesty's sake, she was wearing her panties beneath it—short and loose equaled a wardrobe malfunction waiting to happen—but still she felt pretty bare.

"I'm not much of a drinker."

"It'll help you sleep."

With him watching her, she sipped cautiously, grimaced at the strong taste of the alcohol, then took a breath and gulped the rest down, determined to get it over with. He was right on two counts: she needed sleep, and she was going to need help to get it.

When she finished, he was regarding her with that slight uptick at the corner of his mouth that, for him, signified amusement.

"What?" she asked, nearly belligerent.

The uptick deepened and expanded into what was almost a real smile.

"I like women who chug their liquor."

"I wanted to get it over with." She set the glass down on the chest. The drink seemed to burn in her stomach, and she had to press her lips and swallow hard to suppress a hiccup.

His eyes were on her mouth. They flicked up and met hers as if he felt her looking at him. She barely had a chance to register the dark, hot gleam in them before he turned away.

"Go to bed," he said.

Then he walked into the bathroom and closed the door.

By the time he emerged, Riley was curled up in the big bed, lying on her side with the covers bunched around her ears to ward off the cold she couldn't seem to shake. The vodka was doing its work: fear and grief and terrifying images swirled through her mind, but none of them stayed in place long enough to be truly upsetting, and despite everything, she was feeling more and more drowsy. She'd turned out the light before getting into bed, but enough light still filtered through the curtains so that the room wasn't completely dark. The comfortingly familiar sounds of the bathroom—flushed toilet, running water—lulled her into a sort of half-awake stupor, and she realized it was because they meant she wasn't alone.

Then the bathroom door opened. Her eyes did, too.

In the brief glimpse she got before he turned out the bathroom light, she saw that Finn was bare to the waist. She got a flash of what looked like acres of muscles and bronzed skin, and then the light was gone and he was no more than a tall shape padding toward her in the dark, almost silent on bare feet.

Riley wasn't aware that she was holding her breath until he stopped at the foot of the bed and she had to exhale—quietly, she hoped. For a second she got the impression that he was looking at her, but he didn't say anything and neither did she.

Then she heard the sound of a zipper being lowered: he was shucking his pants.

Her pulse quickened, and she felt a welcome infusion of warmth along with an acute awareness of his every move.

His pants hit the floor. A moment later, he did, too, settling into his makeshift bed.

Closing her eyes, she listened to him breathing, and felt her tense muscles slowly begin to relax.

Halfway between wakefulness and sleep, she realized that it wasn't the fact that she wasn't alone that she found comforting.

It was Finn.

He made her feel safe.

———————

FINN WAITED until the soft sounds of Riley's breathing told him that she was asleep. Then, being careful not to wake her, he got up, put his pants back on, grabbed his shirt and shrugged into that, too, tucked his gun into the back of his waistband, and left the room. He had his cell phone with him, among other necessary things, and used it to call Bax as he went. So he was slightly impatient as he waited for his temporary partner to haul his ass out of bed and answer his soft tap on the door, which Bax finally did by pulling it open with an alarmed "Oh, shit, what now?"

Going into Bax's room would have meant leaving the door to his own room vulnerable, and Riley unprotected—not that he expected her to be attacked while in his company, but just in case. Thus he kept one eye on the hallway as he stood in the open doorway to Bax's room and brought him up to speed. As Finn recounted the night's events, he noted that Bax slept in a full set of pale blue cotton pajamas; he apparently liked to leave the TV on mute while he slept, and, judging by the series of yawns that he kept apologizing for, he had a far harder time coming fully awake than Finn did. None of these observations were unexpected, and none of them gave him any reason to change his mind about what he wanted from Bax. Trusting came hard to him, but under these limited circumstances he was prepared to trust Bax. To get done what he needed to get done, Finn had little choice. He wasn't about to leave Riley, and he couldn't make the arrangements that needed to be made while in her company.

"I want you to head up to Mack Alford"—referring to the medium-security correctional center in Stringtown, Oklahoma, where George Cowan was incarcerated—"and set up a visit for Riley with George," Finn said. "Anytime within regular visiting hours. I don't want this to go ringing alarm bells anywhere. Make arrangements for a private area for them to meet in, and get some surveillance in there."

Bax blinked at him. "But—it's a prison. It'll already have surveillance."

"Yeah. This is private surveillance. Nobody's going to see it but us." Finn outlined what he needed Bax to do. "I want to have eyes and ears on everything Riley and George say and do. Audio and video. Got it?"

Bax nodded. "Uh—does this mean you don't trust her?" The question sounded almost timid.

"I don't trust anybody," Finn replied with perfect honesty. "Except, right now, you. I'm trusting you to do this, and not to fuck it up."

"I can get it done." Bax sounded resolute.

"I never doubted it." He gave Bax a level look. "I'm assuming that since you just filed your report with your boss, you won't need to file again for a few days. As in, after this prison visit's over and we get a chance to see what's what. Am I right?"

"I'm supposed to report everything you do." Bax looked unhappy. "That's my job."

"I know. And you can report it, just not right away. That work for you?"

"Yeah," Bax said. Then he nodded, and added more firmly, "That works."

"Look at it this way: your assignment is to help me find the money. That's exactly what you'll be doing." Up until this point, Finn had humored the joint agency arrangement that had the FBI (Bax) monitoring his every move (a lack of trust between government agencies was pretty much par for the course), but now he needed to operate on his own. Just in case, as his gut kept telling him, Riley was more involved with the missing money than anybody in officialdom knew. If she was, he didn't know what he was going to do, but he did know he wanted to get a solid understanding of the situation before he played a part in throwing her to the wolves. That particular motive, though, wasn't something he was prepared to share with Bax, or anybody else. If, later, his playing his cards close to his vest in this way proved to be a problem higher up the food chain, he could always say that he'd been worried about leaks. Everybody in the Alphabet Kingdom was always worried about leaks: it was the excuse that kept on excusing.

"I will be, won't I?" Bax sounded relieved. Then he frowned. "Who gets the car?"

"I do," Finn said. "You take a taxi to the airport and get a rental. Get started right now, and you should be on the road to Stringtown within the hour. We'll probably be about five to six hours behind you." Finn reached into his pocket and drew out a burner phone—he kept a collection in his suitcase for precisely this type of situation—and handed it to Bax. "When everything's set, use this phone to call me and let me know. Don't use your regular phone." Which the Bureau might very well have somebody monitoring. "Got it?"

Bax nodded. "Got it."

"Good man." Finn clapped him on the shoulder in the kind of *gosh-we're-buds* gesture he knew Bax could relate to, which seemed to please him.

"I'm on it," Bax said again as he closed the door. Finn headed back to his own room.

Where he got to lie down on the floor and, instead of falling instantly asleep as he'd trained himself to do, tried to keep his mind off how much he wanted to crawl into bed with the woman he suspected of lying to him with practically every word she uttered.

It didn't help that, when he'd opened the door to reenter his room, the wedge of light from the hall had fallen squarely across the bed.

Riley must have gotten too warm, because she'd kicked off the covers. Sound asleep, she was lying on her stomach with his T-shirt hiked up around her waist. The sight of her sweet, sexy ass in nothing but a pair of tiny pink panties hit him like a lightning bolt to the crotch.

After years spent in the highly dangerous, highly stressful world of an undercover operative, he'd learned the art of snatching a few hours' sleep, whenever, wherever, and however he could. Lots of times, he'd figured he wouldn't live out the next twenty-four hours, and still he'd slept like a baby. Right now, though, sleep proved to be beyond him. Why? Because he was tormented by images of a truly world-class ass in a pair of itty-bitty, silky pink panties every time he closed his eyes.

— CHAPTER —

TWENTY

When the alarm went off on her phone, Riley sat bolt upright, startled awake. She was groggy, and it took her a moment to assimilate her surroundings: big, rumpled bed, not hers; gloomy, unattractive room, also not hers.

A tall, buff guy wearing nothing but a white towel hitched around his waist appearing along with a puff of steam in the lighted bathroom doorway to frown at her.

Definitely not hers.

Finn.

She blinked at him, bemused. Then, grabbing for her phone, which was chiming insistently from the night table beside the bed, she shut the sound off.

Last night, before falling asleep, she'd set her alarm for 6:30 a.m. It was, she confirmed with a glance at her phone, a few minutes past that time.

Emma. The events of the previous night came crashing down on her.

I have to tell Margaret.

Her stomach knotted. She took a quick, pained breath, drawing the air in through her teeth.

"You snore," Finn said. There was no identifiable expression on his face as his eyes ran over her.

The covers were bunched somewhere south of her feet: she must have kicked them off during the night. His too-big T-shirt had twisted around her as she slept. A downward glance told her that the white cotton hugged her breasts closely, molding the soft curves to the point where the jut of her nipples was clearly visible against the fabric. The hem was hiked up above the top of her thighs, giving him an unimpeded view of her bare legs and, she feared, even a peek at her panties.

"I do not." Adjusting the tee with a quick tug, she scooted off the bed. Then she remembered the screwdriver, and frowned. Against all odds, once she'd fallen asleep she'd slept like the dead. So, maybe—"Did I?"

"Like a chain saw."

"If I did, it was the vodka. So you can just blame yourself," she retorted, keeping her composure even as the intimacy of the situation threatened to render her tongue-tied. Or maybe it was the sight of Finn in a towel: heavily muscled shoulders, brawny arms, a wide, honed chest above a noticeable six-pack. A nice wedge of black chest hair that narrowed down to a slim line that disappeared beneath the towel that rode low on his lean hips. Innie belly button. Long, strong legs. Bare feet.

Her pulse was picking up the pace, Riley realized. And her breasts were tightening and swelling against the fabric and her body was quickening.

It occurred to her that neither of them was saying anything, and her eyes flew to his face to find that he was looking at her breasts.

He must have felt the weight of her gaze, because his eyes lifted to meet hers.

In that brief, unguarded moment, his eyes gleamed with unmistakable sexual intent. As she recognized that, her heart beat faster. Unexpected little darts of excitement raced through her bloodstream.

Awareness hung in the air between them, hot and steamy as the vapor drifting out of the bathroom around him.

All of a sudden, she was possessed by a nearly irresistible impulse to grab the hem of the T-shirt she was wearing and pull it over her head and let it drop to the floor. Naked except for her panties, she would walk over to him, tug at that towel . . .

His mouth hardened. A kind of shutter seemed to drop over his eyes. They went unreadable, opaque.

She wasn't fooled. She'd seen the fierce carnality in his gaze.

He wanted her. She had no doubt about that whatsoever. What made it so difficult was that she also wanted him.

And they were alone and half naked and there was a bed and . . .

Stop.

"I'm done in here. Be my guest," he said, as cool as if he'd never heard of sex, as if the air wasn't thick with it.

"Thanks."

He moved to the closet and opened the door, and she walked past him into the bathroom.

And made the mistake of glancing at him as she did.

He had his back to her. A few stray water droplets glistened in his hair, and his shoulders—his wide, bare shoulders—flexed as he reached inside the closet for his clothes. His strong back, the classic V of his torso, the slightly damp bronze of his skin, drew her eyes, made her breathing quicken and her pulse flutter.

He was so very male.

He was naked beneath that towel.

She wanted to touch him. No—she wanted to fuck him.

There it was, the truth, put in the crudest possible terms.

Forget it. There's too much at stake to—literally—screw it up.

Closing the bathroom door and shutting herself in against temptation, she found herself wrapped in the warm, steamy air from his shower. She smelled the faint scent of menthol, saw his razor on the vanity, and realized that he had shaved: his square jaw had been minus last night's stubble.

She was just getting all intrigued at the thought of Finn shaving when she saw something else on the vanity: her purse.

It was a small purse, expensive, quilted black leather, discreet designer logo. A long, cross-body strap. The top closed with a zipper. The zipper could be locked closed by securing the pull with a small leather tab.

Last night, she'd taken it with her when she'd

gone into the bathroom, and left it there. She hadn't thought a thing about it.

Until now, when she saw that it was zipped tight and the leather tab was snapped closed.

She never, ever used that leather tab.

Finn had gone through her purse.

Outrage flooded her, and reality followed close on its heels.

He might be protecting her, and she might be depending on him to save Emma and keep the bad guys from the door.

But she couldn't trust him.

He was still an investigator, and she was part of his investigation. The key to it, even.

The stupidest thing she could do would be to let herself forget: *we're not on the same side.*

If she'd been toying with the idea of laying the whole sorry story out for him, of asking his advice on how best to handle it, of throwing herself and Margaret on his mercy, she was now officially over it. Telling him that she knew where the money was could only end in 1) all the money, including Margaret's, falling into government hands; 2) at best, klieg lights of suspicion focusing on her and Margaret; or 3) the loss of any leverage she had to get federal authorities to help in saving Emma. Without the giant carrot of the missing money to keep them interested, Finn—and whatever resources he was bringing to bear to find Emma—might well disappear.

Knowledge is power, she reminded herself grimly. Once she shared what she knew, her power to get anybody to do anything would be gone, too. She would basically be at the mercy of the government.

Of Finn.

Yeah. Not gonna happen.

Blocking Finn and everything else out of her mind, she made quick preparations for what was sure to be a long and harrowing day: she took a shower, washed and blow-dried her hair, applied a minimum amount of makeup from the small kit in her purse, and popped more Tylenol. The only thing she had to wear was her dress from the night before, and it was in the closet. Wrapping herself in a towel, she stepped out of the bathroom.

Finn stood in front of the window—the curtains were open now, allowing pale, early morning sunlight to flood the room—talking on his cell phone. He was wearing one of his white shirts with charcoal-gray trousers, and, having apparently heard the bathroom door open, he broke off his conversation and turned to look at her as she emerged.

Sweeping him with an unsmiling glance, feeling his gaze on her all the while, Riley retrieved her clothes from the closet and went back into the bathroom to dress.

Even though she'd done her best to brush it off the night before, the sparkly evening dress still had dust on it. She put it on anyway: she would change into clean clothes at Margaret's. Her ruined pantyhose had been discarded the night before. Without them, the bruises on her legs were noticeable, but there was nothing she could do about that.

Slipping her bare feet into her too-high-for-daytime heels, she picked up her purse and left the bathroom.

"Ready?" Finn cocked an eyebrow at her as she walked out into the bedroom. He was knotting his tie in front of the mirror over the chest. It was such a domestic kind of thing to be doing, and he looked so damned sexy doing it, that her heart picked up the pace and she felt herself growing all warm inside simply from watching. As soon as she realized where her unwary libido was taking her *again,* she stiffened and her indignation at him bubbled up before she could put a lid on it.

"Did you find what you were looking for?" she asked. She was standing near him, just a few feet from the chest. Her tone was polite. Too polite, as she watched him raise his clean-shaven, deeply tanned, and way too masculine chin as he pulled the long end of his tie down through the knot. He threw her a bemused glance. "What?"

"In my purse. When you searched it."

He frowned at her as he eased the knot up into position and smoothed the tie with one hand. "What are you talking about?"

"I know you were in my purse. You made a mistake: I never snap this little tab." She wiggled the tab in question at him by way of illustration.

His eyes as they met hers were totally unreadable. "When I went into the bathroom, your purse had fallen over on its side. Some things were spilling out. I pushed them back in and zipped it up so it wouldn't happen again."

The explanation was reasonable. It might, Riley thought as she held his gaze, even be true. Then again, it might not be. She couldn't actually remember whether she had zipped her purse closed before leaving the bathroom the night before, so she had no way of knowing for sure.

"Oh," was what she said. Kind of anticlimactic, she had to admit.

"Yeah, *oh*."

"I'm sorry if I was wrong."

"You should be."

His gaze swept her. She turned away, walking toward the window, and was conscious of him watching her as she stopped to look out. It was going to be another hot one. The sun was already bright and it was—a glance at the clock told her—not quite 7 a.m. Traffic was moving along the street in front of the hotel. She could see a gas station with a convenience store attached, a strip of small businesses including a pizzeria, a payday loan establishment, a dry cleaners, and an apartment building.

Somewhere out there, Emma was enduring God knew what.

Her hands, which had been casually resting on the windowsill, clenched into fists.

Finn said, "You always dress like that for work?"

Her brows twitched together. She swung around to face him. "Like what?"

He was shrugging into his shoulder holster. Who would have guessed, she thought semi-bitterly, that she apparently had a thing for men with guns?

"Like you're on the hunt for rich husband number two."

"What?" That was so outrageous that she glared at him. "For your information—not that it's any of your business—I had no idea Jeff was rich when I met him. He was just this really sweet, cute, kind of lonely guy. And as for husband number two"—she laughed— "that's a joke. You couldn't give me one on a platter, rich or not. And yes, I always dress like this for that particular job. Don expects me to."

"Oh, yeah. Don." Finn was in front of the closet now, pulling on his jacket, solid charcoal gray like the trousers. "Mr. Cowboy Hat with the five kids who can't keep his hands off you. He who you're after?"

Sparks shot from Riley's eyes. He met her furious glare blandly. She was just about to let fly with a suggestion for what he could do with himself and his dirty mind when something about his expression, about the quirk at the corner of his mouth, about the way he was watching her, clued her in to the truth. Her anger dissipated like air escaping from a balloon. Her expression must have changed, because he lifted his eyebrows at her and said, "What?"

"You're just trying to distract me, aren't you?" Remembering the comment about her snoring, which had come right on the heels of the morning's first alarmed thought of Emma, and, with more reluctance, last night's incendiary kiss, she was sure of it. She eyed him crossly. "Stop doing that. I'm not five years old."

"Worrying yourself sick isn't going to do Emma any good," Finn said, in a tacit admission that she was right. By underlining that he could tell when she was thinking of Emma, it was also an admission that he was far too good at reading her, which she made a mental note to remember. "At this point the people who took her don't have any reason to hurt her, and we've got the best agents in the world pulling out all the stops to find her. I need you to focus on what you're supposed to do."

"Get George to tell me where the money is." Her voice was flat.

"That's it." Pulling his zipped and apparently packed suitcase out of the closet, he said, "You got everything? We need to go."

Her purse hung from her shoulder. She picked up her phone, which was on the table beside the bed. She'd brought nothing else.

"Yes." As she followed him to the door and, when he opened it, preceded him through it, she absorbed the significance of his packed bag. "You're not planning to come back here?"

"Don't know." They walked to the elevator. "I'll have to see how things work out. We'll stop by Margaret's house, then head for Stringtown and—"

The elevator arrived, interrupting. There were other people in it, and more in the lobby partaking of the free breakfast. The buzz of conversation, of activity, filled the air along with the scent of bacon and toast.

Finn nodded at the buffet. "How about we grab a coffee and a couple of doughnuts to go?"

Riley was too tense to be hungry. She was already thinking ahead to how she would tell Margaret about

Emma, and the knot in her stomach multiplied by about ten. But she nodded. If they didn't get something to eat here, she had little doubt that Finn would stop at a drive-thru on the way.

She could understand. He was a big guy. He needed food. Didn't mean she had to participate.

A few minutes later, armed with coffee and, in Finn's case, a couple of chocolate-covered doughnuts, they were in the car pulling onto the expressway. Traffic was already heavy. An anxious glance at the clock reassured her: there was still plenty of time before Margaret got up.

"How is this going to work, exactly?" Riley asked, watching as Finn, with one hand on the wheel, demolished his second doughnut in maybe three bites, then took a gulp of coffee. As much as she needed the caffeine, she'd taken a couple of sips of her own coffee and put it back into the cup holder. Her stomach was rebelling against even that small amount of liquid. "I'd rather you didn't go in with me. I'd like to talk to Margaret in private."

"I wasn't going to go in with you. The less you're seen with me, the better." He chugged more coffee. "It's possible that whoever is holding Emma is watching Margaret's house, although the team on that is reporting no evidence of surveillance. But I'd rather not take the chance."

Riley shivered inwardly at the idea of what her being spotted in Finn's company might mean for Emma. But without him, she was positive that Emma's chances would be far worse.

You did the smartest thing. . . . She knew it, but still she couldn't help feeling afraid.

Stay cool.

She said, "You have a team watching Margaret's house?"

"At this point, we have a team watching everything."

Riley wasn't sure how she felt about that. But she was for whatever it took to get Emma back and keep Margaret safe.

It just means I have to be extra careful.

"While you're in there, pack a bag." Gulping coffee, Finn glanced in the rearview mirror, then changed lanes. "You'll be gone overnight at least."

Riley hadn't thought of that.

"I can't leave Margaret alone tonight," she protested. In fact, leaving Margaret alone to go with Finn immediately after breaking the news of Emma's kidnapping struck Riley as a really bad idea, too. Margaret would be distraught, to say the least.

Finn drained the last of his coffee. "Can't be helped. It's a seven-hour drive to Stringtown. No way are we making it there and back, and then you have to meet with George."

Riley watched him put the empty cup into the holder. "I thought the FBI flew its agents all over the place."

"Car's way more anonymous. We want to stay under the radar. I'd have to request a plane, which involves a lot more people, which means a lot bigger chance of it getting to the wrong ears."

At the thought of what those "wrong ears" might mean for Emma, Riley felt a fluttering of panic. She instantly resigned herself to traveling by car and being gone overnight.

As they reached their exit and Finn turned down the off-ramp, Riley unsnapped and unzipped her purse, and pulled out her phone.

Braking for the red light at the intersection, Finn looked over at her. "Calling somebody?"

"Bill Stengel," Riley said, having hit on what she considered the best solution under the circumstances. "He'll be glad to come over and stay with Margaret while I'm gone. He'll keep her calm if anybody can."

Finn looked a question as the light changed and he drove on.

"Family lawyer," Riley explained, already punching in Bill's number. "He and Margaret are good friends. In fact"—she broke off as the truth of what she was about to say truly hit her for the first time—"I've always thought Bill had a little crush on her. I think he'd like to be more than friends. At some point. When Margaret's ready."

"Hmm." Finn didn't sound particularly interested in Margaret's love life. "You planning to tell him about Emma being kidnapped?"

Riley gave a slow nod. "At least, I think Margaret will want to. He's one of the few who's stood by her through this whole thing." She looked worriedly at Finn. "Do you see any reason why we shouldn't tell him? He won't be able to be much help to Margaret unless he knows."

"Not as long as you trust him to keep his mouth shut and stay the hell out of it."

Bill's phone was already ringing. Final decision time: she nodded. "I do."

But Bill didn't answer. Riley left him a message asking him to come to Margaret's house as soon as possible, hoping as she disconnected that she would be able to stay until he got there. Then she called in sick to both her jobs. She hated to do it, but there was no other choice.

By the time she finished, Finn was pulling into the strip mall closest to the entrance to Margaret's subdivision.

As he drove through the nearly deserted parking lot around behind the Kroger that anchored one end, Riley was surprised to see a yellow cab parked beside an overflowing dumpster.

She frowned.

Finn said, "I told you, I don't want you to be seen with me any more than necessary. If there is surveillance that we just haven't spotted yet, they'll be busting their asses trying to identify me if I drive you home."

What felt like an icy finger ran down Riley's back. "They'll know I went to the FBI."

"Yeah." Finn pulled up beside the cab. "Take the taxi to Margaret's house and have him wait while you're inside. Then have him bring you back here." At what must have been the alarmed look on her face he added, "I'll be keeping tabs on you, don't worry. The only time you'll be out of my sight is when you're actually in the house."

Riley took a deep breath and nodded.

He asked, "You have money?"

To pay for the cab, he meant. From that, Riley surmised it was a real cab, and not some kind of FBI plant. Probably. And not that it mattered.

She nodded. "Yes."

He stopped the car. She was about to get out when he said, "Riley. You need to bring me Jeff's SIM card. There might be information on it that can help us find Emma."

TWENTY-ONE

Riley got out of the car without answering.

Jeff's SIM card.

Finn's tone made it clear that he was sure she had it. And that he thought she could bring it to him when she returned.

She never would have admitted to possessing it, never would have given it to him, but Emma's kidnapping had changed everything.

It was, indeed, in Margaret's house, hidden among Riley's things. Which wouldn't be hard for him to surmise, especially if he had gone through her purse looking for it and had come up empty.

She would comb the SIM card, go through everything that was on it as best she could in the limited amount of time she was going to have, delete anything she found that needed deleting, and then hand it over.

And pray that he and/or the team going over it wouldn't find anything incriminating that she missed.

Jeff might have been looking at something she

didn't even know about when he was killed. Maybe there was something on there that would lead to whoever had killed him, and maybe whoever had killed him now had Emma.

The thought made Riley's breath catch. It made her go weak at the knees.

If they killed Jeff, would they . . . ?

Get a grip.

The best and only thing she could do for Emma now was keep a cool head.

Since there was already a squad car in the driveway, the cab parked on the grassy verge in front of the house. The neighborhood was awake by this hour, with people out walking their dogs and picking up their newspapers and getting into their cars on their way to work. The sun was still only a little way above the horizon, pale in the cloudless blue sky. The heat was already oppressive. Somebody nearby was out cutting grass: the scent of fresh-mown grass and the growl of a lawn mower hung in the air. Around here, people got their outside chores done early to beat the heat.

Finn had said he would be watching her, and she had no doubt that he was, but she couldn't see him.

Conscious of what she must look like to anyone interested enough to watch her cross the yard—that would be just about everyone in sight; the Cowans were big news these days—Riley kept her head high and took long strides toward the small brick house.

She even waved at the cops in the squad car, who looked her up and down as she passed and who, when she waved, waved abashedly back.

If there'd been a news crew around, and thank God there didn't seem to be one, she would have been expecting to have her image heading home, wearing what was clearly an evening dress on a bright, shiny Saturday morning, flashed all over the nation as a perky announcer chirped something like "Riley Cowan takes the Walk of Shame!"

Ordinarily she would have railed inwardly about her life as a tabloid headline, but she didn't have time as she entered the house and fear and dread immediately replaced annoyed embarrassment. As soon as she closed the door and the cool shadows of the living room swallowed her up, she heard faint sounds that could only be Margaret moving around at the end of the hall where the bedrooms were located. The smell of coffee was further confirmation that she had miscalculated: Margaret had been up for at least a little while.

"Emma?" Margaret called. The worry in her voice told Riley that she had discovered Emma's absence. Her voice sharpened, grew louder. "Emma?"

Riley hurried into the hallway.

She had been right: Margaret was standing in Emma's open doorway, one hand on the knob as she looked toward the top of the hall in response to the sounds of Riley's approach.

Seeing some of the tension leave Margaret's face as she spotted her killed Riley. The last thing Margaret would be expecting to hear was Riley's terrible news.

"Riley." Margaret sounded relieved. She was wearing white slacks and a navy blouse, and Riley guessed that she'd gotten dressed and put coffee on before checking on Emma. "Emma's not in her room."

"I know." Riley reached her and took Margaret's hand. It was thin but felt warm, and it returned her grip affectionately. Then Margaret's eyes flickered over her face. At what she saw there she frowned.

"Are you just now getting in?" Margaret asked.

A knot formed in Riley's chest.

"Come here," she said, and drew Margaret into the bathroom.

"What's wrong?" Margaret's voice rose fearfully as Riley closed the door behind them, turned on the tap full blast, and then gently pushed her down on the closed toilet seat and crouched in front of her. Margaret stared at her with wide-eyed horror. "My God, what's happened?"

As gently as she could, Riley told her everything. By the time she finished, Margaret was whimpering like a wounded animal and rocking back and forth with her head in her hands. Riley's heart ached. Margaret's pain tore at her insides. She wanted to whimper herself.

Margaret's head came up. Her eyes were wild. "That money. That cursed money. It killed Jeff. Now it might kill Emma. Oh, please, I can't lose Emma, too." The cry sounded as though it came straight from her heart.

Riley took her hands, which were cold now and trembling, and gripped them tightly. "I know. I told you what we're going to do. All you have to do is keep it together. We'll get Emma back."

Even though she could see the older woman was in no place to hear it, Riley kept talking and walked Margaret meticulously through her plan, going over what she intended to do until she was sure the other woman understood. She'd fine-tuned it so that Margaret was required to do nothing more than keep her mouth shut about what they'd done, because she'd known that in the aftermath of hearing about Emma, Margaret would be barely able to function.

Clearly, she'd been right.

"Are you sure we shouldn't just tell them?" Margaret's voice shook. "Just give them the money, and tell them, and be done?"

"Until we get Emma back, if we're going to give it to anybody, it's going to be to whoever has her," Riley reminded her. "If we tell the FBI, the government will take control of the money, and it'll be up to the government whether or not to trade it for Emma. And they'll suspect us of being involved in taking it, or at least of knowing where it was all along and not reporting it, which is probably obstruction of justice. And then—I took that ten million dollars, and you withdrew thirty thousand of it. We'll probably go to prison."

"I don't care about that," Margaret said fiercely. Tears glimmered in her eyes. "All I care about is getting Emma back safely."

"I know." Her own eyes welling up, Riley hugged her. "That's all I care about, too. But I really think this is the best way. Remember, the FBI could find Emma at any time. They know how to deal with kidnappings. Emma won't be harmed."

At least, she prayed not. And Finn had said that Emma wouldn't be. But Riley knew perfectly well that there was no way to be sure. Still, that was the last thing Margaret needed to hear at the moment.

"This man—" Margaret said, and Riley knew that she was referring to Finn. Riley had told her that the FBI agent who'd come to her rescue after the attack on her at her apartment was the one she had called in the aftermath of Emma's kidnapping "—is he competent? Do you trust him?"

The first question she could answer unreservedly, the second was more complicated. But there was only one answer she could give Margaret to both.

"Yes and yes."

"All right." Margaret still trembled from head to foot, but she sat up and visibly tried to pull herself together. "Bill is coming, you say? And I can tell him about Emma being kidnapped, but I'm not supposed to tell him that we already found the money or—or anything like that."

"That's right. You can tell him everything except that," Riley said. She released Margaret's hands and stood up. "I have to get ready to go. Do you want to wait in the living room for Bill?"

Margaret took a deep breath and nodded.

Riley left her on the couch with a shawl around her shoulders, a cup of coffee and a muffin on the table beside her, and a program Margaret liked playing on the TV. Then she hurried to do what she needed to do.

Quickly and carefully, she told herself.

First, she pulled on a pair of rubber gloves from

the kitchen. Then she extracted George's black book from Emma's painting, and took it into Jeff's bedroom. Looking around the familiar room made her stomach tighten with grief, but there was no time for anything except the task at hand. Loading the machine with fresh paper from an unopened package beneath the desk, she used the copying function on the printer to copy each page in George's book. Jeff had brought the printer from George's Oakwood office with him when they'd moved into this house, which was what had given her the idea of how to circumvent the problem with the fingerprints. The copied pages wouldn't have any fingerprints on them because she was wearing gloves, and if anyone bothered and was able to trace them back to a copying machine it would be to one that George would have had access to. No one would find her and Margaret's fingerprints on the original black book.

Once that was done, she grabbed a cigarette lighter from a drawer in Jeff's desk, set George's black book alight, and dropped it in the brass incense burner that Jeff had used for God knew what purposes to burn. She never would have suspected that one day she'd bless her ex-husband for keeping his drug paraphernalia handy.

The faintly rubbery smell worried her a little—she wanted to leave no trace of what she was doing—but there was nothing she could do to mask it. Fortunately the smoke detector was at the other end of the hall.

While the book burned she grabbed the SIM card from its hiding place and replaced the one in her

phone with it. It was a simple procedure: pull one out
and click the other one into its place.

She was multitasking—clicking through everything she could access on Jeff's phone while making
a dash for the bathroom, where she dumped the fine
black ash that had been George's little book down the
toilet and flushed it away—when she made the first
disturbing discovery.

Two emails had been sent to Jeff on the day he
died from an account she'd never seen before. Of
course, Jeff, being Jeff, had lots of contacts she didn't
know about, and the fact that she didn't recognize the
account wasn't what alarmed her.

One message, sent at 5:17 p.m., read, *Hi from
Paris,* no greeting, no signature, and the other one, sent
at 5:23 p.m., read *We'll always have Paris.*

Reading them, Riley froze in the act of turning on
the water in the sink. All kinds of alarm bells went off
in her mind.

Hours after receiving the two emails, Jeff had died.

Jeff had read them, but he hadn't earmarked them
in any way. He hadn't saved them. He hadn't forwarded
them.

He hadn't told her about them.

He obviously had not picked up on the message,
because *that* he would have told her. But she did, immediately.

The emails seemed to be clear references to Emma's
painting.

In other words, to the location of George's black
book.

Her heart skipped a beat.

Who had sent them? George? But she didn't think he had access to email in prison. Certainly not unsupervised email. And she was pretty sure that any account from the prison would be labeled as such.

So who? She couldn't begin to hazard a guess.

But if someone had known about them, would that have been enough to, to use Finn's words, *stir the pot*?

The mere thought was enough to make Riley's nerves tighten.

Should she delete them? she wondered feverishly. Would they provide Finn or whoever went over the material from the SIM card with enough information to tell them where George had hidden his black book, which was in essence his map to the money? Could they possibly lead investigators to Margaret and her?

Riley thought hard about that as she left the bathroom with the now clean and dry incense burner.

Unless someone knew specifically about Emma's painting, she didn't see how those emails could lead back to it.

"Riley? Is everything all right?" Margaret called anxiously. Her voice was unsteady, and Riley had little doubt that she was hanging on to her composure by her fingernails.

"Everything's fine!" Riley called back, and, pocketing her phone for the moment, went into Jeff's room. Margaret needed someone to be with her, and Riley felt bad for leaving her alone when she was in such distress, but there was nothing else she could do. She had to move as quickly as possible. Things would go far more smoothly if she finished everything she needed to do before, say, Bill arrived, or before so much time had passed that Finn started wondering what she was doing.

Putting the incense burner back in place, she picked up the copied pages and folded them into as small a square as possible.

Then she headed back for the kitchen.

"Can I get you some fresh coffee?" Riley called as she passed the doorway to the living room. Margaret was sitting where she had left her, huddled on the brown couch, the coffee and muffin untouched beside her. The TV was on, but Margaret had turned the volume down so that Riley could barely hear it in the kitchen. She was as sure as it was possible to be of anything that Margaret was not actually watching it.

"No. Thank you," Margaret responded with dignity. Margaret's good manners were as natural to her as breathing, but under the circumstances they broke Riley's heart all over again. Even while she was clearly in anguish, Jeff's mother was class to her bones. "Riley, what—"

The sound of the front door opening caused Margaret to break off and sent a rush of alarm through Riley.

Who—?

"Bill," Margaret said in a thankful tone, alleviating most of Riley's fear. Her only concern about the new arrival was what she needed to get done before Bill came in search of her. She quickened her step as Bill answered Margaret with, "My dear, what is it?"

Margaret said something that Riley didn't catch because she was too busy easing a pewter urn off the top of a cabinet, where it stood sentry over a fern and a clay figure Jeff had made in elementary school. The urn contained the cremated remains of Horatio, the family's beloved Scottie, who had passed away some six months before George was arrested. George would have had access to it, and to her knowledge no one had bothered it since it had been placed on top of the cabinet. As a hiding place for the copied pages, it would work.

Unscrewing the lid, she dropped the pages in among the ashes, muttered, "Sorry, Horatio," screwed the lid back on, and replaced the urn.

Her work done, Riley had just stripped off the rubber gloves and tossed them in the trash when, as she had predicted, Bill came into the kitchen.

"Margaret told me what's happened." Bill frowned at her as she walked toward him with a quick nod of greeting. His usually florid face was pale. "She said you're working with the FBI on it."

"Yes." Riley stopped to put her hand on his arm. It was Saturday morning, and Bill was still dressed like he was going into the office, in a suit and tie. "That agent who helped me after I was attacked: I called him right afterwards. He's waiting for me now."

"What's that taxicab doing out there?"

"It's possible the house is under surveillance. The agent didn't want me to be seen with him, just in case. We're going to meet up somewhere else."

"Margaret says you're going to visit George."

"Yes. I'm going to see if I can get him to tell me where the money is. If I can, then we'll follow the kidnappers' instructions when they call."

"What if George won't tell you? What if he's telling the truth, and the money's spent?" Bill asked.

"I don't know. I guess we'll cross that bridge when we come to it."

"Holy moley." Bill shook his head. "Just—holy moley."

"I have to get changed." Acutely conscious of the passage of time and Finn waiting for her, Riley gave his arm a pat and moved past him. "I'm going to be gone overnight. Stay with Margaret, will you please?"

"Of course I will."

Riley went into Jeff's room, changed into a yellow sundress from the suitcase she'd never gotten around to unpacking, zipped the suitcase up, and, pulling it behind her, left the room.

"You be careful," Margaret murmured as Riley hugged her good-bye. "And call me."

"I will," Riley promised, and went out the door.

In the cab on the way to her rendezvous with Finn, Riley was starting to take Jeff's SIM card out of her phone and replace it with her own when she remembered something: she never had taken a good look at those pictures Jeff had snapped right before he died.

Glancing out the window to gauge where they were in relation to the strip mall, she realized that she didn't have much time. Clicking on the photos, she looked at the first one that came up, which would have been the last one Jeff had taken: two men, walking toward the camera, deep in the shadows of night. They were wearing baseball caps and windbreakers—given the heat, that was suspicious right there. Their faces were indistinct because of the darkness, but Riley was pretty certain that she didn't know them. The second picture was of the same two men a little farther away. Of course, it would have been taken before the other one.

The thought that she might be looking at Jeff's murderers as they closed in on him made her palms grow damp.

She was suddenly glad that Finn would be seeing these pictures.

Then she clicked on the third picture. It, too, had been taken not long before Jeff died, and it, too, was of a man wrapped in darkness.

Her heart skipped a beat.

There was no mistaking this man's identity: it was Finn.

TWENTY-TWO

She looked like a sunbeam, was the stupid-ass thought that first assailed Finn as he watched Riley slide out of the taxi and come walking across the asphalt toward him. Bright yellow dress, vivid red hair—no wonder that, for a moment there, it was like she was all he could see. The taxi took off—she must have paid the driver before getting out. He would have gotten out of the car to relieve her of her suitcase but caution prevailed. The word was that she wasn't under surveillance by Emma's kidnappers, but the word had been wrong before, and anyway Emma's kidnappers weren't the only players in the game.

It was better all around if anyone who might be watching never got a chance to get a good look at him. Not many people in the business knew who he was, but all it took was one photo and a lucky hit with facial recognition software and his identity, along with the Agency's interest and involvement, would be all over the international spook community about as quick as somebody could click a mouse.

Anyway, Riley was handling her suitcase just fine. For all her slender build, there was nothing fragile about her. The gauzy dress with its sleeveless, figure-molding top and long, flowy skirt was superfeminine, as were her strappy high heels. With her ivory skin and delicate features and banging body, *she* was super-feminine.

Good thing he was becoming too well acquainted with her to be fooled.

This magnolia-by-way-of-the-Steel-Belt had cast-iron balls.

She was looking right at him. Her expression was unfriendly. Her luscious, full-lipped, kiss-me mouth was . . . downright grim.

Fair enough.

He was feeling kind of on the grim side himself.

He'd had ears in Margaret's house, and Riley had done her drag-the-other-woman-into-the-bathroom-and-mask-their-conversation-with-running-water thing again.

He doubted she'd done that to tell her Emma had been kidnapped. No masking necessary for that con-versation.

Not long after, he'd gotten a notification that Jeff's cell phone had just been turned on. Seeing as how Jeff's cell phone was in an FBI lab missing a vital part, that seemed unlikely.

What seemed way more plausible—in fact, he was willing to bet his life on it—was that the SIM card that was in essence the brain of Jeff's cell phone had been activated.

He didn't even have to ask himself by whom.

He damn well knew.

————————

FORGET OFFERING to help her with her suitcase. Instead, Finn stayed inside the car, popped the trunk as she approached, and waited.

Which was fine, Riley told herself. She didn't need his help. She could heft that suitcase into that trunk perfectly well by herself.

If, once her suitcase was in there nestled beside his, she slammed the trunk hard, it was because she wanted to make sure it was latched.

Then she yanked open the door and slid into the passenger seat beside him.

"Put on your seat belt," was how he greeted her. A growl. Which was perfect, because it matched her mood. As she complied—she might be angry, apprehensive, and a whole host of other emotions too tumultuous to name, but she wasn't an idiot—he slid on a pair of Ray-Bans and drove out of the parking lot.

She gave him a long, hopefully not obvious, look. Not helpful. Bottom line was, he looked hot. He looked cool. He looked like a fricking federal agent that she would be a fool to trust any farther than she could throw him.

Which was, not at all.

The question was, was she afraid of him?

For a few moments, as he negotiated the local

streets and got the Acura onto I-45 North heading for Dallas, neither of them said anything. With the sunglasses concealing his eyes, his rough-hewn features were impossible to read. He seemed to be concentrating on the road, which at that moment was a free-for-all as the crazy East Texas traffic whizzed in and out around them. When finally they were clear of the city and the traffic settled down, he glanced at her.

"You tell Margaret about Emma?" The growl was gone. There was nothing at all in his voice now.

She wanted to yell at him. No, she wanted to accuse him. She wanted to plug that SIM card back into her phone—it was at that moment in a zippered pocket of her purse—and show him that picture of himself and shout, *explain this*.

But it had occurred to her that she didn't really know Finn Bradley at all. He was a big, buff, good-looking guy who turned her on. They had sexual chemistry so electric that even now, when she was suspicious out the wazoo of everything he said and did, she could look at his hard profile and uncompromising chin, at the stern lines of his mouth, at the breadth of his shoulders in the tailored charcoal suit and the powerful length of his legs bent to accommodate the gas and brake pedals, at his tanned, capable hands on the wheel, and feel herself starting to go all hot and shivery inside.

So was she afraid of him?

He'd saved her life, come to her rescue when she needed it. He'd held her when she'd cried—God, she hated remembering that!—and kissed her dizzy. More than once.

She'd called him at the darkest moment of her life, and she trusted him to save Emma.

What she didn't know was what his picture was doing on Jeff's cell phone.

And that bothered her. It made her wonder. It made her cautious.

At the thought that he might, perhaps, have had something to do with Jeff's death, she was alternately frightened and furious.

At the moment, he was helping her, protecting her. What she couldn't let herself forget was that he was doing it for reasons of his own.

What happened when he no longer needed her to help him get what he wanted?

She had no idea. But until she did, confronting him, letting him know that she'd seen that picture—that she knew he'd been in Jeff's vicinity shortly before Jeff was murdered, a fact that he had never once mentioned—would, she concluded, be dumb as rocks.

So she didn't. She kept her mouth shut. If he was using her for his own ends, so be it. She was using him for her own ends, too.

The key was not to lose sight of that.

To stay cool.

Keep her guard up.

Play her own game.

"Well?" he prodded, slightly impatient now. And she realized that she'd been staring at him—not glaring, hopefully—without answering.

She had to behave as though her discovery of his picture on Jeff's phone hadn't sent panic licking up her spine. She had to behave as though her discovery of his picture on Jeff's phone hadn't happened at all.

"Yes," she said, calm as could be.

When she said nothing more, his eyebrows went up. "So?"

Riley shrugged. "She was upset. Of course she was upset. I was glad Bill got there before I had to go. I would have hated to leave her alone."

"So you took her into the living room, sat her down, and gave her the bad news."

"More or less."

He waited a minute. "That all you're going to tell me?"

"What do you want, a blow-by-blow account? I told her about Emma, I changed clothes, I left."

"You were in her house for a while. I just wondered what went down that took so long."

"Well, now you know."

A pause ensued. His lips firmed as he seemed to concentrate on the road ahead. Then he glanced her way again.

"You get that SIM card?" His voice had a definite edge to it.

God, she hated to admit she had it! But there might be information on there that would lead to Emma. She had to turn it over. The thought of what Emma must be enduring was a constant, heavy weight in her chest. It scared her clear down to her toes, made her sick, made her sweat. None of which would help Emma.

Keep your focus on the job at hand.

She was in a quandary, though: she couldn't point

out those emails to him without revealing that she had accessed the SIM card, and if he knew she had accessed the SIM card, if he was the one who checked the information it contained, he would inevitably see the picture of himself and conclude that she'd seen it, too. The result would be the same if someone else checked the SIM card and told him about the picture.

By letting him know that she had, indeed, seen his picture on Jeff's phone, she might be putting herself in danger.

Which raised the question one more time: was she afraid of Finn?

It was difficult to look at him and find herself wondering if he was capable of murdering Jeff. If he was capable of hurting—or worse—her.

"Damn it, Riley—"

"It's in my purse." Okay, that maybe sounded a little surly. The last thing she wanted to do was give him reason to suspect that she was harboring serious doubts about him.

"Care to hand it over?"

Not really, was the honest reply to that. But she fished in her purse, extracted the small plastic rectangle, and put (did not slap) it down on the palm of the hand he held out to receive it. Glancing at it, he stowed it away in his jacket pocket.

He said, "So I was right about you taking it out and pitching Jeff's phone in the tub yourself."

Riley didn't reply.

"How about you tell me why you felt you needed to do that."

He was asking like he thought she might actually be going to tell him.

Fat chance.

"Well, you know, Jeff and I were married once," she said in her best coy Southern belle persona, which she could assume at will after seven years of hanging around the finest flowers of the South. "I hated to think that anything I might have"— she was practically batting her eyelashes here—"sent him . . . might still have been on his phone for anyone to see."

Finn's head snapped toward her so fast that she hoped it hurt his neck.

"You're saying you went to the trouble of taking that SIM card out of Jeff's phone because you were afraid there might be naked pictures of you on it?"

"It wasn't any trouble," Riley replied. "Snapping a SIM card out is easy." She gave him a sweet-as-pie smile, and was rewarded by the tightening of his jaw. She added, "I'm guessing you weren't able to get the information on Jeff's phone off iCloud after all? Because if you'd been able to do that, then you wouldn't need the SIM card."

That retaliatory poke at him didn't garner a response beyond a slight grimace. Well, she didn't need one: she knew the answer.

All of a sudden, a way to give him the information she wanted him to have without revealing that she'd seen what was on the SIM card hit her, and she went with it.

"You know, you should probably check out Jeff's email. I seem to recall him saying something about getting a couple of strange emails the night he died."

That interested him. He looked at her. "He tell you that when he asked you to meet him at Oakwood?"

Lying was getting easier and easier. "Yes."

"He say what bothered him about them?"

"Not really. Just that he didn't know who they were from. Oh, and that they mentioned Paris."

She could sense him perking up.

"Anything significant about Paris? Had Jeff been there recently?"

Riley shook her head. She tried not to do it too swiftly. This was dangerous territory: she wanted to point him toward the correct emails so that he could determine the identity of the sender sooner rather than later, not hint him toward some kind of missing-money connection to Paris. Not that he or anyone else was likely to ever figure out what that connection was. "Not since he was a teenager, as far as I know."

She thought he was looking at her, although it was hard to tell with the sunglasses.

"You know much about what Jeff was up to in the final weeks of his life?" he asked.

Riley shrugged. Thinking about Jeff hurt. It probably always would. "Nothing special. Like I told you, he was looking into the deaths of those four associates of his father's. Other than that, he was trying to piece his life back together. It isn't easy, if you've been used to having oodles of money, to find yourself dead broke."

"Doesn't seem to have bothered you particularly.

Unlike Jeff, you managed to get yourself a job. Two, actually."

"The difference is, I wasn't all that used to having oodles of money. Before I married Jeff, I was strictly a paycheck-to-paycheck kind of girl."

"A finance degree must have come in handy once you became George Cowan's daughter-in-law."

"A finance degree came in handy after I stopped being George Cowan's daughter-in-law. Wait, how do you know what kind of degree I have?" She scowled at him. "You did a background check on me."

"That's right." He didn't even have the grace to sound abashed. "You got to admit, an ex-daughter-in-law with a finance degree is pretty interesting, when you think about all that missing money. Help me out here, since you have some expertise in that field: if you wanted to make a billion or so dollars disappear, how would you do it?"

"I don't know," Riley said coldly.

"Take a stab at it. Where would you hide that much money?"

"I never deal in hypotheticals." Riley's voice was even colder than before. "People tend to read too much into them. Look, do you mind if we don't talk for a while? I have a headache, and I'm just going to close my eyes."

She didn't wait for his answer. Instead she leaned her head back against the back of the seat and did exactly that.

While mentally flipping him the bird and cooing, *interrogate this.*

———————

SHE WAS lying. Finn knew she was lying. He just wasn't sure how big in scope her lies were, or exactly what she was lying about.

One lie was, the reason she took the SIM card out of that damned phone.

Much as he hated to admit it, the mere idea of Jeffy-boy having naked pictures of Riley on his cell phone was driving him around the bend.

Exactly why he didn't like it he didn't care to speculate. The fact remained, he *really* didn't.

He was pretty sure she was lying even about the existence of the naked pictures, but he couldn't be positive. The worst thing about it was, it was not entirely outside the realm of possibility that naked pictures of Riley might actually be on her ex-husband's cell phone.

He was fairly confident that they hadn't had that kind of relationship at the time of Jeff's death, but there was always a chance the pictures were old, from when they were still married.

The images that he couldn't keep from flashing through his mind every time he thought of her pathetic excuse for an excuse—mental snapshots of Riley naked; worse, ones of Jeff looking at Riley naked—weren't helping.

But his thoughts on the subject were clear enough so that he was sure that whatever her reason for taking the phone from Jeff's body in the first place, and the SIM card from the phone in the second, concern about naked pictures of herself being discovered on it wasn't it.

Whatever she was hiding, Margaret had to be in on it. That was the only explanation for the carefully masked bathroom conversations. They were colluding about something—and it had to be something to do with the missing money.

What it was he didn't know, and it was pretty obvious that Riley had no intention of telling him.

Which left Margaret.

She would be far easier to break than Riley, no question about that. A possible option would be to have a team pick Margaret up, ask her some pertinent questions, see what they could find out. No threats, no torture, nothing like that. No physical or mental coercion needed: given Margaret's background, and temperament, to say nothing of the trauma of her son's death and daughter's kidnapping, he was pretty sure the job could get done by confronting her with what they knew and using plain old official government intimidation to do the rest.

But even as he had the thought, he knew he wasn't going to go that route. First off, Margaret was a woman: scaring—or bringing in other people to scare—women wasn't how he rolled. Second, if Margaret confessed all, and if that confession involved Riley being part of George's schemes, it wasn't something he wanted officialdom to know, at least not until he'd had time to think about it. And third, getting Margaret to tell what she knew only worked if Margaret knew what he wanted to know: where the hell the money was.

Otherwise, that course of action would do more harm than good.

Picking Margaret up would alarm and alienate Riley. It would also alert her to the fact that she and Margaret were under close surveillance. And increasing suspicion.

Which could be counted on to make Riley far less easy to keep tabs on, as well as far less likely to cooperate with the government (in other words, him).

For now, it was better to go with what was already in the works: while the team that had been deployed to find and rescue Emma did its job, he would take Riley to George and see if she could worm the whereabouts of the money out of him.

If she could do that, they could all go home happy.

If she couldn't—well, then he would work from there.

A vibration on the cell phone in his pocket had him casting a quick glance at Riley before checking it.

She'd fallen asleep. A look reassured him that, no, she wasn't faking it to get out of talking to him. Her body was totally relaxed, with her hands lying limply in her lap. Her head rested against the headrest. Her face was turned toward him, bright hair tucked behind an ear, long dark lashes resting against soft cheeks, rosy lips slightly parted.

She didn't snore—and hadn't last night, he'd been lying about that—but her breathing was deep with an occasional catch in it.

She was wary of him, he knew, but still she trusted him enough to go to sleep in his company.

That touched a chord in him. He acknowledged that it did with reluctance.

Careful, he thought with wry comprehension of his own susceptibility. *She's beautiful, she's vulnerable — and you're a guy.*

It was a combination that had brought down whole kingdoms.

His phone vibrated again, and, glad to have his thoughts interrupted, he scooped it out of his pocket to see the message he was expecting: A1.

An arrangement to hand off the SIM card for analysis at a prearranged spot had just been confirmed.

He didn't have to reply, didn't have to do anything but show up.

The exit he wanted was some fifty miles up the road. He'd let her sleep until then.

His eyes slid over her again. Her posture, in conjunction with the neckline of her dress, allowed him a nice glimpse of some pretty spectacular cleavage. Her breasts curved enticingly toward him, with just a hint of her nipples pressing against the thin fabric of her dress. Her waist was slim above the loose skirt that hid her killer legs.

The shaft of desire that went through him simply from looking at her caught him by surprise. That was his body reacting spontaneously, and with an intensity that made him grit his teeth and tighten his hands around the steering wheel. A damned glance, and he wanted her so much he ached with it.

Not good. Even worse: the instantaneous memory of how she felt in his arms, how soft and silky her skin was beneath his hands and lips, how hotly she'd kissed him.

He had no doubt at all that she would be even hotter in bed.

The ache intensified to the point where it was almost unbearable. Faced with the unwanted boner from hell, he found himself in the miserable position where all he could do about it was wish he was wearing looser pants.

That was the effect she had on him. He cursed himself for being a fool, and a horny one besides.

Then his gaze found the bruises on the side of Riley's throat that her bright hair didn't quite hide. Another small bruise was visible on her shoulder, peeking out from beneath the strap of her dress. And her legs were bruised, too, he knew, although he couldn't see the marks.

At the sight of those ugly discolorations on her smooth skin, Finn felt a flush of cold anger that didn't quell but at least redirected his present bad case of burning lust. He didn't like seeing women get hurt, but that wasn't the source of this sudden urge he felt to commit extreme violence on the perpetrators. The thing was, the bruises on Riley felt personal. She might be, as he was beginning to fear, up to her neck in George's scheme, but it didn't matter: she had his protection now. The next asshole who tried to hurt her was going to have to go through him.

And he would take the motherfucker apart.

What that said about the state of his relationship with Riley he refused to think about. Instead, he kept his gaze focused on the road, and turned his thoughts to exactly how he was going to find the damned money if Riley's visit to George didn't pan out.

Ten minutes later, they reached the designated exit, and he pulled off the interstate. Not far outside of Dallas, it was one of those freeway pit stops with a Super 8 motel, a Denny's, a McDonald's, a couple of gas stations, and not much else.

He had a date to meet an intelligence operative in the Shell station's men's room.

TWENTY-THREE

The ladies' room at the Shell station was on the side of the building, accessible from the parking lot. The door was brown metal, the inside was grungy and smelly, there were no windows, and it had two stalls. Finn walked in behind her, totally oblivious to both her protest and the havoc his presence might have caused if anyone else had been in there, and checked both stalls and the rest of the room to make sure it was empty.

Leaning against the sink, arms folded over her chest, Riley watched him with a mixture of speculation and alarm.

Would a man who was thinking about hurting her go to this much trouble to make sure she was safe?

He backtracked to the door, checked to make sure it had a lock that worked. It did.

"What, do you think some kind of bad guy might follow me in here?" Panicky visions of how quickly Emma's kidnapping had gone down flashed in her mind's eye, only to be immediately dismissed: she wouldn't be able to function at all if she allowed herself to think of that.

He shrugged. "I don't, but why chance it? Lock the door behind me, and don't come out, or open it for anyone, and I mean anyone, until I come back and you're sure it's me. Got it?"

His expression told her how serious he was. She'd been feeling a little drowsy from her nap in the car, a little achy, a little out of it, but now this reminder of present danger snapped her wide awake.

She nodded as a thrill of apprehension raced through her. "Got it."

"Good." He exited, pulling the door shut behind him. As it closed the last inch or so he added, "Lock it."

She did. He tried the knob—the door didn't budge—as a test, then gave a single sharp rap on the door and said, "I'll be back."

Everything she needed to do, including tidying her hair and refreshing her makeup, could be accomplished in minutes. She did it. After that, she waited.

The knob rattled once, which made her stiffen and stare at the door, but no one spoke and whoever it was went away. Not, she concluded, Finn.

By the time he announced his return with a knock and an unmistakable "It's me," she was beyond antsy.

Pulling open the door and walking through it into the wall of heat and car exhaust smells and sounds of traffic that were typical service-station-during-a-Texas-summer stuff, she frowned up at him.

"I was getting worried."

Unexpectedly, that uptick of a smile of his teased her. "About me?"

She was stepping off the curb, heading for the car, and his hand slid around her upper arm right above her elbow. It was an automatic masculine courtesy that she'd experienced many times from many different men, but this time was different. She was acutely aware of the warmth and strength of that hand, and how good it felt against her bare skin. She was acutely aware of *him*, and how good it felt to have him beside her, her shoulder brushing his arm, her steps matched with his. A big, bad federal agent who was acting as her own personal bodyguard. *Remember the picture,* she warned herself, and she did, but even that didn't keep her from being glad he was with her.

How she would have gotten through this without him she couldn't imagine.

She also couldn't imagine him hurting her. But then again, she reminded herself severely, maybe that was just because she lacked imagination.

"About me," she clarified tartly, irritable because she was feeling totally conflicted. "I was starting to worry that I'd be stuck in that bathroom forever. What took you so long?"

"Angel, you don't want to know."

Angel? She cast another swift look up at him, not irritable at all now, but he appeared unaware that he'd said anything out of the ordinary as he walked her to the car and opened the passenger door for her.

When he closed it behind her and walked around the front of the car to get in, she watched him with a little bit of trouble in her expression, even as she pulled on her seat belt.

That *angel* uttered in his dark, gravelly voice had done funny things to her insides. Looking at him as he walked around the car did funny things to her insides. She'd never particularly liked big, muscular men. She'd certainly never liked bossy, aggressive, overtly masculine ones. Her taste had run toward lean, debonair, smooth-talking types.

Tastes change.

It was a scary thought.

As he got in beside her, started the car, and began pulling out of the lot, she was way too aware of him. Aware of the amount of space he took up, and of how, at, she discovered with a glance at the dashboard clock, not quite 1 p.m. his jaw was already starting to darken with the first faint signs of stubble. She was aware of the springy thickness of his short, coffee-colored hair, and the less than delicate contours of his hard cheekbones and straight nose, and the stern lines of his mouth.

He must have felt her gaze on him, because he glanced her way. The Ray-Bans were tucked into the breast pocket of his jacket, and what she was suddenly aware of most of all was the cool blue-gray of his eyes.

To her bemusement, her heart started beating just a little bit faster as she met them.

"You hungry?" he asked. The prosaic question smacked her right back down to earth, thank God.

Riley started to shake her head—the mention of food gave her an instant flash-thought of Emma, who at best was certain to be so upset and frightened that she wouldn't be able to eat even if whoever had her provided her with food—but then she reminded herself that she had to keep herself strong in order to do what she needed to do.

"Sure." They were on the road that led to the freeway ramp, and she cast a look around. The pickings were slim. "Denny's or McDonald's?"

"Your call."

"McDonald's." She wasn't enthused, but she'd eaten plenty of McDonald's over the course of her life and she could do it again.

He pulled in to the McDonald's and got in line at the drive-thru. When he ordered a large coffee for himself in addition to the food, she frowned at him and realized that he was looking tired. Of course, he'd gotten approximately the same amount of sleep she had—not much—and hadn't had the advantage of being able to nap in the car.

"I can drive for a while, if you want to rest," she offered, when he settled her Diet Coke into a cup holder in the console between the seats, handed the rest of the bagged food to her, then took a long, appreciative swallow of coffee as he pulled away from the window.

She took the snort with which he answered that as a big *no*.

"Macho much?" she asked with a disdainful lift of her eyebrows as he stopped at the edge of the parking lot to let a semi rattle on by.

"You want to drive?" Settling the coffee into the

empty cup holder, he pulled out onto the road and headed toward the on-ramp. "I'd be glad to let you—if you think you can evade a carful of armed goons trying to force us off the road, or keep the car on the pavement in case someone should shoot out a tire, or—"

"Seriously? Are you expecting something like that to happen?" Riley had been lifting the food out of the sack and unwrapping it, and the smell of burgers and fries now filled the car. She paused in the act to look at him with widening eyes. Then, unable to help herself, she cast a nervous look at the vehicles around them as they merged into the traffic on the expressway.

"Probably not." He plucked the Big Mac she'd been holding suspended out of its wrapper and her hand, and bit into it with obvious relish. "But just in case, we're both better off if I'm behind the wheel."

"Fine. I only offered because I thought you looked tired." While he was devouring the first of his two Big Macs like he was starving, she was looking at her plain hamburger with near distaste. The knot in her stomach that had been there since the previous night made her almost afraid to try it.

"If I do, it's because your snoring kept me awake." He was busy chewing, but the faint deepening of the lines around his eyes told her that he was teasing her. They were barreling down the expressway by this time, tucked in among pickup trucks and semis and passenger cars zooming in and out of the four lanes of traffic. Ordinarily, she might have been nervous to find herself traveling at such speed with a man at the wheel who was busily engaged in devouring his lunch, but, she discovered, she had every confidence in Finn. Or in his driving, at least.

She would have argued again that she didn't snore, but that seemed like a waste of breath. Instead, she took a small bite of her burger and forced herself to chew. Swallowing required an act of real willpower, and she followed up with a quick drink of Diet Coke to wash it down. Her inability to eat had nothing to do with the food, and everything to do with Emma: she was so afraid that—

"Stop worrying." His tone made it an order. "If it makes you feel any better, the team searching for your sister-in-law has a promising lead on that van. The route they took away from the scene went right past an ATM, and the vehicle was caught on video."

Riley stared at him, transfixed, as hope bloomed inside her. Then her eyes narrowed suspiciously. He was telling her that because, once again, he'd clearly been able to read her like a book.

"Is that the truth?" she asked.

He was gulping coffee. When he came up for air, he said, "You know, sometimes I get the feeling you don't trust me."

Riley didn't bother to make the obvious reply. Instead she asked, "How do you know that about the van?"

"I met an operative at the gas station back there." He returned the coffee to the cup holder, snagged a trio of french fries, and scarfed them. His gaze slid in her direction. "Guy I handed the SIM card off to for analysis. He told me."

That would explain why he'd been gone so long. It also alleviated a small degree of her worry about the SIM card: if Finn wasn't checking it personally, it was far less likely that the fact that his picture was on it would come to his attention. But at the moment, none of that mattered. Turning in her seat so that she faced him more fully, voice eager, she asked, "What else did they say? Do they have any idea who took her or where she is? Oh, my God, do they know if she's safe? Are they close to finding her?"

"There's no reason to think she's not safe, but other than that I've told you all I know." His glance flicked down to her barely tasted burger. "We'll get her back. Eat your food."

Riley wanted to ask more, but if that was the extent of his knowledge there wasn't much point. She knew she needed to eat so she picked up the burger and took another bite and then a third. Swallowing—it was like trying to choke down mouthfuls of toilet paper—she made a face at him. "Happy now?"

"Keep eating," he said.

"Are you always this bossy?" She managed yet another bite as he provided her with a sterling example by polishing off what was left of his second burger with apparent enjoyment.

"Only when I'm babysitting."

She was in the act of swallowing as he said that. His words, laced by an unexpected touch of humor, made her choke. Quickly she reached for her Diet Coke.

"Babysitting?" she asked, too politely, when she could speak again.

"Whatever you want to call it." His voice was wry. "This thing I'm doing with you."

"Not babysitting," she warned him. "And for the record, I'm not a fan of bossy men."

"I'll keep that in mind." The afternoon sunlight was blinding as it reflected off the pavement and the shiny surfaces of the passing vehicles, and he hooked his sunglasses out of his pocket and put them back on in self-defense. Not having brought any with her, Riley had to make do with lowering the visor to block the worst of the sun. He continued, "Speaking of how much you like bossy men, I'm curious: how's your relationship with George?"

That was not a topic designed to stimulate her appetite. Giving up on the whole lunch thing and slipping what was left of her burger into the bag to be discarded later, she sipped at her drink.

"I don't like him, he doesn't like me."

"Why is that?

Riley shrugged. "Does it matter?"

"It might."

"I don't see how." But then, because she didn't see any reason not to tell him, she added, "When Jeff brought me home with him to Houston, we'd been married three months. He hadn't even told his family about me, which I didn't realize until we stepped inside Oakwood. Margaret was shocked, but she was welcoming, and Emma"—Riley's voice caught as she thought of Emma—"was great. She said she was glad to have a sister. George, on the other hand, pitched a fit, the gist of which was I wasn't good enough to be part of his family. He never changed his opinion. I encouraged Jeff to stand up to him, and he didn't like that, either. George bullied Jeff. Well, he bullied everybody, Margaret and Emma, as well, but Jeff worked for him so that made it worse. George wanted him to be a hardheaded, tough businessman, which Jeff just wasn't. He tried to dictate his every move, and it was obvious Jeff was afraid of him, although he never would admit it. I think a lot of Jeff's problems—" She broke off. There was no point in going into that: Jeff's problems were history, over and done with, rendered irrelevant by his death, a reality that she faced with a pang. "Well, it doesn't matter now. But George and I are not what you'd call best buds."

"Then what makes you think, if he actually has the money, he'll tell you where it is?" Finn's tone was silky smooth. Nonetheless, the question jolted Riley.

She was surprised at herself, she thought wrathfully: she actually hadn't seen that coming. She'd thought they were simply talking, getting to know each other, maybe, and come to find out he was *interrogating* her again.

"He loves Emma," she said shortly. Then as Finn started to ask her something else she decided enough was enough, and interrupted with "Hold it. I'm tired of talking about me. Let's talk about something else." Her eyes glinted at him. "Like, say, you."

She thought he glanced at her, but it was hard to tell with the sunglasses in place.

"Me," he said. It wasn't a question. It was more of a skepticism-laced statement.

Oh, yeah. Time to turn the tables.

"Yes," she said with relish. "You've been questioning me since we met. I've got a few questions I'd like to ask you."

"Have at it." His tone made it clear that he was prepared to humor her.

"How old are you?" she shot at him.

"Thirty-seven."

It occurred to her that there was something she didn't know that she really should find out. "Married?"

Again she got the impression that he was glancing at her. "No."

Much as she hated to admit it, that was a relief.

"Ever been?"

"No."

"Children?"

"No."

"Girlfriend? Significant other?"

"Not at present."

"When was your last serious relationship?"

"Forget it. No comment."

"You did a background check on me. I'm guessing you know just about everything I've ever done in my life, including all about *my* relationships." She took his silence as an admission that she was right, and pressed on. "Last serious relationship?"

His mouth tightened. "It's been a while."

"How long?"

"I don't know. A while."

"You do too know."

"You're pretty damned interested in my love life."

"You're pretty damned defensive about it. That makes it interesting."

He made a sound of exasperation. "Her name was Jennifer. We broke up about three and a half years ago. Okay?"

"Why?"

"Jesus. She wanted to get married, start a family. I didn't."

"Why not?"

"Because I didn't."

"So you've just been casually dating in the three and a half years since?"

"I'm done talking about this subject. You got something else you want to ask me about?"

Riley considered. There was still a ton of stuff she wanted to know, so she decided to move on in the interest of keeping him from clamming up.

"Parents?" she asked.

"Yes. Two."

Her eyes narrowed at him. "Ha-ha. What are their names? What do they do for a living? And don't tell me you don't know that about me, because I know you do."

"Robert Bradley. An accountant. Died when I was five. Janet Bradley Oppenheimer. A schoolteacher who got remarried to a dentist when I was seven."

Looking at the hard-faced, hard-bodied, armed and dangerous man beside her, it was difficult to imagine him as the son of an accountant and a teacher.

"Is your mother still alive?"

"Yes."

"Where does she live?"

She thought he hesitated for a second. "Seattle."

"Is that where you grew up?"

"Yes."

"Do you have siblings?"

"Three younger sisters. Well, half-sisters."

Riley stared at him. He'd grown up in an upper-middle-class household in Seattle with a teacher mother, a dentist stepfather, and *three little sisters*.

Okay, she was finding it increasingly difficult to be afraid of him.

"You just officially blew my mind," she said.

"And why is that?" There was a note of testiness in his voice.

"That sounds so"—*great, appealing, wonderful*—"wholesome."

"Yeah, so?"

"I just—" She shook her head. "I'm having trouble picturing it. Are you close with them? Do you visit?"

"I make it home for the major holidays."

"You don't live in Seattle, I take it?"

"No."

"Where do you live?"

"Wyoming. On a small, run-down ranch I'm trying to get up and running again. And yes, it snows a lot in the winter and no, I don't mind. Anything else you want to know?"

He was sounding testy again. Riley looked at him consideringly.

"So how did you end up becoming an FBI agent?"

A subtle tension in his face caught her attention. "I got recruited out of college."

There was more to the story, she could tell. "And?"

"And, what? I signed on, got trained, went to work. Here we are."

She gave him a long look. "That leaves out a lot."

"What do you want, a blow-by-blow?"

She recognized the same smart-ass response she'd given him earlier right off the bat, thank you.

"So how long have you and Bax been partners?" Her eyes narrowed. "Where is he, by the way?"

"He's off doing his job, and, not that long," he replied, his tone making it clear that he wasn't going to elaborate. She was getting ready to probe for more anyway when he veered into the slow lane and got in line behind a lumbering car carrier. Even as Riley gave him a questioning look, he gestured at a rest stop sign and added, "I need to stretch my legs. We're pulling off here for a minute."

Which, she thought, was his way of saying, *I'm done talking*.

— CHAPTER —
TWENTY-FOUR

After that, once they'd stopped and were back in the car, they came to an agreement: if Finn wouldn't interrogate her, Riley wouldn't interrogate him. Still, after a few miles passed in seething silence, they ended up talking, on such neutral but diverse topics as the state of the economy, the current political situation, religion (he knew about her background; she discovered that he was raised Methodist), speed dating, college majors, favorites (movies, TV shows, books, foods) and the merits of living in Texas versus Wyoming, with a few observations about Philadelphia and, as they passed the WELCOME TO OKLAHOMA sign, that state, too, thrown in for good measure.

They were just pulling into what a dusty green sign announced was Stringtown when a faint buzzing that seemed to be coming from Finn silenced them both. He frowned, Riley looked at him in surprise, and then as he reached into his pocket she realized that the sound came from a cell phone set on vibrate that was accidentally reverberating against the side of the plastic console.

In other words, making a sound that she could hear.

"Uh-oh," Riley taunted, because it was clear from Finn's sour look as he fished it out that the phone had been set on vibrate precisely so she *wouldn't* hear it. As he glanced down at the caller ID then pressed the button to answer, she realized that the call must be important and any last trace of a desire to tease him fled. Instantly she thought, *news of Emma.* Tensing, she looked at him with worried eyes.

"Riley's right beside me," was the first thing Finn said into the phone, which of course told her that he wanted the caller to be careful of what he said in case she should overhear. Then he mouthed "Bax" at her. From Finn's side of the conversation—mostly monosyllables—Riley couldn't make heads or tails out of it, and the few words she could hear of Bax's end—*today, hospital*—only alarmed her. When Finn disconnected without so much as a good-bye, the first thing he said, before she could even ask, was, "Nothing to do with Emma, so you can quit looking at me like that."

Once again, her face was clearly way too easy for him to read. Riley slumped a little in her seat as some of her tension ebbed. Her fear for Emma was a hard, cold knot in her chest that wouldn't go away. She'd hoped the phone call might be good news, but from what she'd overheard and the look on Finn's face, no such luck.

"Remember, nobody's going to hurt her as long as they think they can use her to get the money," Finn reminded her, and Riley nodded dispiritedly.

"So what was that about?" she asked.

"George was attacked today. Stabbed. He's in the prison hospital. You won't be able to talk to him until tomorrow."

Riley's mouth dropped open.

"Dear God," she said. "How bad is it?"

"Bax said he's going to survive." Finn's voice was grim. "This time."

"*This* time?" Riley felt cold all over. "It was because of the money, wasn't it?"

"At a guess, I'd say yes, but nobody's talking. Not George, and not the guy who did it."

"They caught him?"

"Yep."

"Can't somebody *make* him talk?" The question came out in a frustrated rush before Riley had a chance to think about it—there really was no way in American society to make someone talk if they didn't want to—but the expression on Finn's face in response startled her. It said, as clearly as words might have done, *I could*. Then it was gone, quick as that.

His face was unreadable again, but Riley knew what she had seen.

She thought of his picture on Jeff's phone. She thought of how he'd known how long it took to drown someone. She thought of the impression she'd gotten that he was dangerous, and what felt like an icy hand gripped her heart.

"Ten a.m. suit you?" he asked.

It took her a second, but then she understood: that's when she would talk to George. As she nodded, Finn pulled off into the parking lot of a Comfort Inn and Suites.

"You're staying with me, so I got us one room," he said as he pulled the suitcases from the trunk. That slight smile of his appeared. "Two beds, though."

She didn't protest. The attack on George had underlined how much danger she and Emma and Margaret were in. In response to Finn's instructions, she walked into the hotel a few steps ahead of him, apparently to keep him between her and any attack that might come from the direction of the parking lot. As she did, she thought, *Without him, I'd be a sitting duck.*

The shiver that slid down her spine was a stark reminder of how very vulnerable she was. And how very dependent on him she was.

Whatever he is, whatever he's done, right now I need him. Dangerous or not.

They got settled in the room—two queen beds, a credenza holding a TV against the wall opposite, plus a small sitting area with a couch, chair, and desk, all decorated in tasteful earth tones—and freshened up. Then Finn took her to dinner.

She wasn't hungry—shades of Emma!—but she kept that to herself and went. He clearly was, and once again she knew she needed to eat.

There wasn't a lot of choice. A café in the downtown area, the ubiquitous McDonald's, and a Waffle

House. They settled on the café. The town was tiny, less than a thousand people. It was a collection of run-down red-brick buildings and a few outlying stores, all mostly there for the purpose of supporting the staff and visitors of the sprawling Mack H. Alford Correctional Center, which was visible as a shimmering mirage of chain-link fences and squat buildings just a few miles down the road. The surrounding landscape was hilly and mostly brown with heat, although a few blades of grass and some valiant trees showed green.

"So how are you going to put this to George tomorrow?" Finn asked. They were ensconced in a booth in the café, and he was seated across from her. The booth was in a corner, Finn having refused the waitress's offer of a prime seat in front of the big front picture window (he didn't say why, but his refusal gave Riley an instant, hair-raising vision of snipers with rifles). From where they sat, she could still see out. She watched as the orange blaze of the setting sun was extinguished by a mass of purple clouds, and tongues of lightning began to flicker in the distance.

The café was surprisingly busy. It was noisy and full of good smells, the air-conditioning worked, and the red vinyl bench seats were cracked but comfortable. The waitress having taken their order, Riley was already sipping gratefully at a tall glass of sweet tea, while Finn drank root beer.

Riley frowned at him reprovingly. "Did anybody ever tell you that you have a one-track mind?"

"With George being injured, you're probably not going to have all day to beat around the bush. It'd be a good idea to be prepared with exactly what you're going to say."

"Tell me what you did with the money, you mean old goat, or I'll stab you again myself?"

The tightening of his mouth told her what he thought of her flippancy. "Riley—"

The waitress appeared carrying a tray, and started putting their food on the table. Finn quit talking until the woman asked, "Anything else I can get for you?" and, when they shook their heads, left them alone again.

"You need to go in with a plan. A few key points you want to make." The fact that he was dumping ketchup on meatloaf—his plate was loaded with meatloaf, mashed potatoes, and green beans—didn't detract from the determination in the look he directed at her.

"I have a plan." Riley dipped a fork into the tuna part of her tuna salad plate and smiled at him across the table. "Wing it."

That got a rise out of him, as it was meant to do.

"Damn it." He put the ketchup down. "This is serious."

"You want serious? Fine. Here's serious: I think I can figure out what to say without you trying to coach me. So stop." She ate tuna.

Clearly exasperated, he looked at her for a moment without replying.

"Eat your food," Riley said, not quite maliciously, and ate more tuna.

He ate a couple of forkfuls, then said, "You're beautiful."

For some reason, that didn't sound like it was meant to be a compliment. "Thank you." She narrowed her eyes at him.

"You're smart, too."

"You want to get to the point here?"

"You're lying to me."

"What?" Riley's eyes didn't widen. She didn't choke on her tuna, but it was close.

Her first thought was, *Pot, meet kettle*. Her second was, *Oh, crap*.

He said, "It's time to come clean."

Riley's chest tightened as guilt bubbled up inside her. Finn was looking at her, his blue-gray eyes holding hers like he could see inside her head. Okay, she told herself to quell the little curls of panic that were starting to twist through her veins, he might be able to read her easily but there was no way he could *know*. Anything. At least, not anything important.

Keep your mouth shut. Stand your ground.

"How did you know?" she asked on a shaky-sounding breath.

Putting down his fork, he looked suddenly grim. "Talk to me, Angel. I'm listening."

That *angel* did funny things to her insides. Actually, she discovered unwillingly, *he* did funny things to her insides. Just like she was still in her yellow dress, he was still wearing the charcoal suit, but he'd unbuttoned his collar and lost the tie. Against the white shirt, his throat looked brown and strong. Stubble darkened his square jaw. His mouth was tense, and his eyes were bloodshot, with the faint lines around his eyes noticeably deeper than before. He looked dark and tired and irritable, he was a federal law enforcement officer who was taking advantage of their forced proximity to interrogate her every chance he got, and he had just accused her of telling him lies.

And, oh, yeah, dangerous or not, she wanted him. Bad.

It was stupid. She wasn't proud of it. But there it was.

"All right, I did lie," she confessed, her eyes wide as she held his intent gaze. "Earlier. When I was in the bathroom, and you didn't come back, and I said I wasn't worried about you? That just wasn't true. I *was* worried about you."

For a moment his expression didn't change. Then it did: his brows snapped together and his mouth compressed and he looked *dire*.

She grinned. A big ol' pure Texas shit-eating grin. She couldn't help it.

Their eyes held. Hers, she knew, twinkled. His did not.

Then his face relaxed, and he smiled. Not that little uptick that she'd started to think was all he was capable of, but a real smile. Even if it was a little wry.

"Funny." He went back to eating his meat loaf. She took a couple more bites of tuna. Then he gave her a level look and said, "Sooner or later, I'm going to find out."

She devoutly hoped not. In fact, she was going to do everything in her power to make sure he did not.

Ignoring the prickle of apprehension that slid like

goose bumps over her skin, she shook her head re- provingly at him. "Like I said, one-track mind."

The waitress returned then, with their check and an offer of coffee. Riley declined. Finn paid, and took his coffee to go.

Outside, it was dark. It had cooled off a little from earlier, but the humidity made the air feel thick. The moon looked like a fuzzy white cotton ball in a field of midnight blue. A few stars played peek-a-boo among the scudding clouds. The night smelled of ap- proaching rain. To the west, the flickers of lightning were bigger and stronger now.

When they were in the car driving the short dis- tance back to the hotel, Finn looked at her and said, "You'd be better off telling me whatever it is you're hiding before I figure it out on my own."

Riley had been reluctantly admiring the strong masculine lines of his profile against the glow of the hotel's security lights.

Almost glad to have her thoughts diverted, she frowned at him as he turned into the parking lot. "You think so?"

He sent her an impatient look. "Cut the crap. I know there's something. You need to tell me."

"Newsflash, Mr. Agent Man: I don't know what you're talking about."

He'd just finished parking. At her response, the muscles in his face contracted, his mouth hardened, and as he shot a look at her his eyes glinted steel blue.

"Yeah, you do. Come on, we don't want to hang around in the parking lot."

As they were walking inside, with his hand on her arm and him a pace behind her, looking for all the world like he was escorting a prisoner to jail, it occurred to her that spending the night alone in a hotel room with a man she'd decided might very well be dangerous wasn't something any minimally prudent woman would do.

She kept walking anyway.

He didn't say anything else, and neither did she. Kicking off her shoes, she went into the bathroom as soon as they reached the room. When she came out, he'd taken off his jacket and had his gun on the night-stand between the beds. He was standing at the foot of the bed nearest to the door and was in the process of unbuttoning his shirt.

His eyes raked her. He was looking tall and dark and ill-tempered, and his sheer size made the space feel surprisingly small.

"It's all yours." She indicated the bathroom, and started to walk past him toward the sitting area, with some thought of turning on CNN and trying to catch the day's news.

She didn't make it past him. His hand shot out to flatten against the wall. His arm formed a barrier in front of her nose, stopping her in her tracks.

Frowning, she looked up at him. "What?"

His eyes were hard. "If you're involved in this scheme of George's, you're looking at prison. That's if the system gets you. If I go away, if somebody who's not part of the system gets hold of you, they'll torture you to get the information they want out of you and then they'll kill you. You understand that, right?"

Riley cast her eyes heavenward. "You are a broken record." Since his arm blocked her from the sitting room, she turned to go the other way.

His other arm shot out, trapping her between them. Her eyes narrowed. She faced him, scowling and prepared to verbally blast him. He didn't quite have her pinned to the wall, there was still some room, but her body brushed his and her hands came up to flatten against his chest to hold him off and her breath caught as her heart started to pick up the pace. His eyes were unreadable as he looked down at her, but she could see the quickening of the pulse in his throat, feel the heat coming off him.

"I don't like bullies," she said. "Get out of my way."

He made a sound that wasn't quite a laugh. "I'm trying to save your ass here."

"Is that what you're doing?" She glared up at him. He was way bigger than she was, taller, wider, strong enough where any thought of a physical contest between them was laughable. Their bodies barely touched, but where they did she knew it. Beneath the cool smooth cotton of his shirt, she could feel the tension in his muscles. She could feel the electricity surging between them, and she could tell by the tightening of his jaw and the darkening of his eyes that he did, too. "Funny, feels to me like you're trying to intimidate me."

"Does it?" His eyes slid over her face, his mouth tightened, and then his arms dropped and he made a be-my-guest gesture indicating that she was free to walk away. She didn't. She didn't want to. She stayed right where she was, her hands pressed to his chest, her face lifted to his pugnaciously. Because now the heat that was rolling off him was enveloping her, too, and her body was quickening and tightening and she was finding it harder to breathe. "What I'm trying to do is help you. You need to trust me."

When hell freezes over, is what she thought as all the reasons she shouldn't flashed through her mind. But her hands were closing on his shirt front and her heart was pounding like she was running and the dark, restless gleam in his eyes was melting her bones.

She didn't trust him, not one bit. But what she did do was go up on tiptoe and kiss him.

— CHAPTER —
TWENTY-FIVE

His mouth was warm, and firm, and stayed perfectly still as hers found it. Riley kissed him softly, parting her lips, moving them against his, loving how unmistakably masculine they felt, loving the rasp of his stubble against the soft skin of her cheeks and chin. Her lids were lowered so that she couldn't see his eyes, but she could see the sharp flare of his nostrils and the sudden tensing of his jaw. Her hands were fisted in his shirt, and she could feel the deepening of his breathing in the rise and fall of his chest, feel the hardening of the muscles beneath.

His mouth moved on hers, kissing her back but only barely, a feather-light molding of her lips that had her mouth clinging to his, wanting more. He deepened the kiss, licking into her mouth, and she shivered and kissed him back. As one hand came up to thrust deep into her hair, he took a step forward so that she had to take a step back, which brought her shoulder blades up against the cool plaster of the wall. Riley felt his long, strong fingers shaping the back of her skull. His other hand gripped her hip bone. She sensed desire on his part, and resistance, too, and was excited by both. Even as her body throbbed with arousal, even as her heart started to slam against her breastbone, even as she swayed so that she was arching up against him, he broke the kiss and lifted his head to look down at her.

"This your way of changing the subject?" The hot, dark glitter in his eyes, the growl in his voice, the rigidity of his body, told her how turned on he was. There was no mistaking his erection: it pressed against her, hard and thick even through the layers of their clothes.

She imagined it inside her, filling her, thrusting deep, and her blood turned to steam.

"What if it is?" Heart pounding, she stared up at him, almost taken by surprise by how much she wanted him. The chemistry had always been there between them. Now it was all but tangible, wrapping around them, flowing from her body to his. He felt it: there was no mistaking that, and yet he was resisting it still for some reason of his own. The hand in her hair tightened. So did the one on her hip. He was holding her in place, studying her face with unnerving intensity. It was clear from the increasing desire that blazed in his eyes that he was getting a pretty accurate read on what she was thinking about yet again.

And that would be sex. The air was laden with it. It was there in his eyes for her to see, and she had no doubt at all that it was there in hers.

"Sleeping with me isn't going to fix anything."

He said it as a warning, in a voice that was noticeably rougher and thicker than before. Besides the heat, there was a careful, calculating kind of caution in his eyes that was echoed in the hardness of his jaw, in the way he was holding her, holding himself back from her. She got the impression that part of him wanted to pull back, walk away, and yet he couldn't quite bring himself to do it.

"Who said I was going to sleep with you?" If she sounded breathless, well, that was because she was. The kiss had been an impulse, a mixture of desire and opportunity and, yes, a need to stop him from badgering her and get the balance of power between them back on a more equal level. The excitement it had roused in both of them was enough to render the reason for it moot. A maelstrom of emotions churned inside her: terror for Emma, grief for Jeff, anxiety for Margaret, fear for her own safety. But they were all receding into the background as, right now, in this moment, the man in front of her was rapidly becoming all she could think about, all she could see.

"Then what the hell is this?" The hand in her hair moved down to cradle the back of her neck.

"A kiss." It gave her some satisfaction to echo the words he'd said to her not so long ago.

"A kiss." There was a flatness to his voice, a patent disbelief. "And that's it?"

"I haven't decided yet."

Something dark and dangerous glinted in his eyes. His face hardened, and so did his hands on her. All of a sudden the wall at her back made her feel penned in.

His big body looming over her made her feel penned in. Even as aroused as she was, she didn't like the sensation, didn't like her sudden awareness that, physically, she was helpless against him and he could pretty much do whatever he wanted to do with her. Quick fantasy flashes of herself at his mercy might make her go all tight and shivery inside, they might make her pulse rate quicken and her bare toes curl into the carpet, but the reality of it awakened her pride, her fighting spirit, her innate sense of inviolable self that had never, ever knuckled in to anybody and never would.

His eyes slid over her face. "Better decide."

"I'm thinking."

"Think fast," he said, and lowered his head to kiss her again.

For a split second there, before their lips touched, while his hand that had been gripping her hip slid slowly up her rib cage toward her breast, she nearly panicked. She had the sensation that she was plunging deep into something she had no experience of, something that was already more than she had bargained on.

You started this, she reminded herself, and it was true, she had, but she could tell, from the fierce tension in his body, from the restless glitter in his eyes, from the way he was holding her, handling her, that she wasn't in charge. And then she had a blinding flash of insight in which she realized why she had always preferred gentler, more pliable men: she'd been the one directing the course of events. Always, all her life, she'd been the one to figure things out, the one to dictate what would happen next, the one to decide.

With Finn, she wasn't. What was happening between them was outside her comfort zone. *He* was
outside her comfort zone.

And that scared her.

She almost pushed against his chest, almost demanded to be let go.

But then his mouth covered hers, and he kissed
her, slow and sweet and not scary at all, and she was
dazzled, and tempted, and finally lost. Eyes closing,
she slid her arms around his neck, and went on tiptoe
and kissed him back with increasing abandon as her
body ignited and then went totally up in flames. He
was barefoot, which actually didn't ease the size differ-
ential much but did allow their toes to touch. His were
warm, and a glance down showed her that they were
long, and tan, with nicely trimmed square nails, and
made a noticeable contrast to her own paler, more delicate, coral-painted ones. She could feel the long, firm
muscles of his legs beneath the well-tailored suit pants.
Higher up, the stiff ridge of his erection was impossible to miss. It was there between them, aggressive in its
sheer size, blatant in letting her know what he wanted.
She responded to it instinctively by moving closer,
fitting herself against him, and then reaching down
to touch him. She stroked a questing finger along the
iron-hard bulge, and it instantly seemed to grow larger
and harder still until it tested the restraint of his pants.
He made an indecipherable sound under his breath and
grabbed her hand and pulled it away from him, settling it back on his shoulder, kissing her with an almost
savage intensity as he leaned into her, full-body crush,

pressing her back into the wall. Only now, instead of being dismayed at finding herself trapped, she was on fire for him, loving the way he felt, the heat and solid strength of his body, the size of him, the weight of him.

Her head spun. Her knees felt weak. Her body molded itself to his, arching up so that she could feel the hardness of his muscles—all his muscles—wedged even more completely against her. He shifted so that the iron hardness she'd stroked nudged the notch between her thighs, settled there, rocked into her, making her mindless, making her move against him, making her shudder and quake.

She wanted him so much that she was woozy with it. The blazing sexual attraction that had raged between them from the first was now a wildfire that was out of control.

His hand found her breast, and any last hope of rational thought she had left vanished. She was blind-sided by sensation, by her own white-hot reaction to his touch. The hungry demand of his lips on hers, the hot urgency of his tongue filling her mouth, the pure pleasure of having his hand on her breast and his body rocking into hers, drove everything else out of her mind. Her bones turned to water. Her muscles dissolved. Deep inside, her body throbbed and clenched. She shivered as he caressed her through the delicate layers of her dress with its built-in bra. Then his thumb found and rubbed her nipple. It stiffened and stood up for him, and the resultant ripple of desire had her arching up into his hand as she wordlessly begged for more.

"Made a decision yet?" He whispered it into the

ear he was kissing before trailing his lips down the side of her neck. The wet heat of his mouth, the prickle of the stubble on his jaw against her skin, the warm, caressing hand on her breast, made her pulse race. They interfered with her breathing.

It took willpower, but she opened her eyes, sucked in air, strove for clarity. Her vision was instantly filled by his dark head bent low over her as he kissed her throat, by the nape of his brown neck, by his broad shoulders in the white shirt curved around her. The faint smell of menthol from his shaving cream intoxicated her. She had to swallow before she could reply.

"Still thinking." Breathy, passion-drugged voice. Coherent answer, even if she wasn't sure it was true.

He lifted his head, studied her face. His eyes blazed down at her. His hand never left her breast.

"Oh, yeah?" The slight uptick of his mouth as it dipped toward hers was so sexy it made her heart beat faster. "Angel, any time you want to call a halt, all you have to do is say 'when.'"

She didn't reply because she couldn't. She was so turned on she could barely breathe, let alone speak. Then his mouth found hers again, and thinking was out, too. All that was left to her was to feel.

They kissed, hot fierce kisses, and while they did she started working on his shirt buttons until she had them undone and she could slide her hands up over his chest. His wide, hard-muscled chest with its wedge of dark hair was a visual treat that seared itself into her mind: honed and tanned and gorgeous, it was, like the rest of him, unmistakably, overwhelmingly male.

His skin was smooth and hot, the hair covering it was crisp, and the muscles beneath could have been carved out of granite. As her hands moved sensuously over him, he thrust his tongue deep into her mouth with a growl and rocked into her until Riley thought she would come right there and then.

Her heart thundered. Her pulse pounded in her ears. She was shaken by delicious little tremors of lust that made her want to go ahead and push him to the floor and jump his bones.

She might have done it, too, if what he was doing to her wasn't so mind-blowingly delicious, and if he hadn't been too damned big to move.

His hand slid inside her neckline to cover her bare breast. The heat of his hand, the abrasion of his rougher skin sliding over the silkiness of hers, the pressure of his broad palm moving sensuously over her nipple, sent a shock wave of pleasure through her. It turned her insides to something with the approximate consistency of Jell-O. Hot, thick, molten Jell-O.

Then the top of her dress came loose and she heard a kind of slither, and felt the whisper of air-conditioning on tender flesh that had until that moment been covered by layers of cloth. Her eyes opened, and she cast a slightly disoriented look down at herself to discover that the movement of his hand on the back of her neck that she'd been vaguely aware of had been him unbuttoning the four small buttons that fastened the halter neck of her dress. The entire front of her dress, built-in bra and all, had dropped, leaving her bare to the wide, snug waistband that still encased her waist.

Her breasts were firm and round. A nice size for her slender frame, they were creamy white with dark pink nipples, and she'd always liked them. Now she contrasted their soft fullness with the big, tanned, blatantly masculine hand that fondled them even as she watched, and felt her bones dissolve.

As her breath caught, she glanced up to find that he was watching what he was doing to her, too. He must have felt the weight of her gaze, because he looked up and their eyes met. His were darker than she'd ever seen them, heavy-lidded, smoldering at her.

"You are the most beautiful thing I've ever seen in my life." It was a husky murmur, uttered as he bent to take the nipple of the breast he was cupping into his mouth.

If she hadn't been clinging to his shoulders for support at that moment, she would have slithered right down the wall to the floor. His mouth felt so good, so scaldingly hot, so insistent, that the spiral of need he'd already wakened coiled tighter and tighter until she was pure liquid fire inside and absolutely his for the taking.

"Finn," she said, too weak with longing now even to start pulling off his clothes, which she wanted to do, or start stripping off the rest of her own clothes, which she also wanted to do, or in fact to do anything else except hold on to him as he kissed and licked and suckled her. What he was doing made her so tight and so shivery inside that she thought she might be going to die from the thrill of it.

"Riley." His voice was thick. His tone was surprising. It was absolutely serious, somber even, as if her name had weight. He lifted his head, looked at her consideringly. His eyes were narrow and hot. His face was flushed and his hair was mussed from having her fingers in it. His mouth was hard and sensual and faintly damp, as were the tips of her breasts from his kisses. Just looking at him made her breathless, made her dizzy, made her heart feel like it was going to pound its way out of her chest.

She wanted to say what she'd started to say, but the way he was looking at her suddenly made it impossible for her to draw enough air into her lungs to speak. She swallowed, tried again.

"Is this you trying to say 'when'?" he asked carefully. His hands tightened on her waist. His face had gone absolutely still. No expression, no emotion at all, except for the dark gleam in his eyes.

She shook her head. She might be making a bad mistake here. In fact, she probably was making a bad mistake here. Bottom line, she didn't care. However this whole thing worked out, she would have at best a night or two with him. She would take them, take him.

Her nails dug into his shoulders. Her knees threatened to give way.

She said, "This is me trying to say, make love to me."

TWENTY-SIX

Finn looked at her for a moment longer, his hard face inscrutable, nothing at all to read in it except the blaze of desire in his eyes. He didn't say a word. Instead he bent his head and kissed her.

It was a deep, slow, hungry kiss that was so hot it practically steamed up the air around them. Eyes closing, she kissed him back passionately, all pent-up longing and urgent physical need. She was so intoxicated by the lush demand of his mouth on hers, by the warmth and firm resilience of his bare chest pressing against her breasts, by the satiny smoothness of his heavy shoulders as she clung to them, that she almost missed the tiny sound of a zipper being lowered.

Then her dress dropped the rest of the way, all the way to the carpet, where it puddled around her feet. She realized that while he'd been kissing her he had unzipped the small zipper at her waist that held up the rest of her dress, which allowed her skirt to slide down her legs to the floor, which left her standing there in nothing but a pair of tiny nude-colored silk-and-lace panties.

He broke off the kiss to hold her a little away from him. The carnal gleam in his eyes was so erotic that she practically melted where she stood as he looked over every nearly naked inch of her. After an immobilized-by-lust moment, she took advantage of his superheated inattention to anything except her body to lean in, press her lips to his wide, warm chest, and reach for his belt.

His abdomen was ridged with muscle. As her mouth opened on his chest, as her fingers brushed the firm flesh around his belly button while she grappled with his buckle, he sucked in air and his already taut stomach tightened even more.

"Damn," he muttered, his focus finally back on her face as the buckle surrendered. She couldn't resist the urge to stroke his ripped belly, but she didn't have a chance to go for bigger game. He caught her hands, his eyes blazing at her. "You're killing me here."

Before she could reply or do anything else, he scooped her up as easily as if she weighed nothing at all, kissed her like he was starving for the taste of her mouth, and carried her the few steps to his bed. His hold on her turned briefly precarious as he yanked the covers down. Settling her into the middle of the mat-tress, he straightened, pulled his shirt the rest of the way off, then unzipped his pants and shucked them and a pair of, she observed with interest, blue boxers at the same time.

He'd deposited her on her back. She propped

herself up on her elbows to watch him strip. Besides the bathroom light, which she'd left on, the twin lamps between the beds were the room's sole source of illumination. With them behind him, he looked almost formidably big and tough. His front was in shadow, but not so much so that she couldn't see vital details. She had just a second to admire the buff body he bared. Heavily muscled shoulders and chest. Corded arms. Six-pack abdomen with a puckered scar below the navel that she vowed to ask him about later. Narrow hips. Long, athletic-looking legs. A nice amount of dark body hair.

As his pants hit the floor, she looked at the long, thick erection that she could finally see, and sucked in her breath.

She'd been able to tell from the first time she'd felt it pressing against her, so it wasn't like it was a surprise or anything: the man was seriously hung.

"Nice," she said, as nonchalantly as if her heart wasn't pounding and she wasn't breathing way too fast and her nails weren't digging into the mattress and her body wasn't burning and quaking inside with anticipation, when she felt his eyes on her and glanced up to find that he was looking at her looking at him.

"I would have said, gorgeous. Sexy. Perfect." His voice was hoarse. His face was flushed with passion, and his eyes were dark with it, and his mouth was hard with it. From the way he was looking at her, she knew he was talking about her. He put a knee on the mattress and then came down on the bed beside her, his weight enough to roll her toward him. Even as, trembling now, she reached for him, he gathered her in his arms and kissed her with a controlled ferocity that told her he was done playing. Wrapping her arms around his neck, she kissed him back, arching up against him, reveling in the feel of his naked body against hers, wanting him so much that she was dizzy with it.

His hand slid between her legs to touch her through her panties. Scorching heat shot through her as he found just the right spot, and she gasped into his mouth. Then his hand was inside her panties and he was stroking the delicate cleft without any barrier at all and somewhere along the way she lost every last inhibition she had. The steely strength of his body against the softness of hers drove her wild.

Clinging to him, kissing him like she'd die if she didn't, she squirmed and moaned in response to those long, knowing fingers, roused to a fever pitch by a man who clearly knew what he was doing, knew his way around a woman's body.

"Finn," she gasped as his mouth left hers to kiss her neck and breasts while his hand still played between her legs. She was on fire, burning up, moving restlessly against his hand, against him, kissing his ear and his bristly jawline and his throat and his broad shoulder. The salty taste of his skin inspired her to lick him, tiny sensuous licks along his shoulder, and then nibble at the firm flesh beneath her mouth. He made a sound and shifted his shoulder and pushed his fingers deeply inside her in sexy retaliation, and that was it: she couldn't stand it anymore. She moaned and reached for that part of him that she could feel lying hot and hard against her thigh. At the same time, he muttered something under his breath and stopped with the petting of her and started yanking her panties down her legs.

Then her hand closed around him.

"Riley." Sounding like he was being strangled, he stiffened and went totally still. She could hear the harsh rasp of his breathing, feel him shuddering against her as he fought to retain control, feel the urgency of his need that rolled off him in waves.

His shaft was hot and smooth and hard and enormous and pulsing in her hand. She squeezed it, then slowly slid her hand up and down.

"I want you," she said, as if what she was doing to him hadn't been enough to make her meaning crystal clear. "Now."

"Jesus God." The savagery of his answering growl made her clench inside. It made her heart pound. It made her shiver and pant.

Then her panties came off and she was on her back and he was covering her body with his and shoving himself inside her, all so fast that all she could do was grab his shoulders and hang on and cry out at the sheer, unbelievable pleasure of it. As he kissed her, as he filled her to bursting and pulled back and did it again, she wrapped her arms around his neck and her legs around his waist and moaned into his mouth. He felt huge and hard and hot inside her, and he thrust into her with a controlled ferocity that had her crying out at the wonder of it and arching her back and moving with him. His strokes were deep and fast, and he drove into her over and over again until she was mindless with passion, shaking with it, throbbing and melting with it.

At last she came with an intensity she had never dreamed she was capable of, and as he drove into her fiercely one last time to find his own release she saw a thousand exploding stars and cried out his name.

"Finn. Oh, *Finn*."

RILEY FELT boneless. She felt like all her muscles had turned to water. She felt warm, and sleepy, and absolutely, positively sated. She also felt like she had glimpsed something, been somewhere, that was totally unknown to her.

Chemistry: that was all she could attribute it to. This big, hard, tough-looking guy had just officially shown her a whole new sexual world.

Finn. Even mentally saying his name made her shiver. It made her insides tighten. It made her toes curl.

Okay, enough already. She could drool over him and what had just happened between them later. Right now, he needed to move.

He was sprawled on top of her, spent, his head buried in the curve of her shoulder and neck, and he weighed a ton.

Even lifting a hand was an effort, but she trailed her fingers down his side. It must have tickled, because he flinched. Then his head came up, and she found herself looking into his eyes. Unlike the last time she'd gotten a glimpse of them, they were once again their usual calm blue-gray. She realized that the lamps were still on, that she could see him perfectly, from the black bristles on his square jaw to the slight frown that was contracting his brows to the heavily muscled shoulders that loomed above her. She realized, too, that he could see her equally well, and had been able to the *whole time*.

Good thing she wasn't shy.

"Hey." He dropped a kiss on her mouth, then rolled onto his back, taking her with him so that she ended up half lying on his chest, half sprawled at his side.

"Hey." She pressed a forearm down on his chest and lifted up a little so that she was now looming above him, and could look down into his face. His expression was absolutely unreadable—*surprise*—but he looked so sexy with his head propped up by a pair of pillows and one arm bent behind it—the other was wrapped around her, with his hand splayed just north of her ass—that she started melting all over again. The feel of his warm, solid body against her, the freedom to be naked with him and squirm all over him and basically do whatever she liked, was intoxicating.

Gravely she told him, "Best. Sex. Ever," and felt a tingle of delight as she watched his inscrutable expression vanish, watched his eyes widen slightly with surprise.

Then he smiled, not that little uptick of his, but his second real smile of the night. This time it actually widened into a full-blown grin. "Oh, yeah?"

"Yeah."

The grin was still there as he pulled her head down and kissed her. Then rolled with her. Then proceeded to give her a demonstration of his techniques for the Best Sex Ever all over again.

―――――――

SHE MUST have fallen asleep after that second round of mind-blowing sex, because she dreamed of Emma. It was a scary, mixed-up replay of her kidnapping and the horrors she might now be suffering, and it got worse as somehow dream Emma morphed into Lorna and died.

Sobbing in her dream, Riley woke up gasping for air to find herself flat on her back with the dark, shadowy head and shoulders of a man propped above her, silhouetted against the faint light coming in around the curtains.

For a moment she blinked at him, still lost in sorrow.

"Riley?"

That gravelly voice, the outline of the broad shoulders, the fact that he was in her bed and she was naked and he was naked, gave her his identity in a flash.

"Finn." She said it on a shuddery intake of breath. Reality descended, and she instantly knew everything, where they were, what was happening. They were both under the covers. The air-conditioning hummed, a constant background noise. At some point, he'd turned off the lights.

"Oh, God, it was a bad dream." She closed her

eyes, which as far as blocking out any kind of mental distress was concerned didn't work worth a dime.

He kissed her gently, lay back down, and pulled her into his arms. Her head lay on his shoulder. Her arm slanted across his chest. One leg curved over his. She could feel the naked length of him all down her body, sexy as hell, but now it was comforting, too.

"You were calling out for Lorna," he said.

The pain that came only rarely now went through her, sharp and bittersweet.

"My sister," she said, forgetting briefly that, thanks to the background check, he was bound to already know that. Anyway, right at that moment it didn't seem to even matter. "I was dreaming about Emma, and then Emma turned into Lorna, and Lorna died."

His arm tightened around her. "Emma's not going to die."

"You promise?" Her voice was fierce. She tilted her head to look up at him.

"I promise."

If she'd been in any state to notice, she would have realized that it said oceans about the change their relationship had undergone that she was willing to trust him on that. She let out a slow breath of relief.

"Tell me about Lorna." He smoothed her hair back from her face.

"She was my sister. She died." The words were abrupt. Her fingers had been lying flat on his chest. They curled into a fist.

"Riley."

He was asking for more. She could hear it in his

tone. So she closed her eyes and gave up and told him about the little sister who had been born with a congenital heart condition, who they'd always known would one day need a heart transplant, who after hanging on valiantly for years, after surviving the death of their mother and everything else life had thrown her way, had finally gotten sick enough to get onto the transplant list, and had then caught a virus and died. Nothing anyone could do, gone in two days.

Riley had lived with it for so long, she didn't even cry. But by the time she finished telling him, her heart was shredded.

"I'm sorry, Angel. So damned sorry."

His arms closed around her. He gathered her close and rocked her against him. She felt his lips in her hair. He soothed her, talked to her, pulled her thoughts away from Lorna and Emma and all things scary and bad by telling her stories about himself, about what it was like growing up in Seattle with three little sisters, about playing football in high school, things like that. She asked him about the scar on his abdomen and he told her he got shot, and then when she wanted him to elaborate he kissed her instead. Riley was just realizing that she was allowing herself to be well and truly distracted one more time when his mouth slid down to her breast. She looked at his dark head nuzzling her, and felt the hot pull of his mouth on her nipples, and promptly forgot about everything except the way he was making her feel.

FINN COULDN'T help it. He knew he was digging himself deeper and deeper into a hole that he might find it impossible to climb out of. He knew she was lying to him, hiding something from him. He knew that when this whole thing finally shook itself out there was liable to be hell to pay. He knew he was facing a bastard of a long day, and he and Riley both needed rest.

He knew all that, and he went ahead and made love to her most of the night anyway. Hell, he'd probably still be making love to her at that very moment if she hadn't, after that last steamy session, fallen into an exhausted sleep.

It had been, he told himself as he carefully disentangled their bodies and slid out of bed, one of those things where you've already so completely fucked up (literally) that you can't make the situation any worse than it already is, so you might as well enjoy it.

He should never have given in to temptation and slept with her.

Too late now.

In retrospect, he could see that sleeping with her had been all but inevitable from the moment he'd decided that they had to share a hotel room. But he didn't see that he'd had a choice about that: putting her in her own hotel room would have been like tethering a goat in the path of a jungle full of hungry tigers. One of them would have gotten to her. Kidnapping was the least of what might have happened to her. She could just as easily have been tortured and killed with him sound asleep in the room next door.

So he'd kept her with him. He'd told himself that

he was a professional, that he had himself well under control. And he did have himself under control. Until she kissed him. That had almost been a temptation too far, right there.

But he still could have saved it. He still could have kept the situation from going completely to hell. He'd observed that she had a problem with masculine aggression, and even knew the reason for it: the background check had revealed her mother's penchant for abusive boyfriends. It had been up to young Riley to protect the woman who should have been protecting her, time after time.

So when he'd seen that she hadn't liked being backed up against the wall, hadn't liked being reminded that he was bigger and she was smaller and sometimes size does matter, and seen that she was starting to panic a little at the thought that she couldn't get away from him, he could have gone with that. It wouldn't have taken much to have scared her off him for good and all, but he hadn't been able to do it. Scaring women wasn't something he did, and scaring Riley wasn't something he was prepared to do. Instead he had gentled her, letting her call the shots until she'd ended up in his bed.

Now he had to live with the consequences, while, not incidentally, keeping her safe and getting the job he'd been assigned to do done.

It didn't help, he thought as he took a moment to look her over to make sure she was still soundly asleep before he tucked the covers around her, that she really was, as he'd told her, just about the most beautiful thing he'd ever seen in his life. The room was dark, but not so dark that he couldn't see the curve of her lashes resting on her cheeks, and her softly parted lips, and the sweetly unconscious curve of her body.

Best sex ever. She'd surprised him with that. She'd surprised him with a lot of things.

Maybe the sex wouldn't prove to be such a disaster after all, he reflected as, having pulled on his pants and shirt, and picked up his gun, he quietly headed out into the hall for one more predawn conference with Bax. Women being what they were, there was a fair chance that she'd be feeling more trusting of him in the aftermath of having been well and truly fucked.

He hoped so, for both their sakes.

Bax, wearing plaid pajamas this time, came to his door blinking and yawning. The TV was silent but on in the background.

"You get everything set up?" Finn asked.

"Yeah." Bax let loose with a giant yawn, covered his mouth with his hand, and blinked at him. "Sorry. Uh—where is she?"

"In my room." Finn knew his face gave nothing away. What had happened between them—that was between him and Riley.

If Bax was entertaining any lascivious thoughts, they didn't show. "Thought so. Best way to keep her out of harm's way." He frowned at Finn. "Without us, she'd be in real trouble. What happens to her once we get what we came for?"

Finn shrugged.

Bax continued, "We have to make sure she's going to be all right once we're gone."

It occurred to Finn that, like him, Bax was opposed to seeing women get hurt.

"I agree. We'll take some steps to make sure she's safe. Count on it."

"In the meantime, she's got us," Bax said, and yawned again.

"She's got us," Finn concurred without allowing any of the irony he was feeling to show. "Go back to bed."

He turned to head back to his room.

"See you tomorrow," Bax called after him.

Finn answered with a wave.

— CHAPTER —
TWENTY-SEVEN

Riley was smiling. Only semi-awake, she lay there in warm comfort while hot images lingered in her mind and warm and fuzzy thoughts about the man who'd figured prominently in them danced like sugar plums through her head.

Finn. He was why she was smiling as she drifted back to full consciousness. It was ridiculous, stupid, and very un-Riley-like of her to smile like a fool over a man, but there it was.

Her body was pleasantly lethargic. It tingled in all the right places. She felt tired, but good. Really, really good.

She'd had sex with Finn. Phenomenal sex. Multiple times. Now she was sleeping with him.

Only he didn't seem to be anywhere in the bed. She stretched out an experimental hand to check: nothing.

She remembered that bed: it was a standard hotel

room bed, queen sized. No way could a man as large as Finn be anywhere in it that she wouldn't be able to feel him.

Her smile faded. Her eyes opened, swept the darkness. She was definitely alone in bed. As far as she could tell, she was alone in the room. A sliver of light shining beneath the door to the hall, plus some moonlight filtering in around the curtains, provided enough illumination for her to be sure. No Finn-sized lump in the second bed. No lump at all: the bedspread was perfectly flat. Could he be in the sitting area? Forcing herself up onto an elbow, she squinted at the couch and chair. Nope.

"Finn?"

No answer.

She looked toward the bathroom. The door was open and the bathroom was dark.

So where was . . . ?

A barely audible buzzing sound intruded on her consciousness. A quiet rattle that was separate and apart from the hum of the air-conditioning. She realized that it had been sounding intermittently ever since she'd woken up. In fact, it might well have been what had awakened her.

She tried to locate it and zeroed in on the bedside table. The sound was coming from inside the table. Inside the drawer.

Scrambling toward the edge of the bed, she opened the drawer.

A phone lay there in the bottom, right next to what looked like a couple of brochures and a Bible. It had to belong to Finn, unless a previous occupant of the room had left it behind.

It was vibrating. The vibration of the hard plastic case against the wood was the source of the buzzing sound. Even as Riley frowned down at it, she remembered how the phone in Finn's pocket had rattled against the car's console previously.

There was a text message glowing up at her on the front of the phone, clearly visible in a nice outlined bubble.

Personal privacy was a concept Riley understood and respected. Reading other people's text messages without their permission was a definite no-no.

She picked up the phone and read the message anyway.

It said: *Urgent. Computer inquiry into ID# 0045386, unable to identify source, possible security breach.*

Riley stared down at the phone. She had no idea what the message referred to. Her first thought, clearly a product of the night she'd just spent, was, *I'll ask Finn.*

Her second, slower, more cautious one was, *maybe not.*

With a quick glance at the door, she scrambled out of bed, went for her purse, and dug out her phone. Then she typed the message into her notes verbatim as fast as she could.

Not to be paranoid or anything, but whatever this was, she wanted to check it out herself. No need to let Finn know she'd even seen it.

He was a stud in bed: there was no getting around
that. He was also protective, considerate, and kind.
She liked him. Maybe more than liked him. Maybe
way more than liked him.

Trust him? She wanted to. She could tell him the
whole sorry story, ask him about his picture on Jeff's
cell phone, ask him what the text message meant,
promise that if he told her everything she would tell
him everything, too, and see how that went.

Of course, if it went wrong, it was going to go
wrong bad.

Alternatively, she could keep her mouth shut and
practice some due diligence.

Still thinking about it, she thrust her phone back
into her purse, returned the other phone to the drawer,
and crawled back into bed.

Which was where she was when he returned. He
came in from the hall, closing and locking the door
quietly behind him. Without turning on the light,
he walked into the bedroom, moving as silently as a
shadow. Feigning sleep, her eyes opening to the mer-
est of slits, she watched as he set his gun down on the
bedside table, then pulled off his shirt and dropped
his pants. Being careful not to disturb her, he slipped
into bed beside her. Lying on his side so that, she
guessed, he wouldn't touch and accidentally wake
her, he was asleep almost as soon as his head hit the
pillow.

Riley, on the other hand, lay awake for a long
time. Finally, when the lightening of the room told her
that dawn was breaking outside, she crept out of bed.

Glancing back at Finn, she saw the gleam of his eyes, and realized he was looking at her.

Damn.

She'd figured him for a light sleeper. It was one reason she hadn't gotten up sooner.

"Bathroom," she said, and he inclined his head and closed his eyes.

She picked up her purse on the way, and took it with her.

It wouldn't hurt to exercise a little due diligence.

Getting the information she was after proved to be surprisingly easy. Advanced Google Search was a miraculous thing. Five minutes later, she was sitting on the closed lid of the toilet staring down at the results of her inquiry: a figurative fist to the gut encapsulated on a tiny cell phone screen.

She wasn't sure which emotion was uppermost: hurt, shock, or rage.

ID# 0045386 took her to a government web site, where a little further sleuthing brought up a picture of the badge of John F. Bradley, Special Ops, CIA.

The photo on the badge was of Finn.

After staring at the thing for a while, she finally managed to get her head around it, then went back over everything he'd said and done from the time she'd first run naked into his arms, and came to a conclusion.

Bottom line: he was a lying SOB.

Other bottom line: Trust R Not Us.

———

TWO SATELLITE trucks complete with TV crews were set up outside the prison's front entrance when they arrived. Finn cursed when he saw them. It was possible that their presence had nothing to do with George, but not likely. Finn's best guess was that they were there to get a story on yesterday's stabbing of the disgraced former billionaire, and Riley was going to show up right smack in the middle of it.

There was nothing to be done about it. Canceling was not an option. His only consolation was that she would be driving right on past them, with only the single stop at the gate before she was inside and completely out of their reach. The reporters wouldn't be able to talk to her. They might not even spot her. Unless somebody had tipped them off, they wouldn't be expecting her, and she wasn't in her own car.

Of course, women who looked like Riley were kind of hard to miss.

"I'll be waiting right here when you get done," Finn told Riley as he got out of the Acura's passenger seat into the steam bath that was this particular morning in southern Oklahoma. At just past nine thirty, the sun was already climbing the cloudless sky. Last night's thunderheads might never have existed. "Come straight back."

The arrangement was that he'd wait for her in the small coffee-and-doughnut shop in the seedy strip mall directly across the road from the prison's front entrance.

"All right." She nodded agreement, looking out

through the windshield at the prison across the way
rather than at him, her hands tight around the steering wheel. If she was tired, it didn't show. She looked
beautiful, as always, with her red hair waving around
her face and a businesslike smoke-gray dress, sleeveless and knee-length, showing off her kickass shape.
But there was something remote about her expression that didn't quite jibe with his expectations. He
didn't know *what* he'd been expecting—well, he did;
in his experience women tended to be all kissy-face
and possessive on mornings after the night before,
especially a night before like she'd had—but Riley
wasn't it.

She'd been polite. She'd even returned the kiss
he'd dropped on her right before they left the hotel
room with an appropriate degree of heat. But she'd
hopped out of bed fast—no cuddling, nothing like
that—and disappeared into the bathroom, closing the
door, showering alone. He'd showered while she'd
done her hair and makeup, and then while he'd gotten dressed she'd gone back into the bathroom to
get dressed in private. Not that big a deal, but, again,
not what he'd expected. After that she'd gone with
him to get breakfast, and listened to his instructions
about what to do inside the prison and what information she needed to get from George without arguing
or smarting off or telling him to stuff it, which from
anyone else he would have expected as a matter of
course, but from her, not so much.

It was possible that she was keyed up about meeting George, and worried about her chances of getting

the information they needed. He knew she was terrified for Emma.

But he didn't think any of those things was it.

He had the feeling that whatever was bothering
her was personal, that it involved him. He didn't want
to ask her if something was wrong, didn't want to push
it, until after she'd talked to George. If she could find
out where the money was, his life got so much easier in
every way. He could say everything he needed to say
to Riley then.

A text message had come in during the night, letting him know that somebody might have figured out
that he was on the job here. That wasn't good. If it
became known that CIA Special Ops had an interest
in the missing money, all kinds of awkward questions
might start getting asked.

Fortunately, his people were the best in the world
at tracking down and dealing with potential security
breaches.

Finn closed the door, smacked a hand down on top
of the car to let her know she should go, and stepped
back. Riley drove away.

Mack H. Alford Correctional Center was a collection of two-story gray concrete structures with a couple of low red-brick buildings out in front. It was a big,
medium-security complex surrounded by tall fences
topped with loops of razor wire. Square guard towers
rose at intervals near the fences. In those complexes,
although he couldn't see them, would be a couple of
armed guards. From where Finn stood, sunglasses in
place as he watched Riley heading toward the complex,

what he could see were acres of parking lot, dozens of cars, some activity as people went in and out of buildings. The one thing about orange prison uniforms was they showed up like beacons amidst all that gray.

He watched the Acura drive across the road, past the TV trucks—no problem, thank God; they didn't appear to recognize her—and up to the front gate, watched it stop while Riley got checked off the list by the guard, then watched her drive on in and park. He watched Riley get out and walk inside the visitors' center.

The only part of the short journey where she'd been at physical risk was from the point where she'd let him out to the moment she'd driven through the prison gates. And he'd been close enough that entire time to intervene if needed.

Now, though, she was out of sight. Some activity in the shopping center, but no one observing him particularly as far as he could tell, Finn concluded after giving his surroundings a quick but thorough survey. Turning away from the coffee-and-doughnut shop—it was called Auntie Sue's—he walked to the dark blue van with Hall's Plumbing emblazoned in bold white letters on the sides.

Bax must have seen him coming, because the back door swung open as he approached.

"Yo," Finn said by way of greeting, and climbed in. He glanced around and, as Bax closed the door behind him, took in the array of computer monitors, all with various views from the prison's front gate to different points inside. "These all live feeds?"

"Yep." Bax sat back down in the chair he'd vacated to get the door.

Finn took the other vacant chair and settled in to watch Riley walk through a metal detector, then hand over her purse to be searched.

TWENTY-EIGHT

The smell was what hit Riley first. As she walked into the hospital ward, she was assaulted by a pungent mix of aromas that included urine, vomit, and some kind of strong disinfectant, like Lysol. The walls were cement block, painted pale gray. The floor was concrete, also gray. Big, barred windows let in plenty of light. Men lay in metal-framed hospital beds beneath thin blue blankets. Two orderlies or male nurses, she didn't know which, in blue scrubs tended to patients. A guard sat in a plastic chair against the far wall. The big guard who had escorted her from the visitors' center was just ahead of her as he led her through an aisle between rows of beds. He was as tall as Finn but paunchy, with a sallow, acne-scarred face. His name was Kevin Brown, and he was a sergeant: it said so on his plastic name tag.

Riley was so tense her jaw ached, and that's when she realized she was clenching it. She had to consciously force herself to relax.

"Prett-eee lad-eee," one of the patients crooned upon catching sight of her.

"Hey, baby, do me, do me, do me, do me, do me."

"Come on over *here*."

Wolf whistle.

The guards paid no attention to the catcalls that followed her. Riley ignored them, too. She'd already been told that George had been put in a private room for his own safety, and when Brown stopped in front of a closed door with a guard sitting in another plastic chair beside it, Riley assumed this was that room.

She was right.

"Knock on the door when you're ready to come out, Mrs. Cowan," Brown said, as the other guard stood up and pushed open the door for her. That's when she understood that while she was in the room with George the door would be locked from the outside.

Of course. It was a prison, after all.

Riley nodded, and walked into the room. It was small and, like the ward itself, mostly gray. The shade had been pulled down over the single window blocking any view of the outside, but still there was plenty of light, both natural and from the overhead fixture, which was on. The smell was not as pronounced in here, possibly because this small room was cooler than the ward.

As the door closed behind her, her gaze immediately went to the man in the bed. The last time she'd seen George, she'd been in a courtroom sitting with Margaret, Emma, and Jeff as George, having just been sentenced to seventy-five years in prison, was hand-cuffed and led away. Margaret and Emma had been in tears, and Jeff had been white and sick with distress over his father's fate. The pillar that the other three leaned on, Riley had been angry at George then for causing them all so much pain, and she had expected to be even more angry now.

But she didn't feel angry.

The man in the bed barely resembled George. The burly bully with the perpetual tan and the carefully kept mane of black hair was gone. In his place was a thin, pale old man with age spots and dry lips and gray hair cut so short he might as well have been bald. He wore a blue hospital gown with some kind of print on it. An IV was in his arm, he was hooked up to a monitor that stood next to the IV stand beside the bed and beeped intermittently, and his right hand was bandaged. A blue blanket covered him to midchest.

"Hello, George," Riley greeted him.

George said, "They told me you were coming to see me. Why you? Where's Margaret? What do you want?"

His voice was thinner than before, and it had a rasp. But the attitude: that was the George she knew.

"Margaret couldn't come. She's fine, by the way, thanks for asking." Riley advanced to stand beside the bed. She could feel her old dislike for him bubbling to the surface. George looked up at her, his expression unwelcoming. His eyes were small and blue. Faded now. But still cold.

He was a shell of his former self. She did not feel sorry for him.

"You've heard about Jeff." Her tone didn't make it a question, because she was sure he had. What she wanted to know was, did he feel any guilt? Any remorse? Any awareness that Jeff would be alive right now if it wasn't for him?

Her anger was back, building up inside like a rising tide.

"They told me." If he felt any emotion at all, he wasn't showing it. "So if that's what you're here about, you can just go away."

Riley's eyes narrowed. She'd thought to break it to him gently, but . . . *mean old man.* Jeff's words. Remembering, Riley felt a shiver of grief pierce the anger.

"Emma's been kidnapped." She laid it on the line, flatly, and watched his face. It seemed to freeze. His eyes were suddenly riveted to hers. "The kidnappers told me I should ask you where the money is. If you don't tell me, they're going to kill her."

For a moment he simply stared at her. Then his mouth opened and began to work, like a fish out of water gulping air. His left hand—the uninjured one—fisted in the sheet.

"Eh-eh-Emma," he stuttered. He licked his lips. His head moved from side to side, a negative gesture. His body twitched. His eyes filled with horror. "Not Emma. Oh, no, not Emma. Not like Jeff."

"Where's the money? For Emma's sake, you need to tell me."

He shook his head. "I can't. I can't."

He almost sounded pitiful. Riley almost felt sorry for him. But see, the thing was, she *knew* he knew where the money was. She *knew* that he could tell her about Emma's painting, and the little black book, and how to access those accounts.

She *knew* he could save Emma if he wanted to.

Sweet Emma was the one person she'd always thought George truly loved.

Her anger turned to rage. She leaned over the bed, leaned closer to him, her eyes boring into his. "I know it isn't all lost like you've been saying. You can save Emma, George. All you have to do is tell me where the money is."

He made a sound of distress.

"It's gone," he said, and she knew then that she would despise him forever. "All gone." He covered his eyes with his hand.

"It's not," Riley hissed at him, and stopped, because there was no point. He was exactly what he had always been, and she didn't need his help anyway.

George's hand dropped away from his eyes. He looked at her, and she saw he had tears brimming. "I made a deal with the devil. He came to me, and I did it. But I didn't know. *I didn't know.* If I could take it back I would, but I can't."

That made her frown at him. "George—"

"I can't," he repeated, and began to sob. "Jeff didn't kill himself. *They* killed him. I tried to fix this and they killed him. And now they've got Emma. And there's nothing I can do."

George shut his eyes, drew a deep, shuddering breath.

Riley stared at him as her heart began to pound.

Maybe he would tell her *this*, and maybe it would be enough to help find Emma. Her hand found his, closed around the cold dry fingers urgently. "Who are *they*? Do you know? If you do, tell me. *They've got Emma.*"

George opened his eyes. But instead of looking at her, he looked at the door. "Guard!" he yelled. "We're through."

"George, if you know something, you have to tell me."

He looked at her then. His eyes were full of tears.

"Go away," he said, then looked at the door again and screamed, "Guard!"

"Jeff deserved better than you," Riley said with quiet ferociousness as the door opened behind her. "Emma and Margaret do, too."

"Get her out of here," George cried to the guard who now stood in the open doorway. "We're through here! We're through."

Riley didn't even say good-bye. Hating him so much she felt sick with it, she turned and walked out the door.

———

"WELL, HELL, there goes that." As Riley walked out of George's room, Finn leaned back in his chair, clasping his hands behind his neck in frustration. In the tight confines of the van, that meant his head was almost touching the opposite wall. Ordinarily he would never have said it aloud, but he'd gotten caught up in Riley's emotion, in the naked pain in her voice and her face, as he'd watched her trying to get the information they needed out of George. He'd damned well *felt* some of that emotion, which said way more than he wanted to think about at the moment about the state of his own emotions where Riley was concerned. One more topic to be pursued later; for now he had to concentrate on getting the job he'd been put on the ground to do done. Which meant, clearly, that he was going to have to go down a new path, because George either really didn't know or wasn't giving up the whereabouts of the money.

Riley had seemed to think he knew. Or else she was a hell of an actress, putting it all out there as she fought with Emma's father for a means of saving Emma.

When he got her back, they were going to have a talk. About trust, and all that.

"Now what do we do?" Bax was watching Riley's return progress through the prison, too.

"Your people got any fresh leads on Emma?" Finn asked. Riley's visit to George having been a bust, Finn wanted to get as much of a handle on the Emma situation as he could before Riley rejoined him, upset about having failed. If the girl couldn't be found before the kidnappers called Riley, maybe the best thing to do would be to fake it, lie and claim George had told them the whereabouts of the money. They could try to arrange an ambush.

Bax said, "The van was spotted on I-45 going south, was the last update I got. People are scouring surveillance video at every exit on down that highway, but it's a slow process."

"Yeah," Finn said, having received the same information when he'd called in to his sources last night. On one of the monitors he watched Riley walk into the back entrance of the visitors' center, then watched the guard who'd been assigned to escort her, who was walking behind her and had held the door open for her, check out her ass as she passed him. His body tensed slightly in reflexive reaction: he didn't like what he was seeing, which was another bad sign about the state of his involvement with Riley.

"If they're not going to kill Emma, if they're really intending to trade her for the money, they won't have taken her too far," Bax offered. "The problem is, there's so much activity typically going on in an urban area that it takes a long time to single out anything that might be significant."

"Yeah," Finn said again. His people were also checking NSA satellite footage of the area, but following a white van on a dark night amidst a sea of other vehicles in pictures taken miles above the earth was apparently proving problematic. He hoped they were having better luck tracking down the source of those emails Riley had pointed out to him, but so far he hadn't heard anything to indicate it.

"Here she comes." Bax nodded at the monitor, which showed Riley walking out of the visitors' center into the parking lot. As Finn watched, his hands closed around the arms of his chair preparatory to levering himself upright. Time to get himself to Auntie Sue's.

"Okay. Get somebody analyzing the footage we

just captured. A couple of the things George said—'I made a deal with the devil and I tried to fix this' are what jumped out at me—might be worth pursuing. Check visitor logs, email logs, phone logs, everything that came to or went out from George at that prison." Finn watched Riley get into the car. He had a problem—Eagle and the powers that be wanted him to find the money. If Riley wasn't the ticket to finding the money, then they would expect him to abandon her and pursue other leads until that money was found. He had the same problem regarding Emma—his mandate wasn't to recover the teen.

Finn discovered that he wasn't on board with abandoning either of them.

Shit.

"You'd better get a move on. She's coming through the gate."

"Yeah." Finn stood up—well, as much as he could, considering that he was quite a bit taller than the van was high. "Head back for Houston. I'll give you a call—"

He broke off, his eyes on the monitor. Having made it through the gate, the gray Acura had been rolling merrily along, until it braked beside one of the news crews she was supposed to drive right past.

"She stopped," Bax said unnecessarily, his tone as dumbfounded as Finn felt. "What's she doing?"

Good question. Finn, for one, didn't know.

He watched as Riley got out of the car. The news crews spotted her, practically dropped their cameras in shock, and rushed her en masse.

"Any way to zoom in on that?" he asked, because this particular camera they were watching her on was capturing her from across the street. The sound wasn't there, either. From the angle of that vantage point, he guessed the camera might be concealed in the front of the van. His chest was heavy with foreboding.

"Oh. Sure." Bax jumped up, banged his head on the roof, said "ouch," and rubbed the injury even as he did something with a computer mouse that brought Riley front and center on that monitor—and upped the volume to where they could hear her.

"—visiting your ex-father-in-law, George Cowan?" the reporter asked. She was a young blonde, smiling brightly while holding the microphone in Riley's face. "Can you give us any details about what happened?"

"I only know that he was stabbed yesterday," Riley said. She looked into the camera, and Finn was struck once again by how pretty she was. He was also struck by something in the determined set of her jaw-line. He remembered the last time she had talked to the media, and his sense of foreboding morphed into flat-out alarm. "I spoke to him, and he's recovering. In fact, I had a question to ask him, and he was able to tell me everything I needed to know."

"My God, does she mean what I think she means?" Bax gasped, while Finn stared stonily at the monitor. "Did George tell her where the money is?"

"You heard what I heard," Finn responded.

"Can you share with us what you asked him?" the reporter said to Riley.

Riley shook her head. "No, I can't. It's personal."

Then she looked directly into the camera again. "But I got the answer I wanted, and I'll share it with the people it concerns." While Finn felt his blood run cold, she glanced at the reporter, and smiled. "Thanks for your concern."

Then she waved, and walked away from the camera, ignoring the questions that were called after her.

The reporter said into the camera, "That was an exclusive with Riley—"

Finn missed the rest of it. Heart thumping like it hadn't in years, he was already striding for the rear of the van and jumping out onto the pavement.

Glancing toward the prison, he could see the Acura coming.

— CHAPTER —
TWENTY-NINE

Riley's pulse pounded. Her stomach was in a knot. Her mind, however, was crystal clear. By telling the media, and through them the world, that she had asked George a question and he had told her everything she needed to know, she hoped to get the word to Emma's kidnappers that she knew where the money was and she was willing to trade.

She was going to pretend to Finn and everybody else in officialdom that George had told her where it was. And she wasn't going to tell Finn and everybody else in officialdom where that was until Emma was free and safe.

She was prepared to give the location of the money to whoever gave her Emma.

Finn, Bax, the FBI, the CIA, and every other agency and government group involved were there for the money. Once someone got it, they might very well pull the plug and all go away.

Without making sure Emma was safe.

She didn't trust any of them.

Finn jogged through the center of the parking lot toward her. Riley spotted him as soon as she pulled into the strip mall. His suit today was a paler gray, and his coat and dark blue tie flapped as he ran. He looked completely masculine, slightly disheveled, and sexy as hell. Also, big and tough enough to handle anything. Her instant reaction upon seeing him was that he was her very own port in the storm, and she wanted to park the car and run into his arms. Then she remembered why that wasn't going to happen, and at the same time got close enough to see his expression. She was instantly alarmed by the look on his face.

Grim didn't begin to cover it.

She braked beside him, put the car in park. He jerked open her door even as she started to roll down her window.

"Get in the passenger seat," he barked, reaching around her to unbuckle her seat belt, grabbing her arm to pull her out. She'd stopped in the middle of the parking lot, which, since it was almost noon, was busier than it had been earlier, with maybe two dozen cars and trucks and vans in it now. A woman was walking into Auntie Sue's, and another woman and a little girl were coming out of Stringtown Souvenirs. Nobody seemed to be paying attention to her or Finn. A quick glance across the four-lane road at the satellite trucks parked down the long driveway in front of the prison gate told her that the news crews were nowhere in sight. She presumed that they were either in or in front of one of the vans.

"What is it?" she asked. Anxiety made her throat tight. Sudden dread gripped her. "Is it Emma?"

"No, it's not Emma." He looked grimmer than ever as he hauled her around the hood of the car.

"Oh, God." Riley felt a flood of relief. "Finn—he told me where the money is."

"What?" He snapped a frowning look at her.

"I know where the money is. George told me."

"*What?*"

His eyes bored into hers, and for a moment they blazed with some emotion she couldn't identify. Then they shut down as completely as if a curtain had dropped, and became absolutely unreadable.

"Get in the car." He opened the passenger door. She got in. A moment later he slid behind the wheel.

"George told you where the money is?" He put the car in gear, and they started to move. "Where is it? What did he say?"

The tension in his face hadn't eased. If anything, the muscles around his eyes and mouth looked tighter than before.

"What's happened?" she asked instead of answering, her anxiety skyrocketing again as he drove maybe a dozen yards before swinging into a parking space beside a blue van. "Finn?"

"In a minute." He slammed the car into park, turned it off, grabbed the keys, and said, "Don't move."

"I'M GOING to need some more firepower," Finn said to Bax, who jumped out of the van to join him on the pavement as soon as the Acura stopped beside it. Finn's heart, which had been pounding, was slowing down, as he had trained it to do when he was going into work mode. "You got any weapons?"

"My Glock," Bax said, showing him by flipping back his jacket, although Finn didn't take the time to look. Following Finn around toward the back of the van, Bax added, "I think there's a rifle in the back."

"Get it. Get all the ammo you have, too." Finn clicked the button that opened the Acura's trunk, grabbed his suitcase out, and slammed the lid. Opening the rear door, he threw his suitcase into the backseat, and said to Riley, who had slewed around to look at him, "Stay there," then turned to accept a rifle and a box of shells from Bax. He put that in the back, too, down on the floorboard, gave Riley a warning growl in case she was entertaining any thoughts about getting out of the car, which, knowing her, she probably was, and said to Bax, "Every damned thug in the universe is gonna be coming after her now. You know those steps we were talking about last night to keep her safe? This is one of them, only instead of 'safe' you should think 'alive.' I want you to come with me, be an extra gun. Two things we need to have clear before you do: first off, you're liable to get killed. Second, can I trust you? Because if you come with me and I find out I can't, I'm going to kill you myself."

"Y-y-yeah, you can trust me." Bax's stuttering made Finn think *not*. The other man unfastened his buckle, pulled off his belt, and held it up with a flour-ish. That was not an action Finn was expecting, and he blinked. Then it hit him.

"You've been wearing a bug." It would have been in the buckle. He'd pulled that trick once or twice himself. Didn't stop him from glaring at Bax.

"I had to. The Bureau wanted ears." He threw the belt into the van, slammed the door, and held out his hands palms up to Finn in the age-old gesture of sur-render. "I blocked you whenever you said anything too sensitive."

"Rattling the damned coins." Finn couldn't be-lieve he'd been so stupid. He'd bugged Bax, Bax had bugged him. Quid quo pro, one fucking government operative to another.

"Yeah," Bax said. "And coughing, and turning on the radio, and—"

Finn's face must have been a pretty accurate re-flection of his feelings, because Bax said, "Sorry," in a meek voice, and added, "I'm good now. I'm with you. Let's go."

"You got people around?"

"Two guys." Bax sounded abashed. "They brought the van, helped set up the surveillance. Right now they're up at the McDonald's, waiting for me to call."

Finn gave him a hard look. *Fucking FBI.* "Call them in about twenty minutes and tell them to come collect the van. And I meant what I said about trusting you: I'd better be able to."

"You can."

"Then let's go."

"WHAT'S HAPPENED?" Riley repeated her question as Finn got behind the wheel, Bax climbed into the backseat, and the Acura pulled out of the parking space, heading for the road. A rifle on the floor of the backseat, Bax in the backseat—she hadn't even known Bax was in Stringtown, and what was he doing in that van? It scared her. "What's wrong?"

"You want to know what's wrong? Let's see: for starters, what the fuck was that?" Finn shot at her by way of a reply. His usually calm blue-gray eyes weren't calm anymore, and they weren't blue-gray. They were the color of steel, and furious. "Do you have any idea of what you just did?"

"What are you talking about?"

"Don't give me that." He accelerated smoothly past the prison, and then they were moving down the road back the way they had come, toward Stringtown, going fast but not so fast that they would attract attention. "You just got on live TV and told the whole damned world that you know where George has that money stashed!"

Her brows snapped together. "I wanted to get a message to Emma's kidnappers. And I didn't tell the whole damned world anything: it was a veiled reference. Anyway, how do you know that's what I did?"

"You remember that bastard who almost drowned you in your bathtub? You remember Jeffy-boy ending up getting himself hanged? You remember that Emma's kidnapped and George got stabbed? To say nothing of those other four associates of George's who died mysteriously?" Finn didn't yell, but instead bit the words out savagely. "The people who do those kinds of things? They're now all after you. Every single one of them. I don't know how many there are. Dozens, for all I know. Billions of dollars provide a powerful incentive for all of them to want to get their hands on you and get you to tell them what you said you know, which is where the money is. Do they care if they kill you? Hell, no. For a lot of them, it'll be fun."

"You were spying on me!"

"You bet your sweet ass I was spying on you!" He threw another of those furious looks at her as he nosed the Acura around the curving on-ramp to the expressway. Riley's chest tightened as the maelstrom of thoughts swirling through her head coalesced into a single, terrible one: he might have been spying on her while she talked to George, too. Panic fluttered: if so, he would know that George hadn't told her where the money was.

The solution that presented itself wasn't pretty, but it would have to do. She could say that George's words had contained a coded message that only she could understand.

Liar, liar, pants on fire.

But what else could she do?

They were heading toward Houston, Riley saw, as they merged into traffic. There wasn't a lot, and what there was sped along easily.

Over his shoulder, to Bax, Finn said in a more measured tone, "There's a zippered gun case inside the top compartment in my suitcase. Get it out, and hand me the Sig. Keep the others out where we can get to them."

"Got it," Bax said.

"You have no business spying on me," Riley said. From the backseat came the sound of Bax unzipping the case.

"I have no—" Finn broke off, and Riley got the impression that he was grinding his teeth. "If I hadn't spied on you, you'd already be dead."

Riley's eyes narrowed. "You were spying on me that night I was attacked in my apartment, weren't you? That's why you showed up when you did!"

"Uh, Finn?" Bax passed him a silver pistol.

"What are you going to do with that?" Riley asked, her alarm ratcheting up to a whole new level. The truth was, when she'd made her televised announcement that George had told her where the money was, she hadn't been thinking of anyone but Emma, and getting a message to her kidnappers. The idea that she'd brought a hornet's nest of assassins down on herself—and Finn, and Bax—made her palms grow damp.

"Shoot the first bastard who tries to grab you. Of course, a Sig only holds a certain number of bullets." Finn patted his shoulder holster through his jacket. "Good thing I have my Beretta. And the backups. And Bax. Let's hope we don't run out of ammo before all the bad guys are dead." Tucking the pistol into the cup holder so that the handle was easily accessible, Finn glanced in the rearview mirror at Bax. "I need to find a pay phone. Think you can get on your phone and find me one? As close to us as possible."

Riley slewed around to look at Bax, who was pulling out his cell phone. Seeing a black strip of what looked like Kevlar that had been unrolled on the back-seat with various guns secured to it by strips of the same cloth, she caught her breath and looked at Finn. "What, do you travel with your own arsenal?"

"You better thank your lucky stars I do." His voice was grim. He shot another through-the-rearview-mirror look at Bax. "You can go ahead and tell your people to pick that van up now."

"I'll text 'em," Bax said.

"He was in the van." Riley got it all of a sudden. She glanced back at Bax, saw as she did that they were cruising past a white pickup that was moving at a pretty good clip itself, realized they were speeding, and then forgot about traffic as her gaze focused back on Bax, who had been working his cell phone but looked up as if he felt the weight of her eyes. "You were in that van, weren't you? What, is it one of those surveillance vans like they use on spy shows on TV?" Bax's expression, coupled with his and Finn's mutual silence, told the tale. "It is, isn't it?" She glared at Finn as her worst fear was confirmed. "You were watching me talk to George, weren't you?"

"Angel, you've been lying to me nonstop from the minute I first laid eyes on you. Why wouldn't I watch you talk to George?"

"You want to talk about lying?" The anger and hurt she'd been bottling up since doing her due diligence on that text message surged through her veins. "What about all the lies you've told *me*?"

It was all she could do not to throw the fact that she knew he was a CIA agent, for starters, in his face, but an innate caution stopped her.

Finn's eyes flashed her way, but before he could reply Bax said, "I've got a pay phone in a Grab-and-Go at the next exit. Twenty-four B."

"I NEED a safe house." The Agency kept safe houses ready to go, not just throughout the USA but around the world, and Finn had little doubt that there would be at least one somewhere between where he was and Houston. "And I'm going to need some backup."

As he spoke into the pay phone, summarizing what had happened for Eagle, Finn scanned his surroundings. The phone was set into the wall of an ancient Grab-and-Go store, located conveniently right next to the restrooms. Riley was in one, Bax in the other. The Acura was directly in front of him. Two other cars waited in the parking lot, one at a gas pump, one parked in front of the store, both harmless. He could see all the way to the expressway exits: nothing concerning headed their way. He had a bad feeling that that was only temporary.

He hadn't wanted to trust even his own agency with the knowledge of where he was taking Riley, but he was fresh out of options. Too many people would be coming after her now that they thought she knew where the money was.

"So she knows the whereabouts of the money?"

Something in Eagle's tone gave Finn pause. "I think she was bluffing, trying to draw out her sister's kidnappers."

In fact, he was starting to think no such thing. He didn't know how Riley knew where the money was, but he thought she did know. His gut shouted it, and as he ran his mind back, every fact he turned over confirmed it. But he wasn't about to tell Eagle that. Eagle was on a mission to find that money. If he thought Riley knew where it was, and somebody besides Finn could get the information out of her faster than Finn could, then he might very well find himself in a pitched battle with his own agency.

Because he wasn't letting them have Riley. Until now, his ultimate loyalty, after his loyalty to his country, had been to Eagle. When he'd saved Eagle's life, it had been a split-second decision: they'd been in the basement of a bombed-out tenement in Libya, meeting with the deputy head of Libyan intelligence and a few of his underlings for a top-secret passing-on of information at the highest levels. A traitor in the Libyan ranks had opened fire. Finn had grabbed Eagle, basically turned into a one-man war machine, and gotten his superior out of there, taking a hit himself in the process that had nearly killed him.

He and Eagle had been the only two in that room to get out alive.

Jennifer, his ex-girlfriend by that time but still a fellow agent, had been in that room, too. She hadn't survived.

Finn was haunted by the knowledge that he could have gotten her out of there, could have saved her instead of Eagle. But Jennifer had been a professional like himself, and when the bullets had started flying he had reacted instantly, instinctively, and as his training had dictated.

He still bore the scars of that night: a puckered wound on his abdomen and a shit-ton of guilt and regret and grief over Jennifer.

He'd retired, and started over.

Now there was Riley. This time, loyalty to his superior and his agency wasn't going to supersede his loyalty to a woman he cared about (and how was this for a moment to find himself face to face with the fact that he cared like that about Riley?). He was all in, committed to getting her out of this, whatever it took.

The object of his thoughts came out of the ladies' room and threw him a guarded look. Finn nodded at the car, threw her the keys. It was too hot to sit in a car for even a few minutes without the air conditioner on, and he had no fear she was going to try to drive away. Riley was way too smart for that.

As Riley got into the passenger seat and reached across to insert the keys in the ignition and turn on the engine, Eagle said, "If she doesn't know where the money is, you're a wasted resource as long as you're with her."

Finn pulled his attention back to his conversation. "I need a little more time to figure this out. If the money's around to be found, I'll find it."

"Time's running out," Eagle warned.

"We need to recover the sister-in-law, Emma."

"People are on it. You think I don't want to rescue a teenage girl from kidnappers? Let them do their jobs. You find the damned money. Hang on."

A minute later Eagle was back on the line with the location of a safe house.

Bax was out of the restroom and leaning against the car by the time Finn finished his conversation and hung up. It was hot as hell, the air smelled like gas fumes and restrooms, and Bax, in a suit and tie, too, was turning red from the heat. Grim as he was feeling, Finn experienced a flicker of amusement as he wondered if the other man was avoiding getting in the car because he didn't want to have to answer awkward questions, or worse, from Riley.

"I got a text from the guys in Stringtown. They're at the van, and they want to know where I am." Bax straightened as Finn approached the car.

"Tell them you're on a field trip." Finn pulled off his own tie and unbuttoned his collar. He would have shed the jacket, but then his shoulder rig would have been exposed and he didn't want that.

"Okay. Right." Bax was texting as he got in the car.

"Checking in with the boss?" Riley asked him

with an edge to her voice as he slid behind the wheel, and he knew she was referring to his phone call.

All right, so he was a sucker for a woman with attitude. At least he was facing his faults.

"I got us a safe house," Finn said. His tone was mild. Blowing up at her was a waste of time and effort—it wouldn't change a thing, wouldn't unspill the milk, wouldn't put her words back in her mouth—so he wasn't going to do it. It wasn't how he rolled. It was a measure of how surprised and scared for her he had been that he'd done it at all. Anyway, if he wanted her cooperation, yelling at her probably wasn't the smartest way to go about getting it. And he didn't want to goad her into blurting out too much—like the whereabouts of the money—in front of Bax. Not that he didn't trust the other man, but—yeah, he didn't. He didn't trust anybody that much.

"A safe house?" Riley looked taken aback.

"You know, a place where we can hide from all the people who want to kill us." As soon as he said it, he told himself that sarcasm should probably be given a rest, too.

They were on I-45 South again, and Finn cast a wary look around. Nothing but ordinary-looking traffic. He kept a cautious eye on his mirrors as he moved over into the fast lane and hit it. They had maybe another half hour on the expressway and then fifteen minutes after that to the safe house.

May you be in heaven a full half hour before the devil knows you're dead: the old Irish prayer popped into his head, and he substituted the words *we* and *the safe house* and *enemy operatives get on your tail* in the appropriate places and sent it skyward, then looked at Riley.

"I need you to take the battery out of your phone," he said.

She'd been holding her purse on her lap. Now she frowned at him and clutched it tighter. Finn realized her phone was in there.

"I can't." The touch of panic in her eyes made his stomach constrict. *A sucker for a woman with attitude, my ass*, he thought. *What you're a sucker for is her. Damn it.* "Emma—the kidnappers said they'd call me on it."

"I arranged to have your calls routed through my phone. When they call, we'll get it just fine." He said it gently and watched her process it. "It'd be easy for somebody to get your number and track you with it."

She knew it: she'd disabled her phone before for just that reason.

"What about your phone? And his?" She jerked her head at Bax.

"Mine can't be tracked that way. I'm guessing his is the same."

A glance in the rearview mirror showed Bax nodding. "Blocked," he said.

Riley's lips compressed, but she unzipped her purse—the little thingy that secured the zipper was indeed not snapped—and pulled out her phone. She looked down at it.

"I can't miss that call," she said.

"You won't," he promised.

"I was hoping they would have called by now."

He said, "Maybe they weren't watching TV," and mentally kicked himself for sarcasm again. She looked so worried that he regretted the words, and their tone, as soon as they came out. To soothe her he added, "It was a piss-poor idea to tell the whole damned world you know where the money is, but if it makes you feel any better, any kidnapper worth his salt will have some kind of flag on your name. If they missed the live version of your press conference, they'll get the word some other way soon enough."

Finn watched her expression change, from what he basically translated as *I've put us all in danger for nothing* to *oh, God, I hope so.*

Being able to read her face the way he could was another telltale sign, one that in retrospect he should have picked up on right away.

"All right, fine." She started to take the battery out of her phone with a quick efficiency that once upon a time would have surprised him. It still impressed him.

"Tech forensics was able to trace those two emails that were sent to Jeff that you earmarked," Bax reported on a note of excitement. "I just got a text. Dude named Ed Harper, from the Dallas area. Local PD picked him up, and we've got an agent questioning him now."

Finn frowned. The name meant nothing to him. But no operative worth a damn would be sitting around in a place where he was known to reside waiting for police to pick him up.

"I didn't—" Riley said, but Finn stopped listening.

Up ahead, one semi was passing another. No big deal, except that in a couple of minutes he'd be running up close behind them, and they—both of them—were blocking the way. Glancing in his mirrors, he saw that on this hilly stretch of highway, traffic had thinned out considerably. Behind him were maybe three other cars. Correction: vehicles. Two big SUVs, one beige, one black, and a white pickup, a big one, a Ford F-250.

Finn frowned, and cast quick, assessing looks around. To his left was a grassy median bisected by a thick stand of trees that prevented him from being able to see the northbound lanes. To his right was wooded hillside. On neither side was there enough room for a car. No easy route of escape.

He felt his gut clench. At about that same time, the semis, now running side by side, began to slow down.

Yeah. Showtime.

"Don't anybody look around. Riley, keep your lap belt on, but come out of your shoulder belt and lay forward. Wrap your arms around your knees and hang on. Lie real flat, as flat as you can." His voice was calm and steady even as adrenaline spiked through his veins. As he spoke he was smoothly changing lanes to position Riley, who looked at him with alarm before she obediently slid out of the shoulder portion of her seat belt, so that any vehicles approaching them from behind would have to come up on his side, not hers. "Bax, this is something I probably should have asked already: how good a shot are you?"

"Good," Bax said in a tight, slightly strangulated voice that had Finn praying he wasn't exaggerating.

"Oh, my God, it's happening, isn't it? Shouldn't I have a gun?" Riley was stretched out as directed. Her face was turned toward him. She was pale and her eyes were wide with fear.

Finn shook his head, not bothering to repeat one of his favorite maxims, which was that guns were best left to professionals, especially when he was sitting right beside the nonprofessional who wanted one.

"Your job is to stay down. That's it, understand?" As she nodded he said to Bax, "When the shooting starts, either aim for the driver or a front tire. Shooting the passenger won't help us. Got it?"

Bax sounded steadier. "Got it."

Finn glanced at him in the rearview mirror. Bax had moved the rifle up to lie on the seat with the other weapons, and he had his Glock out. *Good.*

Finn said, "They want to kidnap Riley, not kill her. Us they'll gladly kill, but not in a way that could kill her, which means they're going to try to avoid making us have a terrible accident. That gives us a little bit of an advantage."

"Holy shit, look out," Bax said. "The pickup's coming up on the left."

The Acura's front bumper was already measurably closer to the rumbling semis, and it wasn't because Finn was speeding up. The semis would continue to slow down. The pickup would come up on the driver's side, and the SUVs would close in from behind, boxing them in. The object of the game, Finn knew, was to stop them so that Riley could be grabbed. He could either allow the Acura to be slowed to a stop, or they'd force him to slow down enough to where if they shot him dead while he was still at the wheel, they could close in tight enough around the Acura to bring it to a stop.

In either scenario, he and Bax were dead. Riley, too, only they'd wait until, one way or another, she told them the whereabouts of the money first.

What he had here was a brief window of opportunity.

"I'm getting ready to hang a hard left," he told Bax. In his side mirror he could see the pickup, a big white monster with a billet grille, roaring up. Two men on board: professionals. Sunlight pouring through the windshield glinted off a silver gun barrel in the passenger's hand. "I'm going to be driving, so you're going to be doing most of the shooting. When we go by the SUVs, you pick: driver or tire. But get one or the other."

Bax said, "I'll get both."

Had to love the guy's optimism.

"Don't get killed," Riley said, staring up at him. He could see how hard she was breathing, hear the tension in her voice. She flicked a glance toward the backseat. "Either of you."

"Hold tight, Angel." With that, Finn drew his Beretta and hit the button that rolled down the windows. As always in a situation like this, he felt a fierce calm descend. His heart rate slowed. So did his pulse and respiration. The rush of hot wind whipping outdoor smells through the car's interior hit his face and sent Riley's hair flying. He could hear the rattle of the pickup, see that its grille was almost even with the Acura's passenger door.

Shock and awe, baby.

Keeping one hand on the wheel, Finn leaned out the driver's side window just far enough to get the job done. With unerring precision he snapped off a quick shot that shattered the pickup's window and caught the driver square in the middle of the forehead: *money shot.* The staccato *pop* was lost in the roar of the wind. Even as Finn withdrew, the driver slumped, the horn blared as his dead body landed on it, and the pickup veered wildly toward the Acura. Finn took advantage of the few seconds before impact to stomp the accelerator and yank the wheel left. The Acura squealed past the skidding pickup with inches to spare.

"Holy Mary, Mother of God," Riley gasped as she was thrown toward him and her body came up off the seat, then was caught by her seat belt and flung back down again.

"Stay down."

Brakes screamed as the SUVs tried to avoid the fishtailing pickup and started sliding themselves. Up ahead, the semis were braking, too. The smell of scorching tires filled the air.

"Suck lead, assholes!" Bax screamed. As bullets pinged into the Acura *rat-a-tat-tat,* making Finn cringe, Bax fired, loud bangs that told Finn he had opted for the rifle.

The front tire of the nearest SUV exploded, sending it zigzagging wildly.

"Way to do it!" Finn yelled.

The rifle banged some more.

The steering wheel shook beneath Finn's hands as he fought it for control. The margin for error was so slight—the wall of trees was inches from the side of the car and the swerving SUVs took up most of the pavement. Trees flashed by the windshield in a green-brown blur, bullets peppered the sides of the car right along with flying gravel, and as they hit grass they bounced like ping pong balls. Then the Acura was flying back the way it had come, partly on grass and partly on the pavement. A glance in the rearview mirror showed Finn that the pickup had crashed into the wooded slope on the right side of the expressway, both SUVs were off the pavement, and the semis were angled across the road, one in front of the other. Finn counted three men outside the vehicles, two rushing toward the pickup and one leaning back against the side of the beige SUV holding his arm, and felt a surge of triumph mixed with relief.

"We did it," Bax exulted.

"Way to get the job done," Finn congratulated him, and glanced at Riley, who was cautiously sitting up. "You okay?"

"Fine. I can't believe we're alive after that." Pushing her hair back from her face with both hands—Finn rolled up the windows so it wouldn't blow anymore—Riley looked at him. Something in her face reminded him that she'd just seen him kill a man. Their eyes met. Finn felt naked: *This is what I am.* He didn't like the sensation. Mouth compressing, he returned his attention to his driving, and eased the Acura back up on the road.

"You saved my life again. Thank you," Riley said quietly, and something tight inside him eased just a little bit. He nodded, and she then slewed around to look at Bax. "Neither of you are hurt?"

"No."

"No."

Riley looked back at the site of the wreck they were rapidly leaving behind and shivered. "Will they come after us, do you think?"

"I only got the one tire," Bax confessed. "Other than that, I don't know what I hit."

"Whatever you hit, it worked," Finn said, glancing at him through the mirror. "Good man." Then, to Riley, "They won't come after us. Not right now," and refrained from telling her that there were probably dozens more exactly like them.

"We're going the wrong way down the expressway," she pointed out.

Worried as he was, her matter-of-fact tone almost made him smile. "I'll get right on that."

— CHAPTER —
THIRTY-ONE

The safe house was an ordinary-looking brick two-story not too far southwest of Dallas. It was in a semirural neighborhood with no near neighbors, set back off the road and ringed by trees.

Four men in two cars were waiting for them when they arrived. The cars were parked on the street in front of the house, and the men got out and headed toward the Acura as it pulled up the driveway.

It said a lot about the current state of her life that as soon as she spotted the waiting cars Riley's heart leaped into her throat.

"Finn." There was warning in her tone. Alarmed, she sat straight up in her seat.

"It's all right. They're backup," he said.

The thought that she now needed all these armed guards was terrifying. But given what had happened on the expressway, she was prepared to accept his judgment that she did.

The men followed them into the house. They were introduced to Riley as Agents Foster, Hagan, Waters, and Silverman. She didn't inquire what agency they were from, and they were pretty much interchangeable in their dark suits and white shirts and ties.

In fact, Finn fit right in with them.

Inside, the house was ordinary looking, too: living room, dining room, family room, kitchen, and half bath on the first floor, three bedrooms and two baths above. The new recruits deployed themselves around the first floor. Riley, Finn, and Bax hit the kitchen, which as it turned out was fully stocked. Tired and shaken as she was, Riley was hungry. It was almost 4 p.m., and she hadn't eaten anything except a nibble of toast at breakfast with Finn. She made herself a bologna sandwich, ate quickly, then headed upstairs, leaving Finn and Bax still at the table. Finn had carried her suitcase into the master bedroom when they had arrived, and that was where she went.

Hungry as she had been, the food felt like a cannonball in her stomach, and that would be, Riley thought as she headed into the en suite bathroom to freshen up, because she was sick with fear. For Emma: the kidnappers still had not called. For herself: she had nearly died this afternoon for the second time in little more than a week, and she was confident that there were lots of people still out there who were prepared to make her dead.

Having washed her face and hands, brushed her teeth, and applied fresh makeup, Riley was brushing her hair as she walked back into the bedroom, and immediately lost her train of thought as she saw Finn stretched out on the bed, his head propped up by pillows as he clearly waited for her.

He wasn't wearing his jacket or tie, and his shirt was unbuttoned at the neck and had the sleeves rolled up to the elbows. His shoulder holster was off: she spotted it on the bedside table. Other than that, he was fully dressed down to his shoes, which rested on the cheerful blue floral bedspread.

Just looking at him made her feel warm all over, which she knew was idiotic. She was willing to bet the rent money that he wasn't there for sexy times.

"Hi," she said, and waited.

"We need to talk." Sitting up, he swung his legs off the bed and got to his feet.

Riley put the brush down on the low oak dresser that right beside her, crossed her arms over her chest, and met his gaze as he stopped in front of her.

She didn't have her shoes on, and he loomed large. Good thing she no longer found him the least bit intimidating.

"So talk," she said.

His eyes slid over her face. His expression was grim.

"As you may have noticed, we have a situation here. We're squirreled away in a safe house because everybody and his uncle wants to get their hands on you and make you tell them where the money is. My boss wants that money, too, and my whole organization, including those guys downstairs and a bunch of others who are a hell of a lot deadlier, will turn on us in a heartbeat if he decides the best way to get it is to torture information out of you. We don't have a lot of time before this turns nasty. I'm on your side, and they'll get to you over my dead body, but that could happen. I need you to stop lying to me, and tell me the whole damned truth." He reached out to grasp her arms. His hands felt warm, and strong, and familiar now. It was the familiar part that got to her. "I know you know where the money is. Tell me."

Right. It was all about the money. For a moment there, she'd almost forgotten that.

"If we're going to talk about truth, why don't you go first?" She smiled at him. Because she really, really liked him, and because suspecting his motives and not being able to trust him felt like it was turning her heart inside out, it wasn't a nice smile. "Mr. CIA Agent John F. Bradley."

The skin around his eyes tightened, his mouth thinned, and the grip on her arms hardened.

"I saw your ID number on a text when you snuck out of bed in the middle of the night and the phone rattled the drawer beside the bed," she said. "And I checked it out."

He grimaced. Message: *busted*. Then his grip eased and his eyes and mouth returned to normal. "John Finnegan Bradley, CIA's National Clandestine Service, Special Operations Group. The Agency doesn't want its interest in the missing money known, so we're conducting a joint operation with the FBI. Bax is FBI, by the way. For real."

"You lied to me."

"In the interests of national security."

She huffed out a laugh. "Does that line actually work on people?"

He pulled her toward him. "Pretty much, yeah. Riley—"

"Oh, no." She put her hands on his chest, freed herself from his grip, walked over to the room's one chair, a denim blue recliner, and threw herself down in it. He followed, and she looked up at him with a frown.

"Your picture was on Jeff's cell phone." Her tone was abrupt. It was a measure of her growing trust in him that she told him at all. As she'd decided before, if his picture was on that phone for the wrong reasons, telling him she'd seen it could go very wrong. "He snapped it the night he died."

His face was impossible to read as he looked down at her. "You've been wondering if I killed him."

She'd never really thought *that*. "More like, I've been wondering if you're one of the bad guys."

He snorted. "Angel, if I'm a bad guy, I'm the one keeping all the other bad guys from your door."

"I know. Don't think I don't appreciate that."

The look he gave her was long, level, and impossible to interpret. "In the interests of clarity, I did not kill Jeff. I was looking for him that night, though. He must have seen me, taken a picture without me seeing him, and then run for it. He knew me, knew what I was there for."

Riley's hands tightened on the arms of the chair. "You *knew* Jeff?"

He sighed, and crouched down in front of her. "This is full disclosure, right? I tell you mine, you tell me yours?"

"Maybe." Riley drew the word out cautiously, and he narrowed his eyes at her. But he continued anyway.

"After 9/11, the CIA had a few of us tracking down some insider trades that happened in the markets prior to the attacks. We developed information that enabled us to use the financial markets to predict impending terrorist attacks. Cowan Investments had a large number of investments from suspect sources, and I was sent down here to check them out. Jeff was a teenager at the time, working in his daddy's office. He didn't appreciate my presence. George didn't, either, but he was old enough and smart enough to cooperate. The fact that I was already familiar with the Cowans and their operation was one of the factors in sending me here to search for the money."

Even though she hadn't really suspected him of harming Jeff, Riley felt as if a small weight had been lifted from her chest.

"Is that everything?" she asked cautiously.

"That I can think of for the moment. And it's all top secret, by the way." He stood up, and before she guessed what he meant to do, he scooped her up and sat back down with her in his lap.

"Hey," she protested.

"It's the only chair, I'm tired, and squatting down

in front of you is making my legs hurt," he said, but she was already settling in, relaxing into his encircling arms, draping her legs sideways across his, sliding an arm around his neck. She had never been a lap-sitting kind of woman but—this was *Finn's* lap.

Their eyes met. Something—hot, but deeper and more profound than that, too—passed between them.

He smoothed her hair back from her face, dropped a quick, hard kiss on her lips.

Her heart shivered.

He said, "Whatever you've done, I'll get you out of it. If you stole the damned money, I'll get you out of it. Whatever secret you're keeping, whatever you've been lying about this whole time, I'll help you fix it. But you need to tell me."

She met his eyes, felt the steady strength of that calm blue-gray gaze, and told him. Everything.

———————

HAVING ABANDONED the Acura, which he judged to be too well known now, Finn was behind the wheel of a black Lexus commandeered from Agents Waters and Silverman. The four agents were in an identical black Lexus behind them (nobody ever said the Agency was creative). Riley was beside him, and Bax, because Bax had earned his trust, was the backup of choice in the backseat.

They were on their way to Houston, to Margaret's house. Still not sure whether he was more stunned by, appalled at, or proud of Riley's chutzpah in siphoning off money from the stolen billions that she'd found when the whole world and its mother had failed to do so, he wanted to get his hands on those papers she'd hidden in the dog's ashes before he told anybody anything. If the information was in his hands, he became the target, not her.

Just thinking about the amount of danger she'd been in ever since she'd found that money put him in a cold sweat.

He was wary of sending a message, of transmitting by even the most secure means, that he had ascertained that Riley really did have knowledge of the whereabouts of hidden bank accounts, or that papers actually detailing those accounts existed, and where. No means of communication was totally secure, and if the word got out there'd be the equivalent of an operative feeding frenzy with Riley, and the papers, both serving as chum.

She was with him, because he didn't dare let her out of his sight. Until the money was officially found, she wouldn't be safe.

"Don't forget that Emma's the number one priority," Riley reminded him as she had at least half a dozen times since she'd told him the whole story. He got the feeling she still wasn't completely convinced she'd done the right thing, and Emma was at the heart of that. Riley was afraid that once the key to the money was in his hands, it would be out of his hands, so to speak, that the Agency would take it and whisk it away rather than use it to ransom Emma.

What he said to her was, "Emma will be saved." His internal answer was more complex: *Emma would be saved if it was humanly possible to save her.* He was still working on ways to get it done.

"I know," he answered, and smiled at her, because she was beautiful, and amazing, and she'd trusted him, and—

Get your mind on your business. This is not the time for that.

Bax said, "Hey, I just got a text. Ed Harper—you know, the guy who sent those emails to Jeff—is claiming George bribed him to send them. He said he was visiting his cousin at the prison like he does every week and George promised to give him insider investing tips if he did that for him. We've got an agent on the way to talk to George about it now."

"Good luck with that," Finn said, while Riley frowned and said with obvious disappointment, "So those emails probably didn't come from Emma's kidnappers."

"It's not sounding like it," Bax said. "I—"

He broke off as Finn's cell phone rang. It was positioned on the console between the seats, because Riley wanted it where she could keep an eye on it. He reached for it, looked at the number, and felt his heart rate and pulse start to slow down.

"This may be them," he said to Riley, who was looking at his phone with a combination of horror and hope. She sucked in air audibly. Her hand shook as she reached for the phone. The call was being monitored and recorded remotely. If this was the kidnappers, top operatives would be listening in, analyzing, and trying to trace the call as she spoke.

Riley took the phone, wet her lips, punched the button, and said into the phone, "This is Riley."

Finn couldn't hear the other end of the conversation, but from the way the color faded from her cheeks he knew who it was even before she mouthed at him, "It's them."

THIRTY-TWO

"You called the FBI." The voice on the other end of the phone was ugly with accusation. It was a man's voice, not foreign. No particular accent that she could discern. She didn't recognize it.

Riley felt panic squeeze her chest. "I know where the money is," she said, without confirming or denying his accusation. "I can give you bank names, account numbers."

"Text them to this number. We'll let her go."

Having pulled over to the side of the road, Finn was on his alternate phone, listening to one of the agents who was monitoring the phone call, while Bax was leaning forward into the space between the front seats, agog with interest. Finn shook his head at Riley, who knew the answer to that without him having to tell her. She'd been coached on what to say when the kidnappers called by, she presumed, the same expert hostage negotiator who was listening in, in a phone call before leaving the safe house. Finn made a winding motion with his hand, which she interpreted as "keep the kidnapper talking." If she could keep him on the line long enough, they might be able to trace the call.

"Texts, emails, they're not secure. You know that. I want to make sure you get what you want, so Emma can come home." She'd been told to try to set up a face-to-face exchange. "We need to meet. I'll give you the list of accounts, and you give me Emma. How about—" She was about to suggest, as she'd been instructed, in front of the zoo.

"We'll call you later tonight with a place."

She sensed he was about to hang up. "*Wait.*"

Finn was mouthing something at her: "Proof of life."

Right. She remembered what she'd been told to do.

"I need to make sure she's alive. I want to talk to her. I—"

"Riley." It was Emma.

"Em! Are you all right?"

"Yes. I'm so scared. I miss Rogers so much. And Kenny—"

Emma made a sound, and Riley heard some kind of commotion, as if she was being dragged away from the phone.

"Em!" Riley cried, her stomach dropping clear to her toes.

"Be ready." It was the kidnapper, back on the phone. Then he hung up.

The sound of dead air was the most terrifying sound of all, Riley discovered. Her eyes locked with

Finn's. Her chest was so tight she could hardly breathe. She felt dizzy, sick.

"Em," she said. It was almost a whimper.

"You heard her, she's all right. They're going to call back. They want the money." Finn took the phone from her grasp, then pushed her head down so that her head was resting on her knees. Riley didn't resist. She was too weak. Her head spun.

"Breathe," Finn ordered, and she did, in and out, while he spoke to the hostage negotiator.

In a few minutes, when her head had cleared sufficiently, Riley sat up.

"Better?" Finn asked. His face was tight with concern.

Riley nodded. "She was trying to send a message," she said. "There is no Rogers in her life. There is no Kenny."

"Are you sure?" Finn frowned at her.

"Kenny Rogers," Bax exclaimed excitedly, while Finn repeated what she'd said to the hostage negotiator. Then Bax frowned. "But what does it mean?"

That was the terrible thing. Riley didn't have a clue. None of them did.

———————

BY THE TIME Riley walked into Margaret's house, it was dark outside. Since talking to Emma, she'd had time to regain her composure. The last thing she wanted to do was upset Margaret more, or infect her with her own terrible fear. When, five minutes out because Finn wouldn't let her do it any sooner for fear of a security breach, she'd called to let Margaret know she was coming, Margaret's voice had broken her heart. It was thin, and quavering, and sounded like it belonged to someone who was very, very old.

"Riley!" Margaret came up off the couch to envelop her in a hug. Her normally fastidious ex-mother-in-law was more disheveled than Riley had ever seen her. Margaret's hair looked like it hadn't been combed since Riley had left, she was wearing what Riley thought were the same clothes except for, and this was despite the baking heat, the addition of a cardigan sweater, and there wasn't a speck of makeup on her face. "I'm so glad to see you."

Riley hugged her back. Margaret felt like skin and bones in her arms. The TV was on, and so were the lamps. They didn't help. The atmosphere in the house felt heavy, depressing.

Like somebody has died.

"I talked to Emma," Riley said first thing. She hadn't been able to tell Margaret that over the phone, again because of security concerns. "She's all right."

"You actually spoke to her?" Still clinging to Riley's hands, Margaret sat down abruptly on the couch. "Oh, my God. Thank God."

Then her eyes went past Riley to Finn, who had come in behind her and was standing discreetly back, in front of the closed door.

"This is Finn," Riley introduced him. He was once again wearing his suit jacket, but he'd left his tie off and his shirt was open at the neck. He looked very big in the modestly sized room, and so toughly handsome that Riley was conscious of feeling a little glimmer of pride in him. She was dying to *really* introduce him to Margaret, in a way that let Margaret know that he was important to her, but these were not the circumstances. "Agent Bradley."

"Mrs. Cowan." Finn took the hand Margaret extended to him as she murmured the appropriate greeting.

"Won't you sit down?" Margaret, with her always impeccable manners, indicated the chair beside the couch.

"Thank you, but we'll only be here a moment." Finn gave Riley a meaningful look. He'd already impressed on her how vulnerable she was in this house, which was a place where she was known to spend a considerable amount of time and might well be under surveillance.

"Where's Bill?" Riley asked. She'd known before she arrived that she needed to be in and out, to grab the papers she'd hidden and go, but leaving Margaret, having seen the way she was, was going to be much harder than she'd anticipated.

"He ran to the store," Margaret called after her, because Riley, steeling herself to do what she had to do, was already heading for the kitchen. "He's been so good to me. He's been here with me the whole time."

The cop car was once again parked in the driveway, so Riley didn't worry about Margaret's physical safety once she left. Instead she worried about her mental state. She'd been through so much. How much could one woman take? But as soon as Emma was safe,

Riley would be back, bringing Emma with her. Hanging on to that thought like a lifeline, Riley headed for the kitchen. She flipped on the light, made a beeline for the cabinet and poor Horatio's mortal remains.

"Do you think they'll let my daughter go, Agent Bradley?" she heard Margaret ask, and then she was listening to the rumble of Finn's deep voice as she went up on tiptoe to reach the top of the cabinet.

Riley had the pewter urn on the counter and was in the process of unscrewing the lid when the back door opened. She looked up, startled, and then relaxed as she saw that the new arrival was Bill, who she presumed had used a key Margaret had given him and was coming in from the store. Unlike Margaret, on whom the strain of the last couple of days had left a visible mark, Bill looked like his usual lawyer self in a navy suit, white shirt, and red tie.

She smiled at him, and he took a long step that put him directly in front of her, pulled a gun out from under his jacket, and pointed it right at her forehead.

Riley's heart leaped into her throat. Her breathing suspended.

"If you make a sound, I'll kill you where you stand," he whispered. Riley stood frozen, her hands still on the urn, staring at him in shock. He glanced at the urn. "You put the papers in there?" He shook his head. "Bring it. Walk out the door. *Now*."

In the other room, Riley could hear the drone of the TV. She could hear Finn's voice, and Margaret's. In the split second that was all she had, her mind explored the situation wildly. The sound of a shot would bring them running. But then she took another look at that pistol—it had a silver thing screwed on the end of its barrel that was almost certainly a silencer. Which meant that he could, indeed, shoot her where she stood and no one would hear. If she screamed, Finn would be there in seconds. But she took one look at Bill's eyes—they were cold and hard in a way she'd never, ever seen them—and knew she didn't have seconds.

If she screamed he would shoot her on the spot.

Carrying Horatio's urn, with Bill's gun trained on her every step of the way, she did what he said and walked out the door.

———————

"HOW DID YOU know I had papers hidden in the urn?" Riley asked as Bill hustled her through the back gate and across the dark yards on the same route she had used previously to enter and leave the house unseen. Windows glowed in the houses they passed, but curtains were drawn. No one was outside. He had his hand twisted in her hair and his gun kept nudging her neck, and he'd already made her give him the papers with the account numbers on them and had stuffed them in his pocket. Horatio's urn had been tossed in some shrubberies.

"Margaret told me everything the two of you did, except where you put the damned copies of those bank account numbers you made, because *that* she didn't know. She was so agitated, you see, after hearing you on TV today that she just couldn't keep the secret any longer, and I was right there." He chuckled. "I've been searching the damned house ever since that TV broadcast. When you called, I knew you were coming for those papers. I told Margaret I was going to the store, and then I watched through the windows to see what you would do. I was right: you went for the papers." He shook his head. "In the dog urn, of all places."

"Bill—you care about Margaret. She cares about you. Our family cares about you. You have a great career, a great life. You don't *need* billions of dollars. Why would you do this?" Riley's pulse drummed in her ears, her heart pounded like a trapped animal's, and she was still so stunned that she was finding it hard to think clearly. Instinct told her that getting him talking to her, reminding him that he was a close family friend and she'd known him for years, was the best tack to take.

"I do need that money. The only reason I'm still alive is because the accounts I brought to the table that lost everything are counting on me to get that money back for them. Some of them are getting real impatient." He pushed her into a jog. Riley saw that they were angling down toward the street. Instead of parking at the next cross street, as she had done when trying to avoid the media, he'd apparently parked much closer. In fact, if she wasn't mistaken, that was his Chevy Impala on the grassy verge in front of the vacant house five doors down from Margaret's. "I admire you, Riley, I really do. I've been hunting for that money ever since George, that pissant bastard, hid it."

"You were working with George?" That was the first Riley had ever heard of it.

"I acted as a broker for him. I brought him big-ticket investors, persuaded them to trust him with their funds, and took a cut. It doesn't matter if they're jihadists, or Ukrainian separatists, or our own damned government funding secret wars, they all want to make money, and they all need a place to stash their cash, to launder it, to make it available when they're ready to use it and to make it come back out looking legit. George didn't want to know the details. When the crash came, and he lost some money, and some of the investors made their displeasure clear, so to speak, he wanted out. You don't get out of something like this, not alive. I told him that, and some of the investors made it pretty clear, as well, and the fucker panicked and hid the damned money because he thought nobody would kill him while the money was lost out there. He was right."

Riley pretended to stumble, trying to slow things down as much as she dared because she knew that Finn would miss her at any second and then all hell would break loose. But this forced march to Bill's car was going fast and Finn would probably search the house first and even when he ran outside and summoned the troops he might not get to her in time.

She was breathing hard. Goose bumps raced over her skin.

"I'll shoot you if I have to," Bill warned, pulling her upright and pushing her forward. "The only good you are to me is if I need a hostage to escape, and it's looking like I may not."

"Bill—they're going to know you did it. Even if you kill me, you can't get away." Riley tried reason as they reached his car. Bill smiled at her. The night sky was black as pitch, the few stars that showed were tiny pinpricks of silver, and the moon was a poor pale thing just rising over the tops of the trees. What little light there was touched his eyes, and something about the way they gleamed at her through the darkness made her blood run cold.

She didn't think he was going to have any trouble at all killing her.

"Honey, far as Margaret or anyone knows, I've been at the grocery store this whole time. I've even got a sack of groceries in my car I can carry in. Nobody saw me take you out of the house. I'll just go on in through the front door and act as upset as can be that you've turned up missing." He smiled at her again, shoved her against the side of his car, withdrew his hand from her hair, and said, "Don't you move."

Riley caught herself with her hands against the smooth warm metal, threw a quick glance over her shoulder to find that he still had his gun aimed at her, and heard a tiny beep.

"Get in the trunk," he said. That's when she knew that the beep she'd heard was the trunk release on his key chain. The trunk opened. For the briefest of seconds, she hoped for the flare of a trunk light, but it didn't come on. The night stayed just as dark as before. Panic surged like an icy tide through her veins as she realized that if he closed her in his trunk, if he put her in there and killed her, he could go back in the house just like he'd said and nobody would ever associate him with her disappearance.

She slid a glance toward Margaret's house. A cop car in the driveway, the Lexus with Bax still in the backseat, and another Lexus with two CIA agents inside parked behind it, her own personal CIA agent in the house, which by the way didn't have any more lights on inside now than it had when Bill had taken her out of it, and she was still likely to be killed right down the street. Her stomach twisted into a knot. Her heart felt like it might explode. She thought of how devastated Margaret would be, of Emma, of Finn, and felt a violent aversion to the idea of dying. *No. Not now*.

Mouth sour with fear, she turned around to face Bill.

— CHAPTER —

THIRTY-THREE

The text wasn't important—it told Finn that the ID number check that had outed him to Riley had been initiated, probably on the basis of facial recognition software just as he had feared, by the Ukrainian operative who'd attacked Riley and was now dead—but it distracted him. Between that, and Margaret's asking him questions he couldn't answer about Emma, a few minutes elapsed in which he lost his focus on Riley.

She'd gone into the kitchen. She hadn't come back.

He covered the distance in half a dozen strides.

She wasn't there. Four walls, stove, refrigerator, sink. She wasn't there.

"Is something wrong?" Margaret was in the doorway behind him, an alarmed tremor in her voice. He paid no attention.

Cold, driving fear filled him.

A small, dome-shaped silver lid rested on the

counter beside the sink. He remembered where she said she'd hidden the account numbers—a dog urn—and identified it with a sinking feeling in the pit of his stomach.

There was a back door. He looked at it. It was unlocked.

Somebody had gotten to her. Taken her. He faced it, felt it like a punch to the gut.

"Stay here," he ordered Margaret, steel in his voice.

Then he went out the door, moving fast but silently through the shadows, over the damned so-dry-it-was-crinkly grass, knowing that if Riley had been taken—and there was no way she would have left the safety of the house, of him, voluntarily—that whoever had her also had the information they wanted, and thus had no reason not to kill her.

If he raised the alarm, if he summoned the backup out front, he might provoke the perp into doing just that.

Dread infiltrated his bones.

Whoever had her had left on foot, there was no other option. She hadn't been gone long. She had to be still nearby. The most likely scenarios were that she was being taken to a vehicle, a nearby building, or that she had been/would be/was being killed soon after leaving the house.

Somebody could be killing her right now, putting a silenced bullet in her head, slitting her throat, strangling her, a thousand ways, and he could be within yards of it happening and not know.

For the first time in forever he found himself praying.

Bursting through the gate, Finn forced himself to slow down and look carefully in all directions. The cars full of law enforcement in the driveway would be a deterrent. The perp had almost certainly gone the other way.

It was too dark. So damned dark. He saw shadows, moving shadows, everywhere.

———————

"I SAID, get into the trunk."

Riley's heart pounded so hard that she could feel it knocking against her rib cage. Cold sweat prickled to life around her hairline.

"Bill, please." If begging for her life would save it, hey, she was ready, willing, and able to beg. Besides, anything that bought her time was a good thing. She slid another glance at Margaret's house. *Finn.* . . . "This will kill Margaret. I—"

He made a contemptuous sound. "You sound like Jeff. *You know what this will do to Mom:* those were practically the last words out of his mouth. Margaret will be sad, and Margaret will get over it. If I don't get this money, I'm going to be dead."

Riley was so surprised she almost gaped at him. "You killed Jeff?"

"Not personally. I have . . . associates. They're as interested in recovering the money as I am. But I was there." He made a gesture with his gun. "Now, get in the trunk."

"But Jeff didn't know where the money is."

"Well, I didn't know that, did I? George had somebody send Jeff some emails, and I thought they probably had some kind of secret code in them telling the kid where the money was, but if they did I couldn't figure it out. Jeff couldn't, either, apparently." Bill smirked. "He died trying." His voice hardened, and he pointed his gun right at her forehead again. "I'm done talking to you. Get in the trunk. You make me say it again, and I'll shoot you right here and then put your dead body in the trunk. Go on. Get in."

Riley looked at him, and saw that he meant it. As slowly as she dared, she moved toward the trunk, glancing back toward Margaret's house, wishing, hoping. . . .

I could run. Would that be better than taking her chances with getting in the trunk?

I have no chance if I get in the trunk.

Breathless with fear, Riley was just facing the reality of that when, from the corner of her eye, she saw a big body silently materialize out of the darkness behind Bill.

A sudden rush of movement, a sickening-sounding chop to the side of the neck, and Bill dropped like an empty suit of clothes, his gun clattering as it hit the pavement.

Riley almost collapsed where she stood. If Finn hadn't caught her, she would have. Instead she collapsed against him.

"Where have you been?" she growled, clinging to him. He felt so good against her, so warm and strong, so safe, that she didn't think she would ever be able to let him go again.

"Having a heart attack. I would have shot him as soon as I saw what was happening, but he had his finger on the trigger the whole time and I was afraid he would reflexively shoot you. I don't think I've ever been so scared in my life. Are you all right?"

His arms were tight around her, and Riley thought she felt the brush of his lips on her hair.

She looked up, nodding. "He—" *Killed Jeff,* was what she was going to say.

But then more shapes loomed out of the darkness. Men, at least half a dozen. Big, capable-looking men in black clothing.

"Finn." Her voice had a squeak to it. He'd already seen. She could tell by the tightening of his muscles, by the sudden tension that she could feel emanating from him like an electric charge.

She knew, suddenly, that he was afraid. She could sense it, feel it in her bones.

Anything that could scare Finn. . . .

Riley felt her blood draining toward her toes.

———————

EVER SINCE he'd entered clandestine services, Finn had known that one day the very agency he served might turn on him.

It was looking like today might be that day. He saw the black-garbed men materialize out of the shadows, surround them, and felt his heart stop.

They weren't there for him. They were there for

Riley. To shut her up, to keep her from telling anybody about what she knew about the secret bank accounts, and about the Agency involvement in the search for them and, now, their recovery. But to get her, they were going to have to go through him.

There were enough of them. Eagle knew him. He was taking no chances.

Riley's arms were wrapped around his waist. He could feel her pressing against him, all soft female curves, as helpless as a baby against these men.

Not wanting to make any sudden moves, he angled himself so that he was between her and them as much as possible. Smart girl that she was, she let go of him and inched away, giving him the free use of his body and his hands.

If he went for a weapon, he was dead.

"Where's the information?" It was Eagle himself. A tall, spare man in his late fifties, he'd left off doing field work years ago. It was a measure of how important he considered this that he was here.

The hell of it was, not seeing a dog urn, Finn didn't know. Answer: somewhere.

"It's in his coat pocket," Riley said, her voice strong and clear, pointing to the man on the ground. Finn was proud of her. No fool, she would know what this was and she had to be scared to death.

Finn felt a surge of savage anger at the idea of Riley being scared. Of Riley being hurt. Of Riley being anything at all except happy, and safe.

Eagle motioned with his hand, and one of the operatives—Finn didn't recognize him, Eagle was smart enough to use fresh-minted agents, men he wouldn't know—bent over Stengel, searching his pockets, coming up with folded papers.

"That all we need to locate the missing money?" Eagle addressed Riley.

"Yes," she replied. "It's all there. Bank account numbers. Access codes."

Eagle was looking at her. Finn recognized the cold assessment in his eyes.

"To get to her, you're going to have to go through me," he said. And he meant it. He was prepared to die, and to kill every one of them he could, in Riley's defense.

"I realize that." No inflection at all in Eagle's voice.

"I saved your life," Finn said.

Eagle looked at him. In the other man's gaze, Finn felt the weight of decades worth of ruthlessly enforced silence, of operatives being sacrificed for the good of the cause, of the code they shared that mandated that the good of the many outweighed the good of the few, and his heart stopped beating.

"I know," Eagle said. "That's why I'm giving you this." He gestured at his men. "Get him. Let's go."

Finn tensed, balancing on the balls of his feet as two operatives moved in to pick up the still-unconscious Stengel, then carried him away. Finn had little doubt that somewhere nearby they had a vehicle waiting. He had no doubt that Stengel would never be seen alive again.

"Keep her quiet," Eagle said, and Finn recognized

in those three words both a warning and a threat. Then Eagle turned and walked away.

One operative walked over to the trunk of the car and closed it gently. Then they all followed Eagle.

For the first time in his life, Finn felt shaky inside. He knew it was with relief.

Leaning back against the car for support until he could regain his equilibrium, he reached for Riley and pulled her into his arms.

———————

BY THE TIME Finn got done kissing Riley, and warning her, and then kissing her some more, Margaret's house was alive with activity. Riley watched as small figures that she knew were Bax and the agents and the cops and the one whose blond hair clearly marked her as Margaret ran in and out.

Finn pulled a phone out of his pocket and called Bax. The activity stopped.

"Stengel's not coming back," he warned her again as they finally headed for the house. His arm was around her shoulders, and hers was around his waist. "You never saw him, he didn't try to kill you, nothing like that happened. You stepped outside for some air, and I came after you. Forget everything else. The key here is to keep the Agency out of it, and keep everything you know about those bank accounts to yourself."

"I understand," Riley told him, which was what she'd been saying variations of ever since he'd first spelled the facts of her new life out to her. *See no evil, hear no evil, speak no evil. I know nothing.* "Don't worry. I've got it. I can do this."

That made him stop, and look down at her. Then he smiled, one of those rare real smiles.

"Angel, I have no doubt at all," he said, and kissed her.

It wasn't until they were on the way to the house again that an epiphany hit Riley.

"I know where Emma is." Excitement surged through her, and she stopped walking. Finn stopped, too, looking at her with raised brows. "Kenny Rogers! Emma is so smart! Bill has a boat called the *Gambler*. He keeps it in a boathouse in Galveston. That must be what she was trying to tell me."

Finn didn't reply. Instead he pulled out his phone, placed another call, and passed on what she had just told him to whoever was on the other end. Then he grabbed her hand as, bubbling with elation, she started to take off for the house to tell Margaret.

"Hang on a minute," he said, his voice deadly serious. Riley was reminded once again of the lethal nature of the secrets she'd learned, and the men who kept them. "This complicates things. If you're right, Emma obviously knows she's being held in Stengel's boathouse, so she's going to at least suspect he's involved. But she won't know anything about the bank accounts, or the Agency, or anything like that. What you're going to have to do is pretend that you think Stengel was a lone wolf after the money just like everyone else. You can never tell anyone anything else."

Some of Riley's elation faded as a hard truth hit her: "Bill was going to kill her, wasn't he?"

"I don't see how he could have let her live once she knew he was involved."

"That bastard." An even more terrifying thought occurred. "You don't suppose he's already. . . ?"

She couldn't bring herself to put it into words.

Finn shook his head. "He wouldn't have killed her until he was sure he had the information he needed, and he didn't get that until he took you."

But Finn couldn't *know* that. Riley's stomach knotted. They were just a few feet away from Margaret's front porch when Finn's phone buzzed. He answered, then smiled at Riley, who had frozen in place as she listened to his end of the conversation.

"They've got her," he said. "She's safe."

Riley felt a rush of relief and joy and thankfulness so strong it made her dizzy.

Then she pulled away from Finn and rushed up the front steps.

Margaret was standing in the doorway between the living room and the hall when Riley burst through the door.

"They've found Emma," Riley cried. "She's safe."

"Oh, thank God." Margaret sagged against the door frame. Then Riley reached her, and Margaret wrapped her arms around her.

Riley hugged her while she wept.

THIRTY-FOUR

Finn had never been a big believer in happy endings. But on this particular Saturday morning he had to admit that things were looking pretty good in that regard. He was in Riley's bed, in her apartment, with Riley tucked cozily against his side.

She was still sound asleep. Not a surprise, after the night they'd spent.

He was in love. For real.

So, she'd told him, and given him to understand in lots of satisfying and extremely inventive ways, was she.

It was now two weeks after Emma had been found.

At Riley's instigation, he'd gotten to know both Margaret and Emma since then. They were Riley's family, which meant that they were now an ongoing part of his life.

There had been a one percent finder's fee on the missing money. Since Riley had found it, the fee was coming to her. It would more than cover the ten million she'd taken from the hidden accounts. Both Riley and Margaret were excited about that, mainly because, from what he understood, that meant that Emma would be able to stay on in her expensive private high school. The problem was, Emma was now saying that the place was too snobby, and she thought she might want to try a public school with hot football players. There was some family drama about that, but it was nothing to do with him and he was staying out of it.

He'd put safeguards in place to make sure Eagle and everybody else at the Agency left him and Riley alone. The most important of them was a kind of poison pill composed of the details of every operation he'd been in on, written down and ready to be disseminated to every type of media outlet available in the event something untoward should happen to Riley or him, like, for instance, the kind of heart attack that had killed Bill Stengel, who'd been found dead, slumped behind the wheel of his car the morning after Emma had been rescued.

He made sure Eagle knew what he'd done.

He also made it clear that he was retiring again, this time for good. He wanted to ranch. He was taking Riley to look at his place in Wyoming, to see what she thought. They were leaving tomorrow, staying for a week.

If she didn't like endless blue skies and cool bright air and the smell of mountains in the distance, well, he was prepared to be flexible.

Because more than he'd ever wanted just about anything, he wanted Riley Cowan in his life.

If she wanted to stay closer to home, to Margaret and Emma, he could make that work.

There were ranches in Texas, right?

———————

RILEY WOKE up to the feel of a firm, warm body against her, and smiled. She was naked, he was naked, and he was in her bed, so she knew who he was instantly, no need to open her eyes: Finn. He wasn't asleep. She could tell by the latent power in the arm wrapped around her shoulders, by the rhythm of his breathing. Her head was pillowed on his wide shoulder, her hand rested in the crisp hair in the middle of his chest, and her leg curved over his muscular thighs. He'd been staying with her for the past two weeks, and in that time she'd discovered many facets to his character that she never would have suspected. Most important of which, right at this moment, was that the man could cook.

"I'm hungry," she murmured, opening her eyes as she ran a caressing hand across his chest and down over his ripped stomach, loving the smoothness of his skin, the steely strength of the muscles beneath.

He tensed. The arm around her shoulders tightened.

"So am I." His voice was a husky, throaty rumble.

She stopped stroking him just short of where she knew he wanted her to go, rubbed his tummy, and tilted her head so that she could see his eyes.

They were heavy-lidded and hot, leaving her in no doubt at all about what he had in mind.

"Best. Pancakes. Ever," she said plaintively, because she really was hungry, and his pancakes really were that good, and—she liked teasing him.

"Are you serious?" The look he gave her combined amusement, dismay—and heat.

"One hundred percent," she assured him, letting her hand wander south until she was renewing her acquaintance with her new best friend. He caught his breath, went hard and still as stone, and she smiled. "But I can wait."

"Good thing," he growled. "Because I can't."

He rolled with her, and she found herself pinned beneath a big, honed body that was approximately as solid and heavy as a Mack truck.

She shivered a little as tiny thrills of anticipation raced over her skin. Deep inside, her body began to throb and burn.

He frowned down at her. "Cold?"

She shook her head, smiled. "Hot." Then as his eyes blazed at her she added, "I love you."

"I love you, too," he said, and kissed her.

They got to those pancakes eventually, but it took a while.

———

THE FOLLOWING evening, Sunday, Finn walked out of his barn and took a wide, sweeping look around. His ranch in Wyoming had to be just about his favorite place on earth. Wide-open spaces. Pine covered mountains touching blue sky. Low-slung, red-roofed house, a couple more barns, plus shelters and out-buildings dotting rolling green fields that stretched as far as the eye could see. Cows, his prized black Angus, grazing in the fields. A couple of horses in a corral were closer at hand.

Riley, leaning against a split-rail fence not far away, was looking at the horses, sexy as hell in jeans and a T-shirt, her red hair blowing in the wind. As he headed toward her, she glanced over her shoulder, saw him, then turned all the way around to wait for him.

"It's beautiful here," she said as he reached her, and smiled at him.

Finn felt his heart do something funny. Like maybe expand a couple of sizes.

She was leaning back against the fence now, her elbows on the top rail, one leg curved as she hooked a boot heel over the bottom rail.

"It is," he agreed. "I was just thinking that as I walked over here. I was thinking that I was looking at every dream I ever had come true."

Her eyes met his. "You love this ranch that much?"

"No," he said. "I'm talking about you."

She took a breath, and pushed away from the fence.

He caught her, pulled her against him, and wrapped her in his arms.

Wherever they wound up, here or Texas or Tim-buktu, as long as he had her, he'd be all right.